# BETRAYED SILENCE

## LOIS SLATER

**Gotham Books**

30 N Gould St.
Ste. 20820, Sheridan, WY 82801
https://gothambooksinc.com/

Phone: 1 (307) 464-7800

© 2024 *Lois Slater*. All rights reserved.

No part of this book may be reproduced, stored in a retrieval system, or transmitted by any means without the written permission of the author.

Published by Gotham Books (October 16, 2024)

ISBN: 979-8-3304-6265-0 (H)
ISBN: 979-8-3302-9623-1 (P)
ISBN: 979-8-3302-9624-8 (E)

Because of the dynamic nature of the Internet, any web addresses or links contained in this book may have changed since publication and may no longer be valid.

The views expressed in this work are solely those of the author and do not necessarily reflect the views of the publisher, and the publisher hereby disclaims any responsibility for them.

# LIZA and LIZZIE

# THE BAXTER LEGACY

Sequel to:  Book 1    Stem of the Wildflower
            Book 2    Love of the Blood

John whose crystal blue eyes will shine throughout eternity

…always Chanda…

# PROLOGUE

Abe gave his grandson a curious look. "Tell me you know nothing about any of this."

"I don't, why would you ask such a thing?" Jeffrey answered in a threatened tone.

"Because you haven't been the same boy since you've started hanging around with those hooligans you seem to be so proud of drinking, making a complete mules hind end of yourself."

"Are you blaming me grandpa for something I know nothing about, are you?" Jeffrey was beside himself.

"I pray for your sake that you're not lying." Abe stated matter-of-factly. "If I find out you're involved in this…the consequences will be far worse than a walk to the timber; grandson or no grandson I'll kill you myself."

"Why are you blaming me!" Jeffrey yowled. "I don't know nothin', I didn't do nothin." Like the devil himself was hot on his tail, he rode his horse at a reckless pace through the arched gate yelling like a madman. "Damn you, Damn you all to…!"

# CHAPTER 1
## 'Nelly'

No matter how many boring tea parties Nelly had gone to, no matter how many beautiful dresses she'd made, and no matter how many nights she'd burned the midnight oil, the domineering biddies in the scant dwellings called Crocker would make a point to turn up their snotty noses at the fullness of the lovely sewn dresses in the latest fabric. The petite dressmaker did her best to explain.

"It's a new fashion. The new *'haute couture'* from back East, well, France actually. It's sweeping the West." A lie that ran from her deceitful lips like melted honey. She'd never been to France back East, or any place else. She gave them an innocent look.

"Surely you ladies want to be the first in Crocker to show off this bold new look! Don't you?" she'd questioned in a candid tone.

She was sure the highhanded group had no idea what *'haute couture'* meant. Still, without much prodding they always went along with her suggestions. For now, she had the self-righteous biddy's wrapped around her little finger. And, they seemed to be far more concerned about competing with each other than the size of their waistlines.

Nelly needed the full look of her needled work so the beautiful fabric would cover her unthinkable mistake to hide the mess she'd gotten herself into. Sadly, she also knew the beautiful fabric wouldn't conceal the secret of her condition much longer. No matter how sleek or full the style was, or how tight she pulled the clinging band around her melon-shaped body, at some point one of the nosey heifers were going to notice the changes going on under her petticoat. And to make matters worse, the last couple of weeks her face and feet had begun to swell. She blamed that on an allergy she didn't really have.

Angrily she scolded herself. How did she get into such a *mess*? She'd been with plenty of men for lots of immoral reasons and nothing like this had ever happened. Somehow, this time, she'd managed to betray herself. She'd lost her focus and let her emotions get in the way of her good judgement. Why did he have to be so convincingly handsome? And those green eyes. Oh! She was jelly in his hands. Green jelly!

Grudgingly, she stepped out the backdoor of her small dress shop, placed her hand on the small of her back, and climbed into the rented wagon. It had become a routine for her to go on a picnic every Thursday,

"That's where I get my best ideas for your dresses," she told the snooty bunch.

She'd make a point to smile and wave at the curious women as she headed the team of horses and creaking wagon out of town knowing they were oblivious to who she really was.

Still, Nelly felt guilty when she thought of the way the ladies of Crocker had taken her in with open arms believing she was this innocent young woman struggling alone to make her way in life when in fact, she was completely the opposite. What was she going to do when the small-town gossips found out she wasn't who she said she was? How was she going to keep face when they found out she'd been lying all this time. Would they shun her? Turn their backs on her?

She'd known from the start Jeffrey wasn't the most popular man in Crocker. He was trouble with a capital T. And out of all the decent men in Crocker who'd tried to court her, this scandalous cheat was her choice. In fact, if the truth was known, she couldn't stand his braggart personality. He was always concocting some stupid get rich scheme in a drunken stupor that was never going to come to light, constantly overreaching his limit in any and all situations. And the smell of sour whiskey lingered within the pores of his skin. If she hadn't needed the valuable information from the loud-mouthed Baxter Jones, she wouldn't be in this ridiculous situation. Spinning her wiles on a bad hunch had backfired.

Deep down, Nelly'd known for weeks she'd needed to handle this unthinkable situation. It was building up enough courage to actually do it. To confront the ornery twin sisters, Liza and Lizzie Baxter. In all honesty, she just didn't want to see the doubt that would look back at her through accusing eyes.

Nelly wasn't afraid of either twin; in her sorted ramblings she'd dealt with worse. Would they believe her? Probably not. Jeffrey sure didn't. When she'd told him she was in the family way he jumped out of her bed like the mattress was on fire! And his accusations were anything but kind. What was she thinking letting her affection toward this scoundrel put her in such a delicate condition?

Motherhood had played a foul trick and now she had the guilty seed growing deep within her womb. The seed of the family she'd been sent to destroy. Angry at the position she'd allowed herself to get into Nelly started to cry. Another weakness that disgusted her!

As Nelly bumped along within the confines of the livery wagon, she knew she'd never wanted to be a mother with a bawling little brat clinging to her leg. Just the thought of it made her want to puke, which she had been doing plenty of lately, too. And, it didn't seem to matter how many times or ways she'd tried to get rid of the baby, she couldn't get it to budge.

In a fantasized state, she'd imagined Jeffrey would take the baby and raise it himself. Become the father he could be, should be. And no matter how much he denied it, this wasn't just her baby. It was his too. Why, he lived on one of the largest ranches in the western territory. He had everything a child could want or need.

Still, deep down in her very being she knew he wouldn't accept his responsibility. Jeffrey Jones didn't think about anyone but himself. He was arrogant and selfish. Why would he take responsibility for a baby he didn't believe was his? As far as she was concerned this vile seed distorting the shape of her body was nothing less than vermin. As she gazed at the wiggling bump, her heart sank, she knew there would be no redemption for this mistake. "Idiot!" she scolded herself.

# CHAPTER 2

Nelly accepted the fact the twin sisters were going to be a pain. They were much too nosy for their own good, and she certainly didn't want to have make them disappear. She gave them credit though; they knew how to manage themselves in any situation. They were quiet, discreet, and very protective of their brood. Strong bred women that had good skills and knew how to use them. She had come close to meeting her match several times on this journey to find a certain outlaw, but with men. Not women. She knew how important it was to watch her back where these distrusting renegades were concerned a trick of the trade she'd learned at an early age.

There was no doubt in her mind these two sisters were worthy adversaries. She'd be foolish to underestimate them. And, there was no denying how much the townsfolk respected them, honestly, she did, too. If they were wrong, they said so, fixed it, then moved on. But if they were the ones that were wronged, well, that was another matter entirely.

Nelly knew it was no surprise to either twin how two-faced the folks in Crocker thought Jeffrey was. Their actions toward the lying scoundrel said it all. Nelly also knew the twins were going to be nothing but a thorn in her side. Going up against this pair would be her last option. But, at this point Nelly didn't care, not today. It was high time that she set the record straight. She was going to tell Liza Baxter the truth about her wayward son no matter how much trouble it caused. Jeffrey Baxter Jones needed grow up and except his fatherly responsibilities. Become accountable for his own actions. Be a man for once in his pathic life.

Nelly smiled to herself, no one suspected she was capable of being a killer, when in fact she'd made a living doing that very thing. The dress shop was a rue. She'd ridden hundreds of miles with little resistance chasing killers. Luring them in with her sexy wiles. Bringing them back dead, or alive. It never mattered to her. Until now. This lump that Jeffrey had planted in her womb, the one that kept distorting her body was going to make things difficult. She didn't care a hoot about the man, and she cared even less about the baby. She was after a much bigger fish with a much bigger payoff.

Jeffrey had told her in another drunken stupor everyone would be tending cattle today, that no one except himself, and maybe a couple of the hired hands would be around the grounds. His grandfather was checking on some strange phenomenon related to the water on the north end of the Red Range and wouldn't be back till around sundown. If that was true, it would give her just enough time to slip the sleeping powder that she carried in her bag into Jeffrey's drink, allowing her to nose around at her own leisure.

It was a great plan except for one thing, the motion of the rolling wagon mixed with the extreme heat was making her nauseated and dizzy. She'd questioned her journey this morning as it was, she didn't feel like her typical self, she'd had cramps off and on all night. And this miserable binding that held back the secret of her swollen torso was too tight. Filled with anger, she took the wide band and threw it into the box of the wagon. Then she pulled off her silk top and threw it in the back of the wagon too, leaving only her camisole to dance in the wind. Now she could breathe.

Why did he have to be so charmingly handsome? Damn it!

With the way that she was feeling there was no way she could make it to the Baxter Ranch, it was a good two hours as the crow flies it wasn't going to happen, not today. All this unexpected visit was going to do, was get her through the front door instead of the back. Right now, on this hot day it all seemed so unimportant. She turned the sweating team toward a large old cottonwood tree that reminded her of a ragged umbrella. She gently pulled the horses to a slow determined stop beneath an azure blue sky.

With purpose, she cursed Jeffrey's name and her weak surrender to his wily charms. She looked down at her once flat stomach, there was no mistaking the movement. And where did those big globs of bouncing flesh she affectionately called breasts come from? "Crap." she mumbled as she straightened out the leaking pods beneath her bodice. Angrily she cursed Jeffrey's name. "What is it about you? I knew you were no good. I was warned on more than one occasion about that, about your scandalous behavior, your muckraker ways. I should have listened."

Discouraged, she sat on the grassy bank trying to decide whether to go forward or go back, she knew the answer. As she sat back in the grass, she had a nagging feeling that something wasn't right. Not that she could see it or put her finger on it, no, she just felt it. Was someone watching her? Had someone followed her? Suspiciously, she looked in a semi-circle and much to relief, she saw nothing.

Shelly let out a deep sigh. "Tomorrow is another day," she said out loud. "And, Jeffrey Baxter Jones isn't going anywhere!" Disappointment filled her soul as she sat on the grassy bank pulling blades of wet grass when she noticed the water seemed awfully high and swift for this time of year. The swirling water lapped against the bank like an escaping prisoner giving off the illusion it was flowing upstream when in fact she knew it was running downstream. An unusual turbulence she wasn't used to seeing. Like a dam had burst from a higher place, dragging waterlogged branches and pieces of broken limbs down the banks rolling below the angry surface.

Blowing it off, she wiped her face with the cool clear water when something unusual caught her eye in the swift water. From where she was sitting it was hard to tell what the object was. A calf or small horse maybe? Instantly, she placed her fingers to shade the sun. Then, a strange feeling encompassed her. She'd have to get closer to tell for sure but was that a body tangled within a long spiny branch? Surely, not, her eyes were playing tricks on her. Why would someone purposely be in water like this? But the further down the muddy bank she walked, the more distinct the figure became. Now, she knew that was exactly what it was. "What should I do? No, no, no, Nelly." she said out loud.

# CHAPTER 3

Hesitantly, she started to wade out into the fast-paced water which at one time she suspected was a creek bed. It was too swift and deep as she stepped back onto the bank. Hurriedly, she made her way back to the wagon and grabbed two lassos. Giving them a quick once-over she was sure they had been lying on the rotted box for some time. Like a well-schooled wrangler, she tied them together, praying that they would hold her weight. Purposely, she tied one of the frayed strands under her arms and one to a metal bracket on the wagon. The thick twine made her odd, shaped figure even more visible as she slipped like an overweight otter into the fast-moving current.

Anxiously, she paddled toward the downed tree stuck on the opposite side of the bank. She was amazed at how light the fullness of her body felt within the moving water. It felt as though the unborn baby was holding her up like a floating bubble. Still, the current was strong and it took little effort to make it to the other side.

When Nelly finally made it to the designated spot she was shocked at what she found. "What in the world, how did you get here?" she gasped water splashing over her face making her gag and sputter. It was plain to see that the downed tree wasn't going to hold the water-logged body much longer. Immediately, Nelly's lightning-fast fingers tied the rope around the cold, limp flesh as she tried to pull the unconscious body backward into the rushing water and away from the submerging branch. But the body wasn't lying on the branch; it was wrapped within the branch. Nelly gave it a good pull again and again and again.

Quickly, she assessed the unthinkable situation! Then, she did the only thing she could think of, and with little thought to her own welfare, she plunged herself under the swirling water several times and untangled one body part after another. The thorny limbs didn't want to let go of the water-logged soul as Nelly yanked and pulled!

The half dead individual let out a slight moan when the thorny limbs finally released the body from within the heavy, wet branches.

Nelly was shocked by the crimson water that ducked and darted down the once dry creek bed now rumbling like a lion! She watched in horror as the water-logged branch disappeared right before her eyes! It reminded her of an unwanted object that was slowing down the waters flight, furiously surfacing then exploding as it disappeared in an instant beneath the turbulent foam that had held it captive.

Nelly was huffing and puffing like a winded horse as she laid the bleeding body's head against her slender shoulder as though it was made of glass. The two of them just hung there bobbing within the rhythmic fingers of the moving current. She felt like a dangling worm on a fishhook waiting to catch a hungry trout.

Nelly wasn't afraid of the turbulent water. Actually, she was an exceptionally good swimmer and the baby seemed to make her even more buoyant. But the person she held in her arms, was a lot bigger and heavier than she was. Nelly wondered how she was going to be able to pull them both back to the other side of the bank against the fast moving current more than that, she knew if the half-drowned body regained consciousness and came up fighting in a state of terror, she'd probably drown them both! To save herself she would simply let the half dead body go. There would be no rescue.

Nelly took a deep breath knowing that they couldn't bob out in the middle of the river forever. After all she was miles away from any semblance of civilization. Deep down in her soul, Nelly knew they were the only two out here.

So, inch by inch she started pulling on the taunt rope, hoping, and praying that the wagon wouldn't slip backward into the rushing water. On more than one occasion she had to stop and catch her breath as she floated to her back like a stuffed otter. She could feel the frayed rope cutting her tender flesh, biting her delicate skin like tiny razors. She knew there would be a rope burn just above her swollen breasts by the time they made it to the muddy bank. But she also knew it had to be cutting into her rescued victim too. Purposely, she clung to the cold flesh like an eight-legged spider. Continuously, she balanced the cold flesh ball against her shoulder.

It seemed like a fruitless task as she pulled the two of them backward against the current. For every inch they traveled upstream, they inched downstream two. Nelly's bleeding palms burned from the constant pulling. In her current condition, she didn't have the strength to pull them both to safety. There was no way they were going to live through this. She was going to have to let go. Overcome with exhaustion, she laid her dizzy head back onto the cool water and floated with the current.

For the second time that day the dressmaker started crying. She just couldn't see a light at the end of this watery tunnel! She wasn't herself! What had she been thinking? She didn't rescue people, she killed them! She should have just let the person in her arms drown! "I'm, sorry," she sobbed. "I might well have killed us both!" Then, she took a deep breath. She'd been in tougher spots than this. "Think!" She scolded herself as they bobbed in the rushing water.

The wagon seemed a million miles away as her eyes scanned the endless distance to the far bank of the swirling river. Once again she started pulling on the wet braided rope when for just a second, Nelly felt a little give. Maybe she'd hit a lull in the churning water. Then just like that, it tightened up again. It was an odd sensation as she turned her head to see what had happened. Perhaps it had gotten stuck on a tree branch and flipped itself loose. But when her eyes found the destination of her question a horrified gasp escaped her lips as her heart jumped into her throat. "No!" she screamed as the floating wagon went flying by her at an accelerated speed. It was as though a dark shadow covered her whole being. Like a frantic child trying to escape a rabid dog, Nelly tore at the ropes that were holding the two of them together. She would have to escape, or they were both going to drown!

Frantically, Nelly's bloody palms pulled at the wet strands but the combined weight of their swinging bodies had pulled the ragged fibers too tight. She couldn't get the knots to budge. Horrified she watched as the team of horses swam in the opposite direction, frantically trying to get away from each other and the floating raft. No matter how hard they swam their hairy hides were no match for the roaring water, their large oval eyes showed their terror, trying for all they were worth to defy gravity. Determinedly, they fought to gain their freedom from the swirling vessel with no results. Their ragged high-pitched squeals of death pierced her ears and she tried to drown out the horrible sound.

In a state of horror, Nelly watched as one of the large animals disappeared under the turbulent water only to emerge several feet downstream. Somehow the leather must have caught and snapped on something as the terrified animal climbed to the safety of the muddy bank. It was as though the devil himself was hot on its heels. His full hairy sides heaved from its predestined flight as he shook himself clean and took off at a fast lope down the muddy bank.

For a flash of a second, Nelly wished it was her stepping up on that muddy bank. That she herself had gained her own freedom. In the back of her mind, she knew that it would only be a matter of minutes before the sagging rope that was tied to the back of that sinking livery box would mercilessly yank their dangling bodies beneath the turbulent water. It would steal every ounce of breath she had and finish what the water had started with her dying captive. One, if not both, would surely die! The thought had no more than crossed her mind when the unthinkable happened.

Nelly tried with all of her might to keep their heads above water, but within seconds the weight of the water-filled wagon pulled them under. They were going to drown plain and simple. Then in the blink of an eye they were bobbing on the surface like two grasshoppers riding on the rim of a wagon wheel.

Nelly clung to the limp body sputtering like a drowning cat. Desperately, she pulled on the rotted rope, hoping that it would snap. The jagged twine held tight. She knew there was no way she was going to drown out here allow a courteous act like this to stupidly take her life!

There was only one horse now trying to flee the moving raft. She knew the inevitable fate of the fighting beast wasn't good. Nelly could hear the horse's terrifying screams as it floated across the top of the water like a skipping stone on its side. Its large body must have gotten tangled within the wet leather harness. It did all it could to keep its head above the rushing water. If she'd of had a knife, she'd have relieved the dying horse of its leather prison, but she wasn't about to let go of the reason she'd gotten into the water in the first place.

Nelly knew it wouldn't be long before they would be back underwater again, maybe for good this time, as she continued to tear away at the strand that bound them. Then, the river seemed to slow as a soft wind whisked across her wet face in the opposite direction. It was an odd sensation watching the clear water turn into a dark slime, rolling backward.

The sudden change of motion made Nelly sick as she threw up the very water that she had been swallowing. But the further downstream they floated, the calmer the racing water became. For some reason, the angry current had stopped working against her and for a brief moment the rope lay perfectly still her quick fingers tearing at the rotten threads. That was all that she had needed. Within seconds, the two of them were free. Like a leaping frog, Nelly paddled as hard as she could toward the cove near the muddy bank. Desperately, she dragged the motionless body along with her.

When Nelly finally made her destination, she was completely spent. Choking and gasping for air she pushed the waterlogged body out of the water onto the slushy grass. Like a spider, she crawled to safety herself just as the struggling horse let out another shrill cry.

"No!" Shelly's desperate scream of denial rang out louder than the terrified horse. "I was coming to get you!" she sobbed.

Horrified, she watched the horse and wagon disappear over the foggy falls like a rolling rock. Nelly sat there paralyzed, struggling to understand what had just happened. The wagon would have dragged them under with no way out. That poor animal could have been them. Why, they were lucky to be alive. She sat there in complete shock, sobbing hysterically as unheeded tears ran down her exerted face. Exhausted, she lay back still as a stone on the wet grassy bank for hours.

Once Nelly gathered her wits about her, the petite dressmaker realized the two of them had traveled a long way downstream in the rumbling water. As she tried to get her bearings, she could hear the person lying next to her moaning. She was grateful they were alive! "We made it!" she exclaimed. "We didn't die!" she whispered.

Nelly shivered scanning the grey sky above them. No denying it, there was a storm brewing. From the darkened clouds, it looked to be a doozy. She was going to have to find some type of shelter. That was if either one of them planned on making it out of here alive.

Nelly made sure her unlikely companion was comfortable before she climbed to the top of the ravine. From where she stood nothing looked familiar. Not a landmark in sight. She was surprised when she saw that the rolling water split, then merged back together completely changing directions. *How had she missed that?* That might have been why this wasn't was familiar! She'd never traveled this way before. Looking up stream at the winding water, she knew they'd traveled a long distance in a short time.

Shrugging off her situation, her eyes scanned the terrain. All she could see was pine trees, berry bushes, and the surviving horse. Nelly's heart jumped for joy. She couldn't believe her eyes. Cautiously, she walked down the hillside toward the waiting animal, hoping he wouldn't run at the sight of her.

When Nelly came within inches of where he stood, she realized why he had stopped. His front foot was caught in a metal trap tied to a tree beneath the dirt. Anxiously, she scanned the timber around her. She knew someone else had been here. Hurriedly, she pulled the horses bleeding hoof from its steel prison the cut wasn't deep. The soaked animal seemed to be as glad to see her as she was to see him. His welcoming greeting sounded like a lost child.

Like a well-schooled doctor, she tore off a piece of her dress and wrapped it neatly around the open wound. Gently, she patted the battered horse on his wet neck.

"Thank goodness we both knew how to swim, huh buddy?" she whispered.

She knew that the makeshift bandage wouldn't hold for long especially if it started raining. But, it would have to do for the time being.

"Ready?" she said as the two of them waddled like two lame ducks back to the waiting survivor.

Nelly knew in her condition that there was no way she could pick up the half-drowned body lying on the bank. So, she angled the lame horse beneath it to where she could pull the water-soaked survivor across the animal's back. It took several tries before she managed to drag the semi-conscious baggage onto the back of the ailing horse. By the time she finished the grueling task, Nelly was winded, and her back ached.

She knew there was no time to waste. The sun was starting to edge its way down behind the red-looking bluffs. And from the sound of the thunder rumbling in the distance, the storm was hot on their heels. Nelly knew the two of them would have to find some kind of safe haven before dark or be left to the changing elements.

The twosome had traveled for hours when the lightning became too intense to ignore. It popped like cooking corn in a hot kettle over their heads, threatening their every step. In a panicked state, Nelly tried to find anything that would protect them until it passed. As she came around a jagged cliff she noticed a small opening toward the middle of the upper rocks. Her heart jumped in her chest as she hoped that it would allow them the slightest amount of shelter for the evening or at least until she could go for help. But the closer they got to the distant opening the wider it became.

When they finally made it to their destination, she was amazed at its size. The opening was certainly large enough for the three of them. Cautiously, she stepped inside the rocky cavern. Behind her the thunder and lightning raged, the relentless wind slamming against the rocks. Moments later it started to rain like someone had thrown a bucket of water from the angry sky.

Between lighting strikes, she could see a lone lantern sitting off to the side of the entrance. Cautiously, she led the exhausted horse through the opening as a lightning lit up the darkness. Much to her surprise there on a makeshift table sat a lantern. Anxiously, her shaking fingers lit the wick as the room filled with dancing shadows. They'd made it. Purposely, she struggled to pull the moaning body off the lame horse. It landed with a hollow thud. As she turned toward the exhausted horse, Nelly's knees buckled beneath her. Fatigue overcame her. Within seconds, she passed out on the cold-stone floor.

# CHAPTER 4

The wind was howling like a murderer going to the gallows the day that they laid Emmy and Charlie's coffins to rest under the large old oak that protected Maria and Becky's graves. At times it was so deafening that a person had to cover their ears. The sound of bending trees and brush as it swirled across the vastness of the Baxter ranch made the onlookers have to cover their faces. It was as though the heavens were angry that the life of the kind cowboy and the breath of the beautiful young wife of Matthew Baxter had ceased to exist. Like their lives had been stolen in such an ugly, unholy, manner that the raging heavens were striking out against the unjustified tragedy.

Most of the townsfolk showed up to convey their condolences over the horrible ordeal. Their disbelieving faces said this was one of the worst travesties to happen in the quiet valley for a long, long time. With heartfelt sorrow, the townsfolk stared at the darkened window of the old log house where the twin sisters desperately fought for their lives.

Several times Jeffrey tried to help Matthew as he covered the empty box of the young woman that had encompassed his entire world.

"Stay away from her!" he yelled at his twin brother, holding the shovel high above his head.

"I don't want your filthy hands touching my goodbye!"

"Matthew?" Jeffrey was offended. "What are you saying?"

"You hated everything about her." Matthew gave his brother a look of distain. "How do I know you weren't a part of this? Huh?"

"What? Don't be ridiculous. She was your wife." But Jeffrey's gut did a complete flip-flop as those words stung his soul. "I would never do something like that."

"Wouldn't you?" Matthew accused, raging as he shoved his brother halfway across the pile of dirt. "Get away from her!" he sobbed as he continued to go through the motions of his expected title.

Within minutes of the confrontation, Abe stood between them. "We'll have none of this today!" Abe said. "Not, today."

The heated glare on Matthew's face said he would hurt his brother if he came near Emmy's grave again. He looked like a hollow reed bent in the wind. Emmy, his wife, his love, his soul mate was dead the heartache on his saddened face said his life was over.

Jeffrey had never seen Matthew act like this in his life. He stood in total silence completely shaken at the whole ordeal. His brother was broken, the way wind snaps a dry twig, leaving only the slightest part of the dangling memory. He didn't want the big-hipped heifer to die killing her had never crossed his mind, he just didn't want her to be a part of their family. She was an embarrassment, a huge eyesore. And who knew Charlie would pick up with his Aunt Lizzie and they'd wind up together.

There would be no restitution for this heinous act. For the first time in his life, he was sorry for his big mouth but, more than that, he knew someone would be knocking on his door wanting payment for false declarations. But, who? Who had listened to his foolishness? The thought of his Aunt Lizzie made him shudder. For a brief moment, he gazed at the twins' bedroom window as an icy chill ran up his spine, he knew they would kill him if they found out.

The identical women were far too sick to attend the burial of Emmy and Charlie not that they didn't try. In a glassy-eyed state, the two identical women demanded to know why they were in the hallway being treated in such a harsh manner. Together, the two determined defenders fought off every human encounter as they drug themselves down the wooden corridor of the old log house, their stubborn determination never ceased to amaze them. Arm-in-arm they crawled along the wooden floor like two black widow spiders with no venom left to defend themselves. They both slapped at the hands of those who tried to stop them from completing their destination, not once letting go of each other.

But their determined quest was cut short as the wooden planks denied them access at the top of the stairwell, hopelessly they reached out the way a captain reaches for the tattered billows of a sailing ship torn by the angry wind of a storm-tossed sea. Their fevered bodies refused them passage, denying them access to the safety of their port. Today, there was no Captain to guide them toward land and no ship to carry them to safety. No matter how hard the sickly duo tried to reach their intended destination the further it faded into a fog right before their distrusting eyes.

"Emmy, Charlie," their voices echoed within the same breath as the two of them lay sprawled out on the hard wooden floor, shoulder to shoulder, arm-in-arm with no strength left as they descended into the depths of darkness.

It was a heart-wrenching sight as Abe and Clinton with heavy hearts begrudgingly placed them back in their feathered prison…twice.

# CHAPTER 5

It was daylight when Nelly came to with a start.

"Where am I?" she whispered as her eyes took in the unfamiliar surroundings. "How did I get here?"

She shook her head trying to make some semblance of her odd position. After a moment or two, the memories of yesterday's harrowing event came crashing back.

As she sat there, she could see the rescued body from the river lying still as a stone on the cavern floor, the lame horse standing patiently over it. She took in a breath of relief as she studied the rise and fall of her passenger's chest. It seemed a strand of leather from the horses harness had somehow gotten wrapped around the leg of her unlikely companion. It had made it impossible for the hairy beast to escape.

Nelly struggled to stand up slowly, stretching her back. Every bone in her body hurt, and the lump she detested was still there.

"Enjoy your stay," she stated in an angry tone, "it won't be for long."

Slowly, she turned in a circle taking in her new surroundings. She was surprised how much larger the cavern was in the daylight than in the dark. Relief flooded her body. This cavern would be large enough for all of them to survive. After all, who knew how long it would be before they could find their way back to the small place called Crocker or the Lazy AB Ranch? She saw the clear-looking stream of water as it ran haphazardly toward the back of the cave. *Quite ingenious*, she thought to herself. To the left of it, sat two large sacks of grain. Neither one had been opened. For a moment, the thought of it made her shudder to think this place of refuge was being used by someone else. To the side of that, stood several cords of dried wood stacked in a neat pile against one of the stone walls.

In the middle of the oversized room was a lone makeshift table with a single lantern on each end. Against one wall there was a small roughly crafted bed with several folded blankets on the end. It was all she could do to keep from crawling under those warm-looking covers, forgetting everything around her and going to sleep. She shook off the feeling and continued her search.

Much to her delight, someone had chipped an inglenook in a bench-like rock for cooking with an iron bar that could be accessed from either side. Toward the west side of the cavern, sat a generously crafted fire pit made for heat. Nelly held her breath for a split second. Now she definitely knew they weren't the only ones using this cavern for shelter.

Nelly took a deep breath as she waddled to where her new found companion laid unconscious on the rocky floor, she needed to get the cold body over to the makeshift bed. All she could do was hope the wooden contraption wouldn't collapse beneath the weight of them both. It took all the strength that she had to get the job done as the pregnant woman sat at the foot of the cot huffing and puffing.

Once she got the survivor settled she walked to where the quiet animal stood staring at her with large oval eyes. She could tell by the disillusioned look that he didn't understand his predicament at all.

"I know," she whispered. "Me, neither."

Gently, she patted his neck as she led the limping horse toward the small stall that had been built just for him. She tossed fresh hay on top of what little was already in the wooden trough.

The surviving horse was glad to have his own place to be. He'd been through a traumatic ordeal. Nelly stood there in total amazement as she watched him take a good long drink of the cold water. She couldn't help but wonder why the animal would want anything to do with water again after what he'd survived. She let out a soft giggle when he started throwing small pieces of the stemmy meal in all directions.

"You'll have lots to tell your friends once we get home." Then she added, "If we get home."

Purposely, she pulled the wooden pole across the opening and walked back toward the middle of the cavern. With the lame horse settled, she made a small fire. It felt good as the warmth began to fill the cozy opening.

Nelly sat there for several minutes as the warmth of the fire started to work its way through her achy body. Then she let out a determined sigh as she started looking through the odds and ends she'd seen lying around.

She was delighted when she found an old coffee pot quickly she washed it clean and set it on the flame. Then she found a small bag of coffee which she added to the boiling water, the aroma that filled the dreary dampness was heavenly. She needed something, anything to warm her cold body. Then, she took off all of her clothing, which was still damp, and laid it close to the fire to dry. As her eyes followed the reflection of the cave wall, there was no way to miss the silhouette of her misshapen body, furiously, she picked up a small stone and threw it at the mocking form the loud noise made the horse jump.

"Stinking Baxter's who needs em!"

Everyone on the Lazy AB ranch knew that the ornery twins, Liza and Lizzie, were in the fight for their lives, spiking high fevers then dropping with icy chills. When they were younger, their resistance to the venom had been much stronger. The poison that had invaded their typically resilient bodies was putting up a determined fight, demanding the right to overtake their souls. So, between Naomi, Matthew, Clinton, and Hattie, they kept a twenty-four-hour vigil on their condition.

It was a worrisome passage of time, and the whole Baxter household prayed that they would live, but mostly they prayed that Lizzie would survive the loss of the famed cowboy. Everyone who placed their feet on Baxter soil knew how the dark-eyed rebel-rouser had felt about the hired cowhand named Charlie, how he had won the wild-hearted filly with a flick of his lasso in his determined hand with those kind, steely eyes.

It was as though he knew when to rein her in and then with the breath of the wind let her run, a feat that no one on the Lazy AB Ranch had seen another cowboy do. The two of them were a good match. Always challenging the nature of their beings, yet neither one overstepping the bounds of the other.

It was a comfort knowing that they were able to take charge of any situation with authority and wisdom. Now the mysterious cowhand was dead, and the free-spirited mystical princess was fighting for her life, every breathing soul on the ranch was sorry. Sorry, that the barren spinster who'd given up her younger life to raise a child conceived out of wedlock could suffer such an unkind fate, knowing she would face yet another emotional disaster. It was a sad state of affairs at the Baxter ranch and not one man, woman, or child liked it.

Albert had been out to the ranch on several occasions. He too was upset about the happy-go-lucky cowhand, and Matthew's lovely wife, Emmy. But his main concern was with Liza. He'd fallen head over heels in love with the sassy twin and his heart was in his throat. She was intriguing and so intelligent, but mostly, she was a comforting warmth in his arms. Her strength was like a wild filly, her heart the size of a mountain. He knew if she lived he'd be asking her an important question.

There were no words to describe how Matthew felt about losing, Emmy. It was as though someone had kicked the guts right out of the middle of him, only his empty blue pools told the real truth.

"Emmy," he breathed as he pitched the last shovel of dirt and fell to his knees sobbing. "I should have been there." he acted like a scorned child. "You were my responsibility, I should have never left you. My Emmy, my wife, forgive me."

Sorrowfully, he looked into Abe's chiseled face.

"My Emmy." He wept. "What do I do, papa? Without, her?" he sobbed.

"Breathe," Abe answered as he knelt beside his broken grandson. "Breathe."

# CHAPTER 6

Nelly sat by the sleeping survivor's side just as the baby kicked her like a mule.

"Sure now that I nearly died you decide to make an appearance," she said in a disgusted tone. "Hey," Nelly coaxed her quiet companion. "Can you hear me?"

There was no missing the fluttering lids as the fevered brown eyes opened. Their gaze shocked them both as their eyes met.

"Nelly?" the voice said in a startled tone. "What are you doing here?"

"The better question is what are you doing here?" she declared her eyes becoming misty. "Thank goodness you're finally awake I thought you were done for."

"What happened?" she questioned.

"Why don't you tell me?" Nelly said. "I found you wrapped around a pile of branches in the creek which by the way is now a river for crying out loud."

"What? How could that be? I can't swim," Emmy fretted.

"Well, you swam well enough to save yourself, at least until I came along. That tree was holding on by a thread," Nelly stated wondering why she had gotten in the water in first place. What had she been thinking, her life would be a lot simpler if she'd let her drown.

"So, Emmy, what happened?"

"The stranger with the green eyes, he tried to kill us me, and Charlie," her eyes became misty. "I think, Charlie's—dead. I don't know for sure; the wagon flipped, rolled, and threw me out, I flew off of the bank into the rushing water before I could…" Emmy started crying at the thought.

"It's all right, Emmy," Nelly assured her. "I'm just glad you're alive." But why would anyone purposely want to hurt the lovely young woman she wondered, unless... they found out the truth about the old cowhand. She gave Emmy a worried look.

"Listen, I'm going to have to set that arm it's broken. Let's just hope nothing else is."

Emmy's eyes grew wide. "Are you sure it can't wait till we get back to the ranch?"

The remark both irritated and humored the dressmaker. "It probably could if I knew where the ranch was," she said matter-of-factly.

"What do you mean?" Emmy's voice was on the edge of panic.

"I mean, I have no idea where we've been, where we are, or where we're going," she said simply. "None, and, you're in no condition to travel for at least a good week, maybe two. And...," Nelly stated in a disgusted manner, "I can't go far in this... this... condition."

Emmy stared into her annoyed looking eyes as she saw the roundness of her belly, "You're pregnant?"

"Appears so." Nelly snipped sharply.

"Is it—Charlie's?" Emmy whispered. She hadn't missed the way that the pretty dressmaker had latched on to the older cowboy. "I saw you talking and dancing at the hoedown."

"Charlie?" Nelly scoffed, repulsed at the accusation. "Don't be crazy, Charlie and I, we had an agreement about a certain legal matter nothing more." Then she added, "Seems we both got blindsided."

"I don't understand," Emmy said confused.

Nelly took in a deep breath. "It's Jeffrey's, the baby. Yeah, it's Jeffrey's."

"Jeffrey?" there was no missing the shock in Emmy's voice.

"That's where I was going when I found you to make him responsible for this, what a joke, no one can make Jeffrey Baxter Jones responsible for anything. I don't know who I thought I was kidding acting all big and bad, I knew better. The devil never finds justice for liars like Jeffrey," she said in a distant tone. "So much for men and their charmed lives."

"I, I didn't know," Emmy said fretfully.

"Yeah, well don't feel special no one knows, only me and now you." Nelly replied. It was plain to see that Emmy's condition at this point wasn't going to allow her any mercy.

"I'm sorry, not for you having the baby, but...." Emmy's eyes were so cloudy looking. She was so close to being comatose.

Honestly, so was Nelly as she got up and placed several more sticks of wood on the fire. Then she came back to the small cot with a bottle of whiskey in her hand.

"What's this?" Emmy asked in a skeptical tone. "Whiskey can't be good for a baby."

Nelly let out a half laugh. "The whiskey isn't for me it's for you. As much as you dislike the idea, Emmy, I have to set that arm. So, drink some of this," Nelly instructed firmly. "It will help with the pain." She gave Emmy a sympathetic look. "Man, bad luck seems to dog your heels."

Emmy stared into Nelly's tired face; she looked a lot different without her makeup, older somehow, harder.

"So," she asked through heavy lids, afraid that if she closed her eyes she'd never wake up again, "you really don't know where we are?"

"Not a clue. The water was fast, Emmy, we floated downstream for a long way before I could get us to shore, honestly I don't know," she sighed. "Maybe when you're feeling better we can walk up on that pile of rocks out there and take a good look around something might be familiar to you, as sure as the sun sets it wasn't to me."

Nelly gave the weak woman a slight smile. "For now, there's enough food here to last us for a good while." She gave Emmy a knowing look. "Someone has been using this cave as a hideout, or maybe just a place to hang their hat I don't know, so let's just hope whoever it belongs to doesn't want it back, at least, until we're gone." She gave Emmy a sympathetic smile. "I'm sorry, Emmy, but I have a feeling, everyone thinks you're dead."

"No." a sick look etched across her face. "But, I'm not." Then as though something clicked in her brain she struggled to sit up. "Matthew, he'll be worried sick!"

Immediately, Nelly placed her hand on Emmy's chest. "You stay put." she demanded. "You're in no condition to be moving around, besides, I have a feeling that if Charlie is dead, they wanted you dead, too. Whoever concocted this bush whacking, this travesty, you're probably safer here than on the ranch. Dead people don't talk Emmy, and if the man that did this finds out you're not dead, well, he certainly doesn't need access to you." She gave Emmy an expressive look. "Listen, I expect Matthew is going to have a broken heart for a while but think how happy he's going to be when he sees you again." Not that Nelly really cared if she saw any of them again.

"I know," Emmy whispered just as Nelly popped the bone into place. The intense pain shocked her as she let out a shrill scream that echoed throughout the cavern.

When Nelly heard the bone snap, her delicate fingers worked like magic on the clean break as she padded, then tied it securely bracing it with wooden slats. "Just lay there a minute Emmy the pain will stop here shortly. Take some deep breaths and sip on that cup of whiskey, yep, just like that, there you go." She instructed.

The two of them sat quietly for some time Emmy taking in deep breaths. Nelly just sipped her hot coffee. "All right Emmy, the clothes have to come off," she stated in a straightforward tone. She could see the hesitation on her ashen face. "I don't care," Nelly said in a bored state. "Look at me, I'm a horse, so don't go giving me that look."

Emmy couldn't help but smile at the outspoken woman as she started to disrobe. Nelly let out a gasp when she saw the healed scars on her chest and back. She'd seen those same marks on someone else, someone she'd loved dearly.

Instantly, Emmy's face turned brilliant red. "The night of the harvest dance," she closed her eyes trying to block out the horrible picture. "I was... mother and I we were..." Tears ran down her pale face as she stared into the stormy dressmakers eyes.

"Did you see their faces?" Nelly's voice sounded so dark. "Did you recognize any of them?"

"No," she said simply. "But, I saw his eyes. They were like looking into a green grave, no expression, only hate," Emmy struggled for the right words. "I think it was," she hesitated for a brief moment. "Jeffrey."

"Jeffrey!" Nelly exclaimed in disbelief. "He's been with me nearly every night since we met, secretly of course until this baby thing reared its ugly head. It couldn't have been him. What time?"

"A couple of hours or so after the Harvest dance," she answered.

"Nope. Wrong man he was drunk as a skunk in bed with me, unless," Nelly stopped talking for a brief moment. "No, that's not even a possibility. What makes you think it was him?" Nelly questioned.

"I'd know those eyes anywhere," Emmy stated. "He hates me."

Nelly sat still for several seconds before she spoke.

"It wasn't Jeffrey, Emmy, but I think I know who it was."

"You do?" Emmy responded.

"Yes," Nelly said in a distant voice.

"Who?" Emmy couldn't believe her ears.

"His name is Jerry Bondes, formerly known as Jerry Bowman, better known as, Jeremiah Jones," she said matter-of-factly, "If any of those names are actually real."

"Lizzie's Jeremiah Jones?" Emmy's voice seemed shocked. "But, he's dead." Emmy couldn't believe her ears. "Lizzie killed him. How would you know such a man?" Emmy asked.

"He's the murderer of two little girls ages four and five and my twin sister, Karen." She gave Emmy a bitter-sweet smile. "He's a monster."

"Why would he come...?" she didn't understand.

Nelly never gave her a chance to finish her question. "I was younger than my sister by two minutes and always a bit jealous," Nelly continued, "I still remember the stories about what a wonderful father and husband he was. Jerimiah that is, *until the door shut behind him*. He'd tell everyone how much he loved my sister. *Loved to beat her.* I hated him and he really hated me. He slit their throats you know, while they were sleeping. Those two little girls were so precious they never hurt anyone, and neither did my sister, I vowed I'd put him six feet under someday, do to him, what he had done to them. You can guess how shocked I was when I heard that he and his supposed twin brother, which by the way was no brother at all, just some dusty cowpoke that looked like him," she stated matter-of-factly." That he'd hooked up with another man in a saloon pretending to be US Marshalls. Can you believe that? I should kill him just for that alone anyway, I was told that he was here wooing the hand of a beautiful young barrenness. I knew with everything that made me holy," she turned and gave Emmy a wicked smile, "Which ain't much mind you, I knew it was only a matter of time before he'd do the same thing to her."

She took a breath and continued. "I was told, Lizzie killed him in a fit of rage. But, I know the slaughtering weasel better than that. He's like a cat with nine lives and a thousand tricks up his sleeve. I know his handiwork. I've seen it up close, and personal. Lizzie might believe she killed Jerimiah and I'm not saying she didn't shoot him, but he's not dead. He's here, and when I find him, I'll finish what I started ten years ago," Nelly said matter-of-factly as she sat and stared at the shocked face of the woman in front of her.

"But, Nelly," Emmy whispered through misty eyes, "Jeffrey's..."

"I know!" she said in an angry tone before she even realized it. "I know. But, it really doesn't matter I plan to kill this parasite Jeffrey's placed in my body when it's born." Nelly missed the strange look that Emmy gave her. "It wasn't supposed to happen a ploy to get information that backfired that's all."

Nelly saw the look of contention on Emmy's disbelieving face.

"Oh, don't think that I didn't do everything humanly possible to try and get rid of this pile of fermented flesh. Even in saving you I hoped it would explode and drown in the muck water where it belongs." Her tone got darker. "But, no it clung there like a clump of dog dung sticks to your boot. I won't bring something that belongs to the devil into this world one, is enough."

"But, it's an innocent baby," Emmy argued, flabbergasted at what Nelly had just said.

"Not to me." her eyes turned dark and threatening. "To me it's a rock around my neck."

"I don't understand," Emmy stated in a defeated tone. .

"All I wanted was information, Emmy!" she retorted with a sharp edge to her.

"About what?" Emmy asked.

"Him!" she all but yelled. "Jerimiah whoever he is, I won't rest until I find that filthy murderer. He needs to pay for what he's done, to my sister, my nieces, to you. Can't you see that Emmy, he needs to go back to the devil's lair where he belongs!"

Nelly's eyes were filled with angry unshed tears.

"I told myself, don't mix up the two, Nelly, don't fall for this Jones guy. Did I listen? No. So, what do I have now? This. This...thing." she placed her hand on her stomach.

"Someone played a dirty trick on me, and, I don't like tricks. It's time to put this whole matter to bed, and finish what I came here to do." Her eyes were void of any feelings, "Put the lying vermin in the ground."

It was plain to see that the effects of the whiskey or perhaps the pain of the break were starting to take their toll on Emmy's senses. She gave the small woman an exhausted stare. "So, you really don't know where we are or is that just another lie?"

"I'm done lying," Nelly sighed.

In a caring manner, Emmy touched Nelly's overly warm hand.

"It doesn't matter, Nelly I'm damaged goods either way you look at me. Thank you for saving me, for all I put you through," she sighed. "For telling me the truth."

It was all Emmy could do to keep her eyes open as she gazed at the small woman through heavy lids. This was a side of the petite dressmaker she'd never seen. Then Emmy drifted off to sleep with Nelly not far behind her.

The fire was nearly out when Nelly came to. She was so stiff and sore that she could barely move and her back was killing her. She took a moment to take in her unusual surroundings as she glanced at the sickly woman lying next to her on the makeshift cot. It was dark now and she had no idea how long they had been asleep.

"Good morning, afternoon, evening," Nelly whispered in a sarcastic tone as she made her way to the firepit.

"What happened?" Emmy asked completely confused. "Where am I?"

"The same place you were yesterday, the day before, and the day before that." Nelly answered annoyed.

"I'm sorry, I just realized," she gave the woman a strange look. "You've done all this work and I'm...? Are you all right?"

"Yeah," she conceded, "It's not your fault." Then she got up and waddled back to the cot. Like a skilled doctor she placed her hand on Emmy's heated forehead. "Hungry?"

"A little," she confessed.

"Me, too." Like a mother duck Nelly waddled to the scant looking shelves and started rummaging through the various collection of odds and ends. Oh how she wished she was sitting at the Baxter ranch sipping wine, eating supper, contentedly enjoying the company of Jeffrey's mother and aunt. The daydream gave Nelly a sense of false position. A place to belong. But, she also knew Liza's son would never confess about his end of impregnating her innocent body.

"Innocent?" What a joke she scoffed after the way Jeffrey had scattered like a shotgun blast nearly tearing the door of her dress shop off its hinges in his escape she was sure he'd never been held accountable for much in his lying life. Nope, dear sweet momma Liza has bailed his sorry carcass out every time.

# CHAPTER 7

"I'm sick," Liza whined as she held her pale hand across her stomach.

"I'm, sicker," Lizzie mimicked her sister's actions.

"I'm so hot," Liza stated as she gave her sibling a grumpy look.

"I'm certain that I'm, hotter." Lizzie echoed returning the gesture.

"You're not sicker than me, Lizzie!" Liza seethed, tired of her sister's constant mimicking. "You have more immunity, remember? You brag about it all the time."

"Not today I don't." she snapped back, acting completely traumatized. "I'm sure, I'm dying," she countered in a pitiful tone.

"No you're not." Liza stated in a heated tone.

"Yes, I am," she continued in her pitifully dramatic state.

"Not without me, and I ain't dying today, or tomorrow." Liza injected stubbornly.

"Yes, I am," Lizzie said completely over dramatizing her situation. "It's just a matter of time."

"Stop being such a skunks butt, Lizzie." Liza accused. "Honestly, I'm being so much braver than you are right now."

"That's because you didn't get bit as hard as I did." she continued to whine loudly. "Have you seen my bite? Have you? It's hideous, I'll be scared for life!"

"It barely broke the skin." Liza said as she threw up her hands.

"Barely broke the skin my as..." she snapped.

"Yeah, well I'm not surprised, how could he have missed it." Liza snapped at her annoying sister.

"I know it's bad." Lizzie ignored her sister's remark.

"Mine is much deeper." Liza argued.

"How can yours be deeper when mine is the worst? Don't be an idiot!" Lizzie argued hotly.

"I'll show you an idiot!" Liza threatened as she reached for her sister.

Both women hit the floor at the same time just as Hattie and Clinton walked into the room.

"Oh, my." Hattie stated as she hurried to the side of the bed. "What has happened here?"

"Liza!" Clinton exclaimed.

"She started it!" they said in unison, furious with each other. "Get off of me."

Both women were too sickly to do much damage to the other, they both had high fevers and could barely move. Together they looked like two turtles lying upside down on wiggling shells. It was all Clinton and Hattie could do to keep from laughing aloud they were a pathetic sight.

"Come," Hattie said to Lizzie, "You two are much too sick to be down here on the floor."

"I know," Lizzie said pitifully. "I'm the sickest."

"Of course you are, honey," Hattie soothed through grinning lips.

Naomi laughed aloud when she saw the hysterical sight as she stepped into the bedroom. In her hand she held a small tray with a cup of warm tea for each woman.

"Now, mother," she said in a very grown-up tone, "You and Aunt Liza need to drink this. It will make you feel better," she coaxed.

They both gave the caring young woman a loving smile. "Thanks," they said in unison sipping the warm liquid. "Did you...?"

"Yes," she answered respectfully.

"Two, teaspoons?" Liza questioned.

"Yes, auntie," Naomi answered.

"Plenty of...?" Lizzie questioned with a raised eyebrow.

"Just the right amount," Naomi concluded.

"Thanks," they said drifting fast asleep.

With care, Clinton covered them both with a clean sheet, and soft blanket as he spoke, "How can two such beautiful women look like angels when they're asleep and so full of piss and vinegar when they're awake?"

"When you figure that one out," Naomi said kissing Clinton's cheek, "You let me know."

The young twosome stopped just inside the door frame as Clinton leaned over Naomi and quietly whispered, "Would you consider a stroll after supper with me tonight, Miss Flying Eagle Baxter?"

"I surely would," she pretended to swoon as they quietly shut the bedroom door and walked hand in hand down the stairway stealing little kisses. When they slipped inside the homey room and gazed into her cousin's sad face, Naomi felt a pang of guilt. She had Clinton and Matthew had lost his everything, his Emmy.

Several hours later Lizzie jumped with a start, the lazy reflection of the hollowed moon shone like a tattle-telling beacon. The moonlit blast danced across the quaintly decorated bedroom. Several hours of dormant sleep had come and gone since the herbs in the warm tea had taken their effect on the two sleeping patients. When she realized that it was dark she shook her sister.

"Liza, wake up they're going on a walk."

"Who?" Liza complained still half drugged as she pushed her probing sister's hand away several times.

"Naomi, and Clinton that's who." she snapped back.

"I'm too sick," Liza whined as she clung to her pillow. "I can't move."

"I'm much sicker than you and look at me, I'm sitting up." But the fact was the room was spinning out of control, Lizzie immediately slid backward against the soft down pillow like melted butter. "We have to follow them," Lizzie pleaded in a puny voice. "You know as well as I do what can happen on a walk." Her cool blue eyes begged for her sister's understanding.

"Nothing ever happened to me on a walk," Liza stated matter-of-factly.

Irritated with her identical sibling, Lizzie snapped, "That's because no one ever took you on a walk."

"Point taken," Liza caved. She desperately wanted to go back to sleep. Then on second thought she continued as she remembered that she was half miffed at her sister for waking her up.

"I think Naomi is old enough to know right from wrong on a walk." Once again she pushed her sister's hand away. "Leave me be."

"Yeah, we thought that about Sarah too and look what happened there," Lizzie mumbled.

Liza got a sick look on her face knowing that her sister was right.

"What are we going to do? I'm too sick to move. I still have a fever." Like a small child she slowly felt her forehead.

"Good grief Liza, you're whining like an old hound dog." Lizzie exclaimed, surprised that her sibling was being such a baby. "Where's your backbone? C'mon I'll show you how it's done."

But when Lizzie stood up and leaned against the wall for support, she was nauseous. It took all the strength that she had to hold up her weak body. But, she was determined to find the young lovers.

"Come on, Liza." she pulled her unwilling accomplice out of bed and into a standing position.

"See, you can do it." she smiled weakly. But, within seconds the sturdy wall that was holding them up started to sway like two wet reeds they both slid to the floor.

Groggy they said in unison, "We'll crawl."

Like twin spiders hobbling on broken legs, one desperately clung to the other as they carefully opened their bedroom door and slid out into the dimly lit hallway. In their white sleeping gowns, they looked like two ghosts making their way down the darkened corridor.

Hattie heard them coming long before she saw them as she glanced toward the stairwell. Typically, the twosome could sneak up behind a person and you'd never know they were there, tonight, there was no missing them. They sounded like two hobbled horses dragging a log across a dry rocky creek bed. But, being the unobtrusive woman that she was, Hattie opted to say nothing whatever they were up to was no good and she wasn't about to get herself involved in that. Besides, she had come to discover that they were their own worst enemies and the more rope you gave them the higher they hung themselves. So, she let the two dark-eyed villains disappear into the kitchen as they half crawled, half fell out of the back door. It was a pathetic sight watching the two of them trying to slip unnoticed into the darkness. She gave Abe a quick nod.

"Do you think she saw us?" Lizzie whispered in a devilishly sneaky tone.

"Who?" Liza whispered as she looked around her like a scared cat.

"Hattie." Lizzie recoiled completely miffed at her sister's idiocy.

"Hattie? What's she doing hiding out here?" Liza questioned.

"Not out here, in the house she was in the house!" Lizzie insisted.

"How should I know?" Liza whined. "My head hurts so badly I had my eyes shut."

"Grumblin' horny toads Liza." Lizzie said as her body swooned beneath her. "You are such a sissy." Disgusted, she clung to her identical sibling for support. "Come on."

Liza gave her sister a disgusted look, but she was much too sick to argue with her. Like two drunken sailors they staggered across the open yard to the well. It was a good place to sit for a moment both women were out of breath and sweating.

"I'm so hot," Liza whined. "Can we go back now?"

Lizzie was just as hot. "Yeah, maybe we should." Then she remembered why they were out there in the first place. "No, she's by the creek."

"Hattie? Why is Hattie at the creek this time of night?" Liza asked in a confused tone.

"Would you forget about, Hattie, it's Clinton and Naomi." Lizzie was fed up with her sister's jabbering.

"Clinton and Naomi, what are they doing out here this time of the night?" Liza's face showed her confusion.

"Oh shut up Liza and come on I swear you get goofier every day are you sure that snake didn't bite you in the head?" As though they'd had one too many slugs of whiskey from the jug they had hidden in the barn. They made their way to the back of the old brown building near the creek.

Abe and Hattie sat with smirks on both their faces as the two disappeared into the night.

"That won't be good," Abe stated matter-of-factly, watching them fade within the willows.

"Nope," Hattie said as they continued their game of chess.

There was no missing the worried look from his chess partner. "If they're not back in an hour, we'll go fetch them." Abe stated.

The two marauding ghosts had spotted their unsuspecting prey about ten feet from the mossy bank. They were able to get just close enough to hear what was being said laying like two clams on the cool grassy earth within the lingering willows. It gave their heads a chance to quit spinning as they watched the brilliance of the stars.

"I'm gonna throw up," Liza whined.

"Oh, stop it, everything is such an episode with you. Look, I'm much sicker than you are and I'm not throwing up." Lizzie gave her sister a dirty look. "Honestly, what has happened to you?" she mumbled as she rolled over onto her stomach and threw up.

"I got bit by a huge snn—aake, Lizzie, that's what happened to me." Two seconds later Liza threw up.

"More like a tiny water snake." Lizzie argued.

"What did you say?" Liza countered. "I swear...Oh, my stomach, quick, scoot over," she demanded.

"Liza," Lizzie sneered at her sibling, "I swear next time I'm leaving you in the house!"

"Alright," she agreed in a whining tone.

But, it was all Lizzie could do to keep from throwing up again, herself.

"One little scratch on your thigh and you act like a two-year-old!" she snapped at her sister.

The snake had definitely bitten them both with a heated vengeance and this time they were both extremely sick. But not sick enough to keep from eavesdropping on the happy young couple sitting by the creek minding their own business.

"Clinton," Naomi whispered, as she leaned against him seductively, "why haven't you tried to take me?"

"What!" Lizzie exclaimed, completely taken aback at Naomi's forward question. "Take her where?"

Within seconds, Liza was on her stomach too giving her sister a shocked look. "She didn't learn that from me." she said in self-defense.

"Are you saying she learned it from me?" Lizzie snapped in a whisper as she slugged her sister in the arm.

Instantly, Liza hit her back. "Shush, we're missing the conversation!"

"I don't know," Clinton said through a crooked smile. "Is that what you want?"

"You know how I feel about you?" Naomi whispered in an inviting tone as she untied the top string to her blouse.

"You little scamp." Lizzie seethed through fevered lips.

"I do," Clinton answered, as he gently kissed the warmth of her sweet waiting lips. "You have made that very clear."

Both women gasp at the same time. "This behavior is not becoming of an innocent young lady." Liza said, completely shocked.

"Is there something wrong with me?" Naomi questioned through cow-like eyes.

"Only that you're the most beautiful woman that I've ever seen," he said adoringly. "And, what does that mean?" she asked seductively as she loosened another string. "Am I not woman enough for you?"

"Naomi," he said simply. "I'm a man with little means all I own is one broken down horse, a saddle that used to belong to my dead father, and a black stallion that was given to me for saving your life."

"What's wrong with the horse?" Lizzie stated, insulted that he included their generous gift in his defense. "I'll take the blasted thing back."

"There's nothing wrong with the horse, you numbskull." Liza insisted. "Just, listen!"

"I don't care about that," Naomi said sincerely.

"She'd better not." Lizzie said. "We raised her better than that!"

"You should," Clinton stated firmly.

"Why?" Lizzie whispered through breathless lips.

"Why?" Liza echoed within the same breath.

"Why?" Naomi asked sounding like a scorned school girl.

Clinton took in a deep sigh before he spoke.

"People talk, Naomi their voices will sound cruel and hurtful. They will accuse me of being some kind of gold digger that came out here to settle a land claim against your family and instead I laid claim to Abe Baxter's only granddaughter, the wealthiest cattle Baron in this territory. They'll say if I couldn't get his money one way, I'd get it another."

"Are you?" the twins whispered in unison breathlessly.

"When in fact, I didn't even know that you existed. I knew a little about your mother and aunt, I was forewarned a hundred times over about those two. But, nothing about you. You, have been the most amazing surprise." His soft hollow eyes engulfed her. "I've loved you; I think from the moment I saw you," he confessed. "But, I, love—you—Naomi, and only, you, not your money, or your land, or the fact that you are a Baxter."

"Oh," the twins said in unison, "He's good."

"I won't have people believing badly of you or trying to muddy your reputation because of me for some quick romp in the grass I'm not willing to spoil anything about you." He paused for a brief moment. "I won't disrespect your mother, Naomi, she's sacrificed enough for one lifetime, and, I won't lie to Abe by pretending to be one person and winding up being another. It's not who I am, I won't do that, Naomi."

"Why would anyone think badly of me if only you and I know?" she questioned innocently.

"I think you're forgetting something."

"How do you mean?"

"There's one that knows everything about us, good, bad, right, wrong. I don't care to disappoint him." He gave her a knowing look.

"The Mighty One," she sighed.

"So you do want me?" she sounded confused. "Just not tonight?"

"Of course I do," he said, surprised at her odd question. "Only an idiot wouldn't want you, Naomi. You're like this lovely flower that no one has plucked one single petal from. You stand straight and strong, defying the elements around you. You're beautiful."

Clinton leaned back against one arm on the lush soft grass pulling Naomi close beside him. He let out a slight sigh,

"Do you have any idea what would happen if I was to do what you ask?"

"What?" she sighed.

"Well, for one thing I don't need a bullet in my foot. I kinda like it."

"He'd better like more than his foot," Lizzie said as she waited like a night-crawler in the wet grass giving her sister a knowing smirk. "I'll scalp him bald!"

Naomi gave him a slug in the arm. "Really, no kidding around."

"I just think that there's plenty of time for you to become a woman, I mean look at you, you're barely old enough," he stated in a justified tone.

"Oh, that ain't gonna sit well," Lizzie said.

"Nope," Liza agreed, "she'll be cranky over that one."

"What is that supposed to mean!" Naomi snapped in a haughty tone. "I am a woman full grown, Clinton Small."

"Not that, grown," Liza whispered.

"You are a strong-willed woman, Naomi," he said sternly. "I will give you that. But, you'd best be for learning that you won't get your way with me all the time, you won't."

"So, you're saying you don't want me." she teased.

"I'm saying that I want you more than anything I've ever wanted in my whole life but, not here, not now, not tonight I don't feel right about it." He gazed lovingly into her disappointed eyes, "There will be plenty of time for us, you, me, this ranch, I can feel it."

"All right, Clinton," Naomi sighed, as she leaned against him. "I just know, I was conceived out here beneath the stars and moonlight," she said in a softer tone. "I just thought, maybe..."

"I know you were, Naomi," he said with love in his eyes, "Cause only magic from the starry heavens that cover this god-forsaken place could have made a flower as beautiful as you.

Besides," he said with a twinkle in his eyes, "who says we can't do exactly this when we get married?"

"I love you, Clinton," she breathed.

"I know," he said. "I love you too, Naomi." Together the two of them cuddled beneath the silver moon and gazed at the wonder of the sparkling stars.

Lizzie looked at her sister, "I knew I liked that boy."

"Yeah," Liza agreed with tears in her eyes.

# CHAPTER 8

Knowing that Naomi was in good hands and satisfied that there would be no shenanigans on this beautiful moonlit night, the duo haphazardly made their way back toward the safety of the old log house. Once again they made it as far as the well.

"I have to rest a minute," Lizzie stated completely out of breath as she pulled her twin to the ground with her. Together they balanced against the rock wall.

"I just need to close my eyes for one second."

"Me, too." Liza agreed.

Within minutes the wandering twosome were sound asleep, head-to-head, shoulder to shoulder leaning against the cool rocks.

"Can you see them?" Hattie asked in a worried voice.

"Yep," Abe answered.

"Are you going to leave them out there?" Hattie wondered.

"Yep."

"For how long?" she questioned in the same worried state.

Abe glanced at the ticking clock.

"I'll give them about half hour, forty five minutes, if they don't come to by then, I'll get Matthew to help me drag them back upstairs."

There was no missing the odd look on Hattie's face.

"They won't remember," Abe stated. "The fever will erase everything, it's your move."

Abe kept a silent vigil on the old clock and was just about ready to wake Matthew when he noticed Liza begin to stir. He gave Hattie a wicked grin.

"They're up."

Liza took a quick look around trying to gather her wits about her when she nudged her sleeping sister.

"Lizzie, someone put us outside."

"What?" Lizzie's tone said she didn't understand.

"We're outside." Liza repeated.

"Why would someone play such a dirty trick? Can't they see we're sick?" Lizzie snapped.

They sat silently for several minutes when Liza grabbed Lizzie's arm.

"Do you think someone tried to kidnap us? That's what happened maybe we're not worth as much as we think."

Again they sat quietly hoping their worlds would quit spinning. Then they looked at each other.

"Maybe, they did bring us back that's what papa always said, if'n someone took us they'd bring us back. When we get better, we'll straighten this out." Lizzie stated matter-of-factly tone.

"You bet! We'll put a knot on their head the size of a melon." Liza stated bravely.

"What are they doing out there?" Hattie asked as she peeked out the window. "Are they talking?"

"No, more like conspiring," Abe stated in a half laugh.

"Abe Baxter!" Hattie scolded. "We need to go and help them."

He looked into Hattie's lovely face she reminded him so much of Emmy. "Just watch and learn Hattie, they, will figure it out, they always do," he chuckled.

Together the sick duo tried to stand up, but the world spun out of control as they slid aimlessly back to the waiting ground. Again and again they staggered to their feet only to wobble like two wet blades of grass sliding backward.

"I can see we got us a hiccup," Lizzie said in a faint tone. "I can't stand up without you, and you can't stand up."

"I don't wanna stand up Lizzie, it makes my head hurt." Liza whined.

"Didn't I just say that?" Lizzie snapped. "Honestly, Liza, just let me think." Lizzie sat perfectly still for several minutes. "That's it, I know what we'll do."

"What?" Liza jumped. She'd nearly fallen asleep again.

"Crawl. Yeah, we can crawl," Lizzie stated in a controlled tone. "We're good crawlers."

"It is a lot closer to the ground if we crawl, it's almost like standing up while we're laying down," Liza agreed.

"It's a good plan," Lizzie said. "You go first Liza, and I'll follow behind. If we go single file no one will hear or see us."

"Yeah, that is a good plan," Liza agreed as she started toward the safety of the log house. It felt like they had been crawling forever when Lizzie looked up it seemed like an awful long ways left to go.

"Are you even moving up there?" Lizzie accused.

"Of course I'm moving!" Liza snapped back just as she threw up. "Don't crawl there, Lizzie," she instructed.

"Oh, for crying out loud here, let me lead!" Lizzie insisted.

"Now what are they doing?" Hattie asked as she watched the arguing pair.

"Deciding who is in charge," Abe smirked.

"How do you know that?" Hattie questioned.

"I raised them," he continued with a smile.

Once again the twosome took off on their trek when Liza started giggling. "Hey, Lizzie, when's the last time you changed those ugly bloomers?"

"What are you rattling about back there, ain't a durned thing wrong with my bloomers." Lizzie wanted to give her sister a good whack, but she knew she couldn't reach her.

"All I know is they look like they done been hanging on the back end of Charlie's old mule!" Liza giggled.

"You take that back!" Lizzie stated, furious.

"Will not!" Liza countered.

"Then, take that, Miss Bloomer head!"

Within seconds, Lizzie turned and pushed Liza over into the dirt.

It only took a moment before Liza punched Lizzie back, two good shoves they both laid like turtles upside-down on their shells. "Now look what you've done we're upside-down again. Pull me over."

"Alright, but when we get up to our room remind me to smack you!" Lizzie insisted angrily.

"If I can remember." Liza retorted.

As Abe and Hattie watched the ridiculous duo out the kitchen window, they couldn't help but laugh. They were a comical sight.

"How in the world did you manage with those two all these years?" The older woman wondered.

"Believe me-some days were harder than others." he had to admit. "But, every day when they woke up, it was like a new adventure, for all of us."

One by one they made their way up the planked steps to the landing. Both women were breathing like a set of wind broke horses.

"I can't go any farther," Liza whined.

"We have to. Come on, we're almost there." Intentionally, Lizzie grabbed her sister's arm and drug her up to the step where she was sitting. "I think we need to rest a minute."

"Leave me I beg you, just leave me." Liza whined. "Let me die."

"I'm not leaving you anywhere you big, daisy. Honestly, Liza, you're a Baxter for heaven's sake, act like it, now come on."

Lizzie tried to open the back door.

"It's stuck," she stated as she pushed at the wooden barrier.

"Stuck? That door never sticks. What are you doing up there?" Liza snapped. "Try again."

Once again, Lizzie turned the knob just as Abe pulled the handle as he and Hattie stepped back into the shadows. They placed their hands over their mouths it was all they could do to keep from laughing out loud. The twins sounded like a herd of cattle as they barely made it into the kitchen.

"Are we inside?" Liza asked in a pathetic tone.

"Yes, just keep coming and keep your voice down!" Lizzie scolded.

"What was that?" Liza's voice was shaky as she froze in place.

"What, what did you hear?" Lizzie asked in an anxious state.

"Someone else is here."

"You sure?" Lizzie questioned. By now she could barely see her sister as she grabbed her arm. Lizzie's head was pounding and every muscle in her body ached. "There's no one in this kitchen but us."

"No! Someone's here maybe…the kidnappers." Like a snake Liza turned her head side to side. Lizzie never moved.

"See anything?" Lizzie whispered.

"Not yet, but my feeling says we are not alone." Liza whispered as both eyes crossed in the corners. "I know these feelings; someone is sneaking around, there's a polecat in this kitchen."

"What's going on with...what's wrong with your eyes? Blast it Liza, how many fingers am I holding up?" Lizzie was frustrated.

"Where's my gun?" Liza asked.

"What gun, did we have a gun?" Lizzie couldn't remember. "If we did you lost it."

"I resent that tone, Lizzie, and if I could crawl faster I'd...!" Liza injected.

There was no missing them as they made their way through the kitchen.

"If you had your gun sister you'd probably shoot me in the butt." Lizzie argued.

"Yeah, well it wasn't my gun that wasn't sighted in." Liza argued back.

"Get up here before I sight something else in!" Lizzie grumbled.

Abe gave Hattie a huge vindictive smile. They sounded like two lumbering elephants as they climbed up one step and slid down two on the wooden planks.

"Shouldn't we help them?" Hattie fussed.

"Nope," Abe stated in a stern tone.

"Will you stop going backward, Lizzie, I can't keep up with you!" Liza commanded.

"I'm not the one going backwards, Liza you are. Here, let's loop arms."

"That's a good plan," Liza whispered.

It took the fumbling duo a good half hour before they finally crested the top of the stairs. "We made it!" Liza said amazed and breathless.

"Shh! You'll wake up the whole house. No one knows we're well enough to be out of bed." Lizzie insisted.

"Are we?" Liza whimpered.

"No, sister," Lizzie answered in the same tone. "But we can't let them know that, just a little ways to go down the hall and into our bedroom. We can make it. Now, c'mon!" she insisted.

Together the two of them crawled down the darkened hallway. Like a mouse, Matthew cracked his door and peeked out. It was quite a sight. There they were the two of them moving like white snails. He could only imagine what they'd been up to. Anxiously, he looked toward the staircase as Abe put his finger to his lips, Matthew gave his father a knowing nod and quietly closed the door.

Hattie gave Abe a heads up. "They're in," she grinned.

"They'll be good and sick tomorrow," Abe stated as they resumed their game of chess moving his pawn. Then he looked into the blonde-haired woman's tickled eyes. "You know, there's almost justice in the thought of that!" he said as he let out a loud laugh.

"Abe Baxter!" Hattie scolded as she placed her long fingers over her giggling lips.

"You don't know them yet someday you'll understand what I mean," he said in humored self-defense. "They are their own worst enemies."

But, Hattie did know the two exquisite young women. She knew that they were hard as nails when they needed to be. That those blue eyes would pull you in and spit you out like a cold dark night if you disappointed them. That the two of them stood for truth and right, it didn't take long to find out what a combined force the two of them could be if you sided against them. Justice was their prevailing hand fair-minded and strong willed, with no time for liars or thieves. They didn't sit in judgment or hold a grudge against a situation that was solved, no, they squared up and took care of it, then let it go.

But more than anything, she'd never forget how the two of them had humbly accepted an old broken-down woman into their home and their hearts with open arms when in fact they didn't have to. How they had given her defiled daughter back her dignity at a time when she'd felt dirty and scorned. She knew Liza and Lizzie Baxter all right, and she'd defend either one of them till her last breath.

True to Abe's word the following days hadn't been any picnic for the two sick sisters. Their fevers spiked and cooled, spiked and cooled. They couldn't keep anything in their stomachs and talked in their sleep shouting out names in anger. Some of the words were in English, some they learned from Chief Mad Dog, and some were not befitting a lady. Through it all not once did they let go of each other.

Finally, at the end of the second week the color started to come back to their cheeks, and when Naomi walked into the sunny room that fateful morning the marauding twins were already up leaning back against their pillows like two queens. It was the most refreshing sight Naomi had seen in weeks. Their eyes were brighter, and they were no longer nauseated. Lovingly, she placed a bowl of Hattie's steaming hot oatmeal on each nightstand.

"You two are looking much better today," she smiled. "How do you feel?"

"I'm still nauseous," Lizzie confessed. "I'll be glad when this feeling goes away."

"Me, too." Liza stated as she grabbed the metal bucket and threw up.

Lovingly, Naomi gave each one a kiss on the forehead. "Mother, is that grass in your hair?"

"Grass?" Lizzie said in surprised tone. "Don't be silly where would I get grass?" Intentionally, she flicked the dried stems off of her pillow as she gave Liza a suspicious glare.

"What are you looking at me for?" Liza whined. "I been right here with you."

"So—you—say." Lizzie countered as she gave her the evil eye.

Naomi gave them both a doubtful look she knew they were scandalous and weren't to be trusted, sick or not.

"Besides, we're both tired of being hold up in this room like a couple of trapped coyotes," Liza injected. "Can we go down to the porch today for a while, you know, blow the stink off'n us?"

"Who are you saying stinks? I don't stink, I've never stinked." Lizzie argued.

"Well you sure as a rotted tree don't smell good, I'm sit'n' right here, downwind."

"By the way," Lizzie said through questioning eyes ignoring her sister, "where is everyone?"

Naomi got a sick look on her caring face as she gazed at her mother. "What do you mean—everyone?"

"What do I mean?" Lizzie scoffed. "I mean where is everyone? How come no one's come to see us? Make sure we're getting better?" she demanded.

"Um, mother they have. All of them," she insisted.

"Blasted snakebite," Lizzie stated, "it makes me all goofy headed I can't remember a dern'd thing!"

"How do you mean?" Naomi questioned.

"Well, I'm wondering why Charlie hasn't been up here to see if I'm dead or alive." she countered.

"Umm," she couldn't believe how faint her voice sounded. "I'm sure he'd like to be," she answered softly.

"Don't tell me father sent him up to the highline, and I bet the rangy scoundrel went. Wait till I get my hands on him."

Then, Lizzie gave her daughter a caring look.

"How long have we been out?"

"Right at the end of three weeks, mother. Give or take a day," Naomi answered.

"What? Why that's longer than usual. Was there complications?" Lizzie was incredibly surprised.

"No, but they were big, snakes, they didn't act normal."

She sat next to Lizzie on the bed. "When I looked down in the canyon I was shocked at their size, and their eyes didn't look right."

"What do you mean, didn't look right?" Lizzie questioned.

"They were black, evil looking." The thought of it gave Naomi the shivers.

"They felt big," Liza chimed in.

"Isn't Emmy helping you with the doctoring?" Lizzie questioned. "I can't remember seeing her either. She will need to learn this you know."

Liza gave Naomi a loving look. "Matthew has more important chores to do than becoming your nursemaid."

"Yes, Ma'am," Naomi's eyes filled instantly with unshed tears. "Mother," she whispered, "Auntie, eat your oatmeal I'll be back in a bit to check on you, maybe get a bath ready. You two stink." Naomi practically flew from the room closing the door behind her like a whirlwind.

"What's that all about?" Lizzie asked Liza.

"Danged if I know," Liza stated between bites of her hot cereal. "She didn't learn that from me."

"So what are you sayin'?" Her tone was anything but kind.

"I'm sayin' you stink!" Liza couldn't keep the smirk of her face.

It was all Naomi could do just to get down the hallway she couldn't breathe. Several times she had to stop and lay her spinning head against the coolness of the wall the heated tears made her journey even harder as she searched for her grandfather. When she rounded the corner of the kitchen, all eyes were on her as she flew into Abe's arms.

"She doesn't remember!" she sobbed frantically.

Abe was so shocked from Naomi's intrusion that he dropped his coffee cup where he stood. It sounded like thunder as it shattered into a million pieces on the wooden floor. "Who doesn't remember what?" he questioned, completely baffled at her uncomposed behavior, holding her close.

It was all she could do to speak. "She asked me where he was." she sobbed uncontrollably. "I... I didn't know what to say, I... I froze. Oh, Papa, she doesn't remember. They don't remember what happened to... to Charlie or Emmy, neither one of them remember anything."

The room became deathly quiet as Abe held Naomi in his large caring arms. Gently, he patted her on the back, trying to sooth her sobbing as his rendering brown eyes scanned the other knowing faces at the table.

"It's all right," he said as he mouthed his apologies to Dancing Bear for the broken cup as she picked up the large pieces. There was no missing the heartache in Matthew's sad blue eyes or the sorrow that draped across Hattie's ashen face.

The twins were better, physically that is, now, the hard part would begin. Now, the real healing would start.

"I knew this day would come," Abe let out a deep sigh of regret. "Although, I'll be honest, I was sure hoping it wouldn't."

He placed his work worn hands over his face. Then, he looked back at the uncertain faces.

"I taught them that white is white and black is black. No gray lines. There's no room for second-guessing you do that, out there, on the *prairie*, you die. Believe what you can see, not what you're told to see. I always told them if you believe long enough and loud enough good will override evil. That you get to see and feel just the slightest glimpse of what you cherish the most in this simple circle we call life. That the reflection that we see in the mirror is the glassed-in window of your soul. How you choose to play out that reflection interprets the core of who we are. How you chose to embrace it tells what you'll become." Abe let out a deep sigh. "They've lived that philosophy since they were old enough to walk. My little, blue-eyed wildflowers."

His eyes scanned the sorrowful faces sitting at the long oak table. Purposely, he sat down on one of the large oak chairs Naomi curled up like a small kitten in his lap.

"I instilled in them the difference between lying and telling the truth. For months I tried to trick them into telling me a lie." Abe scoffed. "After a few weeks they had turned the table and were testing me." He laughed. "But that's a story for another day."

The kitchen was quiet and now everyone sitting at that table understood how good old fashioned grit and determination had built a dynasty, that his strength was their strength, their strength was his. No one sitting at that breakfast table wanted to change places with this self-made man named, Abe Baxter.

He took in a deep breath. "I told them, pounded it into their brains that the edge of reason is a fine line that you and only you decide, good…or…bad the judgment is yours to carry. That's where I'm going to have to go with this, over the edge of reason, the fine line will snap, for a tender heart it will be a harsh and unforgiving journey."

Everyone knew that his heart, his soul, his reason for being, his breath lay within the two ailing women resting comfortably upstairs.

Abe looked at Matthew's tear-stained face and held those blue-water-colored circles within his own. Lovingly, he continued to pat Naomi's trembling back.

"Those of us sitting at this table—here—today, its best you know that we will lose Lizzie for a while," he said sadly. "Even the hardest stone will crack when it rubs against itself with an intense emotional force. Liza will have no choice but to go with her their life light won't allow anything less." He gave Hattie a sympathetic look, knowing that she knew exactly what he was talking about.

Abe let out a deep exhausted sigh, "I know it's up to me to stand firm and let truth untangle a broken heart, Lizzie won't believe anyone else. She's been that way since they were young they both have."

Intentionally, the rapacious man walked Naomi to where Clinton sat at the table as he handed her weeping body over to the arms of the waiting mapmaker. Affectionately, Abe rubbed the top of Matthew's curly black hair.

"So, until the time comes, it will be my responsibility and mine alone to tell her. If she asks, which she will, dodge the question at all costs and tell the riders to do the same. No one, and I mean no one, is to say a word about, *'Charlie'*, no one. Now, if you'll all excuse me."

His command was final, which was graciously accepted with those sitting at the table. They didn't want to tell Liza and Lizzie the sad news about Charlie and Emmy. But more than that, not one person wanted to walk in Abe Baxter's boots, not today. The kitchen was completely silent until they heard the closing of the solid oak door to the den.

# CHAPTER 9

Emmy sat with a slight smirk on her face as Nelly battled with two freshly caught trout. Since their disagreement over the fate of the baby, the dressmaker's temperament had long ago changed from friendly to distant.

"What a picture," she said kiddingly. "If I could only paint!"

As Nelly placed her hand on her aching back, she smiled at the tall blonde. "How ya feeling? Think you can travel soon?"

Nelly was quite an exceptional woman and the two of them had formed a common bond of survival. She was not the timid, faint-hearted seamstress that everyone thought she was. No, this little lady was strong as an ox and hearty as a horse.

"I've told you fifty times that I'm fine, and I think that maybe you should slow down and take it easy for a bit." Emmy took the fish from Nelly's weary hands and placed them in the hot skillet.

Emmy knew there was no way she was going to allow the petite dressmaker to kill the innocent pod of flesh that had stretched her body into an odd proportion. So, over the past two weeks she'd done anything and everything she could to keep the woman in her good graces.

Nelly sat and watched Emmy's disillusioned features across the fire as night fall began to tip its hat. Emmy was working on some kind of scheme. Nelly was sure of it. She could feel it in her gut, her gut had never failed her. Once she finally settled on a spot to ease the pain in her lower abdomen, Nelly stared at the glowing fire, her thoughts lost in the flickering flame.

"It's only fair that you know the truth about me," the dressmaker offered from out of nowhere. "I see the way you judge me when you think my back is turned. I'm not a monster. I know you think I am because of what I said about the baby. But monster or not, Emmy, I'm not going to change my mind."

No matter how hard Nelly tried to deny the pain in her lower abdomen she knew there would be a baby born tonight. "I'm not a dressmaker," she confessed in a cunning tone. "I only do that to disguise who I really am."

There was no missing the ache in Emmy's eyes. "Maybe you should be," Emmy said frankly, "No one could have done for me what you did."

Her sincere compliment took the dressmaker off guard. "Blast it, Emmy! I've tried so hard to dislike you, but you make it impossible!"

"I do?" Emmy was shocked at her tone.

Nelly continued. "I've heard told it takes a killer to catch a killer."

All Emmy could do was stare, horrified at the concept of what that statement really meant.

"I've been sent here by Baron Grand, an extraordinarily rich man from further West than here," she stated matter-of-factly.

"I know who he is," Emmy stated.

"How do you know?" Nelly's tone was quick and shocked.

"We sell him cattle and horses. What does he have to do with this?" she questioned.

"That would make sense, but I don't know much about cattle, Emmy. I'm a hired killer." Her cold hollow eyes stared into Emmy's shocked face. "Believe me, it's true I've been trained by the best. Well trained. Baron Grand's wife was my sister. My twin sister. I loved her and her two little girls. That's why I'm here. Redemption!" She let out a painful sigh. "Seems the Baron didn't have any success sending a man to do the job he wanted done. He knew I was a killer for hire and he made me a very handsome offer. You see he had this notion a woman would be able to offer a somewhat different approach to get close to him." She had a darkness hidden deep like a canyon within her tone. "Pay me or not this time it's personal."

"Job? What kind of job?" she sounded so confused. "And, close to, who?"

"He's here," Nelly stated as she flicked a small rock across the uneven stone floor.

"Who's here?" Emmy was struggling to keep up with the confusing conversation.

"The man that killed Charlie and supposedly, you," she stated matter-of-factly.

Doubting her tale Emmy questioned. "How do you know who—*he*—is?"

"Because he didn't get to finish what he started," she stated matter of factly. Her demeanor was sharp and curt.

Her answer was so frank that Emmy knew the woman wasn't lying. "I don't understand."

"Of course you don't understand!" Nelly snapped. "Why would you?"

"What didn't *who* get to finish?" Emmy asked, still not sure of the woman's intentions.

"Killing, Liza. He always kills his lovers. She was the lucky one."

Her eyes were so cold.

Emmy couldn't help herself. She was flabbergasted. "You heard the story all wrong, Nelly. Jerimiah didn't marry anyone; Jacob married Liza."

Stirring the fire with a stick, Nelly's tone said otherwise. "Is that so?"

Emmy continued. "Everyone knew Lizzie was quite smitten with Jerimiah I was told she loved him deeply. He told her he couldn't marry her on account he was already married, the rat."

"Really? You sure about that?" she asked.

Emmy was puzzled by the dressmaker's question.

"Yes. Lizzie and Naomi were doing a ride about, they did that a lot. Something about teaching her the lay of the land."

"She was young then? Naomi?" The dressmaker continued to stirring the fire.

"Oh, yes. But that didn't matter to Lizzie that little girl went everywhere with her. Anyway, they stopped to rest Lizzie's horse for a bit on a small plateau. I guess you could see pretty much the whole valley in all directions. That's when she spotted a lone rider. I swear she has eyes like an eagle!"

"Just one rider?" She could tell by Nelly's posture that the woman didn't believe her.

"That's what she said. Anyway, she followed him to the Old Willow Pasture, watched him disappear down a deep rocky ridge, then in a blink, he rode out the other side."

"Sneaky," Nelly said. "Humph."

"You can't cross that ravine. You have to go around. It's just holes in the ground, jagged rocks, and small canyons. So, she followed his horse's hoof prints and sure enough, there was an opening. I guess it was a hollowed out rocky cave of sorts that a horse could barely fit through. Honestly, I'm surprised the twins didn't know about it they know about everything else."

"That I believe," Nelly commented.

They both watched as sparks jumped then drifted slowly to the cave floor.

"Lots of times they threatened to burn the old white house to the ground. They hate that place. You know it's where their younger sister got killed. They didn't know about Naomi then. It was a sad time," she said, her eyes misty. "Anyway, she snuck into the cave and sure enough there he was I'm thinkin' he wasn't alone." Emmy let out a deep sigh. "I guess he tried to shoot Naomi, but Lizzie shot him instead."

"That's quite a story." Nelly's tone said it was a bunch of lies. "Lizzie might have shot him but let me tell you the animal isn't dead," she concurred.

"How can that be?" Emmy's voice had a quiver in it.

"Emmy, you've got his handiwork written all over your body. I recognized the marks when we cut out your dress. He does that to all of his victims. He's sick in the head! He's like a rabid dog, getting pleasure from hearing the sound of ripping flesh. I know, I've hunted the deranged maniac for close to ten years now. You're lucky he didn't kill you and your mother."

Emmy's face showed the horror. "Are you sure?" she whispered.

"I wouldn't lie to you about that!" Nelly snapped. "I want him dead!"

"Honestly, Nelly," Emmy paused for a moment, "There are days I wish he would have killed me. Slit my throat. What that stinking monster and his gang of thugs took from me the night of the harvest dance, I'll never get back."

"Like I said, lucky."

"I don't feel lucky," she whispered.

"There's been four women in all. At least four that I know of anyway. Knowing him, the way I do, there's probably more I just haven't found them all yet. It's a relief to know I can quit looking now. Let me tell ya those two men caused enough heartache for a lifetime for too many women with their twisted minds trading their identities back and forth. It's time for him to go back where he came from just like his so-called brother!" Nelly stated full of rage.

"So, how do you suppose you'll catch him? I mean with you here, and him out there?" Emmy asked a sinking feeling in the pit of her gut.

Nelly was going to kill her.

"Well, whichever one it is, Jacob or Jerimiah, he thinks you're dead. That gives me the leg up. He'll get careless and bold. That's a part of his pattern, too. He and brother dog-licker will go to the ranch. They'll hide like the cowards that they are. He'll be waiting for both twins. He won't blink an eye as he watches them die by his hand. But I'll be there just inside the shadows to place a bullet right between his murdering eyes! The dirty liar will never see it coming. He'll never get close to either one of them." She gave Emmy a cunning glare.

"You said accomplice? Would that be Jeffrey?" Emmy questioned.

"Jeffrey!" Nelly could hardly contain herself. "Don't be naive! He doesn't have the brains to wipe his own nose. Or, the patience." Then she gave Emmy a menacing look. "Are you sure that Jeffrey and Matthew are twins? They certainly don't look like it. I don't see the resemblance."

Emmy gave the woman a sad look. "Yes. And now I think you're reaching. I'm sorry about your sister and her young children. That's an awful thing, but, who would help kill someone else for something that they weren't even involved in?"

"Who said that she wasn't involved?" Nelly snapped.

"She? His partner is a woman?" Emmy questioned.

"Yes." Nelly said.

Emmy couldn't believe what she was hearing. "The other killer is a woman?"

"That's what I'm saying." Nelly gave Emmy an odd look as she ran her hand across the bulging flesh sitting like an old stump in front of her. "I had no idea how it would feel having power over another human. To be held accountable for every good or bad thing they do. Protecting them just because they're yours actions and all, baked like bread in your body. But now that I do, I don't want it. I don't want this baby it was a mistake from the beginning." She continued telling Emmy how she had used Jeffrey for information. "And let me tell ya for a rich son with a big mouth, he sure don't know much. I got too involved he sucked me in." Nelly explained.

It was easy to tell she was mad at herself. "How could I ever go back to Texas knowing the infant cradled in my arms was the baby of the outlaw I was sent to kill? How do I explain that?" she gave Emmy a strained look. "I can't."

The two women sat in silence for some time. Emmy knew that Nelly wouldn't hesitate to kill her if she tried to save the baby, but she also knew she would try everything in her power to keep her from doing it.

Nelly on the other hand, knew, from the determined look on Emmy's face that she would never let her kill the unborn baby in her womb. They were at a definite crossroads.

Emmy saw a sadistic look wash across Nelly's tired face, a cold darkness that sent shiver's up her spine.

Then, from out of nowhere, Nelly magically pointed a pistol directly at Emmy's chest. "I'm going to have to tie you up, Emmy," she said plainly. "I see that look on your face I can't trust your thoughts anymore. I'll kill you if I have to." Instantly, a pain etched its way across her bulging abdomen. "You're a good person," she struggled to say, "Don't make me do that."

"But, who will help you with the birthing of the baby?" Emmy asked as tears started welling up in her confused eyes, knowing that she and the baby might have the same fate.

"I've already told you, there won't be any baby!" she yelled. "Ooh." she moaned. "It hurts."

"Please, don't kill the baby." Emmy begged. "Let me raise it I can't have children because of what happened to me. Please, I won't tell anyone I swear I won't."

"Shut up!" Nelly screamed as she-half walked, half-stumbled to where Emmy sat. "You make me sick being so nice all the time. Don't you get tired of being all good and proper? Just shut up!"

"So," Emmy said with contempt in her voice, "Killing me is part of your plan then?"

"Maybe!"

"Then why did you bother saving me if you were going to kill me?"

"I don't know." Nelly was baffled herself at the question.

"I'll give you whatever you want," Emmy stated plain and simple. "Name it." Emmy's tone was so desperate. "It's yours."

"Anything?" Nelly mused.

"Yes, anything." she was so hopeful.

"Would you trade Matthew for this baby?"

Emmy's reply was instant. "Of course not." What an odd question she thought.

"Did I hear you wrong?" Nelly's eyes penetrated deep into Emmy's.

"N..." she said in a confused state.

"You did say anything, right?" Nelly jeered.

"Yes. No!" she was frustrated.

"Correct me if I'm wrong. You just said anything that I want, but what I want you're not willing to give me. Is that right?"

"He's my husband." Emmy's voice said Nelly had tricked her.

Nelly continued. "He seems like a good man. I've never had one of those."

"I could never do that," Emmys voice was definite.

"So you're like everyone else then going back on your word?" Her tone was so hostile.

"No." her answer was simple and honest. "Like I said he's my husband, he's not for sale at any price."

"That's what I thought!"

"No!" Emmy shouted.

With one quick blow, the butt of Nelly's pistol hit Emmy hard across the side of the head. Her world went black as she sank to the floor like a wet sack of grain.

"What is wrong with me?" Nelly stated as she stomped her foot on the rocky floor. "All I did was cause myself more trouble and lost time." she confessed, as she stared at the downed woman. "You were dead once, stay that way this time!"

But before she could get the patient horse saddled, a racking pain etched its way across her abdomen. Nelly was beside herself; she knew the baby was coming her eyes were wild with pain.

"Great!" she yelled as she fell to her weak, pain-stricken knees. "Get out! I want you out of my body the likes of you don't deserve to live!"

Within seconds of her loud blast, a small bloody infant made its way into the world. Nelly gave it a quick kick away from the puddle of blood that had pooled at her feet as it plopped like a sinking stone into the rocky pond.

"Good!" she screamed as though she was possessed. "Drown you little rodent!"

But, the savage words had no more than left her white tormented lips when another pain ripped through her body like a streak of lighting. Crying, she closed her eyes and laid on her back, as another small infant found its way onto the bloody cave floor.

"Devil's gate!" she yelled, raged with pain, reaching for one of the larger stones lying next to her. "There's two of you? I'll crush your skull before I let you live!"

But, just as she was ready to split the baby's head like a ripe melon, a set of deep yellow eyes appeared from out of nowhere within inches of her hand. Immediately, she dropped the rock. As she stared at the snarling muzzle, she wasn't sure if the animal was real or not.

"Where'd you come from you stinking ghost?" She reached for the stone again as the wolf pounced within inches of her body, this time with a deadly growl, Nelly froze.

Slowly, she wiped the dripping sweat from her angry brow as she stared at those sharp white teeth.

"What do you want?" she said in a low tone as she stared at the huge female wolf. She was a hundred fifty pounds if she was an ounce. There was no fear in those menacing eyes as she crouched low to the rocky ground.

Nelly didn't move an inch, in fact, she wasn't sure she was breathing. The wolf's distrusting stare never left Nelly for a moment, purposely she licked her large hairy mouth with her long bloody tongue and stared at the screaming baby. It was plain to see that she wanted it.

"I'm glad you showed up. Take it." She said in a toneless voice. "Eat them both for all I care!"

Hesitantly, the wolf smelled the screaming infant as she gently picked it up with her powerful jaws. As though the animal was in a hunting stance, she crouched down and moved backward holding her prey securely.

Like a snake, Nelly slid away from the bloody mass leaving a trail of red liquid on the cavern floor. She let out a painful yell as a round mass left her body. She never bothered to look.

Nelly was nearly to the protection of the flaming fire when the female wolf made her presence known again. Nelly froze in her tracks.

"There's no more you hairy glutton!"

The wolf snarled at the crazed woman. "I gave you all I had! Take them! They're all yours! What better place for vermin to die than here? You did me a favor."

Holding another rock in her hand, she flung it like a rocket at the crouching dog as it disappeared right before her eyes. She let out a painful moan, holding her abdomen as she walked toward the standing horse. There was no need for her to stay in this rock prison any longer. Her work here was done.

Purposely, she took the gun and aimed it directly at Emmy's head.

"You should have minded your own business. You and those stinking Baxter twins you're so fond of. I told you that there'd be no baby. My word is my bond." Nelly placed her hand over her aching abdomen. "You should have minded your own..."

Bang!

"Now look what you made me do!" Nelly yelled.

Like a burglar leaving the scene of a crime, she reached for the nervous horse, painfully she pulled herself up then rode out of the small cave into the waiting darkness.

# CHAPTER 10

As the self-made tycoon, Abe Baxter sat alone in his study, he couldn't help but ponder this unfathomable situation. Several long weeks of worrying about the two ramrods upstairs had come and gone and now he could take a breath knowing that they were on the mend. They'd come through the worst of it even though he hadn't wanted to admit it, the wily twosome had given him quite a scare.

Doctor Slater and his wife, Gail, had been out to the ranch several times, unannounced, to check on the two sickly women. Not that his medical attention had been wanted, or needed they just showed up.

"So, how are our patients today?" he asked in a jovial mood.

When Abe told him the two ornery women would likely survive the sly doctor tried to hide the disappointment in his voice. He always acted so vexed at the strength of survival that the two women lying quietly on the four-poster bed in front of him possessed. It made Abe wonder was there an ulterior motive for this visit.

"Any normal person would be dead by now," the doctor said to Abe in a baffled tone.

"Maybe, but we all know they aren't normal," Abe said with a hint of humor in his voice.

"Ain't that the truth." the doctor stated as his wife started to unwrap the bandages.

"Don't do that!" Naomi said in a sharp controlling voice, she had their healing well in hand, and didn't need the duo's help.

The meddlesome man jumped a foot, where had she come from? "I need to see," Doctor Slater demanded. "We don't know there's no infection under those wrappings."

"I know," Naomi said in a contentious voice as she walked to the side of the bed edging the doctor's wife out of the way. "And, that's all that matters!"

"Surely you jest, why, you're no physician!" he stated in a high-handed arrogant tone.

"I doubt that you're much of one either!" Naomi snapped back.

The doctor gave her a vexed look. "I see you've taken on your mother's perception of me."

"No, I have my own *'perception'* of you," her facial expression said it was time to go.

"Then, I assume my presence is no longer needed here," he seemed so put out.

"Your so-called presence was never needed—here." Naomi's eyes said it all.

"Gail, gather our things, I know when it's time to leave," he said in a huff.

Immediately, the scant woman picked up her instruments and placed them back into the dark leather bag. She gave Naomi a pensive smile as she waited patiently by the bedroom door.

As though the man couldn't take no for an answer, he added. "We'll be back sometime next week."

"That won't be necessary. They'll be up by then, unless..." Naomi had a half smirk on her knowing face, "You'd like to deal with them personally."

The doctor gave Naomi a perplexed look. "Well, now that I think of it, I do have a full schedule next week. Perhaps the week, after?"

"Like I said before. If you come back, I'll let you talk to them personally. No? Then maybe you best go tend to the folks that think they need you," she said as her back dismissed them both. "I don't."

Within minutes, the sound of the doctor's wagon echoed across the empty yard.

"Mark my words, Gail," the doctor said in an angry tone. "Someday, they won't be so high and mighty. Blasted Baxter's, who needs em!"

The folks in the small community were relieved to hear that the twins would recover. The solidity of the well-known family had been through a terrible ordeal and there wasn't a person in the valley that didn't sympathize with their loss.

It was late evening a week after Doctor Slater's visit when Abe stepped out onto the wooded porch to stretch his fatigued limbs. The cool night air felt good as he stared into the darkened void. It gave him a sense of purpose standing there alone, filling his lungs with the fresh air that made this ranch worth fighting for. Playing the same mind games over and over he wondered if coming to this untamed land and the loss of the people he loved had been worth it. Especially now, when he'd nearly lost the nucleus of what made him whole.

Something about the famed doctor's visit had been bothering him all week. It wasn't anything the man did per say but more his annoyed attitude. Abe had never really been friends with the man. And yet he seemed to know an awful lot about what was going on here, how? He was sure no one on the ranch had conversations about their family with the informed doctor.

Abe stood quietly looking at the stars, taking in the landscape before he even noticed his daughter sitting alone on the porch swing. A red checkered shirt placed beneath her trembling chin was as though it were some kind of magic cloak. The darkening shadows had covered her invisible existence until the tattling moon gave away her solemn silhouette.

Regretting the inevitable, he sat on the wooden swing and pulled her fragile body within his arms. "What-cha doing out here all alone?" he questioned. Feeling the emotional shudder of his weeping daughter against his broad chest was unnerving.

"Waiting for Charlie," Lizzie said, questioning her own statement in a faint voice as she lay quietly in her father's arms, wiping her nose with the soft fabric.

Now, no matter how many times they'd pushed it aside, the day of reckoning was here. Where truth would come knocking on their door like a broken skeleton, demanding its turn to be heard.

"I see," Abe said quietly as he noticed Liza curled up in a small ball on the other wooden swing. He should have known that she wouldn't be far from her ailing sister. They'd never been more than a breath apart their whole lives.

When the distance between father and daughter collided, the identical twin had a steady stream of grief-stricken tears running down her shaken face that matched her sister's. The tortured look brewing in her wary eyes told him all that he needed to know. Abe gave her a discerning smile as Liza pulled her knees up under her trembling chin.

Lizzie heard the constant beating of her father's heart. It had a way of soothing her distress just like when she was a little girl.

"I've been waiting here for hours and I know that any minute Charlie's comin' outta that there ole barn and will be lookin' just for me," she stated through hopeful lips as she placed the shirt back under her chin. The scent of pine mixed with aspen drifted across her senses, it smelled just like him.

"No," Abe said in a sober but firm tone. "He's not, Lizzie."

He didn't want to be the one to shoulder this responsibility. He wanted to lie to her just like he'd told the rest of them to. That her cowboy had rode away. But, he knew better, he knew her, and the only remedy to sooth her wounded soul was the truth.

"It's like I can feel him watching me just inside the shadows. I'm sure that's where he is. He has to be father," she sniffed.

"He's not there, Lizzie," Abe said gently as he caught the glimpse of a shadow to the side of him. When his eyes scanned the distance, there stood Naomi and Clinton. The heartsick mapmaker held the younger Baxter close within his arms as silent tears slipped from their saddened eyes. Naomi had never seen Lizzie like this before, and Clinton hoped he'd never see it again.

"Are you sure?" Lizzie whispered in a doleful tone. Her voice sounded so empty.

"Yes," Abe's tone was steady.

"Are you?" she countered placing her hand across her heart.

"Yes," he answered again as he placed his chin on the top of her head.

"I swear I can see his steely eyes looking right at me," she whispered.

"He's not there, Lizzie. We buried Charlie over a month ago." Abe said in a fatherly tone as he saw Matthew standing just inside the doorway. He had tears running down his disbelieving face holding on to Hattie's trembling hand. Luke stood like an old oak leaning against the porch rail his chiseled face was ashen white. Abe took in a deep breath, they were all here to bear witness as the blue crystals shattered like frozen ice on the dry dusty wood from the fallen princess's cheeks.

"I can still feel the warmth of his breath when he whispers my name." Like a child trying to block out a bad memory, she closed her red swollen eyes.

"No, Lizzie," Abe said in a staying tone. "His breath is still."

"Please father, tell me that's not true!" she sobbed as her shoulders shook from the heartache. "It can't be true it just can't, it can't." A deep shutter filled her body as her voice faded.

Abe didn't miss the soft whimper that escaped Liza's trembling lips when she heard the desperation in her sister's voice. He gave her a look that said she would need to be stronger than ever now.

"It's true, Lizzie," Abe continued firmly.

"Father," she sobbed, "How can that be? I see his face every time I close my eyes. He's all around me, his breath—his smell—his arms. I can't—breea..."

"Charlie is gone," Abe said softly but firmly.

"Why?" Her voice sounded odd as though she couldn't believe that the betraying syllables had been formed from her own lips.

Gently, Abe held his hurting daughter even tighter in his large protective arms letting out a deep breath. "No one knows where the dust will settle in this savage land, Lizzie, or how the wind will shape its destination."

"You have to know, father, you always know," her tone sounded so hopeful.

"Only the Mighty One knows which roads get traveled and which roads lead to a greater destiny," he answered in a caring tone. "I know how much you thought of Charlie, but, his destiny took a different path than yours." He hated having to be the one to tell her again and again. Abe could hear Liza's soft sobs in the distance. "I'm sorry, Lizzie, I am," Abe said in a heartfelt tone as he held her close. "I'm only a man I can't change destiny."

"I miss him, father I miss him so much," her voice quivered.

"I'm sure he misses you, too," Abe stated matter-of-factly. "And in my heart I know he's out there roping those red-eyed, snot-blowing, longhorn cattle riding old Redbone beneath the star-filled sky." He knew how Charlie had felt about Lizzie. It showed in those steely eyes every time that he looked at her. "I'm sure he's wishing he was here holding you instead of blowing across the Western sky like a tumbleweed."

"He forgot to say goodbye," she whispered in a voice that said reality had found its way back into her soul.

"He'd of never done that, Lizzie. Do you remember the first words he said to you?" Abe knew that there was no way anyone would be able to seal the dam of destruction that was going to pull Lizzie into a watery prison except to tell her the truth.

"For the brand," she let out a whimpered sob.

"Charlie made sure his *goodbye* was the same as his *hello*, Lizzie."

"Father," Lizzie whispered. "I need to tell you something."

"I know," Abe whispered for her ears only. "I've known for a while now."

"How do you know, father?" she wondered.

"Oh my beautiful broken wildflower," he whispered as tears filled his eyes. "The wind tells me of many things past, and many things yet to come, some we can't change. And it tells me of the truth that will shine through the sun, I've always listened to its wisdom. You needn't worry, Lizzie the truth will reveal itself in its own time. And like the wind changes directions in a moment, this ache will too."

Both twins had lost weight because of the snake's venomous bite and tonight beneath the crystal-clear sky Lizzie looked especially thin. "Maybe it's time we should all go in," Abe said as he pulled the blanket up around her bony shoulders.

"Emmy must have been terrified running the horses like that," Lizzie said to no one in particular. "The wagon was too heavy, she knew better. She was running from someone."

"What do you mean?" Abe asked, startled at her obvious conclusion. "How do you know she was running the horses?" At the sound of his dead wife's name, Matthew's head jerked around.

"There wouldn't have been any other reason for her to go off of the trail unless Charlie was already shot," she sighed. "He wouldn't have let anyone hurt, Emmy, he loved Emmy and she loved him like the father that she never had. No." Lizzie said simply. "She was afraid there was something else a-foot. Emmy was a strong, level-headed young woman she was scared. She was running from someone, running for her, life." She sat quietly for several seconds. "Mother, Sarah, Maria, Emmy, Charlie, who's next father?"

"Only the Mighty One knows such things," Abe whispered.

Then, from out of nowhere through tortured lips Lizzie said, "I've got a bad misery in my heart father it hangs like a noose around my neck it's choking me. Choking me so bad that sometimes I can't breathe."

"There's no reason for it to linger now, the truth will help you breathe," Abe stated matter-of-factly.

"Father, do you think that I'm cursed, have I done something so horrible that it causes the people that I love to die? Was this my fault?" she whimpered through trembling lips.

"No," Abe answered firmly. "And, don't ever say that again."

"Then why?" she asked, brokenheartedly.

"We can't control this life, Lizzie, it controls itself. It lingers like a baby's breath then vanishes before our very eyes. We don't get to say who stays and who goes. We only know that this is today, this is now. We need to live in the now, embrace it, and learn from it."

"Tell me, father, what has been learned from this heartache?" Once again she started crying. "What have I learned?"

"Love," he whispered. "His love set you free to fly."

"Father, if I find the person that killed my, Charlie," she paused for a brief moment as her voice broke, "There won't be no hanging, just lead between their murdering eyes. Just lead," she said in a barely audible tone as she held Charlie's shirt to her shaken lips. "Father, tell me how do I live without him?" she wept.

"You breathe," he said softly as he held her close. "My beautiful wildflower. You breathe."

"Lizzie," Liza whispered in a heavyhearted tone as she held out her hand, "It's time to go in now; Charlie's not coming."

"I know," Lizzie said pitifully as she clung to the red checkered shirt with one hand and her sister's thin waist with the other. "He's never coming back Father said and he'd never lie to me about that."

She let out a forlorn sigh like a dying bird falling from the protection of its nest as she gazed like a small child into her sister's sad face. "My heart hurts."

"Mine, too," Liza said in an affectionate tone as tears ran down her face. "Mine, too."

Like a small child, Lizzie took comfort in the protection of her sister's arms as she gave her father a look of contentment. "Thank you, father," she whispered as the two of them walked into the old log house. She was sorry, sorry, for all of them. Purposely, she patted Matthew's large trembling hand as her sad blue eyes swallowed Hattie whole. "I know Emmy and Charlie are together I just wish they were here."

Abe stood and watched the twosome in complete awe as they walked up the long stairway. Their strength was held like a brimming bucket of water guarded by the perimeter of each other's hand. He was always amazed how they could disappear right before his eyes into one silhouette.

Abe knew that Lizzie was broken, she reminded him of a China cup that had been dropped. It was going to be up to all of them to gently glue the pieces back together. But then, he also knew no matter how hard they tried, she would never be the same, actually neither one of them would. There would always be a sharp edge to the twins that would draw blood when their voice pricked your skin. No one would ever touch Lizzies heart again the broken vessel would stay closed like a stone in front of an abandoned cave. The whole picture made Abe's soul ache as he listened to the familiar sound of a closing door.

For several minutes, Abe sat alone on the old wooden step gazing at the hallowing moon, staring at the starry sky. Purposely, he ran his large work-worn hands through his thick dark hair.

There was no question in his mind that Lizzie would never get over the loss of Charlie. *Why did the messenger of death have to keep taking and taking and taking? Why did there have to be so much sorrow? Why couldn't life just stay the same?*

Abe felt like his chest was going to explode as he stared out at the darkness, he wished Charlie would step out of the shadows and put things right. Swoop his daughter up, spin her round and round and let their laughter ring like a lullaby throughout the large yard. His family had lost so much…and, he'd nearly lost them.

Until today, he'd never questioned whether it was worth trying to make a better life for his family as he sat and listened to the night sounds. Not once did he second guess his choice. The path was so clear to him, now, sitting here he wasn't so sure.

Then from out of nowhere a dark whispering wind taunted him, "Surrender," it said.

"No!" he shouted back furiously. "I won't surrender, not to the likes of you, and, I'll never give up!"

"How much more must I take before you see I will win?" the dark voice lectured.

"I won't let you win, I won't cower to your sinful ways, and I won't quit!" he shouted angrily. "This is my heritage, my purpose in life, my destiny!"

"My destiny for you is much richer," the voice swooned like a sultry woman.

"I don't need your riches, all the riches I need are right here." Abe place his huge work-worn hand over his heart.

"I can give you unlimited power." the taunting voice whispered again.

"You? I'm driven by a much stronger power than the likes of you. You can't even show your face. You hide in the wind like a little girl." he stated matter-of-factly.

Suddenly, the wind had a cold chill to it. "Who are you to stand there and throw insults at me when I know your deep dark secrets? I know where your breaking point is." the voice snapped back angrily. "I know what drr—ii—ves you." Abe heard a high-pitched screech. "I nearly stole it right from under your self important nose!"

"You know nothing about me," Abe scoffed in a confident tone. "I have the protection of The Mighty One, he's the one that wakes me for a new day, every day when the sun rises, and the stars go to sleep, not you. I know life comes with a price I've lived it over and over day by day. I've walk in it till my boots are worn thin." Like a mighty warrior he shook his fists. "Whoever you are you don't get the souls who live and love on this ranch. You get nothing!"

Abe made a slight circle before he spoke again. "Do you see me? Do you hear me? This is my home given to me by The Mighty One. He is wise, smarter than you could ever think of being. You are nothing in his sight. Nothing. This ranch is where my children sleep and their children sleep and those yet to come will sleep. This is his land, it's not for sale at any price!"

Justified in his fury, he walked back into the safety of the old log house as a swirling dirt devil snapped at the back of his heels whipping across the aging wooden planks, trying its best to snatch his feet from under him. Tiny particles of dirt and rocks slapped against the frame of the old wooden house as he slammed the door behind him blocking the destructor's path. The hungry whirlwind fell to the wooden porch in a disappointed heap as it left the particles of waste behind.

In the distance, not more than fifty feet away, a set of sea green eyes watched with unbridled rage as they hid in the darkness. Once again, Abe Baxter's good medicine had defeated his evil efforts the way a father would scold an innocent child. Blast you!

"I've turned this house upside down, inside out, and still you refuse to surrender." the wicked voice hissed. "Next time I'll finish what I started here. I will smother the very breath that gives you life, I will snuff it out, crush it. You won't walk away from that!"

# CHAPTER 11

Every day for several weeks, the townsfolks baked goods and the likes when they caught wind that Liza and Lizzie were still battling the sickness from the snake bite. Like they needed to be a part of the healing process from their horrible brush with death. They needed to share their heartfelt condolences for the two headstrong rebels. They needed to be a part of the healing process, see that they were breathing with their own eyes.

Abe knew it was just an excuse to make sure the two rebellious outlaws hadn't really died. The small place called Crocker had come to respect the two unruly Baxter women no one wanted to see them die.

As weeks slipped into months, the Baxter household was quiet. Inside the kitchen of the old ranch house there were no unruly episodes at the breakfast or dinner table, no bickering, no loud outbursts of anger, nothing. The twins were quiet as two mice. Not even Jeffrey, who seemed to be preoccupied when he made one of his rare appearances, could get a rise out of either one of them. It seemed the sun had forgotten how to shine its beaming rays into the windowed hearts of the twin Baxter women.

"Papa," Naomi said. "Dancing Bear and I want to come with you today and help, can we? Please, papa."

"I could sure use the extra hands," he said honestly as he stared at the pale faced woman at the end of the table. The work on the ranch was piling up without the well-schooled hands of the twins. They always knew what needed done before it needed done.

"Where will you be?" Lizzie questioned through empty eyes. She was still feeling quite nauseous from the snake bite.

"We're going to catch that corner down by the Old Willow pasture block that section of ground out for good," Abe concluded. "If the vultures want it, let them fight over it." Everyone waited for some kind of explosion to erupt over the location, when there was none, Abe continued. "We'll leave in about half an hour or so."

"Where's Clinton?" Lizzie asked with no emotion.

"He had business in town," Naomi stated. "He'll be back by supper."

"Matthew, where's he?" There was no missing the worry in her eyes.

"Doctoring cattle on the high ridge, he'll be back tonight as well," Abe stated.

"They can go," Lizzie stated with a warning in her voice. "But, make sure you take your pistol and your rifle, ya hear? I don't want you out on that god-for-saken prairie alone and unarmed!"

Liza gave her sister a strange look for she too felt the ache that ran across her twins' heart when those words escaped her barren lips. She knew how much Lizzie loved this land. It wasn't its fault that Emmy and Charlie had died. No, it was the back shooting cowardice cur that hid like a scared rabbit.

Lizzie gave her father a puzzled look. "I don't know why I said that, father. What's wrong with me? I love every inch of this ranch. Forgive me, Mighty One, I didn't mean it." Lizzie's eye's filled with unshed tears. "What I meant to say was, be watchful."

"Yes, ma'am," Naomi said with a smile. This had been the most her mother had spoken in weeks.

"And…mind the smell of the, grizzly," she warned through black eyes as she held her stomach.

"Yes, ma'am," Naomi answered in a knowing tone.

It was late afternoon as Naomi and Dancing Bear pulled the last wooden post from the back of the wagon. Abe wiped his sweat laden brow with the arm of his dirty sleeve leaving a black mark across his forehead.

"Why don't you two call it a day and head back I'll be along in a few hours. Besides," he said off handedly, "It looks like we've got a storm brewin'."

"You this sure?" Dancing Bear questioned. "Tire not. We wait."

"Me neither," Naomi added. It had been so nice to get away from the confines of the ranch. "I've enjoyed the fresh air."

He gave them both a thankful look. "You two have saved me several days of work by helping today, but your Mother and Aunt will hang me by my heels if you don't get going. She might act sick, but you can bet that she knows everything that's going on around this ranch. Don't worry, I'll be along directly."

"All right, Papa," Naomi said in a cheerful tone. "Come on, Dancing Bear." There was no missing the concerned look on the lovely Indian woman's face.

"I'm fine," Abe said honestly. "Now, you best git I'll see you two later."

Naomi took the reins of the waiting team and headed back toward the ranch. The warm wind had a slight edge to it today as Dancing Bear smiled at the enchanting young woman next to her. "You most beut day," she said in broken English. "Father, you proud."

Naomi's eyes filled with affection as she gazed into the soft brown face of her loving chaperone. "Thank you," she said. "I love you, too."

Dancing Bear was always amazed at how the young woman could read her mind. At how perceptive she was in all things around her. "Mother goot you, Lizzie. Teach lessons much goot. Much love."

"Yes, she has been a great mother sometimes though, I wish I could have known my real mother," she sighed.

"Real mother like fragile flower wind too much for soul quiet be. Heart too much lonely. Too much divided," she stated.

"How do you mean?" This was the first time that Dancing Bear had said much about her real mother.

"Love very deep like canyon, Flying Eagle much snap in eyes." She gave Naomi a loving smile. "Fear there live, much fear. Bring home me, be mother Flying Eagle say, I take. I do told. Love much I give, heart." Lovingly she placed her small hand on Naomi's chest. "You, heart, see?"

"What was she afraid of Dancing Bear? Papa? Liza? Lizzie? What?" she held her breath.

"Dark magic," Dancing Bear whispered.

"What?" Naomi questioned.

"Bad magic hide in pebble rocks snatch you!" she made a popping sound with her tongue. "Not, see when comes."

"That sounds scary," she said honestly.

"Bad magic live in man friend best, dark heart." Her deep brown eyes turned sad and forlorn. "No see it come. Like dead fish bellies under frozen pond no reach through."

"Willie," she breathed. "Papa won't talk about him."

"No talk fix, badger rip out tricked heart."

Naomi sat silent for several minutes. "I love Aunt Lizzie. I wouldn't trade her for anything in the world." The twosome bobbed along the rocky trail just enjoying the chirping birds. "Dancing Bear, why did Aunt Lizzie never marry when she was young? Was it because of me? Was it my fault?"

"No you, broken chest, here," she put her fist over her heart. "Deep skin hurt hide no heal." She looked into Naomi's uncertain face. "Broken like dry arrow."

"I'm sorry she never fell in love," Naomi whispered. "It's such a grand feeling."

"Who say no love, Lizzie?" Dancing Bear questioned.

"But you said that she..."

"Love, broken," she said. "No same."

"Of course, I should have known she really did love Charlie; she just didn't want us to know."

"No, Charlie, Jerimiah. Very love much for him, he say, no room for love living in beating chamber. She much ashamed of tricked heart."

"Didn't he love her back?" Naomi asked.

"No he leave."

"What!" Naomi couldn't believe her ears.

"He say she no good woman he have one more other. He try steal light from eyes, beating chamber crack. She stomp out breath, she kill." It was as though Dancing Bear's statement was final.

"Light? What light?" she asked.

Dancing Bear gave Naomi a loving look. "You. You light save heart like sun. No more taking." Then she let out a deep sigh. "Charlie come soft like otter, gentle like wind. Much happy there for two."

"And now...he's dead," she gave Dancing Bear a sad look.

"Broken, too much, no find way back," Dancing Bear sighed.

Just then the wheel made a cracking sound. "Well, it looks like that's not the only thing broken." Naomi set the wagon brake and jumped from the seat like a jackrabbit as she stood beside the wheel. "Great!" she said in an exasperated tone. Instantly, she gave Dancing Bear a doubtful look. "Well, we'd better unhitch one of the horses and ride home that way. Neither one of us are strong enough to pick this darn thing up and slide the hook back in."

So, Dancing Bear began unhitching the team when in the distance they could see a slight cloud of dust.

"That must be, papa," Naomi said in a relieved tone. "Wait, Dancing Bear, he can help us." Patiently the two women waited as the small party got closer and closer. It didn't take long to realize that it wasn't Abe Baxter.

"Trouble?" the large overweight man asked as he stepped down from his horse.

"Nope," Naomi answered bravely, "Just waiting on my grandfather to catch up."

"Really? I didn't see anyone behind us." He turned and stared at the men sitting on horseback.

"Then you must be blind." Naomi stated unafraid.

"You fella's see anyone back there?" The men shook their heads no as the bandit gave Naomi a wicked smile.

"Young lady, I'd say you got some troubles here," the sadistic man said as he rubbed his bristly chin. There was no mistaking the meaning of his words.

"The only trouble you're going to find here, Mister, is down the barrel of this shotgun if'n you don't just keep on a goin'." Naomi stated matter-of-factly with no fear in her darkening eyes.

"Mighty big words for such a pretty little lady," he quipped.

Naomi stood her ground as Dancing Bear's deep brown eyes followed the men's hungry stares. She spoke to the woman in her native tongue as Dancing Bear edged toward the team.

"If you think I'm bluffing, just take one more step," she threatened as she pulled back the double hammers.

"Now, don't go gettin' all hasty," the man said as he remounted his horse. "I know when we're not welcome."

In slow motion, he began to turn his worn-out horse the other direction. Then, like a madman, he spun the surprised animal around like a corkscrew and ran the spooked critter straight into Naomi. Startled, she let out a loud yelp as she fell flat to the ground. The jammed rifle lay helplessly at her feet as she struggled to reach it. Within seconds, one of the other men had Dancing Bear with a knife to her throat.

In one quick scoop, the heavy-set man roughly grabbed a handful of Naomi's hair and drug her backward to her dazed feet. "Oh, you're tough all right!" he laughed in a menacing high-pitched tone. "Tough as a kitten."

"I'll show you kitten!" she mumbled under her breath.

"What's that honey?" he said as he slobbered on her cheek showing off for his men.

Like tangling with a bobcat Naomi's teeth dug deep into his bottom lip as she stomped on his foot. Instantly, he let her go as Naomi ran and jumped on the back of the lead horse.

"Get up!" she yelled as the animal tried to jump forward within seconds Naomi laid like a sack of grain on the hard ground. The break on the wagon was set, the terrified horse couldn't move.

Once again, breathing like a wind-broke horse the bandit pulled her back to her feet. "Honey, you get to ride with me."

Like a fighting cougar, Naomi pushed and fought against the man's steely grasp but he had her at a disadvantage, winding her long berry-colored hair in his hand like a coiled rope. Uncontrollable tears ran down her terrified face.

"Let me go you sorry dog!"

"Sorry dog am I?" he breathed lustfully in her ear. "Keep talking like that, and I'll show you what this sorry dog can do."

Naomi let out a loud gasp at the insinuation of his words. "Pig!" she seethed as she stomped on his foot again.

Recklessly, he pulled her toward his waiting horse. "So, my nephew seems to be quite taken with you. He can't seem to stay away from you, can't keep his nose out from under you skirt. I saw you in town you little snot, wouldn't give me the time of day just like your so-called, Mother!"

The heavy-set man remembered all too well the unfriendly conversation that he'd had with the fearless dark-eyed Baxter. There was no mistaking their superior presence as they stood like two hissing snakes on the wooden porch.

Lizzie had recognized him immediately. "Ben Parks," she'd said in a distasteful tone as she held her rifle across her arms. "What an unpleasant surprise."

"I thought we told you to never trespass on this property again," Liza had injected.

"Listen," Ben said trying to figure out which one was which hoping they would grant him a little relief. "I think we got off on the wrong foot, so to speak I came out here to set claim to a certain piece of property for my client. That's all I want to do, then, I'll be on my way."

"And what property would that be?" Lizzie asked.

"No one holds claim to any property of ours," Liza added.

"The Old Willow Pasture it belonged to..."

"Vermin!" Both women said in icy voices at the same time.

The intense hatred of it caught Ben off guard. "It belongs to my client and I'm here to lay claim to it!"

"Listen, Mr. Parks," he remembered Lizzie saying as she took a step down from the porch, "The only thing you're going to lay claim to is a wooden box with your name on it if you don't get off of this property."

There was no denying the fact that the cagey-eyed women would have done just exactly what she threatened to do as the two of them cocked their rifles in one swift motion. His men had backed their horses away from the dangerous duo as soon as the first hammer clicked. They were crazy women his men wanted no dealings with the she-devils.

"Cowards!" he hissed at his men when he saw where they waited. He could tell that there was no way they were going to tangle with Liza and Lizzie Baxter.

"All mighty, Baxter's!" Ben stated sarcastically. "Well, little lady, I'll bet your momma has time for me now."

"Time to kill you!" Naomi hissed.

Roughly he tied Naomi's hands behind her back and tried to gag her mouth as she kicked him in the shin.

"Agh!" he yowled like a stepped-on cat. "Dirty little...!" he yipped as she kicked him even harder in the other one. "Quit!" Furiously he threw her to the ground. Naomi landed face- first bouncing on her chest in a pile of cactus. "Tie that Indian up she'll slit your throat if you give her a chance!"

"Don't you worry none boss we're gonna look her over real good like, make sure she ain't hidin' no weapons." He let out a hideous laugh.

"We gots plans forn you," one of the men said laughing as he grabbed for Dancing Bear. When she hissed at him like a rattlesnake he nearly fell off of his saddle. Shocked, he slapped her hard across the face. "She's a fighter," he said proudly.

With little effort he threw Dancing Bear over the saddle and climbed up behind her. Roughly, he ran his hand across her backside. There was no denying the lust in his greedy eyes.

"There's no time for that!" Ben said hotly. "And you!" As if Naomi was a blade of grass, he yanked her backward. "Try one more thing and I'll put a bullet right through her head. Understand?"

Naomi hissed at him again.

"Good! Now, we got us a understandin'. Let's move, they'll figure out you're missing soon enough we need long gone by then!"

Hurriedly, the party disappeared down the rocky trail on the back side of the Old Willow Pasture. When they rode into camp there were two cagey looking men waiting. "Where's Clinton?" the scruffy-faced bandit asked.

"Hasn't showed up yet said he had papers to file in town. Don't reckon he's gonna be too happy with you, ain't that his girl?" the marauder asked.

Ben gave him a sloven look as he edged his horse in the opposite direction. "This little thing? Found her waitin' just for me out on the prairie far as I'm concerned, finders...keepers."

"Clinton's gonna be madder than a rabid skunk I don't care what you say." The arrogant man threw his hands up in the air. "It's you're funeral." Then like a proud peacock he walked to where

Dancing Bear laid helplessly over the front of the horse, recklessly, he pulled her to the ground.

"Well, well, what have we here?" Dancing Bear, scooted backward as the men mentally undressed every inch of her. Then the outlaw walked to where Ben sat on his tired horse. "I think I like the one you got better." Anxiously, the man reached to drag Naomi off of his horse when Ben kicked him square in the jaw. The surprised bandit landed on the ground with a thud holding his bleeding nose, cowering like a beaten dog.

"I'm tellin' all of you, this one is mine!" he said in a stern, greedy tone. "No one touches her cept me! Is that understood?"

The men backed away from the rider as he dismounted. They were afraid of the burly scoundrel. You just never knew what he would do. There were days he'd just a soon shoot ya as look ya.

"Do whatever you want with that one I don't care, but, this little filly, she's mine. It's time that snotty nephew of mine learned how to share." Recklessly, he pushed Naomi from the front of the horse to the ground.

In a fit of rage, she kicked him hard in the shin again. In an angry stupor, he grabbed her shirt and gave it a good yank. Naomi let out a shocked yelp as she stood stark naked with no way to cover her bare chest.

"Pig!" she hissed, Naomi was terrified she'd never been in a predicament like this before. Thoughts of what these drifters would do ran through her terrified mind, they had to escape and the only way to do that was if Dancing Bear could get away, get back to the ranch. It was risky, but if her guardian could only make it to the trees, they'd never catch her.

The sun had come back out like a fire and the shadows were hours away. In a determined tone, she spoke to Dancing Bear in her native tongue. The beautiful Indian woman gave her a strange look refusing her command, she wasn't about to desert her brother's only child. Naomi, told her to run and hide in the darkening timber. Again Dancing Bear refused to move. In a fit of rage, Naomi said it again as her wild-colored eyes turned black.

Without hesitation, Dancing Bear turned and started running like the devil himself was on her tail, it looked like her feet had wings. One of the men grabbed a horse just as Naomi ran smack dab into the skittish animal within seconds it unloaded the rider in the dirt.

"Run!" she screamed as Ben backhanded her hard, Naomi fell to the ground in a heap. The last thing she saw was Dancing Bear as she disappeared over the ridge. Now, she understood how scared Emmy must have been.

"Run!" Naomi wept. "Run Dancing Bear!" Then, as darkness surrounded her she wept, "Mother, save me."

# CHAPTER 12

Clinton walked from shop to shop searching for his Uncle Ben with no luck. The few people he'd talked to hadn't seen him which to Clinton seemed a bit peculiar since the older man had never learned how to keep his big mouth shut. He wanted the pompous ass to know that he'd have no more dealings with him. Even if he was family.

The psychotic relative was out of control, and Clinton was done rescuing him. He was through nearly getting his head blown off every time that they went someplace new. Paying off debts that sometimes took months of demanding work which his Uncle never contributed to. It was time for him to suffer for his own bad decisions.

Clinton had found the family he'd been looking for his whole life since the hideous massacre of his own. They took him in like he belonged there, they respected his documental abilities. His God-given-talent. And lately, Naomi had become the nucleus of his life if she'd have him for a husband, he'd love her forever.

As he rode out of Crocker, he had an odd ache brewing within his soul that he couldn't explain. Something ugly was going to ruin the sanctioned peace that typically filled his being, he could feel it. A warning sat deep in the pit of his gut and chilled him to the bone. There was trouble brewing in the restless wind and darkening sky that he didn't like one bit.

Nonchalantly, Clinton rode at a slow lope as he made his way toward the Baxter ranch. "What the devil?" he said aloud when he saw two horses hitched to a broken-down wagon. "What happened here?" he thought to himself as he cautiously rode closer. He could see where the lead horse had tried to drag the wooden contraption several feet, but the strain and weight had been too much.

The closer he got the more familiar the team seemed, those were Baxter horses he was sure of it, how long had they'd been standing there? The stranded team gave Clinton several welcoming nickers when he rode up.

"Hey, fellas," he said in a reassuring tone.

They didn't seem to be any worse for the wear, a little hot maybe. Clinton studied the scene for several minutes as he unhitched the team and turned them loose. Like two hungry pups being called for supper they took off at a fast pace toward the ranch leaving nothing but a cloud of dust behind them.

Curiously he looked into the empty wagon box he didn't detect any foul play and yet something was amiss. Suspiciously he looked at the different tracks that surrounded the broken wheel when out of the corner of his eye he saw the small medicine bag that Dancing Bear wore around her neck for protection lying on the ground. Why would her leather pouch be lying way out here? There was no way the over-protective maiden would have accidently left that behind.

"She wouldn't!" Answering his own question Clinton picked it up and put it in his pocket. *"Damn!"*

Clinton's heart sank in his gut as he mounted the black horse he prayed these weren't the band of thugs that his uncle had befriended. But, more than that, if his Uncle participated in this, there would be a price to pay. There was just enough light left to follow the hoof prints. "Please, don't let me be too late."

Like a cat hunting prey he snuck up on the unsuspecting party. He could see his Uncle sprawled out on the ground, leaning against a barky log, staring at the dancing flames of the yellow fire. In the distance he swore he saw someone tied to a post or maybe it was a stump. It was hard to tell from where he sat, probably some bar tramp he drug out here for entertainment. When he rode into camp his blood ran cold. Clinton jumped from his horse and ran to where his Uncle was sitting with a face full of unbridled rage he accused. "What do you think you're doing?"

"Nephew," the drunken slob slurred. "I wasn't expecting you to show up but now that you're here you can enjoy the show along with the rest of the men," he let out a drunken laugh.

"Show? What show?" Clinton questioned suspiciously.

"You can't see, what, ya blind as well as stupid?" Ben asked arrogantly.

Clinton stared across the fire through the dancing flames was that who he thought it was? No, it couldn't be. "What's wrong with you?" Clinton stated angrily as he recognized the battered woman.

"Nothin' a little whiskey and a good woman won't fix." he slurred.

Clinton was beside himself. "You know who that is?"

"I reckon I do," he was so proud of himself. "I'm the one what took her."

"What are you trying to prove?" he asked flabbergasted.

"I don't have to prove nothin' to you ya damn skirt licker!" he slurred angrily.

"Let her go." Clinton demanded. "Let her go now you filthy underhanded hide!"

"I will not, finders, keepers!" Then he gave Clinton an evil look. "You need to learn to share."

"Share? Don't you get it, are you really that stupid? If you hurt one hair on her head they will hunt you down and kill you." He thought for a brief moment. "They'll hunt me down. They'll think I'm a part of this ugly travesty why it's ludicrous." He gave his Uncle a crude look. "I don't want to imagine how painful they'll make your death."

"They'll try," the older man said in a cocky drunken tone.

"They'll succeed!" he yelled. "I won't be privy to any of this, I'm finished with you and your band of thugs!" Clinton was beside himself.

"You need to calm down boy and show me the respect I deserve." Like a lumbering elephant Ben came to his feet.

"You don't deserve the air you breathe you rotten liar!" he yelled.

Purposely, his uncle placed a hard right to Clinton's unsuspecting jaw, but the younger man didn't fall; he simply wiped the blood from his mouth and walked toward the beaten woman hanging like a wet reed on the barky pole...

It was dark when Naomi began to regain her dulled senses. Her arms were tied securely around a barky tree and her fingers were completely numb from the lack of circulation. As she regained sight in one eye she let out a startled gasp, she was completely naked.

Why was she naked and where were her clothes? As she lifted her head she could barely see two men standing within the dancing shadows of a dimly lit fire, she couldn't hear what was being said but they seemed to be arguing. One of the men was frantically throwing his arms in all directions screaming at the top of his lungs.

The shorter man looked terribly angry and awfully familiar. "Clinton," she whimpered. "You found me."

Furiously, Clinton grabbed a blanket from one of the bedrolls as he started walking to where Naomi hung like a baked piece of meat his face was white as a sheet and his throat was so dry he couldn't spit. To think his flesh and blood would do something this hideous. He should have shot the old goat where he stood no one would miss the lying heathen.

The looming shadows from the firelight hung like death as Naomi tried to figure out where she was, she was so thirsty, and her head felt like a lead ball. She yanked at her wrists trying to see if she could secure her freedom, but no matter how hard she tried the bands draped across her body felt like sharp cactus digging deep into her delicate flesh, she couldn't move.

Once her eyes adjusted to the darkness she looked around for Dancing Bear. She was nowhere to be seen, she got away. That's why Clinton was here she'd made it. But, wait, where were the others, Liza, and Lizzie, where was everyone else?

As Naomi studied her surroundings, she tried to make sense out of the predicament she was in, she couldn't remember what happened or how she'd gotten here everything was a blur. She jerked her head when out of the corner of her eye she caught a glimpse of a man laughing as he walked from the darkened hillside when their eyes met, she knew, Dancing Bear didn't make it back to the ranch. She knew the fate of the loving woman's journey as she let out a yell that rattled the ground.

The life of Dancing Bear had been taken by scavengers sent by the devil himself. The mere thought of it made Naomi wretch.

She hung her head as the clear bile escaped her stinging throat and ran down her bloodied chest. "No," she screamed. "No!" she sobbed.

Naomi jumped when she heard Clinton's voice, "Don't cry, Naomi." He said in a horrified tone. "I'm here, I'm right here." He could barely speak. "I saw the wagon and came straight away, I'm going to..."

But, before the young mapmaker could finish his sentence the sound of gunfire echoed across the vastness of the prairie. A bullet fired directly in his path stopped him dead in his tracks, he turned and faced the inebriated killer again.

"I should have known that this so-called little job wasn't on the up and up that it had nothing to do with boundaries or borders. It had to do with, money, blood, money!" Clinton accused his uncle furiously as he turned and walked toward Naomi again.

"I wouldn't do that if I was you, Clinton." Ben said, in a cold calculated manner as he fired another shot. "I told you finder's keepers."

Clinton was beyond reasoning. "I won't be a part of this!" he yelled. "I won't! Emmy, Charlie, did you kill them too, uncle, did you?"

His Uncle gave him a queer look. "I'm sure I don't know what you're talking about."

"Of course you do the old man you tried to kill in town, the one who defended the young girl that you were trying to drag into the barn that night. Did you kill him?" he hollered, completely out of control. "What are you some kind of animal!"

Instantly, Clinton turned and placed the blanket over Naomi's naked body. "Don't worry, I'm here," he said through angry eyes as he snipped at the wiry looking rope that draped across her body. "I'm here, don't cry," he soothed. "I'm right here."

"Help Dancing Bear," she whimpered through dry cracked lips. "They have her Clinton, they..."

"I plan on doing exactly that as soon as I cut you down." Tears of hatred ran down his angry face.

"I said don't do that, Clinton." Ben warned again.

"And why not you savage backstabbing liar?" Clinton hollered.

"I kind of like the view," he gave Clinton a sickening smirk.

"Haven't you done enough damage?" the stocky built man demanded, unafraid of the drunken brut. "You and those disgusting barbarians are nothing more than a pack of rabid wolves!"

The young mapmaker was livid and ignored his uncle's outlandish threat as he continued to cut at the ragged looking rope. He gazed into Naomi's shocked circles, "I'm not a part of this I would never hurt you I'm going to cut you down, take you home. Oh, Naomi I didn't know." His eyes showed his misery as his gaze covered her terrified face. "Thank goodness you're not dead, I don't..."

Bang!

The words had no more than left Clinton's lips when he felt the stinging bite of cold steel dig deep into his unsuspecting flesh. The protector fell to the ground with an anguished thud.

"Are you crazy?" He raged as he rolled in the dirt holding his leg moaning profusely. "You shot me you ignorant cattle thief!"

"You don't listen boy, I said I liked the view just the way it is, now leave it be!" Ben spit at the young man in a cocky drunken state as he held the bottle of whiskey in one hand, and a steaming pistol in the other. "I told you my spoiled nephew you need to learn to share!"

"The devil I will!" Clinton yelled as he pulled the scarf from around his neck and tied it around his leg, then he hobbled like a lame duck to his feet. In a determined state, he reached for the knife at the bottom of Naomi's naked feet to cut the braided rope that held her bleeding wrists.

"Don't cry, Naomi, I'm sorry, so sorry." he pleaded through a pain racked face. "I would never agree with this kind of reckless behavior, let me..."

Bang!

Like a three legged dog Clinton lurched forward like a piece of crumbled paper on the hard ground.

"You murderer!" Naomi let out a shrill scream.

The second bullet lodged itself in his right shoulder, but, once again he staggered to his feet and stood directly in front of Naomi as he faced his Uncle, a stream of blood ran like water between the fingers of his hand.

"What is the matter with you?" he hollered furiously. "I'm not a part of this I'm not a killer, or a violator of women, and children." Anxiously, Clinton reached for his pistol.

"I said leave her be!" the older man said again in a threatening tone as he walked toward the piece of wood that held Naomi hostage.

As if she was his private property, he took his filthy hands and roughly cupped her heaving breasts as he pulled her red matted hair backward like a crazed maniac. Roughly, he placed his sour smelling mouth on her hers.

Like a fighting cougar she savagely bit his lip. Instantly, he threw his head backward as he spit blood on the taunting ground. Like a crazed madman he slapped her bruised face with the back of his bloodied hand. Her body fell forward in a heap of berry-colored curls.

"No!" Clinton yelled, horrified at what he had just seen, his face was dark with rage. "Get you're filthy hands off of her!" Once again he staggered to his feet it was getting hard for him to focus as he blinked back the fading light. "Don't touch her again you filthy no-good dog!" he hissed as he pointed the loaded pistol at the crazed man. "Don't you touch a hair on her head!"

With no regret Ben took the handle of his pistol and slammed it hard into Clintons accusing face. Blood splattered out of the side of the young man's mouth like rain as the ringing pistol fell to the ground with Clinton right on top of it. Then, the drunken marauder took his boot and slammed it hard into the side of the downed man's ribs, the young map maker let out a loud groan.

"You'll pay for this." the older man mimicked. "Just like your dead mother did," Ben hissed.

"What?" Clinton said through cloudy, disbelieving eyes.

"For being such a smart boy you sure are ignorant." Ben's voice bellowed. "Did you honestly believe that I was your Uncle, did you think for one minute that I really cared about you?"

"Your deranged mother started shooting like some kind of warrior and put a bullet right through me, she... shot...me you self-proclaimed...! She meant nothing to me, and, she sure wasn't my, sister."

"And you? You believed everything I told you, gobbled it right up the whole sad pathetic story. Doctored me back to health with your own two hands, how stupid do you feel now?"

"It was you all along?" Clinton could barely see the man standing in front of him.

"Yes, it was me all along, the sad thing is you won't live long enough to tell anyone," Ben stated matter-of-factly. "You'll bleed to death by morning. I'll make sure of it."

Bang!

Laughing, he yanked Naomi's head backward in a drunken stupor as he stared into her sunburned face. "We've got all night you and me so I'll deal with you later, princess!"

Like a drunken sailor the cutthroat made his way back to the campfire and took another long pull off of the whiskey bottle, after he'd drained the brown liquid dry he tossed it into the fire and pulled another one out of his saddlebags.

In a drunken state he sat alone and studied the young woman's naked body. She was a beauty with all that long strawberry hair, and those striking eyes. He'd never seen eyes quite like that before. They were haunting.

"I think," he said, "that you will warm my bed for several nights to come." Ben let out a long hideous laugh, proud of his catch. "I came for land and landed two Baxter's," he slurred. "By the way, where is that boy?"

# CHAPTER 13

Like a bandit's bullet, Jeffrey flew through the back of the bar and headed for the livery with a fifth of whiskey in each hand. He knew that if he stayed around the ranch much longer Lizzie would eventually kill him. She hated him and had turned his mother against him, too, his own flesh and blood.

"You'll see." he mumbled. "Someday, you'll be sorry, you'll make a mistake and I'll be the one on the other end of the gun."

He dreaded going into the small livery because he disliked the man that owned it not because he was a bad man but because he was in love with his mother. "Dirty, scum!" he slurred.

But, he needed his horse, and he needed it now. No more waiting around, dragging their feet, the pack of trouble makers needed to leave right away. He'd give the filthy bandits whatever it was that they wanted but, come fire or brimstone tomorrow he was heading for California.

Albert saw Jeffrey right away when he walked into the cool barn there was no love lost between the two men, that's for sure. But the kind liveryman had promised Liza that he wouldn't hurt her troublemaking boy, so he ignored the drunken parasite. Still, there was something about him tonight that made the livery man take notice, his actions were fidgety and reckless. Not just from the booze, but there was something else brewing within those lying eyes, like a burr stuck beneath a saddle blanket. Albert gave him a suspicious nod just Jeffrey jumped onto his horse and tore out of the large wooden opening.

The thunder boomed like falling rocks in an empty canyon as it shook the ground like an earthquake beneath the fleeing horse's feet. There was something bad brewing in the Western sky tonight, it seemed like the wind and stars were angry as they popped in and out of the lightning strikes. But, Jeffrey ignored the warning signs after tomorrow he would leave this cursed place and never look back. He would show his family that he didn't need their money to survive, that someday when they least expected it he would come back filthy rich. He wasn't a rancher, but more than that he wasn't cut out to be a father he'd never wanted to be one.

As he rode like a madman towards the small camp droplets of rain splattered against his face, Jeffrey pulled the brim of his hat down to counter the raindrops. As he contemplated his journey he wondered why anyone in their right mind would want to live in this god-for-saken place just as a blast of wind nearly knocked him off his horse.

"Pick up your feet!" he yelled in an irritated tone as he rode toward the small camp.

He could hear the men in the distance laughing and hooting in a good-ole-boy tone. He couldn't help but wonder what the celebration was about they should be packed up and ready to go. Jeffrey stared into the darkness as he rode closer to the tattle-telling-flame of the fire pit. Confused he shook his head, surely his eyes were playing tricks on him, for there in the distance he swore that there was a woman tied to a barky tree.

The young woman who seemed to be unconscious was a disturbing sight, she was completely naked her long hair hanging over her face as her chin nearly touched her chest. Her motives must have been underhanded to make Ben angry enough treat her like that.

In the distance he saw a man walk out of the darkness zipping up his pants. His probing eyes scanned the distance as lightning lit up the camp like a summer day.

"What the…" He thought to himself when he saw an object lying perfectly still face down at the naked woman's feet. From the stillness of his body Jeffrey assumed he was dead, but the longer he stared at the downed object something seemed vaguely familiar about him.

The disturbing scene irritated him as he stared at the large figure sitting next to the fire. He was here on a mission, not a rescue and if some dumb pilgrim was stupid enough to walk into another man's camp uninvited well that was their problem not his.

"Hey, Jeffrey," the heavy-set man said in an inebriated state. "Where ya been, boy? You're missing all the fun."

"I see that," Jeffrey replied in an irritated tone, completely unimpressed. "What's going on here?"

"Not much, just waiting on you with the money so we can get headed for, Californy." He gave the young man a cunning smile. "The men were a little restless." he laughed till he choked. "We saw these two on the prairie there tryin' to fix a broken wheel on their wagon." He took a swig from the half empty bottle. "I decided they might need a hand. Know what? That high-fa-lutein tramp pulled a gun on me, said she'd blow my head off!"

Jeffrey didn't care, what was this idiot doing, they needed to be ready to move in less than five hours. "I see," Jeffrey said quietly as a sinking feeling started its way into his chest.

"Yeah, I'm saving that one over there," he pointed at the naked woman leaning against the tree, "For later. I told the men no one touches her but me," he boasted proudly. "Private property don't ya know."

"I see that someone didn't believe you," Jeffrey stated matter-of-factly as he stared at the lifeless body.

The older man continued to ramble on in his drunken state. "Mr. Do-gooder, thinks he's all big and bad now that he's hanging on the Baxter shirttail," Ben let out a hideous laugh. "He don't look so big and bad now does he?"

"He looks, dead," Jeffrey stated, frankly.

"That nasty nose poker will think twice before he makes me deal with two disrespectful hotheaded women again," Ben rattled from out of nowhere. Then he paused for a moment. "No wonder you want to get out of here."

The sinking feeling in Jeffrey's gut went to the next level as he took a closer look at the young woman hanging lifelessly still. "Who might you be showing exactly?" he asked hesitantly as the darkened sky thundered like a cannon over his head. Instantly, he pulled his collar up higher to keep the chilly rain from running down the back of his neck.

"Why, that dirty skunk, Baxter," he stated in a shocked manner. "What, you can't follow the talkin' boy?" Ben was irritated that

Jeffrey didn't know who he was talking about hadn't he just made that perfectly clear?

Jeffrey wasn't sure if he was scared or had a moment of irritated stupidity. "Of course I can follow you ya dull-witted simpleton I'm not stupid!"

"You mocking me, boy?" Ben warned in an arrogant tone as he struggled to stand up.

"No." he answered. He didn't want Ben to change his mind.

"Then shut your yap!" he threatened as he swung the bottle of whiskey around like a liquid whip.

"I want those two devil Baxter women especially that one with the big mouth, cut the back of my neck with some kind of knife hidden inside her shoe. She thinks she's all big and bad, well, I got something big and bad for her lying right here!" he made an obscene gesture as he howled like a hyena. "I guess I showed her today."

Then he smiled at the young man in front of him. "Are ya followin' me now boy?" He paused and took a good pull off of the half empty whiskey bottle.

"How so," Jeffrey asked. His heart was pounding like a thousand drums in his chest. He knew there wouldn't be a hole deep enough to hide if he messed with his mother or his Aunt Lizzie.

"I done told her what she could do with that there ranch land that she seems to think is hers," he boasted. "Told them both, I didn't need no map, or mapmaker for that matter, changed my mind, I was headin' for Californy." He slapped Jeffrey on the back as slobber ran from his thick lips. "Thanks to you, son," he slurred. "I'm sure glad you're nothing like them."

"You didn't happen to tell them who you were going to California with did you?" Jeffrey felt a chilly wind slide up his back.

"And tattle like a sissy girl? No, I ain't no squealer!" the drunkard seemed surprised at the question.

Like the thunder that boomed its warning over his head Jeffrey shuttered as he stared into the inebriated man's face. "I don't have all of it," he lied convincingly. "But I'll be here with the rest early in the morning."

"That's good!" Ben said in a half coherent tone as his body swayed back and forth. Smiling he whispered to Jeffrey through cupped hands. "Side's, I have enough to keep me busy till then."

"Listen," Jeffrey stated, "I best get back before they miss me, don't want anyone getting suspicious, don't go having too much fun tonight we got us some gold to find."

"Damn, straight!" Ben slurred.

With that being said Jeffrey climbed back on his horse and nonchalantly rode out of camp. As soon as he was out of sight, he pounded the sides of his horse until he couldn't breathe. That was Naomi, he couldn't even think about what they had done to, Dancing Bear.

Harder and harder he pushed his horse till he rode into the yard of the ranch like the devil himself was on hot on his tail. Like a chased rabbit he climbed the stairs two at a time to Lizzie's room he threw open the door as he stared into his aunt's startled face.

"Please don't kill me, Aunt Lizzie!" he begged as his rain-soaked clothes dripped water onto the clean dry floor. "It's my fault I was going with them to California, to pan for gold. I didn't know that they were going to...!"

Lizzie walked toward the young man with a horror-stricken look on her face. "What are you talking about?" she asked in a suspicious tone. "What did you do?" Her voice was threatening and calculated.

"Liza," Lizzie screamed in a commanding tone. "Liza, get in here!"

Like a gunshot Liza flew through the open door. "What!" she exclaimed. "What?"

"Seems your son has gotten himself into something else," Lizzie stated in a mistrusting manner.

"Mother, I didn't know what they were capable of." he sobbed. "I would have never let them hurt her!"

"Hurt who?" Lizzie asked as she stood inches from his terrified face.

"What are you talking about?" Liza questioned as she stepped in front of Lizzie, fearing for her son's life.

"I hate it here." Jeffrey confessed like a small, threatened boy. "I hate everything about this place it's suffocating, you're, suffocating, I can't breathe. I wanted to go with them to get away from you and you." he confessed like a murderer going to the gallows as his sea green eyes were full of regret. "Anything to get out of here but now they have her, I, I couldn't do anything, they would have killed me so, so I came here." he fell to his shaking knees sobbing. "Please, please, please don't kill me, Aunt Lizzie!"

"Liza," Lizzie said in a distant tone, "We best saddle up. I have a feeling someone is going to die tonight."

"Don't let her kill me, Mother." Jeffrey begged like the coward that he was as he hid behind his mother's back. "I didn't know...."

"Didn't know what?" Matthew asked as he walked into Lizzie's room.

"That's what we're trying to find out," the twins said in unison.

"Well, hurry up papa wants to know why Clinton's black horse is down by the barn." Matthew stated. "And, has anyone seen Naomi I can't find her."

Within a breath Lizzie's intimidating blue eyes probed the skin of the young man in front of them like a thousand needles as he cowered. "What do you mean you can't find her? Dancing Bear and Naomi are with, Father."

"Papa just rode in," he stated in a hesitant tone. "They're not with him he said they should have been home hours ago. They had the wagon with all of the supplies in it." Matthew got a sick look on his face. "What's going on Jeffrey?"

Lizzie turned and stared into Jeffrey's ashen face, her cool blue eyes turned black like a viper as they traveled the distance between them. He'd never been this afraid of his Aunt before. He'd never actually seen that vivid transformation, not up close, but now those dark black eyes were choking every ounce of air from his lungs.

"That's what I've been trying to tell you, Mother we need to go and fetch Naomi and Dancing Bear back to the ranch before they kill them both."

Lizzie let out a horrifying scream that nearly deafened everyone in the house. "You little, rodent, you'd sell your own soul!" Lizzie came within inches of the young man as she pulled him to her chest. "If she dies, so will you."

Jeffrey pulled away from his angry Aunt as he shrank back against his Mother. "I didn't know!" he screamed at Lizzie through a reddened face. "That wasn't a part of the plan." he sobbed pitifully. "She must have done something to make him...he would never have intentionally...you made him mad!" he accused. "It's your fault, if you weren't so mean and, and nasty all the time and...!"

Matthew reached over his mother's lean shoulder before his twin brother could finish his sentence as he grabbed Jeffrey by the front of the shirt. "Where are they?" he hissed in a deep threatening tone as he slammed him against the wall. "Where?" he demanded as he threw his brother halfway down the hallway. "You'll be sorry if they've harmed one hair on her head."

Jeffrey didn't know what to do as he tried to escape his brother's grasp and run down the hallway, he had to get away from all of them, escape. Terrified, he ran smack dab into, Abe.

"What's going on here?" He saw Lizzie's ashen face. He knew it was bad. "Lizzie? Liza?"

Lizzie walked past her sister, Matthew, and Abe as she grabbed Jeffrey by the back of the neck. "Come on you lying back-stabbing slug." she seethed.

"Mother," he screamed frantically. "Mother, help me."

"You're going to think, mother." Lizzie hissed as she practically threw him onto his waiting horse. "I swear Jeffrey if she's hurt I'll kill you with my own two hands!"

# CHAPTER 14

In a determined hurry, the riders headed toward the unsuspecting party. When they rounded the ridge it was evident what had gone on, Naomi was still tied tightly to her wooden prison like a spider in a web, it was a disturbing sight. From what they could see she her body was naked, her head was resting in a forward position, her chin nearly touching her chest. Her long berry-colored hair was the only protection covering the front of her body. Lizzie's heart sank in her gut.

There was a stocky looking man lying completely still on the ground at her bare feet, he looked dead from where they were standing. There were two men passed out to the side of the buckboard and one large man sitting by a dimly lit fire. It was an unimaginable sight.

Lizzie said in an icy tone. "Jeffrey, you ride down there just like you were supposed to if you make one wrong move or if I think that you have, I'll put a bullet right between those deceitful green eyes."

Liza twisted his arm backward as she hissed like a snake in his ear. "And know this you stinking weasel we won't miss. "Wipe your face you lily-livered coward and try to be a man for once in your pathic life!" she threatened through thin lips that said he might not make it to the fire alive.

"Yes, mother," his voice trembled. "I'm, I'm sorry," he whined.

"You have no idea just how sorry you are…yet, shut your mouth you lying rodent, or I'll gut shoot you right now!" Lizzie hissed like a snake.

Jeffrey stared at his mother he was terrified. "Mother?"

Like a scared rabbit he did what he was told, he knew there would be no restitution for his lurid act this time, these men he'd tangled up with had gone too far, now they would all pay the price, himself included. As Jeffrey rode into the camp the older man staggered to his feet.

"What you doin' back so soon scaredy ghost get ya?" he laughed in a teasing manner. "Voodoo—hoodoo after ya?"

"No." he said in a business-like tone. "I've been gone about six hours what the corn digger's hoe have you been doing? I thought you were going to be ready to ride out when I got back, I've got the money. Where is everyone?" he said in a disgusted tone.

"Man, I must have passed out," Ben apologized in a drunken state shaking his head wondering where the time had gone. Through glossy eyes he continued, "I didn't even get to finish my business." Purposely, he scanned the distance to make sure that his caged prey was still where he had left her.

But, when the older man rubbed his bloodshot eyes and tried to refocus he looked directly into two slender silhouettes that danced back and forth outside the shadows of the fire. They stood with their legs spread, hands on their hips. The shock made him jump as Jeffrey stepped away like a scurrying rat.

Liza cocked her pistol and aimed it directly at her cowardice son, "I don't care if I am your mother, move one more inch and I'll drop you where you stand." Her eyes were dark and foreboding. "And remember this my traitorous son, I never miss."

Jeffrey froze in his tracks; she sounded just like Lizzie. His mother had never behaved this way towards him before, and from the look on her face he knew she'd do exactly what she had threatened.

As he stared at her within the fire's haze he couldn't tell one from the other. "Mother?" he whimpered.

The sinister sight had a sobering effect on the heavy-set bandit. "What the...?" he stated in a disbelieving tone. "Where'd you two come from? What do you want?"

"Redemption," they said in unison like a freezing wind that stings your face on a frosty winter night.

They reminded the cagey outlaw of two black-eyed vipers, coiled and ready to strike. Their dark eyes snapped the venomous authority that lay like a deadly poison within them. The taunting flames were deceiving as Ben reached his hand toward the fire he was sure that they were close enough to touch, and yet they were several yards away. Together standing there in the shadows of their personage they looked like a destructive entity wrapped one within the other like a braided vine. It was an odd feeling of deception. As Ben stood there swaying back and forth their silhouette's melded into one giant shadow with a look of destruction written all over their determined faces.

"What took you two spiritual witches so long?" he demanded.

There was no doubt in Ben's inebriated mind who was waiting on the other side of that fire. He knew the Mighty One had sent two fearless warriors to do his bidding, that tonight he would pay for every heinous act he'd ever committed, his number was up.

Here on this open prairie he would answer to the man upstairs, there would be no redemption for his misdeeds Liza and Lizzie Baxter would see to that, even Ben knew he'd gone too far this time. These valiant warriors were going to send him straight back to hell where he'd come from.

As the drunken kidnapper tried to focus his lethargic eyes, he swore that there was someone untying the naked girl. Forgetting all about the threat standing in front of him he hollered in an angered tone.

"The last man that tried to do that is lying dead at her feet unless you want to join him you thieving bandit you'd best get back!" Fearlessly, the drunken thief reached for his gun. It never made leather; he pulled back a bloody hand with two missing fingers. Ben yowled like a frightened cat. "Heathen witches!" he screamed as he held one hand within the dripping blood of the other.

"Is she breathing?" Lizzie hollered.

"I think so," Matthew answered.

"Yes or no!" demanded Liza.

"Yes!" Matthew yelled back. "Naomi," he whispered through pale lips as he cut the ropes to her bleeding wrists. "It's me, Matthew."

Naomi stared at her cousin with no expression of recognition in her hollow eyes. They looked like two empty pools. Her small delicate nose had blood dripping from one side of a swollen nostril. Matthew grabbed his hanky from his pocket and gently dabbed at the red dribbling liquid. Her bare chest had tiny cut lines like someone had tried to wrap some kind of braided twine around her to keep her restrained. Her bottom lip had a small cut that ran to her chin as though the tender flesh had been sliced with a sharp object, her upper lip was swollen twice its size. Her typically pink colored cheeks were burned a brilliant red from the flaming sun and she had tiny slivers of rope ground deep into her ankles, it looked like several of her toes were broken.

Anxiously, he covered her bare body with a soft cotton blanket as he laid her gently on the waiting ground, then he turned over the familiar looking body lying still at her feet. If he was still breathing, Matthew would slit his throat.

"Clinton!" Matthew gasped in shock as he recognized his face. "No, not you! You were her..." Immediately Matthew hung his head. There was nothing he could do for the mapmaker he'd be dead by morning.

Intentionally, he pulled Naomi into his large sobbing arms all he could think of was Emmy, and how afraid she must have been the night of her attack. "I'm sorry Emmy, so sorry."

The scene around Matthew seemed to be moving in slow motion. Like everything was jumbled together, nothing seemed real. Overwhelmed, he sat on the ground with Naomi cradled in his large arms, he couldn't believe the sight in front of him. The lightning snapped as the thunder rumbled like falling boulders shaking the wet ground. For him it was too much. Shocked and grief-stricken Matthew watched his grandfather carry Dancing Bear's lifeless body like a piece of broken glass and place her in the back of the wagon. Angry tears ran down his rain soaked face as he covered her dead body with a blanket. There was a look of death and destruction on the older man's ashen face that Matthew had never seen before.

# CHAPTER 15

In a fit of rage, Abe took one drunken slob lying by the back wheel of the wagon and tossed him like a stone into the raging wind, his feet never touched the ground he landed with a loud thud onto the hard muddy soil. The lightning and thunder seemed to echo Abe's fury as it pounded like horse's hooves within the darkened sky above them. When the filthy bandit regained his senses, he let out a high-pitched squeal the intensity of his yowl woke the other bandit lying a few feet away. Like he was nothing, Abe tossed his drunken body in the same direction, the confused outlaw landed within inches of the other. Like two startled cats they jumped to their feet and squared up at the swaying image in front of them pulling their guns.

With little thought and careful aim, Abe placed a billet of steel right between both of their eyes before their shaking fingers could pull the trigger. The sound of the blast echoed across the ringing camp like a hollow tomb, they were dead before they hit the ground.

Matthew clung to Naomi as she jumped at the loud blast of gunfire. Her only recoil was to get away from the person that held her prisoner, like a fighting grizzly she scratched Matthews's face as he held both of her hands at bay.

"No, Naomi." he said in a shattered tone. "It's me, Matthew." The young man couldn't believe what was taking place. Even after all she'd been through his cousin fought like a trapped cougar. "It's me," he whispered as he held her even tighter. "It's me, Matthew."

"Matthew?" her empty eyes wept. Then Naomi quit fighting and lay like a rag doll in his large protective arms, her silent weeping nearly tore his heart from his chest. "Don't let me go." she mumbled. "Don't let me go."

He could barely hear her voice. Not knowing what else to do Matthew held Naomi close joining her rhythmic sobs, and watched the display unfold in front of him. It was all he could do to keep from jumping to his feet and ripping his brother's heart out.

What had he been thinking getting tangled up with a pile of trash like this? Vermin, that's what they were nothing less than vermin. She'd never done anything to Jeffrey look what he'd caused.

But, not only did the blast wake the determined escape from the young woman in Matthew's arms, but the man lying next to him came to life with a vengeance.

"Don't touch her you filthy dogs!" Clinton garbled through a raspy throat. "Keep your hands off...I'll kill every mother's—sons of you." then he passed out again.

The kind mapmaker had tried to save his lovely young cousin his wound had been inflicted for a different reason and now he might very well lose his life because of it.

There was no stopping the fiery rage that ran through Liza and Lizzie's blood. The disbelief and hurt boiled within their enraged beings. It had been years since they'd been this angry, the kind of anger that steals the life of a soul and ages you tenfold.

This man had violated the sanctity of life in general, he stole something that wasn't his. They'd already lost Sarah, Emmy, and Charlie to backstabbing men just like these. There were no words to express the worried hurt that engulfed them at the thought of the young Baxter's demise.

The twins had made a sacred oath as sister's years ago that they would protect Naomi with their dying breath. That they'd never allow anyone to try to kidnap or hurt her again, in fact the last man that tried died with Lizzie's bullet in his heart. His bones are lying in one of the caverns beneath the decrepit white house in the Old Willow Pasture.

This outlaw would pay the same price he was just too prideful to know it. This lying bandit had no idea how wide the gates of hell were going to swing to engulf his lurid being.

"I know all about you!" Ben arrogantly hissed in self-defense seemingly, unafraid even though his heart was pounding like a beating drum. "The boy has told me all I need to know about your hoodoo—voodoo crap." he stated as his bulky body swayed within the fiery perimeter pretending to be much braver than he felt. "How you two high and mighty-heathen lovers believe you're some kind of God's. How you ramrod an outfit that was handed down to you and the rest of those uncivilized-heathen-loving misfits."

"Are you referring to Emmy and Charlie?" the blood in Lizzie's veins felt like molten lava she could barely breathe she was so hot. "The two innocent people you bushwhacked you murdering scum? There's not enough good in your whole body that could ever compare to the lives of the two lives you stole."

"Killed?" The drunken man had an odd look on his face, not of denial but of doubt. "I ain't killed anyone," he paused for a brief moment, "Here."

The twins looked at each other completely baffled. It was the only thing that the dishonest bully had said that they actually believed, so who killed Charlie and Emmy?

Ben continued his rant. "What, you think I'm afraid of a couple of stinkin' cow-lickers that don't know when to keep their big fat yaps shut, nothing more than stinkin' women tryin' to be men instead of their God-given place?" He looked from one twin to the other. "You two belong in the kitchen making men like me supper fussing about my needs." He wiped his sleeve across his slobbering lips. "I'm not afraid of you!" he hollered like a madman at Lizzie. "Or, you!" he shouted at Liza.

"And," he hesitated for a brief moment. "Especially, not you." he stated to the large looming shadow right behind them. "What? You send your girlies to do your job…again, take care a ole Ben?" he laughed.

With no remorse on their cool calm faces they stepped to either side, "Father." they said in unison. "You ya worthless cattle thief should be very afraid."

"Why? Cause you brought your daddy to protect you, the man that let two misfit, outlaws, run his ranch?"

"No, because he is the ranch." Liza stated in a calm tone.

"And you, you crossed the line," Lizzie said in dark tone.

"What line, there ain't no line out here? If you want something, girlies, you reach out and take it, survival of the fittest, that ain't you!" his words were like a branding iron searing their skin.

"There are lines all around us," the twins stated in unison. "Right. Wrong. The one between living and dying." Their voices were so calm.

"What are you saying cuz I don't listen to no-cocko-headed women. Never have never will, like I said go back to the kitchen where you belong." Ben put on a rather good show as he searched for a way out. "Or, maybe the bedroom." he laughed hideously.

"What do you think sister?" Lizzie asked.

"I don't reckon I like the kitchen so much," answered Liza. "You?"

"Never much liked it there either." Lizzie stated.

"We never much cared for either place," their voices sounded like hissing snakes.

"So what, you gonna kill me, out, here, in cold blood? What line does that cross you disrespectful..." It was obvious that there was no place to run so with the eyes of a hunting hawk he zeroed in on the images standing like iron in front of him. "Baxter's!" he hissed. "Who needs em!" Intentionally, he drew his pistol and fired.

Matthew sat in awe as he watched the flashing display of gunfire, it looked like a formal dance. Three shadows ghosted by a flickering flame that gave off the appearance of one silhouette drawing their guns in perfect rhythm, cocking the steely hammers, placing the precise pressure on the waiting trigger, hearing the firing pin as it slammed into the back of the waiting bullet. One bullet, one movement, one destination. Their cold demeanor held no remorse, no regrets, no forgiveness, just one intended bullet preciously aimed, purposely ejected, determined in its journey, securing its target. The three of them stood there together and watched the outlaw fall as they placed their pistols back in their leather holsters.

There was no missing the look of shock on Ben's face as the spinning steel ball of lead ended his life of destruction and mayhem. The impact flipped him backward onto the hard unforgiving soil, it was a ghastly sight.

Matthew stared in complete shock as he closed his eyes and clung to the small woman in his protective arms. He could hear the raging thunder's anger every time the earth shook from its mighty blast. Even with his eyes closed he could see the lighting dance across the darkening sky like an ignited lance ready to strike whoever was foolish enough to challenge its fury. He felt the rain as it started to pour down like a child's tears soaking everyone to the bone as though it was trying to cleanse the ugliness from the soiled dirt.

There were three dead men here, where had they come from, why had they singled out their family? The marauding thieves didn't deserve to live, not after the innocent lives they'd stolen. There was only one word to express what his grandfather, his mother, and aunt had done here tonight: Justice!

Terrified, Jeffrey tried to run from the unthinkable sight but before he could take a step Lizzie pulled her gun from her holster and put a bullet directly in front of his feet anticipating his every move. There was no escape for Jeffrey he knew his destined fate, Lizzie was going to throw him into one of the deepest ravines she could find and enjoy watching him die.

"I'll put the next one right through your traitorous lying heart if you move one inch," she threatened through icy disconnected lips. Her eyes were hollow looking.

Liza walked to where her cowardice son stood trembling like a leaf, bawling like a baby, as he cowered behind her. Like an old oak she stood in front of him. "I'm afraid I'm not going to let you kill him, Lizzie." she said with checked lips.

"Step aside, Liza," Lizzie said with no emotion in her voice.

"You know I can't do that," Liza said fearlessly as their dark eyes collided like the thunder above their heads.

Bang!

Lizzie put a bullet right between Liza's feet. "Step aside, Liza," Lizzie said again in a louder voice. "This isn't your fight."

"My son will always be my fight, sister," she whispered as their black eyes surrounded each other like an empty circle. She certainly didn't blame Lizzie for wanting to kill Jeffrey after all of the things that had happened because of the boy and especially what had happened here tonight, honestly she would have welcomed the relief. But, that's not how his life would end, not today, not tomorrow, not by her sister's hand, at the end of the day he was still her son.

"Lizzie," Abe said in a calm tone as he stood behind her. "Give me the gun."

Bang!

"Step aside Liza," Lizzie said again as she put another bullet squarely between her sister's feet.

There was no stopping the inevitable disaster that was about to unfold. "You know I won't," Liza stated plainly.

"Lizzie," Abe said again in a sterner tone. "Give me the gun."

Bang!

Mud splattered on her sister's pant leg as she fired again. The bullet looked as though it had streaks of lightning blasting from the barrel. Their dark threatening eyes never left each other, neither woman budged.

"Lizzie we need to get Naomi to a doctor," Abe whispered, hoping his words would penetrate her closed off brain. Even he was worried that she might actually kill Liza to get to the boy, after all, Lizzie hadn't been herself for several months now. There was only one thing he could think to do to get her attention. "We need to go and get, Doctor Slater."

As though she'd heard her father's soothing voice for the first time, Lizzie shook her head as her sordid being walked back to reality. For a moment in time, it was as though she'd stepped completely outside herself, her eyes pleaded for Liza to understand her distress.

Then she said in an icy tone, "No one touches my daughter but me I'm the doctor not that mule's hind end." Then she gave her father a knowing look. "But you'd better take this, father," intentionally she handed him her gun, "or I'll kill him for sure."

Abe took in a big sigh of relief as he held the cocked pistol in his waiting hand. In the state of mind that Lizzie was in, he knew she would have shot Jeffrey with no remorse.

"Liza, are you all right?"

"Why wouldn't I be father," she answered with no fear in her voice, somewhat miffed at his question.

"Are you hurt anywhere?" he fretted.

"She would never hurt me." she stated matter-of-factly with an edge to her voice.

"Then you best take that boy home before she changes her mind," Abe said in a commanding tone.

"Plan on it." Liza answered in an angry voice.

Like a snapping viper she turned and faced the pitifully sobbing boy behind her. "Jeffrey, if you weren't my son," she said in way that would have made even the heavens shudder, "I'd...Now get on that horse you conniving backstabbing coward!"

"Why are you mad at me, Mother?" he demanded. "I didn't do nothing."

"You never do!" she said angrily as she half threw him into his horse. "You never do."

# CHAPTER 16

The loud clap of thunder startled Emmy as she struggled to see in the darkness, her head was foggy from the pistol blow. Was she dead or alive? In a woozy state, she wondered how long she'd been unconscious then she felt the large knot on the side of her head. It felt like an egg and made her wince just as the brilliant lightning lit up the open cavern, there was no Nelly, no horse, and no baby. She knew deep in her heart what Nelly had done.

The coals to the fire had long ago burned down as she stirred the dimly lit embers and added more dry twigs. After a few minutes, a small flickering flame seemed to appear from out of nowhere. As if it were made of glass Emmy gently added small pieces of the small sticks blowing gently until she could get a good flame going.

She took a good look around once her head quit spinning and fire shed a dim light. She couldn't help but notice several puddles of blood on the rocky floor toward the side of the watering hole. Immediately her heart sank Nelly must have given birth and drowned the baby.

"No." Emmy breathed as she slowly made her way to the watery opening in the cave floor.

She knew that the heartless woman had dropped the baby in the pool and left it to drown. Even though Emmy's head was still spinning from the impact of the pistol blow she regrettably looked into the clear water. But much to her surprise there was no baby, only the reflection of her bruised face.

Emmy let out a deep sigh wondering whether to laugh or cry, she was relieved the baby wasn't in the pool, so where was it? The joyful feeling began to fade as her searching eyes focused to the elusive darkness, there was no missing the distinct blood trail to the very place that the horse had been standing.

Emmy pounded her fists against the rocky floor, Nelly must have taken the newborn with her to the river, the wily woman had done exactly what she said she was going to do. Heartbroken she looked up toward the roof of the cavern. "I don't understand why she would get something so precious. She said she didn't want it, she said it was a curse, she called it vermin, a sweet innocent baby why would she do such a horrible thing?"

"It's not fair that I get nothing." Her voice quieted. "I know Mighty One, that Liza and Lizzie did everything in their power to save me, for what? I don't understand this path laid out before me, I know you do that's why I've embraced it with courage and faith accepted it with a broken heart." she wept. "That perfect little baby was practically lying in my arms. I could feel its warm little body snuggling me, the sound of it breathing; now I feel nothing."

The thunder echoed through the cavern. "Why do I get nothing? Even if Jeffrey is the baby's father." She couldn't stop the tears. "Why do I still get nothing? Why?"

# CHAPTER 17

"I'll take her," Matthew insisted as the wagon came to an abrupt halt in front of the old log house. He refused to let anyone else carry Naomi's mistreated body for fear that she might wake up fighting like before. He was in shock himself from the brutal attack on his lovely young cousin, and the bestial death of Dancing Bear. After seeing all of the destruction that these savage heathens had caused he could only imagine how alone Emmy felt with no rescue in sight. "Dirty, bloodthirsty dogs!"

He'd never seen his mother and aunt act as ruthlessly as they had tonight. Not just against the man that had hurt Naomi but each other. There had been tales of their rough-shod ways, but he'd never believed it until now. The reality of that ugly picture rattled him, too.

With the grace of a sure-footed mountain goat, Matthew climbed the steps two at a time and hurried into Lizzie's room. Like a fragile flower he carefully laid Naomi's battered and bruised body on the large, overstuffed bed praying that they hadn't done to his beautiful cousin what they'd done to Dancing Bear. There was no mistaking the questioning heartache in his crystal blue eyes as he looked at his loving aunt.

"I know," Lizzie whispered in a soft tone as she gently touched his shoulder. "I know."

Then, without being asked Matthew hurried down the hallway like a runaway locomotive and out to the well, with little thought he drew a fresh bucket of cool water and took it back upstairs to his aunt's room poured the clear liquid into a small porcelain basin then exited the room once again. When he re-entered he held a soft white cotton gown with worn-looking pink flowers. "This one is her favorite," he said in a brotherly fashion turned and exited the room once again, this time to find his brother.

As Matthew headed out the front door it felt like he couldn't breathe, his chest hurt, his head hurt, his heart hurt. The unbelievable picture of destruction rolled over and over in his mind, the ugly scene replaying, replaying, replaying he couldn't shut it off. The thunder boomed when his boots touched the dirt as he hurried toward the barn, lightning lit up the night sky.

All he could think of was what a lying coyote his brother was, nothing more than a filthy predator. Naomi didn't know how to deal with men like that why would Jeffrey put his family in such jeopardy steal from his grandfather when all he had to do was ask?

When he finally made it to the lighted barn Jeffrey was in a state of panic trying to get one of the horses saddled before anyone came looking for him. He needed to make a quick exit and get in the clear get away from this ranch.

It only took seconds for Matthew to close the distance between them. "Going somewhere you lying cull?"

Within seconds Matthew had Jeffrey by the front of the shirt as he threw him halfway across the barn. His twin landed with a thud in the dirt, but much to his surprise Jeffrey was quick to get to his feet. "You're not leaving until you pay for what you did!" Matthew hollered.

Jeffrey wasn't afraid of his brother he knew Matthew would never really hurt him. "And what about you being so perfect and all, the one mother runs to. What makes you think you're so much better than me?" he hollered back as he charged his brother like a caged bull.

Together they landed on the dirty floor rolling like two tumbleweeds. Purposely, Jeffrey slammed his fist into his brother's face, he was quick, but Matthew was beyond reason as he slammed him right back.

Boom, thunder shook the ground as the lightning raged.

His brother's fist slammed into his jaw, the blow stunned Jeffrey as he flew backward. "Please," he begged. "No more."

Pitifully Jeffrey struggled to his wobbly feet, "Help me up brother, I'm sorry, I am."

But when Matthew gave him a hand up, Jeffrey sucker punched him in the side of the head, Matthew laid still for several seconds.

"Now who's a cull?" he yelled just as Matthew kicked his legs out from under him.

Over and over the two of them rolled landing under one of the startled horses. There was no one here to stop him, hold him back, to protect his brother, so without restraint Matthew pounded his fist into Jeffrey's face over and over with a vengeance.

All he could hear was Naomi's whisper echoing through his denying brain. "Don't let me go. Don't let me go."

"You dirty dog!" he sobbed. "Filthy animal!"

Like a dream he could see Emmy's warm smile and laughter as she waved goodbye that fateful morning. Matthew tried to shake off the memory of his grandfather carrying Dancing Bears dead body beneath the scolding heavens.

"I'll send you to your maker you, you filthy scum, you're not a man you're nothing but a infectious maggot." he said over and over. "I know you shot them, and today you nearly killed her you don't deserve to live!"

Matthew had no idea when his grandfather came into the barn and pulled him off of his unconscious sibling. "Matthew!" Abe hollered. "Matthew, you're going to kill him!"

"I want to after what he's done he deserves to die!" Matthew raged.

"Stop! Stop it! We've had enough bloodshed for one night. Matthew!" Abe yelled.

"It's the only way!" Matthew hollered back through bloody lips and muddy tears. "He'll never listen, he'll never learn any other way!"

Abe stood in front of his grandson. "Enough!"

Matthew leaned on one of the stalls out of breath sobbing as Abe shook Jeffrey back to life. "What happened?" the twin said in a dazed tone.

Abe gave him a disgusting look. "Jeffrey, you are your own worst enemy."

As the twin came to his feet he couldn't believe what Matthew had done. "You tried to kill me, me, your own brother, what, you were gonna beat me half to death?"

"You don't deserve to live I should wring your neck like a chicken." Matthew was beyond reason.

"We're one and the same you and I." Jeffrey was shook.

"I'm no kin to you." Matthew yelled.

"What kind of brother are you?" Jeffrey hollered back. "One that would kill his own brother?"

"The kind that's gonna make you pay!" he threatened as he plunged at Jeffrey catching him at the waist as the two of them broke through the stall leaving splintered wood in their path. "I'm nothing like you. You're worse than the critters that crawl beneath the dirt!"

"Stop!" Abe yelled as he grabbed Matthew by the back of the shirt holding him back using all his strength he had to keep the battling brothers apart. "We have bigger problems to deal with right now."

"I—can't—let him live!" Matthew yelled through broken sobs. "He killed my wife I know he did."

"I wouldn't put my hands on that filthy cow you called a wife!" Jeffrey countered.

Matthew struggled trying to pull his pistol, he was going to place a bullet right between his brother's lying eyes.

"She's nothing more than pig-squalor!" Jeffrey was overcome with anger. "She wasn't fit to be a Baxter someone did you a favor."

The two brothers squared up at each other as Matthew gave him a threatening look. "Your day is coming brother you'll pay for what you've done here tonight." Matthew grabbed his hat and started to exit the large open door. "From this day forward you're no brother of mine, and," he said in a dark tone, "Someday, I'll finish what I started here."

"I'll be waiting!" Jeffrey argued back. "I'm not afraid of you!"

"Shut up!" Abe demanded. "What's wrong with you, boy? What got rattled in that brain of yours? You don't ever go against family!"

"You know what old man...!"

Within seconds, Jeffrey lay sprawled on the barn floor knocked out cold.

# CHAPTER 18

Lizzie's heart was in her throat as she stared at her daughter's bloody, bruised skin. Her typically sound fingers shook uncontrollably as she gently wiped the dirt from Naomi's blistered face. Each stroke was like the feather of an eagle. Then, she very gently dabbed at the blood on the side of her small swollen nose thankfully, it wasn't broken. Then, like a mastered physician she wiped at the tear along the outside of her rosebud mouth. She let out a deep sigh knowing that there would be a definite scar where the soft skin would have to be stitched.

Silent tears of remembering Emmy's unthinkable fate rolled down her ashen cheeks as she finished cleaning the dirt from the rest of her daughter's battered body. Seeing Naomi hanging helplessly from the rotting bark like a bug caught in a spider web was just too familiar.

Tediously Lizzie placed her special salve on Naomi's blistered lips, the same salve they had concocted for Sarah years ago for her crimson skin. She knew that they would be very sore when the scabs started to form. As though her nose was made of crystallized glass she lightly wiped the magic salve over the swollen mass then through angry tears she rubbed the homemade concoction on the pin-like cuts on her chest.

Lizzie had surmised that the stupid cutthroat must have wound a piece of straw-like rope around her naked body to keep her under control. As she leaned Naomi into a sitting position there were matching marks on her back as well, silently she cursed the dead man's name.

Like an eggshell she lifted Naomi just enough to slip on her nightgown, lovingly Lizzie gave her a kiss on her reddened forehead as she slid into the old rocker like a bag of wet grain and stared at her pride and joy as a river of uncontrolled tears exploded from her eyes. Her heart hurt like a festered splinter was lodged deep inside the beating vessel, a pain she couldn't get rid of.

She wasn't herself losing Charlie had been too much for her soul to accept, she was emotionally exhausted. This beautiful girl lying in her arms was the only child she'd ever have. And their own blood triggered by revenge, tried to take it away. "You won't live I'll see to it."

"Mother," Naomi whispered as their eyes met when she finally came to.

"Naomi," Lizzie sighed lovingly.

With little effort the young woman curled up in her mother's warm affectionate arms. She placed her head on Lizzie's sturdy shoulder and let out a deep sigh. "Mother," she whispered again. "I was so afraid I prayed and prayed to the Mighty One that you would come, that you and Liza would find me."

Those words nearly tore Lizzie's heart out of her aching chest, how many times had Sarah wished for the same thing only to be sorrowfully disappointed? "I would walk through the fire of the burning gates for you." Lizzie stated through a broken sob as she covered her with a homemade quilt. "You're my daughter. Mothers are bound to protect their children at all costs. I feel that I failed you as a mother."

"No," Naomi said as she lay in her mother's loving arms, "You came for me."

It was all she could do to speak. "I will always come for you." Lizzie held Naomi even closer. "Sister and I thought you were with, papa Jeffrey was the one who showed us where you were."

"Jeffrey?" she whispered. "How would he...? Why would he?"

"Your cousin was afraid of dying by my bullet, he still might it's a long story for another time I will tell you when you're well, all that matters now, is you're safe in my arms."

"Oh, mother," Naomi cried.

Together the two of them let their emotions out as they shared the pain of their heartache. Lizzie hushed her daughter's humiliated sobs as her heart skipped a beat when she asked, "Did he hurt you?" Her aching eyes asked the unspoken question.

"Not like that," she answered in a faint tone.

Lizzie let out a huge sigh of relief.

"Dancing Bear?" Naomi asked.

"She's dead," Lizzie whispered as she lovingly stroked Naomi's berry colored hair.

Naomi sobbed even harder at the unbelievable news. Then, her odd circles completely absorbed her mother as she asked the question that she feared the most.

"Clinton?" she wept. "He was so mad mother he tried to save me and his uncle shot him." she cried even harder. "Is he dead, too?"

"Liza is tending to, Clinton," she said matter-of-factly. "I tend to you."

"He, he didn't listen to any of them," she sobbed. "Is he going to die, Mother because of, me?"

"I don't know his condition, but it wasn't because of you," Lizzie said truthfully. "I believe his Uncle would have killed him either way."

"Please don't let him die, Mother," she wept softly, "For me, I've seen what you and Liza can do, your hands are like magic. You can do anything," she rattled on through her sobs.

"You just close your eyes and let us worry about that," Lizzie soothed her heartbroken daughter.

Several hours came and went when Lizzie heard a light tap on her bedroom door. Naomi had long ago fallen asleep in her arms as she cuddled the young woman the same way she did when she was a little girl. "Come," she said softly.

"Lizzie," Liza said quietly, "I need you."

When their eyes met there was no denying the sorrow that engulfed them both. "What has happened?" Lizzie asked disturbed at the worry on her sister's face, yet not wanting to leave her daughter alone.

"I can't get the bleeding to stop. I've tried everything. He's dying, sister. I can't do this without you," she said in a discouraged tone.

Lizzie let out a deep sigh as she laid Naomi's sleeping body beneath the covers of her bed. Begrudgingly, she let go of the slumbering girl. "Sleep well my, Little Feather."

"I'll see to it," Hattie's warm voice echoed behind her. "Like she is my own," Hattie's face was full of heartache. "Go, both of you save the boy."

Liza walked over and placed a kiss on the young woman's forehead. "I love you too, Little Feather."

When the twins' eyes met they were both sorry. Sorry, for this travesty that had risen up from nowhere. "Was she…did they?"

There was no missing the relief in Liza's eyes when Lizzie spoke. "No. Not like that."

When they entered Matthew's room it was plain to see that the young mapmaker was fighting for his life. His typically tanned skin had a melon-like hue to it and his breathing was coming in shallow bursts. His brow was sweating like he was still lying in the pouring down rain, and it was plain to see that the fever had already found its mark.

Liza had bandaged both of his heavily muscled thighs where the bullets had gone completely through the skin, but the blood was still finding a way out of the bandages. Lizzie gave her sibling an odd look.

"That's not even the worst of it, look at his shoulder, I can't get the bleeding stopped there either," Liza stated hopelessly.

"Matthew," Lizzie said in a tone that he had never heard her speak, "go out to the barn put several of the red-hot coals into the small round bucket, put the long thin iron that hangs by my bridle in the coals, when they get a yellow-red hue you high-tail it up here as fast as you can."

"Yes, Auntie," he said as he hurried from the room.

"And, Matthew," Lizzie stated.

"Ma'am?"

"Tell Luke to keep several of them ready."

There was no missing the discoloration that had begun to show on the outline of the bullet hole. Lizzie shook her head as she pulled the jagged skin away from the mushy opening. "I need more light," she instructed her sister. "It looks like something is stuck inside there."

"I know," Liza said. "But, every time I try to pull it out, blood just flows like a river from that hole."

"Then we'll do it together." Lizzie laid her hand on top of her sister's. "Together Liza, we always do what needs done together. When Matthew brings the iron, I'll grab the piece of—I think it's a part of his shirt, anyway, when I do that you sear that opening with the heated iron."

"What if it gets infected?" Liza asked.

"Do you have the poultice made?" Lizzie questioned.

"Of course," she replied, put-off at her sister's flippant question.

"It won't get infected with the poultice, besides if we don't use the iron he'll die, and I promised Naomi we wouldn't let that happen. We have to stop the bleeding—infection or not."

"You're right," Liza stated. "I'm not thinking straight. I've got the poultice ready to go into the wound, and we'll use the iron we've done it before." It was as though Liza was repeating her own words for her own comfort.

Lizzie placed her hand on her sister's trembling fingers once again. "Nothing has changed between, us."

The doctoring duo had no more than planned their mode of attack when Matthew came bounding into the room. "Here, Auntie," he said in a panicked tone. "Be careful it's really hot."

"Ready, Liza?" Lizzie asked.

"Yep."

The two acted like the operation that they were about to perform was second nature. Their fingers worked like magic one within the other in perfect time, there was no hesitation, no second guessing, only precise movement.

But just as Lizzie pulled the cloth from the gaping hole she noticed something else within the fleshy mass. "Wait, the bullet's still in there."

"What!" Liza exclaimed. "I swear I took it out, look."

"It must have splintered, give me the tweezers, quickly," she demanded. "I'm sorry Clinton," Lizzie said aloud. "I've got to get that bullet."

Clinton let out a deep moan as he tried to move but Matthew held him still. "No!" he hollered, "Get your filthy hands off of her, I'll kill you!" Then he passed out again.

"Get ready, Liza! I almost have it, yes, now, do it now!" Lizzie said urgently.

Immediately, Liza pressed the heated iron against the open wound, the smell nearly made Matthew throw up where he stood. Lizzie was relentless in her quest to save the young mapmaker she, and Liza both knew if it hadn't been for his love for Naomi her daughter would be dead or worse.

"That should do, Liza," Lizzie said. "Now, let's get that poultice in there before it starts bleeding again."

Instantly, Liza's fingers went to work. Dip, dip, she placed a layer on the wound, dip, dip, she placed another layer, she did that several times until the wound was packed full of the wet poultice. Then she carefully tied a heavy white cloth around his arm and shoulder to keep it still.

"Do we need to do the same thing to his legs?" Lizzie asked. "They're still seeping."

Liza looked into her sister eyes they knew the answer. "Matthew," Lizzie instructed, "reheat the iron."

"Liza," Lizzie said, "You should have come sooner this was a big job for one person."

"You had your hands full enough," she whispered through thin angry lips. Like a wounded cougar she snapped her head upward, "If he wasn't my son Lizzie, this would have ended out there on the prairie, she's ours yours and mine our sister sacrificed her life for hers. What in thunder was Jeffrey thinking hanging around hooligans like that?"

"Liza," Lizzie said in a soft tone, "I don't blame you I would never blame you."

"It was like a repeat of the past like we'd been thrown right back in time. Why, I nearly died at the sight." Liza wept. "It was just like looking at...Sarah."

"I know, I've seen the same picture, but right now we need to save this boy he's the reason that our Naomi is alive," Lizzie said in a controlled tone surprised at her sister's emotional state. "Besides, if we lose Clinton, on top of Emmy and Charlie, why I don't even want to think of the consequences."

"I know, I—know, I'm undone because you're undone, and, and we're never undone. What kind of spiteful hatred has taken place here to one of our own." Her tone was fearful. "By one of our own? It's taking all of my breath."

"Mine, too." Lizzie whispered.

When their eyes walked across the distance they both knew that the time would come when Lizzie would expect retribution. That each breath Jeffrey drew was bound to be his last. With one bullet, Lizzie would place his soul next to the devil where it belonged. Sadly, Liza would never allow it.

As they worked diligently on the dying map-maker, Lizzie gave her sister a puzzled look. "Did you see the surprise on Ben's face when I asked him about Emmy and Charlie?"

"Yes," Liza said as her fingers held the fleshy wound tight. "He acted like he had no idea what we were talking about. What a liar he knew exactly what we were asking."

"No, I don't think that he did," Lizzie stated in a knowing tone. "Someone else did that." She stared into her sister's ashen face. "Someone that knew exactly what was going on that day and where the wagon would be, but more than that…where…we would be."

"No." she exclaimed, shocked at her sister's accusation. "He would never do that."

"Wouldn't he? Put it together Liza, all of the drunken nights that he never came home, stealing money out of father's safe, our father's safe! Getting ready to run off to, California." She gave her identical sibling a skeptical look. "And what about the bruise on his shoulder where did it really come from?"

"How did you know about that?" Liza questioned in a leery voice. She'd certainly never told her sister about that.

"I know, Liza," Lizzie answered in a tired tone. "I see what you've been trying to hide just like you see what I hide. We're one and the same you and I there's no hiding life between us, from us. So if he's been lying about all of that, what else has he been lying about?" she challenged. "How can you be so sure?"

Liza gave her sister a weak look. "I can't, it's like I don't know him he's like a crooked trader that talks from both sides of his mouth making promises he doesn't intend to keep."

Together they finished doctoring Clinton and without another word they tucked the wounded man beneath the warm covers as their shattered eyes met. "Jeffrey wouldn't have killed Emmy and Charlie he wouldn't have betrayed our family like that."

"Yet that is exactly what he did tonight, sister." Lizzie stated.

"Why would he do that? For what reason? No, it has to be something else." Liza stared at her sister in disbelief.

But, Liza knew from looking at the hardened features on her identical siblings face that Lizzie would expect him to pay a price for what he'd caused tonight. That she did believe it was Jeffrey who had betrayed their family and put them in harm's way. Liza knew that Lizzie's method of discipline would be brutal and harsh, only death would comfort her soul.

Liza knew that she would never allow her sister to kill, Jeffrey. Good or bad he was her son, the only way to save him would be the unthinkable it would be the best day and the worse day of her life.

"Goodnight, Liza," Lizzie said in a quiet tone through heartbroken eyes.

"Goodnight, Lizzie," Liza answered with a voice full of doubt as the two of them walked back to their own rooms.

# CHAPTER 19

For three long days and nights, the storm raged as Emmy made plans for her journey homeward. She knew she was on the wrong side of the river, that was a given. And with the past several days of drenching rain she knew that the river would be crowding its banks like a pile of hurrying people going to a hanging. She'd have to be smart, pay attention to her surroundings, leave markers encase she needed to find her way back. But most of all she'd have to be brave, brave enough to cross that dangerous threshold of liquid between herself and the riverbank. She let out a deep sigh, getting across the swift water would be the trick, especially since she didn't know how to swim.

Tears etched their way down her cheeks. "Oh Mighty One how do I get through this one?"

"Then from out of nowhere Matthews's strong voice reminded her, "We're tall people, Emmy, the water's not deep for us." Emmy let out a deep sigh. "I sure hope you're right."

As she contemplated her situation, she couldn't help but wonder if the mystery man would be coming back and planned to live here himself through the winter. Whoever had been using this place for whatever reason had it well stocked but there wasn't enough food to last her all winter.

As Emmy's eyes searched the unusual looking shadows on the cavern wall, she made a conscious decision, tomorrow come hell or high water she was going home. "Time to get busy Emmy." She said to herself.

Purposely she took one of the ragged blankets and made a makeshift pack. She carefully added one small bag of coffee, the pot, two jars of peaches, a knife, a small bag of flour and just a little sugar. Then she folded one of the good blankets and stuffed it in on top. She'd found a shotgun in the corner behind the bed but here were no bullets at least she hadn't found any yet. After all who would leave a shotgun for protection with not bullets? All she could figure was Nelly had either thrown them down one of the darker caverns or hid them.

As she pounded the side of the makeshift pillow, Emmy swore that she heard the faint sound of a baby crying. Like a snapping willow she sat upright and strained her ears to listen. She couldn't hear a thing but the pounding thunder and constant rain. "It must have been the wailing wind." She whispered to herself as she laid her head back on the wadded-up material and praying the storm would end soon. She needed to get home why; Matthew must be worried sick.

As she stared out the cave opening, she hoped there wouldn't be snow on the ground when she woke up that would make her journey home even harder.

Like a squirrel in a nest, she settled down beneath the warm covers as her head snapped around, there it was again that same sound someone else was in this cavern. The thought of it made her shake.

Like a thief, she slowly made her way toward the faint noise. Was that a baby's cry, no, Nelly wouldn't have hid it way back here, would she? No, she'd have killed it before she did that. "It must be something else." She whispered.

Like a thief, she slowly made her way toward the faint noise. Carefully, she planned every footstep so she wouldn't make a sound but, the further down the corridor she went the louder the whaling became. She could have dropped a boulder, no one would have heard it. She knew now that it was definitely a baby's cry and the closer she slipped down the darkened corridor the louder it became.

Terrified she peeked her head around the corner of the stone wall her heart skipped a beat as she witnessed the unbelievable sight, there lying in the dirt were two pink, bare-naked infants and one newborn wolf pup. She couldn't believe her eyes.

Emmy squatted there in complete shock. "Babies? A pup? How in the world?" She whispered as she snuck even closer. But, her intuition said, "Stop!" She stayed within the shadows as a huge grey wolf practically lay on top of the small infants, Emmy let out a silent gasp. "She'll kill them." she whispered. But, as soon as her long tongue touched their delicate skin the whining became non-existent. She watched in awe as the female wolf rolled their tiny bodies with her long nose until they found the intended food source that she offered. This animal had been taking care of them all this time right under her nose. Emmy was stunned as she watched the large wolf affectionately lick each child as though it were her own pup, they knew her touch.

Emmy sat hidden within the walls of the dark corridor for what seemed like an eternity she didn't know what to do, she didn't have any bullets to kill the lone wolf and take the infants. She also knew wolf-to-human that she would be no match for the huge animal, it was a hundred fifty pounds if it was an ounce. Besides, she didn't want to kill the wolf even if she had bullets, death wasn't the answer for a good deed.

As she sat like a dark speck in a large hole, she wondered how she could steal the newborns away from the mother wolf if she could rescue them at all. She knew that her attempt would have to be swift in the stealing and even swifter in the leaving. Then on the other hand if she did get brave enough to approach the mother wolf she just might kill the babies, it was an unnerving situation.

She took in a deep breath; the babies were safe for now, still the female wolf seemed nervous and distracted as she stared into the darkness directly in Emmy's direction. Like her feet were made of cotton she made her way back to the main part of the cavern. She'd have to act fast encase the wolf decided to move them to another part of the cave to a place she might never find.

As she built the fire even higher, she added several cups of powdered milk to her pack and four cans of cream. Not that she had a clue as to how she would get the liquid down the babies tiny throats but when the time came she'd find a way.

With several hours of preparation behind her, she made her way back down the darkened corridor it was nearly daylight when she finally made it back to where the babies laid. Her heart sank as she dropped to her feet, they were gone, all of them.

"No." Emmy whispered, as she inched her way closer to where the infants had lain.

Frustrated, Emmy started to cry when she heard a faint sound, instantly she crouched down into the darkened shadows. Not more than fifteen feet away from her stood the large female. It looked as though she was getting ready to go for a hunt, Emmy stopped breathing.

The wolf stood silent frozen like ice for several minutes smelling the air in front of her. All Emmy could do was hope that she was hungrier that curious. After what seemed like an eternity the wolf bolted out of the side of the cave and disappeared. This was her chance!

Like greased lightning she ran to where the two babies lay cuddled around the lone pup. All Emmy could hope for was they'd stay asleep. With trembling fingers, she carefully picked up each baby, they never made a sound as she pulled the makeshift carrier off her shoulder and placed them securely within it. Then, she threw the pack over her back, grabbed the shotgun, and started out of the safety of the only shelter she'd know for weeks.

"Please, Mighty One, I beg you be with us." She said out loud as he headed toward the river constantly looking behind her hoping that the female wolf wouldn't follow.

# CHAPTER 20

Several long weeks crept by as Liza and Lizzie kept a constant vigil over the broken mapmaker. The two of them made sure that his wounds were clean and well dressed, they monitored his fever constantly and either one or the other was with him all the time. They did everything they could to keep the mapmaker alive, after all if it hadn't been for his selfless act trying to save Naomi who knows what would have happened.

Every morning one of the hands would walk to the bottom step of the old log house to hear if the brave young mapmaker and the lovely berry-headed woman would pull through only to be turned away with a shake from Abe's head and worried eyes. It made the hired hands restless knowing that the two young people in the main house were holding on for dear life. But, more than that they knew if Liza and Lizzie the self-proclaimed doctors were concerned they had reason to be, too.

Everyone on the ranch wanted the young man to live. He'd proven on several occasion that he could pull his own weight without complaint, carry his end of any workload. The men had grown quite fond of his happy-go-lucky ways, no they didn't want the mapmaker to die.

And then there was sweet, Naomi the princess of the Lazy AB Ranch who lay struggling trying to win her fight against a raging nightmare that never seemed to end. Her screams could be heard in the middle of the yard. They all loved Naomi with her sweet kidding nature. The men that rode for the brand were overprotective of the beautiful young, Baxter. But, more than that, they felt as though the people that surrounded the existence of the Lazy AB Ranch had suffered enough heartache. Sarah, Charlie, Emmy no one wanted to see Clinton and Naomi added to the list of deaths.

The men held a constant vigil at the Lazy AB Ranch arch. No one that didn't belong here passed through those gates. If they tried, a bullet was their ticket out.

On the fourth day Clinton finally woke up. "Hello," Lizzie said in a motherly fashion. "It's about time you came back to us." Her smile was warm and reassuring. "I was starting to get a little worried."

Clinton gave her a weak smile, he should have known that Liza and Lizzie would doctor him back to life. "I was in the hands of angels with you two taking care of me, why would I worry?" He had the kindest smile. "I'm sorry, I didn't mean to cause," his hoarse throat stopped him in mid-sentence.

Lizzie carefully propped up his head as she let him take a small sip of water. "Not too much now I don't want you getting sick and undoing my sister's fine needlework."

"No, ma'am," he sounded like a small child. Then his fevered eyes held hers, "Did he kill her, is she dead?" his pale face said his heart was broken. "Please, tell me my so-called uncle didn't kill her," a quick sob caught in his throat. "I tried, I did, but..."

Just then Naomi paddled into the room like a bird. "Is he awake?" she asked her mother in a caring tone for the hundredth time.

"See for yourself," Lizzie answered as she stood up from the bed. "Only a minute now."

There was no missing the look of adoration and relief that passed between them. His eyes were open, his fever was down, and he was alive. "I thought you were..."

"Dead," he whispered as he stole the words from her blistered lips. "I thought the same."

"No," she sighed as she took his hand in hers. "I'm quite fine— now."

He ran his warm hand across her scaly face as he spoke, "Like Matthew would say that's a different look for you."

She knew he was teasing as she replied, "Mother say's I look like a snake getting ready to shed its skin."

"Not a very attractive thought," he mused as he held his side. There was no doubt that several of his ribs were broken.

"I know." Then on a more serious note she said through heartfelt eyes that said she was sorry that he'd gotten hurt. "Thank you for trying to save me."

"Ah," he said sweetly, "It was better than a shot in the foot."

Clinton held out his arms as Naomi gently fell into them, her soft sobbing etched a scar in his heart. "I thought he killed you," she wept. "There was nothing that I could do. You're mine and I thought he killed you." There was no stopping the flood of tears. "I, I tried to get lose but," she wept even louder, "I couldn't."

"I thought when I woke up your mother would tell me that you were dead." Tears filled his reddish eyes. "I would never have been able to live through that, I love you Naomi, you're mine and as soon as we're both well we're gonna make that official."

Together, the two of them lay sharing their tears. Naomi was careful not to open his wounds and Clinton was careful not to tear her skin, their tears mingled like the love that they openly shared for each other.

Everyone on the Baxter ranch was relieved the day they heard Naomi, and the mapmaker were going to live, it had a way of lifting the spirits of those left wondering. Smiling and laughing, they passed around a bottle whiskey, each taking a good swallow, it was their way of celebrating a miracle.

But, they also knew that there had been a traitor linked within the deceitful ways of the male Baxter-Jones twins, that perhaps he had been the reason they'd lost Charlie and Emmy. Not that Jeffrey had openly admitted anything the townsfolk all secretly hoped they'd be someplace else when the day of reckoning came back tenfold screaming like a raging banshee ready to purge his troublemaking soul into darkness. Jeffrey had crossed the line of no return he had gone against the ones who loved him, cared for him now, there would be a price to pay. His life!

# CHAPTER 21

Liza sat broken-hearted in the old oak rocker and stared at the brilliant green eyes of her disobedient son. "Do you have any idea what it is that you have done?" she asked in a voice that wasn't her own.

"Mother," Jeffrey whispered through begging lips. "I swear, I didn't know that they'd kidnapped Naomi and Dancing Bear I didn't!"

"You have divided me against myself," she said in a dead tone as she stared at the framed portrait of one of Sarah's paintings hanging on her bedroom wall. "Against, myself!" she shouted furiously. "I will need every trick that I know to save you and I'm not sure I want tata…!"

The storm raged over the old wooden house with angered vengeance, lightening cracked like the end of a bullwhip lighting up the night sky. Thunder boomed so loud over the ranch that it shook the very ground of its foundation, on and on the angry storm expelled its fury.

"I'm sorry, Mother," Jeffrey interrupted. "How was I supposed to know that they would kill, Dancing Bear? I didn't know that they would do something like that, I wasn't with them I swear."

"I will lose my breath by the time this day is over," she whispered in a far-off tone ignoring her son's whining words. "One way or the other, it will be gone."

"No, mother no." he begged. "You didn't do it, I did."

"You have no idea what you did!" she snapped as she stared into a face that she no longer wanted to know. Lizzie was right if he lied about this what else has he been lying about.

"Mother, I love you," he sobbed hoping to gain back some of her grace.

"We have drawn the same breath since you were born," she whispered softly as one lone tear ran down her tanned cheek. "My sister and I we share the same blood."

"I share your blood," Jeffrey insisted hoping to drag her out of her tranced state.

Liza stared at the boy again with hollow eyes. "You have no blood of mine, and soon you will have no breath either."

"What?" Jeffrey said startled at his mother's accusation. "What does that mean, Mother?"

"It means, I don't know if all of this is worth the saving," she whispered matter-of-factly. "You have caused a crack in my sister's heart like melting ice, and in mine."

"You would choose her over me?" he said completely taken aback at his mother's words.

"Because of you our blood will be divided, it will spill from our aching hearts like rain onto the sacred ground that we call home." Liza tried to make her son understand the impact of what he had done. "I can't let her kill you."

"No, mother," he said with hope in his voice.

"I should for what you've done, for acting like the backstabbing fool you are, for all of your hatefulness and lies, I should. You went against us, against our family." Liza's eyes were full of hurt. "Against me. Why?"

"I can make it up I can!" Jeffrey insisted in a panicked tone.

"There's no making nothing up now." Her voice had become low and bane as she walked to where her son sat. Gently she ran her hand across the top his blonde curly hair. "I was so proud the day that you were born Jacob, your father was going to kill me and Lizzie both in cold blood steal Naomi for some kind of ransom from people we didn't even know. Can you imagine? He stood just inside that closet right there hoping that I would die naturally in childbirth, he was a coward just like you, Lizzie refused him access. My sister, my flesh and blood unselfishly saved my life and yours too she sacrificed her own body to save me, used it as a shield."

"What?" he said shocked at the confession. "What are you talking about?"

"Jacob hated Lizzie from the moment he met her and she him. She refused to move one inch even when the barrel of his gun was stuck like a knife in the flesh of her beating neck trying to brand her into submission. Of course it didn't work, your father's bullet missed me and hit her. I was the one that killed your father that day Jeffrey not your Aunt Lizzie, me, I shot Jacob."

Jeffery was appalled at his mother's confession. "My father would never have done such a thing, and neither would you this is just another ploy to protect, Lizzie."

Angrily, Liza grabbed a fistful of Jeffrey's golden curls and yanked his head backwards. She was livid. "He not only would do it; he did do it and so did I! I am the one that killed my own husband before he killed me, and now," her dark eyes collided like thunder with his as she stared at disbelieving eyes, "I will do the right thing by being a mother protecting my offspring because he doesn't know how to get out of his own way. Taking his side because he is my flesh and blood that makes me divided against myself because of your selfish actions. Liza studied her son's face; do you have any idea what that means?"

"You can take her, mother." he said in a vain pumped-up tone. "You're stronger."

It was as though the man standing in front of her had no clue what she had just said. "You lying excuse of a man!" Finally, Liza allowed herself to lose her temper, angrily she slapped her son hard across the face. The unexpected blow took him off guard as he landed in a sprawled-out heap on the floor shocked at the powerful intrusion all he could do was stare.

"She's my sister, my lifeline, my breath!" she screamed uncontrollably. "Do you know what you have done?" Liza strapped on her holster. She knew that Lizzie would be doing the same thing waiting for the inevitable.

"You have turned us inside out pitted our soul's one against the other." Sadly, Liza knew even with all of Jeffrey's misgivings there was no way that she was going to give up the boy.

"Mother," Matthew urged through misty blue eyes, "Please don't go I can talk to Aunt Lizzie; she'll listen to me."

"It's not about the listening now Matthew, it's about the doing." She gazed into her son's strong kind face his caring blue eyes said that he understood but in reality he didn't want to. He had grown to be a good man, a Baxter through and through any mother would be proud to have a son like, Matthew.

"Mother," he asked as he choked back his tears, "What if you don't come back?"

"She'll be back." Jeffrey said in a prideful tone. "Aunt Lizzie is nothing more than an old dried-up cowpunchers has been whose not worth spit."

"Shut up!" Matthew yelled at his annoying brother. "Shut your filthy mouth you double-crossing piece of dirt." Matthew's face was so red. "Are you that naive? Do you think this is another one of your pathetic range games? It's because of you that our mother in this mess, you! You're an ignorant, prideful loudmouth who doesn't care about anyone but himself!"

Jeffrey backed away from his raging brother he hadn't forget the beating he took in the barn. "I said I was sorry."

Matthew anxiously turned and faced his mother once again dismissing his brother's lame apology. "Let Aunt Lizzie have him, Mother. It's time for him to be accountable for his actions." He turned and stared with a heated vengeance at his sibling. "He's not worth it." Then, he gazed into his mother's ashen face. "What will we do—without you I mean?"

"Your Aunt will finish the raising that we have started, right along with Naomi. I expect your brother will be dead by then." She gave him a strained look of disgust.

"I don't want you to go, mother," Matthew said through trembling lips. "I don't want Aunt Lizzie to finish what you started I want you to finish it. We've lost so much already I can't bear the thought of losing you, I love you, Mother."

"And I, you," she said lovingly as she touched his cheek.

"What about me, mother? I love you, too," Jeffrey asked in a rejected tone.

"You?" Liza answered shocked at his question. "It's impossible to love someone like you, Jeffrey. My son you bring heartache to all those around you, befriend men who hide in the dark and rip our family apart like a worn piece of paper. Looking at you now I realize no one can believe a single word that comes out of that big mouth, and today, at this very moment I'm not sure you are my son, my flesh and blood. The Mighty One knows, by all that is just and written I wish you weren't." Liza stated matter-of-factly.

Liza held her head high and walked from her room into the late afternoon light of the long hallway. Dread filled her being like she was sinking in a pool of mud with nothing below her feet but emptiness. Today, she was divided against herself.

On the other side of the large old house Lizzie had her own struggle going on. "Mother, Lizzie," Naomi said in a genuine tone, "I didn't get hurt."

"You're battered and bruised don't tell me you're not hurt I see what he caused." Her tone was anything but kind. "He would already be dead if anyone would have hurt you in that way.'

"No one touched me, not like Dancing Bear." There was no missing the onset of tears that rolled down her scaly face. "Look at me, I am healing fine." Her sorrowful eyes pleaded for her mother to understand.

"Jeffrey has divided me against myself," Lizzie said in a dead tone to no one in particular. "He has no idea what it is that he has done."

"But Mother Lizzie, I am all right I didn't get killed, I'm right here." Naomi said in a knowing tone as she tried to make her mother understand. "And, and you're not well."

"I tried to make him one of us, he didn't want to be one of us. I tried to make him understand the meaning of tradition of family, he has no love for family. We tried to teach him good over evil, he chose evil. "He's the master of the dark magic's son, he'll never be a Baxter."

"Maybe there is still hope," Naomi said softly. "People can change."

"Flying Eagle said that stormy day that he brought you to us, *'It's not the understanding but the love of the blood that will meld you together.'* Jeffrey never learned what that meant and he never will. His heart does not beat with the rhythm of ours, he does not bear our bloods strength."

Regrettably, Lizzie strapped on her holster and loaded gun.

She knew that Liza was doing the same thing. She knew that her sister would never give up the boy she didn't blame her, but Jeffrey had gone too far this time, he betrayed their family and put them all in harm's way. She knew every motherly instinct would tell Liza to protect him that was her right as a mother. Lizzie's motherly instinct said, "Kill him," It was her right to protect her own.

Still the Mighty One wasn't pleased Jeffrey'd stepped over the line of redemption. He'd walked into a world where he had no business being, trying to hide his hideous acts behind the moon, the moon rejected his lies and sent justice to prevail. She couldn't prove it but deep in her heart she knew Jeffrey killed Charlie and Emmy and now he would pay for his bad decisions.

"Mother," Naomi wept through trembling lips, "I can't let you go what if you don't come back?"

"Then your Aunt Liza will finish what I have started." Lizzie's eyes were void of any emotion.

"I don't want Liza to finish it I want you to," Naomi whispered.

"Today I have been divided against myself, my way of justice will vanish, as will my sister's." She gave Naomi a loving look, "There will be no winner we both lose."

"Please don't go," Naomi whispered breathlessly. "I love you."

Lizzie ran her work-worn fingers across the lovely young woman's forgiving face. "I wish I could stay right here forever," she breathed with tears in her cool blue eyes that reminded a person of moon drops on a lost forgotten lake. "But I can't, you see, I made a promise, pledged your life on my sister Sarah's soul, that you would be mine, that I would protect you with my dying breath, that I would raise you as if I gave birth to you, I became a mother, your mother Naomi because my sister Sarah died. You are my own, my only own. What kind of a mother would I be if I didn't follow through with the promise of life that the Mighty One gave to me? To fall short of that promise that I made to him years ago? I won't do that to the guardian of my soul."

Lizzie was still tired and nauseous from the snakebite. For her the venom from the rattler had been much harder to shake off this time and she couldn't get rid to the effects of it. Plus the ordeal of losing Emmy and Charlie plagued her.

Liza and Lizzie stepped into the hallway at the same time, they both had a look of regret on their sober faces.

"Is this travesty duty or pride?" Liza asked looking straight ahead.

"Neither," Lizzie answered. "It's justice."

# CHAPTER 22

Much to Emmy's dismay, when she reached the river the rushing water was pushing at its banks. She knew that trying to get across to the other side with the two babies strapped to her chest was going to be impossible, so she headed up the semi-traveled trail toward the top of the endless mountain.

The unfamiliar path was quite pretty, and the rain had left everything well-watered. Much to her excitement it was getting warm out, very, warm. The tall pines always seemed to show up with their gracious shade at the perfect time and she was more than grateful. The remaining leaves from the falling aspens reminded her of the floating feathers from her wedding she couldn't help but giggle remembering all of the familiar faces that she loved so much.

By the time she made it to the top of the grassy knoll she was panting profusely, from where she stood she could see for miles but much to her dismay nothing looked familiar and there was no mistaking the storm that lingered like a hangman's noose over the large ridge. She gently touched the tops of the babies' heads, she needed to find shelter for them before night fall.

Emmy continued her uncharted travels when she spotted a hollowed-out log. It was quite large, and she was sure that someone or something had made it for the reason she would be borrowing it for the night. Carefully she laid the sleeping babies within the protection of the hollow space as her distrusting eyes scanned her surroundings.

Knowing that her pride was secure she started gathering semi-dry pieces of wood for the fire. Within minutes she had a roaring flame going and made a flat dough as she placed it within the heated skillet. "Good ole, Charlie," she whispered. There was no doubt that the baked bread was going to taste just as good as the coffee smelled.

After the hunger pains had been satisfied, and the babies asleep, she decided to walk down to the bottom of the stream. She could see the tree clearly from where she stood and was amazed at how far she must have traveled down the engorged creek, nothing in front of her was familiar. No notched tree trunk, no pool of boggy mud, nothing, she had no clue where she was or how she could have survived the rushing water.

Emmy let out a slight sigh, only by a quirk of fate had Nelly seen in her the raging water and decided to save her from drowning.

So with a clean cloth she wiped her dirty face and gave herself a good once over. As she finished her bath an uneasy feeling washed over her like someone, or something was watching her from just inside the shadows. A feeling much like the one she had on a particular Harvest Dance night.

"Stop it!" she scolded herself. "There's no one out here for miles. Do you see anyone? No!"

Thankful for the shelter the Mighty One had provided she purposely placed more sticks of dried wood on the low burning fire. In the distance she could see there was another storm churning its web of destruction. She watched the lightning snap within the dark rolling clouds even though Emmy knew it was miles away, yet close enough to know it would be a doozy.

So far all the storms she'd experienced out here had been bad. "Wherever here is," she said to herself as she stared at the rushing water below her. "Mighty One," she whispered. "I don't know how to get home, I don't know where it is." Her anguished eyes filled with unshed tears. "I'm not brave," she said as her eyes cast toward the heaven. "I've never been brave my whole life, I'm afraid, did Nelly tell me the truth about her, and Jeffrey are these innocent little babies his daughters? She lied about killing the babies why not about Jacob, Jeremiah, and Jeffrey?" She shook her head it was too much to take in, too much to deal with right now.

Emmy let out a deep sigh, she was exhausted. Purposely, she stuck her head inside their scant sleeping area to check on the babies when she stopped dead in her track. "What are you doing here?"

# CHAPTER 23

As the twins stepped onto the wooded porch their eyes searched the beautiful landscape of the distant horizon in complete harmony. They had been each other's lives since the time of conception. They were sisters. Soul twins. Blood twins. One body. One breath. One beating heart. The span of time that had passed before their eyes since childhood were one and the same. They loved each other unconditionally not even death would change that.

They ramrodded this ranch, the rich black dirt beneath their feet fed the passion of their beings this was their home. Still they both knew there could be only one survivor, and after tonight one of them or maybe both of them would no longer be able to say that. There was no angry hostility between them, only love.

The twins hugged each other for what seemed like an eternity, then turned and walked thirty feet in the opposite direction, today they were divided against themselves, neither would win this battle.

As they stepped into the center of the large yard their eyes held nothing but the utmost respect for each other as Lizzie squared off at her sister. "You know why I'm here." She said in an uncaring tone. "I want the boy, Liza."

"No." Liza said simply.

"Our lives can't go back to normal if you don't give him to me," Lizzie stated matter-of-factly.

"After today, our lives will never be the same," Liza answered truthfully.

Naomi, Clinton, and Matthew stood together at the end of the large wooden porch, all three were in shock. Abe stood one step down holding onto the back of Jeffrey's shirt making sure that he saw the sacrifice that was taking place on his behalf. Tears of regret poured down Jeffrey's wooden cheeks mumbling inaudible words that floated away at the hands of the restless wind.

"So be it." With a disgusted sigh Lizzie swished her hand against the dry dusty ground, instantly a whipping wind rose into a large dirt-devil as she waved it towards her sister. The dust-filled circle did as it was commanded, flying across the ground at a fast rate of speed, skipping and jumping like a jack rabbit gathering every little stick and stone the harrowing swirl could carry. There was no missing the sound of destruction it brought with it.

"I wish you wouldn't do that, Lizzie," Liza replied as she fell to the ground narrowly escaping the dusty trap. Then, with the snap of her fingers she commanded the dust devil back at her sister's unsuspecting face.

Lizzie blocked it with one swish of her hand, instantly it dissipated. "I will stop if you give me the boy."

"No." Liza's voice was stern.

"Then what you're saying is you will take his place?" Lizzie reached up toward the sky and pulled two sunrays into her fingertips as she threw them at her sister's feet. They exploded like dynamite, knocking Liza backward in a heap Lizzie was playing for keeps.

"Mother!" Jeffery screamed, shocked at his aunts wizardry.

Liza shook her head for a brief second as she sat quietly on the ground. "I can't do that he's my son, Lizzie." Liza dusted herself off and stood up she never raised her voice.

"He turned against our family." Lizzie yelled like a squawking vulture as she waved her hands high against the sky. "He's never been one of us."

"He is still my, son," Liza said with no emotion.

Everything turned black as hail started falling like rain. "Is he worth all of this, sister?"

Lizzie looked into the young boy's face as he stood on the bottom step, her eyes were black, void of any expression her tongue looked forked just like a snake ready to strike, it appeared to be inches away from his terrified face as it floated against the wind waiting to snatch him away within its powerful jaws.

Jeffry let out a loud scream and did all he could to get loose from his grandfather's grasp. But Abe Baxter wasn't about to let go of the backstabbing, lying coward.

"I don't think so, Lizzie," Liza spit back as the dark clouds dissipated and Liza threw her sister a little something of her own.

From out of nowhere, a thousand-winged moths flew into Lizzie's face, blinding her of her prey, within a heartbeat the illumined shadow disappeared as she stared at her sister's cunning face.

Naomi, Clinton, and Matthew stood spellbound watching the vexing show. Never in their wildest dreams had they been subjected to such a display of trickery or witnessed a battle like the one taking place right in front of them. The two younger Baxter's had no idea that their mother's possessed such power.

Abe knew what the girls were capable of he'd seen them square off like this once before when they were far younger and less knowledgeable, they nearly killed each other then, today they probably would complete that task.

Then he also remembered the warning that went with dividing themselves one against another, their sacred skills were never to be used against each other—ever. Only bad would come from that. Chief Mad Dog, the one who had taught them such trickery would be angry with the twin daughters' decision.

"My, my, Liza, wasn't that impressive," Lizzie hissed as she made a swooning noise. Within seconds there were a thousand birds in the yard their beating wings surrounded Liza like a tunnel pecking, swishing, and dive-bombing her.

But, Liza wasn't thrown off guard from her sister's sneaky attack, no with one swoosh of her hand a mighty blast of wind threw them out into the field like dried up leaves, within seconds they disappeared from sight.

"I won't let you kill my son Lizzie he's my flesh and blood the very one that you alone saved. Every night for month's you sat with him making sure he didn't die in his sleep." Liza was panting and sweating. It was plain to see that the fatigue of her sister's power was wearing on her. "Why did you save him only to kill him?"

Jeffrey looked at his grandfather's face. "Is that true, she's the one that saved me?"

"Yes."

"No wonder I'm cursed." Jeffrey whined. "She put some of that hoodoo voodoo in me."

"Shut up!" Abe shouted as he gave him a good shake.

Lizzie was panting and sweating just like her sister their bodies hadn't had time to fully heal, they knew the fight would be long and drawn out, the fatigue was setting in. "Now, I wish I wouldn't have."

"You don't mean that," Liza stated in a disappointed tone.

"Yes, I do." Lizzie's voice was tired and dark. "Are you so blind? He doesn't look like us, he doesn't act like us, he's never been one of us, can't you see that?"

"You're the one who brought him into this world you saw him first how can you say that? He's as much yours as he is mine!" Liza countered, she was tired of her sister's bullheaded attitude.

Lizzie stated in a disturbed tone. "I don't know maybe Mr. Horseflesh's crawlers split somehow his digits didn't add up as Luke would say."

Both women stood their ground staring at each other for several minutes. It was like time stood still then in the same motion they waved their hands high in the air and chanted several words that no one had heard before as a thick heavy fog began to envelope the ground around them like a heavy blanket.

Abe knew what was coming, he heard the familiar sound long before he saw them. He never dreamed it would go this far but it had and now he knew he couldn't stop it. Soberly, he spoke to the others on the porch as he held on to Jeffery's collar even tighter.

"Naomi, Clinton, Matthew, you kids step back slowly and get on the swing, put your feet underneath you, and sit as close together as you can. Whatever you do don't hang your hands over the rail just hold on to each other things are going to get ugly now," he said regrettably.

The three of them gave each other a queer look wondering how things could get any uglier, but they did as they were told. It was an odd feeling; the fog had a way of wrapping itself around them as they anxiously pulled their feet up into the swing just as the back of a long black snake appeared out of nowhere, Naomi let out a slight gasp.

"Papa," Jeffrey said in a scared tone.

"Hush," Abe retorted, "You're the reason they're here!"

"But, I didn't do nothin'." he whined pitifully. "All I wanted to do was pan for gold."

Abe tightened his grasp even more. "We know it was you that killed Charlie and Emmy, Jeffrey," Abe accused in his ear. "You might not have pulled the trigger, but I know it was you're doing."

"No." Jeffrey said in a scared denying tone.

"Clinton, Matthew, I want you to take off your belts and buckle them together as quickly as you can," Abe said in a serious tone. "Then, I want you to toss the belt over to me."

"Yes, papa," Matthew said as they did what they were told.

"When I tell you kids to hold on tight, you do it, don't let go of each other no matter what." he commanded.

"Yes, papa," Naomi whispered breathlessly as one of the snakes bumped the bottom of the swing. She let out a startled yelp it was plain to see that the three of them were prisoners.

As though Abe was in a contest for time he hurriedly wrapped the belt under Jeffrey's arms and around his own waist. Then, he took his belt and buckled them to the pole of the porch. "I hope this holds or we will both be spending the rest of our lives in the hereafter."

"I want the boy," Lizzie hissed through the thickening fog.

"No," Liza hissed back through the thickening fog.

"I don't want to kill you, Liza," Lizzie hissed. It was impossible to see her sister through the thickening mist. "I'm here to defend what is mine."

"I don't want to kill you, Lizzie," Liza hissed. It was impossible to see Lizzie through the thickening mist. "I'm here to defend what is mine."

The scene was unthinkable as the heavy mist swirled like a cloud on a storm-tossed sea at the bottom of the twins' feet. There was no doubt in anyone's mind that something deadly was moving beneath that threatening haze. The two souls that were bound together on the bottom of the step and the three companions that sat on the porch swing were hypnotized at the sight when the fog lifted enough to see the identical women from the waist up.

To the right and left of Lizzie, sat two large black snakes hissing and snapping on their long scaly tails in the direction her identical sibling stood. Their heads were wide with black colored scales and their eyes were crimson red, Lizzie stroked their clammy heads like trained dogs as they stood ready with the wave of her hand to do their masters bidding. Their long-forked tongues looked like tiny sparks of lighting as they snapped back and forth trying to intimidate their prey.

They stayed within the perimeter of Lizzie's requested domain and never offered to stray. Their scaly circles never once moved from their intended target. Standing in front of them were several rows of smaller snakes that acted like ridged well-trained soldiers, they never took their dead pan eyes off of Liza, they stood ready to serve their newfound masters command.

To the right and left of Liza were two large diamondback rattlers hissing and snapping on their long scaly tails in the direction her identical sibling stood. Their heads were wide with green colored scales and their eyes were crimson red, Liza stroked their clammy heads like trained dogs as they stood ready with the wave of their master's hand to do her bidding. Their long-forked tongues looked like tiny sparks of lighting as they snapped back and forth trying to intimidate their prey.

They stayed within the perimeter of Liza's requested domain, their scaly circles never once moved from their intended target, standing in front of them were several rows of smaller snakes that acted like ridged well-trained soldiers, they never took their dead pan eyes off of Lizzie, they stood ready to serve their newfound masters command.

Hissing and snapping one group faced the other both prepared to do battle at the commanding force of the two mighty generals.

"I am growing weary of this battle, Liza," Lizzie said in a hissing tone as though she was bored with the whole scenario. But in reality her strength was fading fast.

"As am, I," Liza agreed. She was also exhausted.

"We can end all of this just give me, Jeffrey," Lizzie said coldly.

"I will give you myself, and only, myself." Liza said again in a firm tone.

"I don't want you!" Lizzie screamed at the top of her lungs as the swarm of snakes began to hiss and rattle, the sound was deafening.

"Nor I—you," Liza said calmly.

Lizzie stood and studied her sister's demeanor she knew she wasn't going to give in. "So be it," she said with no emotion.

With one swish of her hand the fog completely covered both women like a protective blanket, there was no emotion in either twin's face. It was a standoff plain and simple their eyes never wavered one from the other. Everyone held their breath as they drew their pistols, each weapon was aimed directly at the other's heart. Their hands were steady as a rock. From this distance neither one would miss.

Abe stared at the unthinkable scene that was about to unravel in front of him, he wanted to let go of the boy that had caused all of this terrible trouble. "Take him! Take him!" he wanted to yell. "Throw him out into the middle of the arena and be finished with him once and for all. Put this nasty business behind them so their lives could got back to normal."

But he knew life on the Lazy AB Ranch would never go back to normal, that from this distance neither one of his daughters would miss, when this day was over his reason for living would be gone.

"Mother," Jeffrey whispered as he closed his eyes and hung his head.

Instantly Abe jerked his head backward as he spoke, "You open those traitorous eyes, Mr. you watch every single thing that happens here, you have been a whining coward since the day you were born." Roughly, he shook the young man standing in front of him. "Watch!" he demanded.

Sobbing Jeffrey did what his grandpa told him as tears ran down his petrified face. Silently he whispered his mother's name. "I didn't do anything." he confessed. "I swear, I was with Nelly all night."

"What?" Abe said shocked at the boy's confession. "Is this the truth? You were with a woman all of this time?" he said again as he shook the boy in front of him. "For once in your pathetic life tell the truth!"

"I swear, papa," he sobbed. "I, I didn't want anyone to know, she didn't want anyone to know."

"Know, what?" Abe demanded.

"About...the baby." he sobbed.

"Baby?" Abe was shocked. "What are you saying? Charlie, Emmy, you didn't have anything to do with that?" he demanded in an angry tone. "Your, cousin?"

"No." he stated through slobbering lips. In a pathetic tone. "I, I just said I was with those men so that everyone would stop treating me like everything that happens on this ranch is my fault I was going to pan for gold, nothing more."

"A woman, Jeffrey? All this hiding has been about a woman and a baby? Why?" he questioned in an angry voice.

"Because I love her and she's married to someone else don't you see we had to keep it quiet he might have killed me." he sobbed. "And, and I don't want to be no stinkin' father, ever."

"Boy," Abe said in a dreadful tone, "what have you done?" Desperately, Abe tried to unknot the belts wrapped around the twosome as he yelled furiously at the twins. "No! Stop! He didn't tell the truth." the belts wouldn't budge. Abe watched helplessly as the nightmare unfolded before him.

Jeffrey cowered under a remorseless grin. "Die!" he whispered under his breath. "Do the world a favor, both of you die!"

Abe knew the Mighty One would be angry pitting sister against sister.

Both women spoke in unison:

*"On this day I am divided against myself."*

*"Good against...," Liza spoke plainly.*

*"Evil." Lizzie answered distinctly.*

*"Light against...," Liza spoke plainly.*

*"Dark." Lizzie spoke distinctly.*

*"Life against...," Liza spoke plainly.*

*"Death." Lizzie spoke distinctly.*

*"Hidden in...," Liza spoke plainly.*

*"The Betrayed Silence." Lizzie accused loudly.*

*"The Betrayed Silence." Liza countered loudly.*

Abe shuddered to think how angry The Mighty One must be watching the twins' hostile behavior summoning the very skills that had protected them for all these years, now, using them against each other. He knew the repercussion's would be unforgiveable calling on the heavens to do their dirty work, he knew this act of defiance was only going to make matters worse, he knew the judgement from the Mighty One would be harsh.

Or was The Mighty One using the heavens to trick his twin daughter's into casting out the evil that had plagued the nucleus of this ranch. Was this an elaborate scheme to teach this boy a lesson he wouldn't soon forget, a way to pull him into the fold? This was unchartered territory for Abe, he'd never encountered such a determined evil hiding in the darkness waiting to engulf them all.

Within seconds of the last regretful syllable that passed the twins' lips the sound of a single pistol shot echoed across the open yard. There was no missing the smoke from the heated barrels as the ejected bullets soared like a shooting star to its designated target. It was as though the raging steel parted the misted arena like a tunnel of fire, spewing their flames of destruction aside to get to their sole target. The lunging reptiles coiled one within the other like strands of braided rope, the hissing sound that they created was deafening.

"No!" Abe yelled at the top of his lungs, the noise in the yard was too loud and the twins couldn't hear the sound of his voice. He tightened his grip even harder on the troublemaker in his hands, Jeffrey could barely breathe. "You keep those eyes open," he said in a steely tone that sounded just like his aunt and mother.

"I swear, papa, I never killed anyone." Jeffrey sobbed uncontrollably, but deep down he hoped they'd finish what they started.

"Kill each other!" Jeffrey hissed under his stagnant breath.

The ejected steel billets were hungry to serve their female masters' hands in their determined quest for honor. The blow would be mighty and unstoppable, the steely billets would tear at the flesh of their intended prey as they penetrated the sacred chamber of their beating souls.

No one moved, no one drew a breath as the earsplitting sound combined by the bulk of destruction riding within the blinding flash of light slammed bullet to bullet. The mighty force of the unbelievable event shook the earth beneath their feet as a wailing cry hidden within the blackening sky exploded, they all knew nothing good would come from this, for several minutes there was an eerie silence.

Then out of the blue something grabbed Jeffrey's leg trying to pull him into the thickening fog. The young man's horrified screams could be heard above the thundering howl, Abe held his grandson tight, they would have to kill him before the nasty serpents stripped his him from his arms.

Abe could see the black heads of the atrocious snakes pulling at the leather straps, with the back of his fist Abe struck one then another until his fist was bloody. Then from out of nowhere, one of the large green snakes attacked the dark menacing serpent. He knew if Jeffrey fell, they would shred his cowardly flesh with their honed teeth, behind him Abe heard Naomi screaming at the top of her lungs.

"Papa, they're after me!" Naomi yelled as she looked directly into the reddened eyes of the scaly serpents hissing face.

"Hang on, Naomi!" Abe hollered. "Don't let go of her Clinton."

Like a fighting grizzly Clinton held Naomi securely in his arms. "I won't!" The shy mapmaker had made a promise to himself that nothing was going to happen to the lovely young girl in his arms ever again.

"Mother!" Naomi's scream echoed across the yard.

At the sound of her voice, the noise stopped as their red eyes fixated on her when out of nowhere one of the serpent's long rattling tails slapped Matthew backward against the swing with a quick flick of his thick tail. For a brief moment, he was completely dazed by the blow and let go of his cousin.

But, Clinton still had a good hold on Naomi using his body for a barrier he clung to her trembling frame with all of his might. Within seconds the diamond back wrapped its tail around the mapmakers throat suffocating him gasping for air he let go of Naomi as he pulled the reptile free.

Matthew had barely regained his senses as he grabbed her and pulled her trembling body tightly next to his as he slugged the scaly serpent several times on the head. "No!" Matthew hollered as he clung to his quaking cousin. "No you don't you slimy... Naomi hold on to me." he demanded. Within seconds it disappeared beneath the protective layer of fog.

"Naomi?" Clinton hollered frantically as Matthew held her within the safety of the swing. The three of them huddled together even closer.

Abe had his own battle going on as he clung to the terrified bandit. It was plain that the scaly serpents had been given a command of death, one...to save, one...to kill from their dark-eyed master's. Abe could feel Jeffrey slipping as he reached his arm around his chest to secure Jeffrey's position when he saw blood on his sleeve. "What the..?" He didn't remember getting bitten.

Within seconds of seeing the blood, Jeffrey passed out the dark black clouds lifted and the fog with it. Abe placed Jeffrey on the wooden porch, the sight that lay before the older man was indescribable. The darkened sky had turned back to its natural blue and the sun shined like a brilliant ball of fire. There were lifeless looking snakes of every color and size lying in a circle in the middle of the open yard one tangled within the scaly skin of the other like braided ropes. Some were stretched like long crooked limbs from a diseased tree within the dirt and lying right smack dab in the middle of that pile of exfoliated skin lay Liza and Lizzie still as two stones.

Angrily, he kicked the lifeless reptiles out of the way as he covered the distance to where the twins lay in the softly trodden dirt. Abe's heart beat like a war drum as the scene laid out before him, it was all too familiar as a memory of a young berry-headed girl with knowing wildflower eyes flashed through his mind, she knew her father had found her, knew he was there to rescue her. This travesty here, he feared would have the same dreadful ending.

He felt like a murderer being drug to a hanging. "No." The mournful sound escaped his lips as he fell to his knees placing one hand on Liza and the other on Lizzie.

There was no mistaking the port of entry as his disbelieving eyes followed the trespassing steel. He knelt there still as a stone as he shook his peppered head and stared at the penetration of their strange wounds. He could see a single bullet hole etched within their tanned flesh at the center of their beating hearts, but…the torn skin wasn't bleeding not one drop of blood oozed from the jagged mark.

"So," a deep heartless voice said from out of nowhere, "They're finally dead."

Abe's head jerked around like a startled cat.

"I guess flesh isn't stronger than a bullet the invincible duo doesn't look so invincible now do they?" His mocking tone was cold and menacing. "They've always had such a charmed life unless they fight against themselves I guess that little bit of information was worth the price I paid for it the world is better off without them."

Abe had been so caught up in Liza and Lizzie's dreaded condition that he hadn't noticed anyone else standing in the yard. He watched in shock as he looked into the haggard face of a dead man. Intentionally Abe rubbed his eyes, surely they were misleading him, but, when he opened them again the image was still there.

"You? You're the one that has caused all of this suffering?" Abe said in a disbelieving tone. "All of this heartache?"

# CHAPTER 24

The tall curly haired man stood straight as an arrow, proud of his intruding presence wallowing in the fact that Abe Baxter had no idea he was alive. His arrogant pride said he had one upped the know it all cattle baron, tricked him like everyone else into believing he no longer existed. Jacob was ensconced in the glory of it, engulfed in the glory of it.

Abe's shocked features said he was talking to a ghost, he stood there wondering, where had he come from, was this the black spirit he'd been dealing with.

"Do you see anyone else standing here old man?" he said arrogantly.

"Where did you come from?" Abe questioned, completely baffled at his presence as his eyes scanned the distance between them. "You're dead."

"So I've been told old man, but I'm standing right here in front of you." his tone was so disrespectful.

"Why?" Abe questioned baffled at his presence.

"Why?" he snapped back fiercely. "Because you have something I want that's why. For a man of your superior intelligence, you're sure not very bright, I always get what I want."

Abe stood and stared at the ghost standing in front of him for several minutes, he was furious. "Nothing on this ranch belongs to the likes of you."

"Oh, you're finally mad now, good, that will definitely work to my advantage because I've already laid claim to one thing on this ranch soon I'll have it all."

"What are you talking about?" Abe demanded.

"Honestly, I didn't want her in the beginning but, the more I was with her the more I wanted to keep her," he let out a long hideous laugh.

"That was you?" Abe said in a horrified tone, "You're the one that defiled an innocent young woman?"

"I'm not so sure I'd call her innocent she seemed pretty willing to me I do have to say it only took a matter of minutes to tame that one," the bold man gave Abe a quick smirk.

"Emmy?" Abe whispered. "You violated Emmy and killed, Charlie?" he said in disbelief. "They never did anything to you."

"Emmy? Charlie? What are you talking about old man? Payback and lies killed, Charlie panicked stupidity killed the girl," he said in a pious tone.

"What are you saying? What have you done?" Abe yelled angrily.

"What have I done?" mimicked the man like a squawking crow. "Seems to me I've 'done' quite a bit, but the daughter you gave me for better or worse, she's mine and I want her back."

When Abe came to his feet he looked like a mountain. "Over my dead body." he said in a threatening tone. "Lizzie has lost enough for two lifetimes."

"Lizzie? I don't want, Lizzie I've come to get my wife the one you gave to me." he stated matter-of-factly. "For better or worse you do remember?"

"Your, what?" Abe couldn't believe his ears. "I've never given you anything."

Jacob gave Abe a cunning look, then he laughed. "You don't have any idea who I am do you? Even now you can't tell the difference between me and Jerimiah, we were that good of actor's weren't we?"

"More like liars and killers." Abe stated. He didn't understand, how could this be?

"That, so?" he scoffed.

"Liza didn't kill her husband, her lover that fateful day those two boils called babies were born, stupid woman, she didn't shoot me, she shot Jerimiah my so-called brother, although let me tell ya he was no brother of mine the stinkin' jackal!" Jacob let out a hideous laugh. "I told him not to go to the ranch that day, told him he didn't owe you Baxter's nothing to hold back till I could figure this all out." Jacob spun around, "Did he listen? No!" He gave Abe a daring look.

"Lizzie put some kind of spell on him with her hoodo-voodo, and he was ready to confess all his sins, tell her the truth that it was all a lie, tell her he wasn't no US Marshal, that he really did love her how sorry he was, stinkin' cull I should have shot him myself. Fortunately my wife took care of that for me, she couldn't tell the difference either, my own wife, but then no matter what you think, neither daughter is all that smart, we fooled them too." Jacob scoffed.

"I'm Liza's husband, Abe, it's me Jacob alive and well, I knew if Lizzie ever found out it was me, she'd kill me, not that I wasn't already dead, but she needed to take her vengeance out on Jerimiah for making her a sick looking, loving cow, which he did." he smiled.

"All these years she thought I was dead, that Liza had killed me and she had killed Jerimiah. What a sweet little bow Miss Lizzie tied, except for one thing, who's the real fool, think about it." he stated. "Not me."

"All these years Lizzie's been mourning over the man she hated, that would be me, Mr. Horseflesh. It couldn't have been more perfect when you think about it, her own sister killed her sister's lover, Liza had no idea the bullet from Lizzie's gun put a hole in Jerimiah's chest, not mine." he let out a loud laugh. "My heart jumped with joy that day! I was in the clear, all I needed to do was lay low and wait, which I did. Now, I'm here to collect what's mine, all of it."

"There's nothing here that belongs to you." Abe countered in an icy tone. "Nothing!"

Jacob blew off his remark as if he wasn't standing there. "I saw Lizzie on the plateau that day watching with that little heathen, I knew if she saw me she'd kill me, at least that's what I hoped, she didn't disappoint me. Her and that little half breed found my hideout, with a little help. I wasn't sure at first if she'd really shoot me, but yeah she did." He laughed even louder knowing he'd fooled them all as he slapped his chest. "Iron is a little hard on a bullet."

"And, that worthless pile of flesh lying over there passed out like the coward he is doesn't belong to me, I won't lay claim to that worthless pile of dog dung. No way I could have spawned something that dense from my loins he must take after the Baxter side," he jeered.

"So, long story short, I want my wife, just...my wife." He smirked.

Abe lunged at the disgusting man only to be stopped dead in his tracks, holding both hands to his throat.

Intentionally, Jerimiah place his palm on the small bag around his neck slightly squeezing it. "It's kinda hard to tell who is who sometimes huh, Baxter? Look familiar?" Within seconds, Abe became immobile. "You're not the only one with hoodoo voodoo," he stated wickedly as he watched Abe struggle for air.

"You filthy...!" Abe gasped.

"I've been called a lot worse," Jerimiah laughed.

But, in the midst of the puffed-up confrontation, Jeremiah didn't see the other three faithful family members of the Baxter ranch as they stood like lodge pole pines in front of Liza and Lizzie's downed bodies.

"What's this?" Jerimiah said in a sober fashion. "You think I'm afraid of a couple do-gooders and little girl?" He let out a hideous laugh. "Don't flatter yourselves."

Purposely, he held onto the small leather pouch and with a swish of his hand he sent Matthew flying through the air like a sprig of dry grass, he landed with a thud a good fifty feet away. Then, he looked into Clinton's angry face as he did the same thing to him. Naomi wanted to rush back and make sure that her cousin and Clinton weren't dead but she never moved an inch her questioning eyes turned dark as she confronted her abductor.

"So, you think you're as tough as your so-called adopted mother?" He let the words linger for a moment. "Maybe...cause your real mother was nothing more than a blubbering coward crying for her sister's to come and rescue her. *'Help me, Liza, Lizzie save me'*, yeah well we know how that turned out, they didn't make it. They didn't save her just like they can't save you now ya little redheaded heathen!" With another swish of his hand he threw a fireball at the standing young woman.

But, Naomi was fast and reversed the flaming rod immediately, catching the man off guard as it angled back toward where he was standing. The sudden impact threw sand into his unsuspecting face giving the twins just enough time to regain their senses.

Liza and Lizzie were both physically spent. It was all that they could do to sit their energy level was drained from their divided confrontation. There was no way they could continue this battle between themselves and fight the evil that was contained within the darkened bag that Jeremiah had circled around his neck. Now, they understood the bad bite from the snake and the oddity of certain happenings around the ranch. Today, instead of settling a score with each other, they would be fighting a much stronger adversary.

Abe could see that his daughters were in trouble in their weakened state as he took a dive at the man that held their lives in his hand. With one swish of the stranger's hand, Abe lay face down on the hardened earth, the force of the blow knocked him out cold.

The distraction gave Naomi enough time to help her mother and aunt to their fatigued feet. Lizzie was completely undone at the image that stood before her. "You can't be here," she said in disbelief. "I shot you…**Dead!**"

"You tried, I'll give you that, but no, I know the pathetic sentimentalist that you are, Lizzie, at least when it comes to love. I knew you'd shoot me in the chest blow away the one thing that had betrayed your stinkin' double-crossing heart, blast me out into the wide-open prairie." He could tell she didn't understand. "Cast-iron it comes in real handy knocked me down good, but it was a long shot from killing me."

"You were the one that ambushed and killed Charlie and Emmy, for revenge?" Lizzie asked in a confused tone.

"Why do people keep asking me that?" he said in a flippant manner.

"Why?" she questioned angrily. "Because you are nothing less than a rotten lying killer!"

"And once again I don't have a clue what you're talking about, are you people all deaf? I'm here for my, wife ain't no one gonna have what belongs to me," he said in a controlled tone. "I don't want none of you's else, Liza has belonged to me from the moment I saw her." There was no missing the darkness in his eyes. "I've come to fetch her home."

"My sister never belonged to you," Lizzie stated coldly.

"Well, sister, I reckon' you're a little off some where's Lizzie cause I sure did marry Liza got the paper right in my pocket."

"Is that right? I've been told vermin like you ain't worth belonging' to," she snapped back.

Her accusations made Jacob mad, "You wouldn't know how to belong to a real man if you had one!" He shot back.

"Would you know a real woman?" they said in unison.

"Oh I see, I've done it, I hurt your feelings." He said in a sarcastic tone.

"I see your lips moving, but do you know which one of us you're talking to." The twins said in unison as they gave him a cunning look. They knew he didn't from the baffled expression on his face.

Lizzie continued the accusations, "If you're referring to yourself or your so-called brother as real men you're a long shot from telling the truth. Real men don't change their names so no one knows who they really are, real men don't butcher their wife and children leaving heartache and death behind, real men don't hide in the shadows and defile innocent young women or leave the old to die." Lizzie gave him a menacing smile. "I had you pegged right from the beginning Mr. Horseflesh, you're nothing more than a two-bit liar and killer."

Trying to hide the shock on his face Jacob wondered how they knew about his past, what he'd done, after all he thought he'd done a good job of hiding his misdeeds and blaming that on Jerimiah. "See, there you go again blaming me for something I didn't do, you don't know me to spread such bitter lies." He said in a whining tone. "It hurts my pride." Damn Baxter's who needs em!

Lizzie's eyes were dark with anger. "I'm glad your so-called brother or should it be partnered killer is dead! Justice served!"

Following Lizzies venomous words, the man threw up his hands as a mighty wind violently funneled around them stinging their skin with its fierce blast. But, Liza, Lizzie and Naomi had joined together as one mind and one soul the three of them stood like a solid pillar of granite rock, each supporting the other arm in arm. As soon as the sandy wind hit the barrier of their mighty shield it dissipated to the ground in a pile of dust.

"I'm almost impressed," Jacob stated soberly. "But, is that all you've got?"

Furiously the twins challenged the lying trickster. "Is that all you've got? I'll die right here before I'd ever let you touch me, again," they said in unison. All this time it had been him, he was the dark magic. If their guns hadn't been lying ten feet away they'd of already put a bullet in him.

Jeremiah didn't miss the look on their angry faces. "What cha thinking, Liza? Feel like a fool?" He couldn't tell them apart.

"The only fool I see is standing right in front of me." Liza stated. "Your arrogance has outweighed your common sense this time," she said in a placid tone. "But you're too full of yourself to see the trouble you're in." Their smiles were cunning.

"That right?" he scoffed.

"Yep." They both agreed in a dangerous tone.

"You wanna shoot me? Believe me, better people have tried," he laughed.

"Yeah, that's what your so-called brother said," Liza taunted as her words mocked the standing man. "We all know what happened there."

"Shut up, you Indian lovers!" he snapped.

"We'd rather love Chief Mad Dogs tribe than a baby killer!" they shouted in anger.

The remark stopped Jerimiah dead in his tracks. "You don't know about that."

"I know you stole a sleeping child from her bed!" One twin stated.

"Or have you forgotten?" the other snapped.

"That ratty redheaded heathen didn't mean a thing to me other than a hefty reward, money I didn't have, nothing more." He was struggling with who was who. If he could make one twin mad enough she'd expose herself and he'd put a knife right through her heart.

"Don't listen to him, Liza, he's a liar!"

"Don't listen to him, Lizzie, he's a liar!"

Lizzie stood her ground as she stared directly into Jerimiah's red face, "You and your kind—they're all done taking anything from this family or anyone else's."

Jacob had been so caught up arguing he hadn't seen the two young men that had silently made their way back toward the three women. "What are you going to do about it Lizzie, shoot me—again?" he challenged.

Just then Clinton took a hold of Lizzie's arm and Matthew took his mother's. The twins could feel the power of the young men's blood surge through their veins like fire giving them the strength they needed to fight the black magic of their enemy.

"Am I supposed to be afraid of this simple display?" With one finger he sent sparks flying through the air. Abe let out a mournful yell when the heated embers hit him in the middle of the back. Naomi wanted to run to her grandfather, but Liza and Lizzie held her firm as they shook their heads no. Their darkened eyes never left their intended prey, neither twin moved, no one blinked so much as an eyelash. This man had stepped into a hornets nest, he just didn't know it.

# CHAPTER 25

Time stood still as the two parties stared at each other in disgust, there would be no happy endings here today. Liza and Lizzie even though they were worn out would fight to the death to save what was theirs.

"You can't beat us, Jacob," Lizzie said in a truthful manner. "The Mighty One always triumphs over evil."

"On the contrary, Lizzie, I've already beat you. I'm the one that caused all kinds of havoc against this family, me, I've beat you tenfold." He sneered.

"The only havoc that you've caused is for yourself," Liza said in a calm voice.

"You'd think so," he said smartly, "and on any other day I might just agree with that, but I'm not here alone," Jacob stated arrogantly just as a berry-headed woman stepped out from behind the shadow of the blinding sun's rays.

"We have come to take what is ours." Her voice was hoarse.

Both women let out a loud gasp as they recognized the crippled woman. "You?" They stood there in shock.

Within seconds they came to their senses. "Nothing here belongs to you," the twins said in unison in a threatening tone as they held on to Naomi even tighter dismissing the old hag's disturbing presence.

The older superior acting woman laughed aloud, "It's a shock to see I'm not lying in any box under a tree isn't it? From the looks on your faces you don't believe I'm real, you can touch me, I'm flesh and blood looking right at you two, not that I'm pleased with what I see."

"We don't care what you see, Becky, we'll never let our flesh touch yours again, you're poison." Their tone said they meant it.

Becky let out a slight laugh, "I see you haven't changed any, worse maybe, but not for the better." All she could do was stare, they looked just like their father. "All this time you believed that your battle was with a stranger?"

"You are a stranger," the twins said in unison.

She ignored their remark. "If it hadn't been for Jacob saving me after your so-called hired hand and that filthy Mexican cook shot me in the barn, I wouldn't be here at all."

"She was loyal." They said in unison.

"He tossed my body down the shaft of the old white house I would have died."

"In the barn? What are you talking about?" Lizzie questioned in a doubtful tone. "You broke your neck years ago."

"They didn't tell you?" the older woman seemed surprised.

"Tell us what?" Liza asked suspiciously.

"I should have known, the back stabbing vultures I guess it doesn't matter now the old crone is dead," Becky hissed.

"No, the old crone is standing right in front of us." Lizzie stated.

"Maria shot me the old hag she hated me from the day I met her. You really don't know about Luke how he dumped Willie's body and mine down the shaft of the old white house?"

"No," the twins said in unison. "But, evidently it wasn't deep enough." they stared at the lying snake in front of them.

"Well he did, Luke killed my sweet darling Willie, my husband!" she screamed as she stared at the two of them for several minutes. "You two were such a disappointment to me," she said in a degrading tone as her heated eyes tried to smother their breath.

"As were, you." they said together. There was no way to miss the bag of bad medicine wrapped around her wrinkled neck.

"All I ever wanted was a couple of sweet little girls that would grow like lovely flowers, want the same things in life that I did, you know, the finer things. I prayed that you two would willingly return to my homeland, a place where young ladies could be raised properly with self-respect and dignity, where they'd learn to be poised, beautiful and elegant. That wasn't too much to ask for was it?"

She paused and stared. "I never understood what your father saw in two little dark-eyed heathens parading around half-naked all the time letting you run wild like two warriors. I was embarrassed to call you mine." she said as she spit on the ground. "You'd rather wash the back end of a horse than try to be ladies. Weeds, that's all I got was weeds."

"You mean like the lady you are?" they said together in a disgusted tone. All Liza and Lizzie could do was stare in disbelief at the hostile woman. This couldn't be their mother. Not the woman that they had spent endless hours grieving over, the woman that their father had wasted half of his life mourning over. This poor excuse of a woman was no relation to them.

Becky continued ignoring their smart remark. "Then Sarah came along, she was enchantingly sweet and smart she had a loving, caring spirit, nothing like you two," she hissed.

"You mean, nothing like you, we're fine with who we are." they said again in unison.

"I sat back and watched how your savage ways affected her simple being. How you tried to take over her sweet soul." Becky accused.

"No Becky," they said at the same time, "that was you wanting her to be someone else."

It was getting harder and harder to ignore their spiteful remarks. "No one could get within inches of the child just like the one you have cradled in your arms now. I knew your father would never let me take her away from here, so when Tom Watkins came to me one lonely moonlit night he accepted my offered flesh in payment for kidnapping my beautiful Sarah."

"From where I'm standing," Lizzie stated matter-of-factly.

"He got the raw end of the deal," Liza finished.

Becky stopped talking as she stared from one disrespectful twin to the other. It was plain to see they'd never change. "But Willy, god rest his soul, got cold feet, afraid that someone would get hurt."

"Someone did." She was not going to get Naomi.

"But, Billy, that sweet boy wasn't afraid not dear sweet, Billy."

"Sweet my butt the man was deranged he's the reason Sarah's dead." Liza said.

"His soul is hangin' like rotted meat off'n your saddle horn Becky, the wolves can smell it ten miles away, they'll be comin' for you next." The two of them stated.

Becky continued to ignore their blaming accusations. "I don't even know what that means!" she screamed.

"Yes you do," they said in unison in a calm voice.

"I felt honored he'd chosen me, a mere woman thrice his age to help him take that walk into manhood and between the two of us we made the ideal plan. I would die, he would disappear until the time was right, and Willie would stay and watch over our investment."

"Is that all Sarah meant to you, an investment?" Liza was furious. "You were her mother."

"You and the drunken snake in the grass, sounds about right." Lizzie stated in an icy tone.

"Me and Willie bless his rotting soul!" she snapped.

"You chose a rotten whiskey drinking liar over the safety of your own daughter? You're disgusting." Lizzie wanted to throttle her.

"I loved him." she snapped again. "He was a good man, my man."

"That's not saying much you," Lizzie concluded coldly through blackened eyes. "You old withered up crone."

"You've never trusted anyone your whole life Lizzie always hiding behind your sister's shirttail. You could never understand the concept of love," she said in a hollow tone. "Love can't penetrate a heart like yours there's no room inside a black empty chamber." She gave the twin a cold hard stare, "I've come for my granddaughter."

Lizzie stared right back at her mother's haggard face so many questions became perfectly clear. The frayed looking woman had been such a disappointing mystery when they were young. The two of them wondered why she'd never paid any attention to them as little girls, why they were with their father scouting out the prairie, today, they knew the answer to that question. No way was this wrinkled-looking old has been going to take anything that belonged to Lizzie or Liza Baxter.

"Well, I'm sorry to have to disappoint you—Becky," Lizzie said in an icy tone ignoring her hurtful remarks. "But you'll never lay your filthy murdering hands on my child." Lizzie tightened her grip on Naomi's arm almost to the point of cutting off the circulation.

Liza did the same thing. They both knew what was coming and they weren't sure they had the strength to fight them both.

"You always were the arrogant one, Lizzie." Becky tried to get a rise out of her daughter so she could cause a distraction and get their hands on Naomi. "Bullheaded just like your father."

"That's better than being a haggard looking old has been like you." Liza stated, frankly.

Becky could see the fury building in Lizzie's dark eyes as she continued, "Letting Chief Mad Dog take over your raising I was horrified at the thought."

"Why, you didn't want to do it." Lizzies tone was matter of fact.

"I am your mother."

"In name only." They said in unison.

She continued, caught up in her own deranged tale. "God knows I hoped you'd been a Willies, I prayed you were his, but…you weren't." she took in a disappointed breath. "The moment I laid eyes on you two with that crop of curly black hair and those blue eyes I, we knew Abe Baxter was your father." She scoffed in their faces. "How high and mighty do you feel knowing your mother was married to another man when she got pregnant with the likes of you two? What does that make you?"

Their voices never wavered. "Relieved." They answered in unison with no emotion.

"You hated me from the start! You never listened!"

"Now we know why." The syllables of their words never missed a beat.

"The only one that could ever control you was your father."

"You mean the only one that loved us was, father." Lizzie added.

"Don't listen to her, Lizzie," Liza said in a stern tone, "she's just trying to anger us into letting go of Naomi she's nothing more than a lying ugly old cow." Liza gave her the once over, "Knowing what I know now, what you were willing to sacrifice, I doubt you were married to either one of them. You weren't any rich girl from a rich family, you were the leftover spoils of a whore weren't you? Nothing more than some painted up tramp pretending to be something she wasn't."

Lizzie saw the mortified look on her mother's face; Liza had hit the nail on the head. "You lied," Lizzie felt the anger well up in her chest. "All these years you lied, why? He gave you everything."

"Not everything." She looked so smug. "He never gave me a son."

"Which man never gave you a son, or were you particular?" Liza asked.

"You dare to criticize me look at you Liza, you couldn't think for yourself when you were young I see nothing has changed. Here you are holding to the very speck of life that makes you whole clinging to the droppings of your sister." She had to make one of them mad to get to Naomi.

"It's because of my sister I am whole." Liza snapped.

Becky took in a deep breath before she continued. "How ignorant do you feel knowing that you took the seed of the man that I'd sent to kidnap your little sister? How stupid do you really feel, Liza?" With a flip of her hand, she blew them off. "Why am I wasting my breath on you two I never wanted either one of you." Her tone was so disgusted.

She took a long wide look around her. "I hated it here, hated it!" she screamed. Then, she stared directly into Lizzie's determined face. "She's not your child Lizzie, she's Sarah's, and Sarah was my daughter, that makes Naomi mine. Nothing good could grow inside of you, so no matter what you think of me she's still my granddaughter and I've come to take her home just like I tried to do with her mother."

Her words cut like a hot razor through Lizzie's heart as she stared at the woman through misty eyes. She was still nauseated from everything that had gone on and she didn't have the strength for much of a battle, but Lizzie stood her ground. "Like I said before you nasty old hide, you'll never take anything that belongs to me or my sister."

"It's your funeral, girls," Becky said in a nonchalant tone as she closed her eyes. From out of nowhere a wicked wind taunted the twins, spitting rocks and tiny sticks into their unsuspecting flesh like splintered glass.

"Hold on!" Lizzie yelled.

"I can't breathe," Liza hollered pitifully just before she passed out.

Within seconds, the raging wind pulled Naomi from their heaving arms. Lizzie let out a startled yell as she threw her exhausted body toward the young girl, but the wind anticipated her move as it rolled her over and over like a leaf beneath its grasp.

Lizzie mumbled several words in Naomi's native tongue, the wind began to fade, like a hunted rabbit she crawled on her hands and knees as she grabbed the young woman's leg. "Give me your hand!" she yelled as she tried to pull her backward.

"I can't reach you!" Naomi screamed as she reached for her mother.

Within seconds, Lizzie grasped Liza's arm as she reached for Naomi's hand, fatigue showed on their anguished faces.

Matthew and Clinton started running toward the downed twins just as Jacob took two of the large dormant snakes, one in each hand and threw them toward the determined men. When the serpents hit their mark they became like a braided rope binding the two of them where they stood snared like a coyote in a trap.

"Naomi!" Clinton hollered frantically. "Naomi, no!" he yelled as he tried desperately to free himself.

Naomi stood alone singled out from the rest of her family as she stared directly into the dark eyes of her menacing grandmother. The young woman knew if her grandmother had an opportunity to touch her flesh that she would perish within the aura of the evil pair. Silently she started to cry, she was afraid as her grandmother tried to snub out her life, and what little strength she had was nearly gone her grandmother was choking the life out of her, she couldn't breathe.

"Help me, mother," she whispered as a dark menacing cloud shadowed her head, the end was inevitable.

"I'll be your, mother," the rolling darkness said in a tempting tone.

Naomi fought the voice with all the strength that she had. "You'll never be my, mother!" she screamed defiantly. "I am the daughter of Sarah Baxter and Chief Flying Eagle; Lizzie Baxter is my mother!"

The shadow became angry as it snapped its fingers sending sparks of lightning toward her innocent heart. The ignited spark nearly penetrated her chest as Lizzie jumped to her feet taking the blow instead. When the streak of light entered her body Lizzie fell defeated at Naomi's feet.

"Run." Lizzie whispered through ashen lips before darkness covered her body.

Naomi watched in horror as her mother sank deeper and deeper into the unforgiving ground. "Mother," she whimpered.

"No!" Liza screamed as she fell over her sister's body just as another bolt of light tried to blot out her life.

Naomi screamed hysterically as she sank to where the twins' bodies laid still as stones. "No," she sobbed uncontrollably as she glanced over at her grandfather's still body.

In the distance, she could hear Clinton screaming her name waving Dancing Bears small brown bag in his hand as the wind ruthlessly whisked it away. Everything around her was happening in slow motion shaking she looked into the kind mapmakers saddened eyes she knew he'd never get to her in time.

Bravely Naomi turned and faced her enemy. "Lizzie has lost enough, I won't let her lose her life for me," she was determined just as a soft brown hand reached out and gently brought her to her shaking feet.

Naomi held her breath. The illusive figure was so handsome with his raven black hair and kind brown eyes that told her not to be afraid. Next to him stood a beautiful young maiden with shiny berry colored hair, pale freckled skin, and wildflower eyes, she had an adoring look on her loving face.

"Mother? Father?" she breathed. Surely, her eyes were playing tricks on her, but their touch was warm and caring as their invisible fingers held the hand of their forbidden love, gently they wiped away her tears.

"Don't cry so," a deep voice said. "Evil will not win on this day of truth."

When Naomi looked up she was no longer holding the hand of her mother or father this man held his head high with honor and position. He had a headband full of eagle feathers with a small sack tied with a yellow satin band in his hand.

"Don't let her die," Naomi whispered softly. "She's been through so much I beg you don't take my mother Lizzie, take me."

"I see she has done her best with you loved and protected you as though you'd come from her womb. She has taught you humility and honor, rest your heart, quiet your soul we know her sacrifice. We know the strength of Lizzies love, and now she dies for you, Liza dies for her. There is no greater honor than that."

Naomi couldn't stop crying as she looked up into the Chief's kind face. "I beg you, don't let them die I can't live without them my life light will surely fade into darkness."

Deep in her heart she knew that none of what was happening here was real how could it be? She didn't understand as she knelt by the quiet bodies of the identical women that had unselfishly given their lives for hers, she knew life didn't get any more real than this.

"Your time is not yet, Little Feather," the figure said lovingly.

Then he looked down on Liza and Lizzie. "Come my loyal children," his voice sounded like a warm wind. In a knowing manner he untied the small brown sack and sprinkled the herbs across Liza and Lizzie's still bodies as he held each of their icy hands in his. In a loud commanding voice he spoke words that no one had heard before. "You have made the ultimate sacrifice on this day of truth you have given your lives for a third heart, and she surrenders hers for both of you. 'I, Chief Mad Dog', say death will not overcome your light on this day."

Liza and Lizzie struggled to their feet as they looped their arms one within the other as they looked toward the brightly lit sky, they knew what they were seeing couldn't be real yet here they were.

Chief Mad Dog placed his hand on the top of both their heads. "I did not give spirit magic to see you destroy the hidden meaning of the of this sacred heritage land." His voice was loud and commanding. "I have warned you of such things, you didn't listen."

Lizzie didn't hesitate, "I will take the blame, I will take the punishment." She felt so weak.

Liza didn't hesitate, "I will take the blame, I will take the punishment." She could feel Lizzie's strength fading.

"The blame is equal for both hearts," the image stated in a gruff tone.

"I was protecting my own,"

"I was protecting my own."

Chief Mad Dog's voice echoed like thunder, "I will watch no more of this bad medicine between sisters with many secrets of spirt medicine."

"Lizzie Baxter you were willing to give your life for your sister even though the separation of your souls divided your heart for a brief moment in time. Your sacrifice has been etched within the memory of the sky and will not be spoken of again."

"And you, Liza Baxter, were willing to give your life for your sister even though the separation of your souls divided your heart for a brief moment in time. Your sacrifice has been etched within the memory of the sky and will not be spoken of again."

Chief Mad Dogs voice sounded like thunder. "I, Chief Mad Dog not give good medicine to sisters of one heart, one soul, one breath, my spirit brothers sacred medicine from land, sky, grasses, wind to silence two what breathe." His eyes were dark and intimidating, "No again, I snatch," he gave them a hard look, "no more Wildflowers."

He turned his attention back to the intruders. "It is true, evil come, needs rooted out like rotted tooth, but I 'Chief Mad Dog' will tolerate no more craziness," he scolded. "Now stand proudly, hold your child of two and watch how good destroys evil."

The menacing sky above them turned coal black as lightning filled the vastness of the darkened sky. It was an odd sensation outside the circle, they could see the brilliance of the shining sun.

Recklessly, Jacob and Becky tried to pull out several of the herbs from the small bag as they backed toward their wagon. They knew their black magic wasn't strong enough to match what was coming, they knew their rein of lies, deceit, and destruction on this earth were over, there would be no forgiveness for what these intruders had tried to do, what they wanted to steal, but mostly for the deceitful heartache they had caused.

The threesome stood huddled together, there was no missing the movement on the ground beneath their feet as the darkened serpents that looked like frozen sticks came to life. Like a well-schooled army they stood high on their tails as they hissed at the two trespassers.

Faster and Faster Jacob and Becky hurried toward the wagon, "Get away from me!" Becky yelled. Anxiously she looked around her but there was no place to run, within minutes the snakes wrapped themselves around the screaming killer.

They all jumped when from out of nowhere they heard the recoiled sound of a rifle as its eerie blast echoed through the silence. They stood in complete shock when they saw Jerimiah's body lurch forward, shocked. Red liquid poured from a gaping hole in the middle of his forehead, his face showed the disbelief as blood spilled down his ashen face.

Within seconds, Becky's life had the same fate as blood ran like crimson water down her confused face. Her startled look said she didn't understand as she fell face first on the ground. Both killers laid still.

Disoriented the twins couldn't tell where the shots came from as they looked at each other in disbelief as everything around them moved in slow motion. Not a leaf swished in the wind, or the annoying sound of a buzzing fly as it darted around their heads, no crickets, no trickling water, the air was dormant nothing but silence, to them time stood still.

# CHAPTER 26

Emmy didn't know what to do about the unexpected company in the hollowed-out log. Immediately, tears of frustration started down her reddened cheeks. Then, something told her to speak to the intruder in Naomi's native tongue. She didn't know that many words so she kept repeating the same ones over and over. As the threatening storm approached Emmy knew that she wouldn't survive out in the cold all night, she knew if she caught phenomena they would all die.

So, in a much braver tone than she felt she looked directly at the snarling wolf and said, "I'll be dogged if I'm staying out here I've been accosted, beaten up, and left for dead I'm cold, and there is no way that I'm sleeping out here in this stinking storm, so whatever it is that you plan on doing to me with those big white teeth ain't gonna make a lick of difference." And with that being said she carefully crawled into the large empty space and sat quietly by the dry wood with one of the wool blankets pulled securely under her chin.

Emmy didn't know how long she'd been asleep when the cracking sound of the thunder woke her. At first she wasn't sure where she was, then, when she saw the deep-seeded eyes of the female wolf, she remembered.

"You're still here, huh?" she said softly to the set of distrusting circles. "Quite a predicament that we're in me here you there. I can see that you haven't hurt them any in fact they seem to know the safety of your touch. How is that? Better yet, how did you get them?"

The large dog didn't move a muscle as her large muzzle wrinkled across her long nose. "Oh, don't worry," Emmy said, "I'm not going to try and take them. I was wondering how in the world I was going to get them fed you saved me a lot of work." The large animal never moved but she didn't seem to be as fearful. As Emmy sat upright her muzzle snarled again. "I'm sorry," Emmy stated in a worn-out tone. "I'm much too tired to be afraid of you tonight my head hurts and I don't know where I am not that you care but it's still the truth." Lovingly, she looked at the two small babies she knew better than to touch either one. Who in the world was going to believe her story if she ever lived through this?

"She's quite pretty your pup," she said. "Only one, huh? Well, that's one more than I'll ever have in my lifetime."

Outside their safe haven the thunder boomed, and the lightning lit up the sky. As she sat there and watched the dark turn to light, then back to dark she couldn't help but think, 'The heavens are angry tonight'.

Just then the wolf jumped to her feet as her growl became threatening. Emmy immediately coward to the back of the tree. But it wasn't her that the large animal was afraid of, there was something outside something that she didn't like an unknown entity that threatened her existence. Like a guard protecting the gates of a prison she laid just inside the opening. Her deep threatening growl was a louder warning than the thunder.

"What is it girl?" Emmy whispered as the dog gave her a wary look. There was definitely someone out there. When Emmy heard the sound of footsteps and listened to her coffee pot sail across the distance, she knew that she was in trouble. Like a bullet the large dog flew out of the opening with Emmy hot on her heels. She could hear the shrill screams of a man as the mother wolf ruthlessly attacked.

Something was amiss here Emmy'd never seen this man before where had he come from? Then a sickening thought crossed her mind, what if he was the one living in the cave that she had just evacuated? As Emmy came to one side of him the man jumped forward grabbing her by the shoulder as he pulled her to the ground, he was strong. Desperately she tried to get away just as he savagely punched her face with his large fist.

But, the heavy dog was hell-bent on destruction as she landed in the middle of him. Instantly, he let go of Emmy's struggling body as she jumped to her feet. Desperately, she hit him in the middle of the back with a large chunk of wood just as he threw the large wolf to the side like it was nothing. The blow didn't seem to faze him in the least like a frenzied animal he ruthlessly kicked Emmy's feet out from under her as she fell to the muddy ground in a heap. As if he was a rabid animal he jumped on top of her rutting like an old boar but once again the large wolf landed in the middle of him ripping and tearing at his flesh in a frenzied state.

Emmy was screaming, crying, trying to get some kind of a grip on reality when she felt the butt of the rifle lying in the mud. Instantly she grabbed the metal stick and pointed it straight at his heaving chest just as the dog savagely attacked him again. This time he was ready for her as his large knife dug deep into her long torso. Within seconds the crazed animal laid bleeding on the ground.

"You blasted killer." she screamed as she took careful aim at his lunging body and pulled the trigger. Nothing. The gun didn't fire.

"Now what ya gonna do girlie?" he hissed.

Frantically Emmy spun away from the attacking man and cocked the hammer and pulled the trigger again. This time the roar of the gun was deafening. Within seconds, the lurching man laid dead in a puddle of mud at her feet his face showed the shock of his demise. No wonder the wolf recognized the hunters scent she was sure the line of wolf pelts that dangled from his belt had been her pups.

Emmy was huffing and puffing like a runaway horse she couldn't catch her breath, above her the lightning and thunder was deafening and in the background she could hear the babies screaming through the howling wind. The dirty rotten scoundrel would have slit her throat in her sleep, she'd be dead if it hadn't been for the intuition of the mother wolf. Who knows what he would have done to the babies.

Sadly, she ran her hand across the dead wolfs body. "Thank you," she whispered through strangled sobs. "He'd of taken my life if it wasn't for you."

Crying and frustrated, she slipped back into the safety of the hollowed-out log. She was soaked from head to toe but like a mother bear she picked up both babies and held them in her trembling arms .No matter what she tried they wouldn't stop crying, then she reached over and picked up the pup within minutes the three of them laid looking into her shaken face. Two newborn babies and one lone wolf pup. Who was going to believe this tale? "Quite an ordeal," she whispered as they all fell sound asleep.

Emmy was stiff when the sun peeked its warming rays inside the hollowed-out log. She had several new bruises on her forearms and across her face. Her back was sore from the fall onto the rocky ground, her head still hurt, and to make matters worse there was a light skiff of snow on the ground. "Great." she mumbled. "How can it be so hot one day and snow on the ground the next?"

Purposely she drug the dead man from the side of the fire and kicked his body down the steep embankment hoping that some animal would eat his filthy hide for lunch.

As she rekindled the fire and boiled a fresh pot of coffee she contemplated her journey home. From where she crested the hill yesterday there seemed to be a shallow bend in the river about a half mile up. If she could get across that at least they'd be heading in the right direction, maybe.

As she held a baby in each arm, she couldn't help but notice how sweet-natured they seemed, it was as though they didn't have a care in the world. She smiled to herself as she gazed into their trusting green eyes. They had long tiny fingers, small button noses, and a skiff of light curly hair. They weren't big babies by any means, but they were definitely hearty after all how many of us could say they were invited to dinner in the wolf's den and not be the main meal? "Unbelievable," Emmy whispered.

After their ordeal of feeding in which she was sure there was more milk on her than in the twins' tummies, the threesome headed out. But, they hadn't gone far when Emmy noticed the small pup lagging behind, she'd contemplated all morning on whether to bring her or not. After all what would everyone think bringing a wolf back to the ranch? That would be like inviting the fox into the henhouse.

The babies were restless and cried the whole way, the pup whined and howled like a banshee when she couldn't go any further. Purposely, Emmy turned around and looked into the small animal's terrified face, it was a baby too maybe three weeks old, she was just as scared in these strange elements as the rest of them. Emmy knew some large predator would eventually find her, kill her, and eat her for dinner. Where would the justice be in that? After all, her mother had just given her life to save them all.

"Alright," Emmy whispered lovingly, "that's enough." Begrudgingly she placed the small pup inside the makeshift sling between the two fussy babies. They quieted down immediately when they felt the warmth of the wolf's soft fur like it or not she knew that the pup would be a permanent part of their party.

When Emmy finally made it to the bend in the river, it didn't seem as fast or threatening as it had earlier. But the angry gray skies acted as though the fluffy white flakes were ready to cover the rocky ground as she put one bare foot in the rushing water, immediately Emmy let out a loud gasp, it was freezing or was it because she was already cold. Either way she was going to have to take the babies across the moving current one at a time to keep them dry.

Nervously, Emmy searched up and down the embankment for a good half hour before she found the perfect spot to cross. It was a lot rockier, slower, it wasn't as deep, at least not for a tall girl like herself. After several near misses she made it to the other side of the bank. Instantly she laid one baby on the back side of boulder then hurried back for the other one. When she finally made it back to the other side, she put on both packs and held the rifle tightly under her arm. There was no way that she could carry the pup, too she'd come back for her.

"You wait here." she commanded. But, the pup didn't understand the desertion of the kind woman as she jumped into the water directly behind her. "No!" Emmy screamed as she dropped the rifle and grabbed the back of the drowning pup.

When the twosome reached the opposite bank, Emmy was soaking wet. "Bad dog!" she scolded. "Look what you made me do I lost the rifle, we needed that gun!"

Emmy stood for several minutes staring at the scolded pup as it immediately laid by the babies. It didn't seem to matter that she was soaking wet she just wanted to be where they were. Emmy let out a deep sigh. "I would have come back I wasn't going to leave you, I'm not mad at you." Once again she reached down and put the three of them in the dry bag and started walking.

The frosty wind had become threatening and colder as Emmy questioned her decision to try and find the safety of the Baxter Ranch in such hostile weather. There were definite grey skies above her and miles of nothing in front of her. She still wasn't sure where she was and what if she was going in the wrong direction, they could very well freeze to death out here. As she sat there in the open, shivering like a dry leaf, trying to feed the screaming babies she contemplated her next move. Should she go back to the safety of the cave where she knew there was food and shelter, a safe haven where the four of them could ride out the winter winds, she'd have to ration the scant supplies. Or should she continue onward into the vastness of the unknown and possibly kill them all.

"What do I do?" she said out loud to the howling wind. "I need to get home I need to get back to Matthew how can anyone rescue me when they think I'm dead," she cried, "but I'm not, I'm not dead I'm right here."

Emmy placed her head in her freezing hands. "Oh, Mighty One show me what to do I'm so afraid and alone," she whispered just as a cold blast of wind mixed with sleety rain hit her hard in the face. "Alright," she whispered through chattering teeth, "I hear you."

# CHAPTER 27

Emmy tucked what was left of the dry blanket over the small infants that lay sound asleep in the makeshift carrier. As she stared out into the vastness of the open prairie she couldn't help but notice the distant trails that led in all different directions. Why hadn't she noticed them before? It was as though they had magically appeared. All she could figure was the dead trapper must have made all of the different paths to check his traps. "Murderer," she mumbled as she thought of the fate of the mother wolf. As her inquisitive eyes followed each path she was shocked when she recognized a familiar sight in the distance was that the cave they had walked away from?

"What in the world?" she said out loud as she stopped at the edge of the deep embankment.

It was like the large black rock had been mocking her. Shaking her long dark finger like a mother scolding her daughter, telling her that she had no business being out in weather like this, especially with three newborn babies. Looking off into the distance she hadn't come as far as she'd thought, all she'd done was make one huge circle. Disgusted at her own geographical ignorance she pounded her foot on the ground as the empty feeling of despair engulfed her. She had to get her small brood to safety, heated tears slipped down her freezing cheeks, she felt like such a failure.

"Which one should I take?" Purposely she looked to see which path was the most foot worn.

But the further down the well-worn trail she walked the steeper it got which made her slid on her rump, she was sure there would be bruises to show for that. Disappointed, she looked back at the crooked trail, she knew it was too steep to climb back up with the babies and the pup. Exhausted she sat against the backside of the rocky ridge watching her foggy breath disappear at the greedy hands of the echoing wind. She had no other choice but to keep going downward. "Oh Mighty One," she whispered, "save us."

Silently, she sat and pondered her situation when she noticed a spot where the trail was worn down even more than the others. "Please let this be the right way," she whispered as she got back up on her feet and continued downward. After several yards of sliding across even more jagged rocks, there was a narrow rooted foot bridge slung across the wide ravine dangling like a spider's string.

"Are you sure, Mighty One?" Now, she wished she hadn't asked. How in the world was she going to get across that unstable looking swing with all of her precious cargo, and, what guarantee did she have that the bridge would hold their weight?

As she sat contemplating her next move, she placed her face in her freezing hands. "What am I doing?" she whimpered. "I'm not brave, and I'm certainly no woodsman."

The babies were getting restless as she readjusted her pack hoping they would stay asleep for the next part of their journey. She was cold and scared as she peeked inside the warm tote, three sets of trusting eyes stared directly at Emmy's tear-stained face.

"All right," she said in a motherly fashion. "Here we go. Just whatever you do, don't look down." Then she let out a loud laugh. "Yeah, don't look down, like that's going to save us if this dangling string snaps."

As though the bridge was made of glass Emmy stepped on one plank then another. Even though the wood was greyed from the months of bad weather and sun, it seemed sturdy enough. Still, she couldn't help but notice there was a definite swing to the roped catwalk. Cautiously, she got down on her hands and knees and started crawling like a hunted animal, praying to herself that the ropes wouldn't break.

"You're an idiot, Emmy Baxter." she mumbled. "You should have just kept going the ranch can't be that far away." Then she told herself. "No, I can't do that what lesson would I have learned by dying because of my own stubbornness? Nobody wins when you do that." Then as though she'd been reenergized the way a lightning bolt streaks across the vastness of a dark sky, Emmy got mad. "I'll be dogged if I'm going to die out here, not now, not today, not ever!"

Feeling a sense of control for the first time in her sheltered life Emmy tackled the bridge fearlessly. Hands to knees, one at a time.

But, no matter how slow she crept across the greying boards or how carefully she crawled, the swaying lifeline still had a definite swing to it. On more than one occasion she clung like a spider to both sides of the weathering wood trying to steady the motion. She was in the middle now and the far bank seemed hopeless she wanted to turn back but there was no room, nowhere to go but forward and she was terrified.

Then from out of nowhere an old familiar tune popped into her head. A silly little song that her mother had sang when she was young and afraid. With each measured step she belted out the cheerful words louder and louder as tears of frustration ran down her frozen cheeks.

**"The sun is out, no tears today, the wind will swish your cares away. Time's your friend and life's a dream, smiles bring sunny days."**

Louder and louder she sang the made-up tune as she crept across the rough lumber. After several bellowing chorus's she started to giggle, the young pup had decided to join in with a high-pitched howl and the babies were trying to mimic the pup. Emmy couldn't be sure if it was the piercing sound of her voice or the howling but between the four of them it was a toss up to determine which one was the loudest.

Not once did she look back or down for she knew that the distance between where she was and where she was going was beyond the reality of her comprehension. She knew that if she got dizzy from her fear of height they would all perish, the bubbling water below would swallow their breath, and no one would ever find them. After what seemed like an eternity and knees full of splinters she finally made it across the jointed planks.

As Emmy crawled up the steep embankment on the other side of the wide ravine she let out a deep sigh of relief, they'd made it. Her whole body shook much like the wispy reeds that bent and swayed at the hands of the rumbling rapids below her as she continued to crawl well past the swaying roped bridge. Desperately she tried to control her shaking as she struggled for air, she was relieved when she checked her precious cargo, they were all safe and sound. Once she'd collected herself she took a good look at her bleeding knees full of splinters she'd deal with that when they got back to the cave.

Nonchalantly, her eyes scanned the distance between where she was and where she'd been, but when her swollen circles settled on the other side of the long bridge, she let out a loud gasp. "You've got to be kidding me!" No wonder the bridge had been swaying, sitting like she had a mouse in a trap, her brilliant yellow eyes drilling a hole right through her intended prey sat a large overconfident, mountain lion. The animal must have been right behind her and when the bridge started to sway got scared and turned back.

There was no missing the look of destruction on her wily face. Her large cotton paws looked like small melons as she intentionally stepped onto the bridge. Each movement she made was carefully calculated on the swaying makeshift crossing, her high-pitched cat-like yowl was meant solely for Emmy, there was no doubt the cat fully intended to kill her.

When the pup heard the cat's menacing warning she immediately wanted out of the small shelter, her natural instinct's came to life. As Emmy reached in to calm the fur ball she stuck her little head out of the makeshift pouch her tiny muzzle was wrinkled like drying mud. What little teeth she had sheltered within her furry muzzle shone like honed razors and the pup full intended to use them. It was plain to see that the baby wolf was just as fearless as her mother had been, and she was determined to protect what she deemed to be hers. The small wolf knew what kind of a threat the large feline posed, and she was having no part of it. Terrified she held tight to the wiggling ball of fur, Emmy was amazed at her bravery, she wasn't afraid, but she also knew one swipe of the cat's massive paw would kill her small protector, Emmy knew there was no way she would allow that to happen.

It was obvious that the large cat didn't know what to think of the growling object, the large feline knew instinctively that the wolf was its natural enemy, she stopped dead in her tracks, trying to figure out the annoying noise, surveying her position, but that didn't stop her, she was hungry and Emmy was supper.

As the large female lion cautiously crept across the wooden bridge, crouched on all fours, her yellow eyes seared a hole right though her terrified prey. The small pup saw her getting closer and closer as she became ecstatic barking frantically in high shrill intervals, trying to get out of the bag. Its erratic behavior scared the two babies, and they began wailing like two stepped on cats their harmony blended with the baby wolf. Within a second of their disturbing behavior, Emmy started singing at the top of her lungs the whole rowdy scenario made the cat stop once again.

"Why does everyone want what's mine?" Emmy sobbed uncontrollably through each word. "Why does everyone want what I have?" Recklessly, she picked up a good-sized rock and threw it like a rocket at the surprised animal. "You can't have it." The crouching cat let out a loud ear-piercing yowl when the stone hit its mark, but the hungry female continued. Emmy grabbed another and another and another, each stone pelting the angry animal's flesh harder than the last. "No!" she screamed again bringing the babies cries to the next yowling level.

It was plain to see that the large hungry lion didn't like the pounding that she was getting from the hardened stones, and she liked the noise even less. There was no sign of retreat as she let out a loud screech that said nothing was going to stop her. She had a determined quest and fully intended to follow it through, with each calculated step the lioness got closer and closer. When she made it within jumping distance, five or ten feet away, Emmy did the only thing that she could think of. She never took her eyes off of the hunting cat as she laid the two bawling babies and the small pup in a crevasse behind her in one of the large boulders. With all of the strength she could muster she reached down and picked up a large boulder.

"You want what's mine you nasty killer!" she threatened like a wounded grizzly. The angry feline stood staring at her, long lines of drool dripping from her salivating mouth. "Then, you come and get it!"

Bawling, Emmy ran to the end of the bridge just as the yellow cat let out an earsplitting scream—crouching down—ready to jump. Breathlessly, Emmy heaved the massive rock with all her might as the small pup ran between her feet like a streak of lightning, teeth barred and barking.

"No!" Emmy screamed just as the boulder hit the rotten wood for a split second it laid on the rotted lumber then disappeared with a loud crash into the swirling water below.

Emmy couldn't believe her eyes as the charging lion and the pup both disappeared into thin air right before her eyes. The rotted hole sucked them both down as the winding rope unraveled like twine through a needle. The collision of rock and wood sounded like thunder in an empty canyon as it exploded into pieces, she had no idea if she'd killed the pup.

"No, what do you want from me?" She hollered like a crazy woman at the threatening sky. "Haven't I given you enough?" Angrily, she pounded the ground with her fists as a flood of tears fell from her tormented eyes. "No, you're not going to win, I won't let you!"

Angrily, Emmy sprawled out on her stomach along the wooded planks and crawled like a bug to the shattered opening. She couldn't help but wonder where the justice was in all of this. What lesson was she supposed to learn that she hadn't learned already? Humility? No. She'd learned that at hands of vultures on a dark summer night. Despair? No, she'd overcome the abuse that her body had taken in. Love? No, she'd found her true love in the arms of a forgiving husband. Then what? Fear?

"Not today," she shouted out loud, "today, I'm fearless!"

She knew it was a long way to the bottom of the river it gave her a little hope that the young pup had survived the fall. Cautiously, she stuck her head through the opening as she let out a loud gasp, Emmy was completely taken aback as she stared at the unthinkable picture below. There swinging like two flies in a spider web was the pup and the lion both of them were tangled within the frayed rope.

What was she going to do? The babies were her first priority, and they were screaming like two banshees. What if the rope broke and they all fell? The babies would die for sure without her care, after all what difference did it really make; it was just a wild dog nothing more.

"I'm sorry," she whispered wanting to crawl back toward the safety of the dirt path. But when she looked into the swinging puppy's faithful eyes it was plain to see that the fur ball didn't understand her predicament she wasn't screaming like the wounded cat, she was waiting for Emmy to rescue her. Those wide trusting circles said it all, Emmy knew she couldn't leave her.

Purposely, Emmy wrapped each foot within one of the ropes behind her, she winced as the barbed strings cut into her cold tender flesh as she stretched her long torso down the jagged opening she struggled to reach the pup. Thankfully the rope gave her just enough length to wind her fingers like a burr within the softness of the dog's furry neck gently, she unwound the rope from her chubby belly. A breath below her the large cat savagely clawed at the two objects above her trying to get her sharp claws on her intended prey, as the band of rope that held them hostage frayed with each attempt.

By now the cat was rabid with fear as she hung above the rushing water. Her threatening cries echoed a definite warning across the vastness of the open void, screaming like a scorned woman. But she was too heavy as Emmy listened to the straw-like braid rip as the furious cat made one last attempt at the intruder above her.

Emmy had one chance to save the pup and herself from the angered beast, terrified she swooped down just as the lion's large paw groped for anything solid. The feline's yellow circles swallowed Emmy whole as her massive paw brushed across her jaw just as she swung her face to the side trying to avoid the impact as the lifeline that held the hunting animal snapped.

Desperately she clung to the frozen pup with all her might as they watched the flailing female fall into the rolling water below. Tears rolled down her frustrated cheeks, she was sorry that the noble beast had to have such a disastrous end to her life but it was either herself or the hungry lion, today she chose herself.

Emmy took in a deep breath as she clung to the small animal in her grasp trembling like a leaf, she wasn't about to let go of the pup as she struggled through the jagged opening. They were alive! She held the furry ball close for several minutes, then she held her small protector up in the air as she spoke, "Man," she giggled, "you're going to be the death of me."

Exhausted, she made her way back toward the screaming babies as she lovingly picked up the small carrier and placed it back over her head. As soon as they felt the warmth of her body, their crying stopped.

"You two," Emmy stated matter-of-factly, "were a great help. Why, that ole cat didn't know what hit her. I'm thinking maybe between the four of us we could out howl the coyotes." It was a stupid joke, but Emmy needed something stupid right now just to keep her sane. "All right," she whispered, "here we go."

As she looked over her shoulder she spoke to the pup in Naomi's native tongue. The pup took the lead as though she were now the mighty leader of this pack strutting down the winding trail, at least until she had to be put back in the carrier with the babies.

But the cave wasn't as close as Emmy had first thought the distance between the endless open arenas in front of her and where she was going was very deceiving. She'd walked a long time and wondered on several occasions where the opening had disappeared to. Her gut told her that the well-worn path had to lead someplace better than where they were, but where? Purposely, she wrapped the dry blanket tightly around her shoulders, rearranged the sleeping babies and leaned into the chilly wind.

Emmy had walked a solid four hours and darkness was starting to come on fast. The constant changing condition of the relentless wind was taking its toll her body was so cold and her fingers were numb from the freezing wind, constantly she rotated the flapping blanket with each hand. All she wanted to do was lay down against one of the large boulders and go to sleep just drift away into the peacefulness of a warm place. But, in her mind Emmy knew if she surrendered the icy wind would steal her breath, and, if it stole her breath she and the babies would perish within its chilly arms it took all of the strength she had to keep going.

After walking a good mile straight up the small party crested the top of a rocky hill, just as the howling wind mixed its hammering blast with sleeting rain, it was on the edge of getting dark as a slow panic started to grow within her like a chunk of smoldering coal.

She had to keep going, she had to find the cave by nightfall, one more bend, one more bend, and one—more—bend. Emmys strength was fading with each footstep as she struggled against the relentless wind, she was ready to give up when she saw an opening at the center of the next slope, Emmy's heart jumped for joy, there it was the destination of her salvation, the warmth and protection of the camouflaged cave.

As though her feet had wings she hurried down the worn path but as she got closer it was evident this was not the same cavern. Exhausted she shook the sleep from her foggy mind, she'd been out in the elements a long time it was nearly dusk the skyline was fading, and she was no closer to safety than when she started.

"The journey I started at dawn," she wept "is this how it's going to end, have I killed us all?" Cold and shaking Emmy got down on her knees, "Mighty One walk with me, show me the way, I'm afraid, I'm so cold and soon I'll lose the light, be my light Mighty One, be my light."

# CHAPTER 28

Emmy pulled the babies closer as she continued walking, putting one foot in front of the other. "I can't fall asleep, I can't."

At first she thought her eyes were playing tricks on her, she shook her head in an exhausted state, trying to clear her vision, trying to push away the nagging feeling to fall asleep. How had she missed the silhouette of the black pointed rock that had been her constant guide, it was right in front of her. Was she hallucinating, had she been walking in circles, was any of this real?

She shook her head again as she continued down the rocky trail when her inebriated brain began to wake up, Emmy stopped dead in her tracks, her heart began to pound as she took a sober breath. "Is that what I think it is?" she said in a baffled tone. "Is that…no, it can't be, this has to be the right place, still something was out of order, turned around somehow, but the closer she got to the familiar rock shaped like a bears head the more she knew her prayers had been answered, the Mighty One hadn't forgotten her.

Then it hit her, she was on the opposite side of the rock pile there was more than one entrance that's how the mother wolf had snuck into the cave without being seen or heard, this fortress is where she'd hidden her only pup.

As Emmy hurried to the large opening she cautiously walked through the small entry. To her right was a holder with a small torch and a lighter. Her fingers were so cold it was all she could do to flick the flint as dancing flames filled the darkness. Once her eyes adjusted to the swaying shadows she could see that there were several jointed paths that looked like fingers. After several minutes of calculating she picked the one that was worn the most, like a ghost she walked along the foot path as she ran her hand along the rocky wall. It wound round and round, like a twisted cork screw for a good hour then, all of a sudden it just dropped. Carefully she struggled to get herself and the babies to the bottom of the rocky floor, by now she was nearly spent, but much to her surprise the narrow path turned into a large open room. A place that wasn't familiar.

"No," she whispered to herself. "Where am I?"

In the distance, Emmy could hear the faint sound of running water as she stayed close to the far wall and followed the flowing echo. After several more twists and turns she walked through one long corridor and then from out of nowhere there it was the warm inviting pool, the large clean table with two lanterns, and her bed. Everything she'd left behind was sitting right where she'd left it, everything they needed for their survival. Like a wet reed she sank to her knees and wept. "Thank you, Mighty One. Thank you."

# CHAPTER 29

Everyone standing in the yard at the Baxter ranch jumped at the sound of the exploding rifle blast even the twins were taken by surprise. The yard was in complete ciaos as the wind blew dust and dirt in wide circles making it impossible to see anything.

"Die you spawn of the devil!" Nelly screamed as she held the rifle in her trembling hands, slobber ran her pain-stricken lips, it was all she could do to stand.

"I told you I'd find you and your evil whore!" Her face was void of any mercy. "Hallelujah the butcher and his queen are dead, murdering liars both you!" Nelly could feel her breath fading. "You killed them for no good reason, just for the joy of it, devil be damned!" she screamed as she dropped to her knees sobbing. "I swore I'd find you, and I did, you got cocky, thought you were invincible, that you were safe, you weren't I snuck up behind you when you weren't looking, you let your guard down, that was a big mistake I warned you, didn't you believe me? I told I'd be there when you did!"

Her lips were paling with every breath. "You thought you were safe, that no one would find out what monsters you both really were for years I've been waiting to put you in the ground. Hallelujah the butcher and his queen are dead!" her lips were white; she could barely hold her head up. "You can't hide anymore neither one of you, you'll live with the dark one now!" She spit on the ground. "You don't deserve any better!" she screamed. "No better!" then she collapsed in a pool of blood, pain showed on her ashen face.

When Matthew knelt down beside her frail body, Nelly was nearly gone. "Nelly?" Matthew gasped. "What? How did you...? Where did you come from? Let me help you, are you shot?" Where had all the blood come from?

Nelly took in a shallow breath as she looked into Matthew's warm caring eyes. "Tell Emmy I did it." She said in a barely audible tone. "Tell her," she coughed as red bile slid from the corner of her mouth. "For the brand." Then as a soft warm wind whisked past her face Nelly took in her last breath.

No one said a word they sat in complete silence and watched as the unruly wind became like a tornado. Swishing and swirling around the downed duo as hundreds of snakes covered the pair of killers like a pile of maggots. The brilliance of the distant light above them became so bright that they had to close their eyes. When they reopened them, there was nothing left but dirt and small pebbles, the silence was deafening.

"You shot me, Lizzie!" Liza broke the silent void with her loud accusation. "That really hurt!"

"You shot me!" Lizzie snapped back. "How do you think that felt? Look, look at my chest I'm scared for life."

"Naomi!" Clinton breathed. Like a fragile flower he held her in his trembling arms as he sobbed saying her name over and over.

"Papa," Matthew asked in an astonished tone, "was that real?"

"I don't rightly know son but if it was and I ever see it again, it will be too soon."

Matthew stared into the kind brown eyes of his grandfather. "What do you suppose Nelly was trying to say? Didn't she know about, Emmy?"

"I wish I knew." Solemnly he shook his head. "I wish I knew."

Like a family of crippled ducks they hobbled toward the old log house. In all of the mayhem they had completely forgotten about, Jeffrey. He laid sprawled out still as a stone on the wooden landing right where Abe had left him.

Lizzie was completely disgusted when she stepped up the planked steps to the wooden platform, purposely she ground her boot into Jeffrey's hand. "Coward!" she hissed. "I still don't believe you ya worthless lowdown stinkin liar!"

Jeffrey came to life instantly. "Ow!" he whined as Abe bent down and pulled him to his feet. "That hurt, Aunt Lizzie you did that on purpose!" Then he looked around trying to make sense of what had happened. "Where did everything go papa? I swear all I wanted to do was pan for gold, I swear that was all." He paused for a brief moment, "I remember snakes…lots of snakes they were everywhere was that real papa?"

"Oh shut up, Jeffrey!" They all said together at the same time in a disgusted tone.

As they walked through the threshold of the old log house, Lizzie stated matter-of-factly, "I'm gonna throw up!"

"Again with the throwing up!" Liza stated in an irritated tone. "The snakebite is gone get over it!"

"You get over it!" Lizzie snapped back.

"Papa, I wish Nelly would have lived long enough to tell us what she meant." Matthews tone was puzzled. "What was she was talking about."

"I can't say but it sure don't seem right somehow."

Quietly they closed the heavy door behind them shutting out the world just as an angry wisp of wind slammed against the heavy wooden door closing the portal as it denied the angry wind access to the sacred building. "You…won…this…time…you…won't…next time!" it moaned

The cave had provided more than enough protection for the four of them against the raging storms that came and went at a furious rate. On more than one occasion it whistled through the large opening stealing the warmth that the glowing fire graciously offered. Emmy remembered seeing a small room that sat alone back where the mother wolf had been protecting the babies and the wolf pup. They were little and she was afraid the constant difference in temperatures would make them sick.

So, she brought the table, bed, chairs, all the pots, pans, dishes, and food into the smaller tavern then she took several of the blankets and tied them together placing them over the opening. The difference was amazing it kept the wind from stealing all of their warmth and for some unforeseen reason the room had a natural venting system which kept the smoke out of the rocked cavern, where it went she had no idea but all that really mattered was they were all safe here.

Emmy's real worry was how fast their food supply was diminishing at the rate it was disappearing, the staples wouldn't last much longer.

The babies on the other hand were growing at a steady pace as was the young wolf pup. The girls were small for their age which made handling them a lot easier. If they weren't in the homemade carrier placed over her protective shoulders they were placed securely one on each hip. Their needs seemed to be small, and they rarely cried. If they did it was at night—well until the wolf pup snuggled as close as she could between them only then would they close those sleepy circles and go to sleep.

There were lots of nights that Emmy sat and watched the tiny beings her two little miracles. She could see both Nelly and Jeffrey in their sweet innocent features, they'd gotten the best parts of both their parents.

She was grateful that the female wolf had saved the two babies taking them in like they were her own, especially since Lizzie told her there would be no babies for her and Matthew. As Emmy sat and contemplated her unusual situation she had a dreadful feeling wash over her, the twins would know she was lying they knew her womb would never carry a child at some point the wily duo would have to be told the truth.

Emmy let out a soft giggle as the wolf's fur tickled the babies' cheeks making them smile. How they'd gotten their sweet dispositions was beyond her neither Nelly nor Jeffrey had a warm caring bone in them. Emmy let out a deep sigh why had fate dealt her the hand that it had, what had she done to deserve the denial of motherhood? The Mighty One gave her these tiny souls to protect they were hers now to love and raise she'd never turn them out and she'd protect them with her dying breath. She knew deep in her heart Liza and Lizzie would except them no matter who their parents were and when she got to the ranch they would know how to manage this delicate situation; they always knew what to do. "Thank you Mighty One and forgive me for my selfishness."

The months drug on and on as Emmy sat in the rickety chair she figured it had to be close to gift and offering season by now a time when everyone joined together for a day of celebration for memories of those that had left them, gone to their own quiet place. How she wished she was in the warm old house sitting in one of the large stuffed chairs snuggled next to her loving husband sipping sweet cream coffee placing a special memory of her own on the tree. She missed Matthew so much but…as she gazed at the two little blessings lying within the makeshift crib, she wouldn't have them, Ivy and Evy if fate hadn't stepped in.

Nelly would have killed them for sure or sadly at some point the wolf would have realized they'd be better to eat than save. No, she was right where she was supposed to be, why, she had no idea, but summer was coming and maybe, just maybe the wind would guide her back home. Until that time came this cave was their home it would provide all the protection they needed. She would take care of these two baby girls and when the time was right she'd find her way back to the Lazy AB Ranch where she belonged wrapped within the arms of her loving husband, Matthew Baxter.

# CHAPTER 30

The snow had been falling off and on for several hours when Liza and Lizzie finally made it to the seclusion of the large barn. They were tired of arguing with their father over the fact that they were going to be the ones that went and cut down the *'Thankful Tree'*, and under no circumstances were they going to have one that looked like last year's twig with broken branches and half the limbs missing.

"Only an idiot would bring home a tree like that!" they'd puffed up in unison.

So, consequently no one said a word when they told them where that tree would be put if the rest of the family didn't get off their lazy butt's and pull out the special decorations that would be placed on the tree from each one of them.

"I'm not saying I don't care about the tree," Abe countered in a distressed tone. "I doubt you two aren't up to snuff quite yet and it worries me that this storm might kick up into something worse I don't need you two getting lost out there."

"Father," they said at the same time in an annoyed tone, "we know this ranch like the back of our hand we're not going to get lost!"

"I thought that same thing once," he warned.

The twins stared at their father's subdued remark. "No one could have predicted that father not even you."

"I'm just saying…"

"We know what you're saying father we get it but, that's all behind us now we're feeling fine." Lizzie stated.

There was no missing the worry in his rugged looking face. "Alright but, if you're not home an hour before dark I'll be looking."

"We'll be back." they said together.

Liza's horse gave her a soft nicker as she walked to where he stood in the warm stall. "Hey, Buddy," she whispered. He'd been ridden hard the day before, picking up lost strays and she was sure he needed a rest, calculating the situation she decided not to ride him, there had to be another horse in the barn she could take instead. As her eyes scanned the airy room, she noticed one of the green broke mares that Luke had been working with she was a tall sturdy looking animal. "You'll do," she said out loud just as Luke came around the corner.

"She's not ready for the likes of you," he stated in a cranky tone which seemed to be normal for him since Maria's death.

"Then...she'd better get ready," Liza snipped back. Why had everyone suddenly felt like they needed to give the two of them orders, they were the ones that gave the orders.

"What's the matter, you still upset cause I beat you in checkers last night?" Luke countered.

"You couldn't beat a tick on a dog's butt without cheating." Liza snapped back

"Oh yeah?" he challenged "I sure as the devil beat you two-legged dog's...! Wait a cotton pickin' minute you're not taking the wagon?" he stated completely frustrated.

"Nah, we know right where we're going." Liza gave her sister a quick wink.

"I do, too," Luke mumbled.

"What did you say?" the two of them said in unison.

"What's that supposed to mean?" Lizzie's dark eyes were smoldering as she gave him a dirty look.

He gave Lizzie a disgusted look. "It means you're going wind up in a snowbank some where's ya lunkhead if not worse, she's ain't ready for the likes of you I'm tellin' ya!"

"I'm riding Charlie's horse." Lizzie stated in an indignant air. "If we do get off kilter, which we won't, he'll know the way home."

On that note Luke turned and started walking away mumbling under his breath. "At least there will be one with some smarts. What in the devil any how's you's two knot heads goin' out in weather like this, I swear I don't know why Abe didn't throw you over his knee more often. Derned troublemakers!"

"Thanks...Luke," they said sarcastically in unison as the older man threw up both hands and walked into the shoeing room.

"You know," Lizzie stated. "I believe some where's along the line we, you and me, have lost some respect around here."

"Yeah and it's darn time we get it back!" she scoffed.

"You said it sister!"

Liza grabbed her saddle as she studied the young mare for several minutes, she didn't appear to be skittish at all. "Luke, what a mother hen!" she said in a flippant manner. The sleek-looking animal stood still as a stone as Liza bridled and saddled her, then she walked her in a circle several times. The mare never made a bobble.

Lizzie gave her an encouraging look. "That old goat wouldn't know ready from a starting pistol c'mon Liza, let's get going."

The wind had picked up slightly as they led their horses out into the yard and mounted up. The melting snow didn't seem to bother the young mare at all actually, she seemed to enjoy it. "She's gonna be a keeper," Liza stated. "I can tell."

"She looks good on you." Lizzie agreed.

"It's probably the way I sit a saddle," Liza answered in a conceited tone.

"You sayin' you sit a saddle better than I do?" Lizzie challenged.

"I never said that why do you always turn my words around?" Liza snapped.

"Because you can be such a snot, Liza." Lizzie snapped back.

"I'm no bigger snot than you are!" she accused.

"A huh!" Lizzie stated.

"What?" Liza asked.

"You just admitted you were a snot." she said matter-of-factly.

"I didn't say nothin' of the kind." Liza argued.

"Yeah, well you won't be sayin' whatever it was you weren't sayin' when you wind up in a snow bank." Lizzie countered.

"If I go in a snow bank Miss Blabbermouth, you'll be going with me." Liza argued back.

As Abe shook his head and watched the twins' body language out the front window he knew they were bickering already.

"I wish I was a mouse in their pocket." he laughed as Clinton and Matthew joined him.

"What is Liza doing riding that mare?" Clinton stated in an astonished tone.

"My guess," Abe answered, "Luke probably told her not to." His boisterous laugh was contagious.

"Why, she's barley been ridden at all." Matthew chimed in completely shocked. "And can she buck!"

"I hope she doesn't tie anything on behind her that'll be a rodeo start to finish," Clinton stated matter-of-factly.

"You both know that's exactly what they're going to do I know those two like the back of my hand. I wish I could be there to see it," Abe said in a humored tone. "Those two never have played by the rules both of them defy authority like a cat repels water." He let out a deep sigh, "There'll never be two more like them."

"Amen," Matthew and Clinton said at the same time as they watched them shove each other's shoulders as they disappeared through the huge looking arch.

"Well, I guess I best go collect my trinkets for the tree," Abe said as he stared into Matthew's sad face. He knew what his grandson was feeling. "I'm sure she misses you too son."

# CHAPTER 31

The wolf pup had been restless off and on all day not that she offered to leave the protection of the rocky walls, but something had her attention.

Emmy had learned quite some time ago to trust the wild animal's natural instincts, the twitching of her long-pointed ears, the way she tipped her large furry head as she sorted out the odd sound around her.

The twin girls noticed it too as their piercing eyes followed the wolf's intense stare as they watched the rhythm of her breathing while she searched for the strange noise, neither child made the slightest sound hidden deep within the dog's sleek shadow as they appeared to be invisible.

It was late afternoon when she heard the animal's protective growl. Instantly, Emmy hushed her for fear that whoever was in the cave would hear and come looking. The well-behaved pup immediately did as she was told respecting the command of her master.

Like a thief in the night carrying the dead trapper's shotgun in her hand Emmy crept to where the intruder made his presence known. It didn't matter that she only had two bullets, it still gave her that little added edge.

As she crept around the corner like a centipede she let out a slight gasp as she put her hand over her mouth. "Jeffrey, what in the world are you doing here?"

Her first thought was to run out and throw her arms around his neck and thank him for finding her what a wonderful celebration this would be, she could take the babies and go home then everyone would see that she was alive that Jeffrey had found them, had saved them. She didn't see a horse but there had to one Jeffrey never walked anywhere she sure that he hadn't come by foot. Home. Civilization. He was her way back to Matthew's loving arms.

But, as Emmy started to expose her position a cold wet nose bumped her elbow, she jumped a foot something in those deep-seeded, distrusting eyes told her to stay put, she did. Hidden like a hunted mouse within the darkened corner of the quiet cave she watched as the intruder's fiery mood changed from bad to worse.

"Butch, you son-of-an-egg-sucker." Jeffrey accused. "Where is everything...Butch?" It was plain to see that he blamed the trapper for the caves barren appearance as his mistrusting eyes scanned the empty room like a thieving rat. "Where are you I told you to stay put, Butch?" Jeffrey took a good look around as his eyes adjusted to the dark cave. "Hey, man. What'd you do with the table, where's the bed?" There was nothing but the sound of his own voice echoing back as he continued his little rant. "What am I supposed to sleep on tonight?" Still nothing. "C'mon, quit fooling around and get out here." Nothing. "I didn't mean what I said I'll give you your cut just come out." He whined in a high-pitched apologetic tone as he kicked at the rocky floor.

Emmy could see his expression in the fading light starting to change. "Don't tell me you done run out on me too, what you and her have this planned all along?" he slurred. "I saw the way she flirted with you when she thought I wasn't lookin' tryin' to make a fool out of me." Nothing. "Don't fall for her, trust her, she's the devil, she'll strip your hide clean off'n your bones, Butch do you hear what I'm sayin'?" Angrily he scuffed his wet boot across the rocky floor, it made an annoying crunchy sound. "I should'a know'd neither one of you could be trusted." He banged the palm of his hand against his head.

"You just had to look like the big man actin' all better'n me didn't you? Well you're not. Did you think you could get away with double-crossing me by leaving me high and dry?" Angrily he kicked at the rocky floor again.

"Stinking devil-woman!" he screamed bitterly. "That's all she is, a woman born'd by the dark one, I know'd better than to fall for her she didn't want me and she dern'd sure didn't want you!" He let out a high-pitched laugh. "Don't we look like the fools; the dirty liar didn't want either one of us."

Jeffrey paused as he took in a deep breath and shook his head as he tried to make some kind of sense out of his uncontrolled rage. "Well," he stated as he brushed off the front his shirt, "Good riddance who needed you two anyways try and make a fool out of me now, Nelly! Oh, what's that you say?" he paused like a spoiled child as he put his hand to his ear. "You can't? Oh, that's right, dead women can't talk."

Emmy couldn't believe her ears. That meant Nelly had made it back to the ranch. Why didn't she tell them where she was, why didn't she let them know that she was still alive? But, as she stood there barely breathing hidden within the darkness she knew exactly why Nelly hadn't told anyone of her whereabouts.

*"Dead people don't talk."* That's what Nelly had said.

Emmy hung her head as a sinking feeling devoured her. That meant the man who killed Charlie and thought he'd killed her was still alive, that man was standing right in front of her. Her body was shaking so hard it took all the strength she had to hold back. It was all she could do not to walk out there and fill Mr. Jeffrey's black heart full of buckshot. But, instead, she waited like a fly on a wall she knew his day was coming.

Emmy sat still as a stone just watching his panicked disposition. Then, as though a rational thought had crowded Jeffrey's inebriated brain, he hurried to where the dishes had been neatly stacked against the small makeshift shelf. Like a madman he pulled the wood away from the stony wall and threw it to the rocky floor. It made a hollow banging sound as it slid across the slick surface in broken chunks. Anxiously, he pushed his hand through a small opening and magically pulled out a ropelike cord with two hard pulls the door slid open like clockwork.

Emmy stood dumbfounded as she watched him slide through a small needle-like opening. Within minutes of entering he exited the small hole as he cradled a leather saddlebag pressed against his chest like he was holding his own beating heart.

"You didn't take it?" he sounded relieved. "I was sure you would have, unless..." Then a cunning look came over his face much like the one the mountain lion had for her. "She killed you before she came back to the ranch. She did didn't she? No wonder I can't find you, you're dead. Well," he boasted, "this has turned out to be a fine day." A broad manipulating smile crossed his face. "I've got everything, it's all mine and there ain't no way you're getting one cent of what's mine. You and that worthless money-grubbing husband of yours I'll see you dead first, both of you!" Then like a raging bull he exited the small tavern, holding the leather bag in hand.

Emmy stood in silence trying to figure out who exactly the drunken man was referring to as she watched him exit the hidden opening. Who was the money-grubbing husband, was that Clinton or Charlie? Her heart skipped a beat if it was the latter that meant Charlie had survived he was alive the gunshot hadn't killed him. The thought brought joy to her heart, but if it wasn't Lizzie and Charlie then who? She thought a moment the next in line would be, Naomi and Clinton they got married without her the thought made her both happy and sad. "Of course they got married without me," she sighed, "I'm dead."

It was an odd feeling sitting in the darkness watching the one person that could save her life and the lives of the babies. She knew deep down that he would just a soon kill her as look at her and how did he know his way around this cave like he did? Maybe, the trapper hadn't been the one hiding in this cavern at all, maybe this was the place that Jeffrey had been spending all of those days and weeks that he hadn't come home. The times when Abe and the twins believed he'd been drinking all night when in fact he'd had a whole other agenda up his sleeve, and whatever that agenda was laid hidden in that leather bag.

Knowing he'd come this far on a night like this gave her the slightest ray of hope that the ranch or Crocker couldn't be that far, she just needed to know in which direction. Now she knew when spring came she could and would find her way home. The thought of it gave her a small glimmer of hope in a hopeless situation.

Emmy waited in the darkness for what seemed like an eternity, contemplating her next move. By now, Jeffrey had a large fire going, she assumed he must have passed out or slipped and hit his head after all what kind of an idiot would stay out in a storm this long?

So against her better judgment, she crept like a small mouse toward the needle-like opening cautiously she listened for Jeffrey. Where was he, where did he go, did he leave? Only an idiot would wander out and about in a storm like this, but then Jeffrey wasn't known for his brilliance.

Still shaking she carefully she peeked around the crook in the stony wall. It was impossible for her to see anything within the small room from where she was standing, it was completely black. Nervously one more time she looked to see if she could find Jeffrey, the man was nowhere in sight so, with trembling fingers she reached down and lit one of the small torches as she slipped within the confines of the stone wall.

Emmy couldn't believe her eyes, her heart filled with hope as she looked at all the supplies everything she so desperately needed to survive the winter was here. There were all kinds of food and clothing like someone had planned on living here for a while. As she took a mental inventory the overexcited woman didn't hear the babbling madman re-enter the large cavern.

"What do you think you're doing?" Jeffrey hollered in an angry hostile tone.

Emmy spun around like a top dropping the lit torch.

"You're my ride out of here what, you think I'm going to let you get away?" With little thought to the condition of the skittish animal he pulled it into the cave.

It was quite evident that the horse didn't want to come into the small tavern maybe he could smell the wolf, maybe it was the fire. It didn't seem to matter what the reason was, the horse was spooked from the get-go throwing his head and stomping its snow bound feet.

Terrified Emmy leaned against the rocky wall trying to disappear within its jagged arms. Her heart was pounding like a thousand drums in her chest he must have seen her. Now, the drunken prowler knew that she was here. And in knowing that she also knew he wouldn't hesitate to kill her.

"I know what you're doing." he yelled at the small opening. "Trying to hide in the dark and run off with the evidence."

Tears of fear ran down Emmy's tortured face. "What's he talking about evidence of what?"

"Trying to make it so that I don't inherit anything?" he scoffed.

"Who is he talking to?" she wondered. "Is someone with him?"

"Well, I've got news for you I'm getting all of it!" In a fit of anger Jeffrey threw the bottle of whiskey in his hand at the small crack in the stone wall. The heavy object smashed against the shadowed rock like an ejected bullet just as Emmy peeked around the corner of the opening.

She could feel several splinters from the sharp glass penetrate her unsuspecting skin as blood trickled down her cheek. Anxiously, she wiped it away. "Another battle scar to match the other one," she sighed as she ducked backward for her own safety. "I can't let him find me."

"At least you had the common decency to leave me some firewood you worthless pile of pig squalor!" he hollered as he started to make himself a small fire, then he disappeared again into the darkness.

"I've got to get out of here." she whispered to herself in a panicked voice as a feeling of despair engulfed her. She could see that the horse was in poor condition and covered with icy melted snow. She couldn't help but remember the tale that she'd been told about a horse that been taken away from him for the very same mistreatment.

Recklessly, Jeffrey pulled the saddle from its bony wet back and threw it several piles of put-up grass. "That ought to keep you ya worthless pile of hair." Then like a sack of wet grain he sat down in front of the burning fire.

Emmy let out a relieved sigh as she placed her shaking hands over her face, he hadn't seen her all he'd been doing was babbling like the raving lunatic that he was. Relieved, she laid her head against the back wall of the rocky tavern as a state of panic started to etch its way into her brain. How was she going to get past him he was like a lying slug directly in her path the only way around him was directly in front of him.

In the distance she could see the small wolf pup watching every movement, but the furry ball never once offered to show herself, she was too smart for that. Emmy believed his smell reminded her of the smell from the trapper and there was no way she was coming out.

From time to time she would disappear then show herself again. There was no doubt in Emmy's mind that Jeffrey would have to kill the lone protector to get to the babies. "The babies." Emmy whispered to herself frantically. "What if the girls wake up, what if he hears them, he can't be trusted I've got to get out of here."

No matter which way she looked there was no path to get past the inebriated man. If he saw her and his dormant brain figured out who she was, it would be over she'd either have to take his life or he would take hers. Either concept was too much to think about she would wait until Jeffrey went to sleep or passed out, whichever one came first then; she would hightail it out of here.

But Jeffrey had other things on his mind as he pulled the yellow papers from within the leather case. As he sat in front of the fire admiring the handwritten documents it was plain to see from the wicked spark in his rat-like eyes that whatever he was up to was no good. As he sat mumbling to himself like a crazed idiot, Emmy anxiously watched as he polished off what was left in another bottle of whiskey. Then he stood up on his unsteady feet, walking in her direction.

"Mock me you filthy liar!" he yelled as he continued toward the opening.

Panic filled Emmy's being as she slipped behind one of the flour barrels just as Jeffrey entered the small room with his flickering torch. In his determined state of mind, he didn't see the hidden figure that shrank into the rocky exterior all he wanted was another bottle of booze.

Emmy let out a sigh of relief she would exit the opening right behind him like a shadow. He was too drunk to know the difference he'd never see her and when she got out she'd hide by the crooked rock and wait for him to pass out, it was a good plan. So, as the inebriated man started to exit the small opening, Emmy stood right behind him like a mouse hidden within the shadows. Like a cat she mocked his every move, making sure she wasn't seen. Emmy could see the dim light from the fire her heart soared knowing that within seconds she would be out of this prison.

"Thank you—thank you—thank you," she whispered just as Jeffrey stopped dead in his tracks in front of the needle-like opening,

Emmy melded within the shadow of the rocky wall praying it was dark enough that he hadn't seen her.

Jeffrey stood there for several minutes acting like he'd forgotten what he'd come to get. Then, he pulled the coiled rope and waited for the rocky door to close behind him. Terrified Emmy ran to where the door was closing her heart sank in her chest. Hysterically she grabbed for anything she could to jam the opening she didn't care if he did see her she had to get out of small room she had to get back to the babies, but much to her dismay there was nothing to grab. Shocked at her own stupidity she fell to the floor, the opening was too narrow for her to slide under there was no time for escape. Within seconds Emmy stood alone in a cloak of darkness. "My, babies!" she sobbed uncontrollably.

On the other side of the stone opening Jeffrey stood for several minutes listening as the counter-weight door closed behind him. He didn't like the dimly lit cavern and he didn't like the darkness that it placed around him, for some odd reason the blackened air made him feel suffocated and alone.

As Jeffrey sat cross-legged in front of the flaming fire he felt like there were hidden eyes following every move he made, the feeling gave him the creeps. Not that he'd actually seen them, but he felt them just the same. On more than one occasion he swore that he heard the desperate high-pitched screams of a woman, but how could that be he was the only one here?

Sitting alone by the flickering fire Jeffrey felt confident that no one would ever find out about the months of lies and deceit that lay hidden inside the saddlebag he held close to his chest as his wicked scheme ran back and forth through his demented mind. He'd planned every minute detail alone, secretly promising a lot of people land for money that wasn't his, not yet anyway.

Disgusted he kicked at the fire as tiny sparks flew in all directions, he was tired of being the bad apple in the family, but more than that he was dead dog tired of being a Baxter, of being someone he wasn't, constantly trying to prove himself only to be shut down flat.

"Hold your head up young man," his grandfather demanded, "start acting like a Baxter instead of a hoodlum." The Baxter name had such stigma attached to it; one he'd never live up to.

Why were they so afraid to take a chance, all he wanted to do was make the ranch pay for itself. Was it such an impossible idea to let water be their main source of income instead of livestock and lumber, to just sit back and collect the money?

No matter how many or how few people came to this savage land they would need water, barrels of it, the Lazy AB Ranch owned all the water in and around the valley. Let the poor pathic life squatters pay to water their thirsty livestock, the wagon trains pay to fill their barrels to the top. His plan was fool proof, at least until his grandfather Abe, his self-righteous mother and aunt Lizzie got wind of it, they squashed the notion immediately.

"Why would our neighbors pay for water, do they not have livestock?" Liza questioned.

"Do they not need it for their crops," Lizzie added.

"No, we will not agree to such a thing." They said in unison, their word was final.

Jeffrey sat there mumbling, drinking the brown liquid that gave him courage. "No one cares about me." he hollered in a pitiful drunken state. "Not even my own mother."

The wolf pup stayed hidden just out of sight in the darkness of the rocky channel, ready to do battle if the intruder threatened her position.

Jeffrey sat entranced in his own self-pity patting the saddlebag cradled in his drunken arms as if it was a newborn baby when his inebriated brain came back to life with a vengeance his voice was loud, angry, and full of revenge.

"I warned you," he shouted, "but you didn't listen, not a one of you, now I don't care about you, none of you." He paused for a brief second. "Wanna know why? Yes? No? Well," he stated in cocky tone, "Let me tell you."

Jeffrey took in a deep drunken breath. "Cuz, come summer this whole cave will be twenty feet under water, there won't be one single shred of evidence that I was ever here, everything that I've hidden from your self-righteous eyes and hands in this cavern will be buried beneath rocks, mud, and red sand.

Like a small child Jeffrey closed his drunken eyes as he cradled the half empty bottle of brown liquid in one hand and the mysterious saddlebag in the other, come morning he would leave this hell hole and never look back. Within minutes the inebriated cutthroat passed out."

# CHAPTER 32

"So, where's this beautiful tree you keep talking about," Liza asked.

"I don't know," Lizzie stated.

"You don't know? Lizzie I thought you knew where we were going." she whined.

"Well, for crying out loud Liza, there's enough trees on this ranch we could cut ten different ones to decorate, and no one would know the difference. I just needed to get out of that blasted, stuffy, house."

Liza wanted to be mad at her fibbing sister, but the problem was she felt the same way. "Yeah, things don't seem the same around here since—you know."

"Yeah," Lizzie whispered. "I know."

"I was thinkin' we'd done caught that darned ole fox but now, I'm thinkin' we got the pup not the big dog. Something's not settin' right with me I thought the culprit was, Jerimiah or should I say Jacob, I did, but now, I'm not thinkin' so much. I got this bad feeling way down deep in my gut," Liza stated.

Lizzie gave her identical twin a worried look. "Me, too."

"Speaking of gut, how is yours doing?" Liza asked in a concerned tone.

"Some days good, some not so good," Lizzie answered with a sigh.

"Do you think father knows?" Liza worried.

"Father knows everything," Lizzie sighed again. "Sometimes, before we do."

"Are you going to talk to him about it?" Liza questioned.

"What for? My reputation is already soiled." Lizzie stated.

"Yeah, that's true," she agreed.

"What's that supposed to mean?" her twin snapped.

"Nothing, gees, Lizzie!" Liza snapped back. "Take a breath."

"I know," she confessed. "I'm not myself I'm all be-gibbered inside I can't seem to control it."

"Been there," Liza stated knowingly.

"So this is what I was thinking, we could go up the sourdough ridge and down the east draw there are lots of pretty pines back in there we shouldn't have any troubles picking one out. And, it's not that far from the ranch, you know, incase this storm does kick up." Lizzie stated.

"Works for me," Liza countered.

The two women listened to the rhythmic sound of the horses' hooves as they plodded through the softly falling snow even with the storm it was beautiful out. The dark grey skies let the rays of the flickering sun slip through the snowy mist. The shadows cast an elusive spell across the powdery flakes making them look like a million scattered diamonds within the white powder beneath their feet. The chilly wind caressed their rosy cheeks as it whipped back and forth testing their determined strength to go forward. They enjoyed being together engulfed within the swirling silence it was a sacred time where their bodies bonded as one soul healing the scars of the aftermath of disappointment left from the spoils behind them. There was no reason to say anything their minds spoke to their hearts without speaking out loud. A time to fine tune the lines that made them one as they cleared the clogged channels of communication that only they shared, it was a sobering effect riding side by side, something they'd done since childhood.

Before they knew it, time disappeared right before their eyes as their destination stood right in front of them. Together, they scanned the distance to the bottom of the ravine. The two of them stared at each other, the same thought crossed their minds, it looked a lot farther to the bottom than they had remembered.

"Buckskin is the most sure footed," Lizzie stated scoping out the distance.

"Umm, I don't know." Liza gave her a wary look. "I'd feel better if you let me ride down there, I don't want Buck falling with you." There was no missing the worry on her frosty face.

"Alright, Liza. I just don't have the energy to argue with you," Lizzie answered.

"Why? What's wrong? Do you feel alright? Don't lie to me, Lizzie!" Liza said in a panicked tone.

"I'm fine I just get tired easy." She answered in an exhausted tone.

"Oh, I use to do that, too," she said relieved.

"Really? Is there anything you haven't '*use*' to do?" there was no missing the strain in Lizzie's voice.

Liza gave her irritated sister a wide teasing smile, "If there is, I'll let you know. Listen once I cut the tree down, we can tie our ropes together and pull the tree up from the bottom."

"I reckon this mare is going to get a good lesson today," Lizzie grinned.

"I expect one of us will," Liza said.

As if they were mending a wound their fingers were in perfect rhythm one matching the other as they tied their lassoes together. Liza would ride to the bottom and Lizzie would throw the lasso down the side of the ridge. The plan was flawless and started out beautifully that is until Liza got to the bottom.

After thirty minutes of deciding which tree Lizzie wanted, Liza was ready to climb back up the slippery slope and knock her twin down the side of the ridge. Finally they agreed on one.

"Throw the lasso, Lizzie." Liza commanded.

Trying to follow her sister's instructions she threw the rope toward the bottom of the snowy ravine, but each time she tried the wind caught it and the strand would land ten feet in front of her.

After several more attempts Lizzie hollered. "Hang on, I'll put something on the end of it."

Lizzie searched for several minutes before she found what she was looking for. "Ah, this is perfect." She half laughed as she picked up the odd shaped piece of pine with two uneven humps to secure the rope, carefully she tied the lasso in a sturdy knot. "That should do," she said to herself out loud.

Round and round over her head she swung the attached object. "Here it comes watch out!" Within seconds, it flew like an ejected bullet down the embankment just as the wind kicked up.

"What is she doing up there!" Liza said to the waiting horse as she shaded her eyes from the sparkling display in front of her.

"Throw the darned rope, Lizzie!" The words had no more than left the twins mouth when a sailing object clipped her on the side of the head knocking her to the ground.

"Yikes." Lizzie stated. "I don't think she was ready."

After Liza's head stopped spinning she scrambled to her wobbly feet, there was no missing the anger in her furious eyes. It was all she could do to keep from riding back up there and pouncing on her sister, condition, or no condition.

"Lizzie!" she screamed. "What are you doing up there?"

"I thought you were ready, I yelled ready!" she defended herself. "Are you alright?"

"I swear when I get back up there." Rubbing the sizable egg-shaped knot that had begun to form she tied the rope to the bottom of the tree as Lizzie took her time reassuring the big mare that she was fine as she tied the rope to the saddle horn. "Take it slow with her," Liza yelled. "We don't know what she'll do."

"What?" Lizzie strained to hear her sister through the wind.

"Slow," she yelled again as she gave Lizzie the signal.

"Go? Man she's bossy I should have come out here by myself." she muttered.

"Slow." Liza hollered again.

"Alright, but I think we should take it slow." In an indignant air Lizzie took the reins and walked the horse forward. "Boss me around like I'm some kind of servant." she mumbled.

The horse didn't budge all four feet were planted securely in the snow. In a slow manner she walked back up to the distrusting mare, talking in a soothing tone. Once again she tried to get the young horse to follow her lead, the horse refused her command.

"Now," Lizzie said in a reassuring tone, "we have to come to some kind of an understanding here there's nothing to be afraid of, nothing's going to hurt you. C'mon now, one foot at a time." The mare refused to budge just as Liza rode up over the ridge.

"Holy cat's Liza you like to scared ten yours off'n my life popping up like that you scared the daylights out of me!"

"What's up? Why didn't you pull up the tree?" her face was speckled with wet snow.

"She won't move it's like she's frozen." Lizzie stated.

"What? Here, you take Buck I'll take her." Like a cat Liza slipped off of Charlie's horse and into the saddle of the jittery mare.

"Don't get too crazy up there," Lizzie stated. "She's got a wild look in her eye."

"Wild look or not, we've got to get going; it's going to be dark soon." Gently, Liza tapped the horse's fleshy sides. Nothing. She patted her on the neck as she did it again. She could tell the green-broke mare was terrified of something but what? There was nothing out here but them.

Like a cat she slid off her horse as she spoke to her sister. "Let's pull the tree up with Buck then tie it on behind her. She needs to learn that it won't hurt her." Twenty minutes later the tree laid on top of the plateau.

"That's a nice one," Lizzie stated matter-of-factly.

"It'll look good in the house," Liza agreed. So, once again Liza tied the rope to the horn of her saddle. "Let's just pray she doesn't throw me off it's a long ride home soaking wet."

"That's why I brought an extra slicker," Lizzie stated proudly, Liza gave her an accusing look. "It's in your best interest, Liza."

Liza gave the mare a gentle nudge and Lizzie a look that said, they had this handled. Then, from out of nowhere a bullet landed directly between the skittish mares' front feet throwing bits of rock and snow into her unsuspecting face. The large horse came completely unwound as she jumped straight in the air.

Liza knew the horse was panicked and her only thought was escape as the startled animal took off on a dead run, it was all Liza could do to hang on. Then another shot landed to the side of the running animal just as the length of the rope ran out and the weight of the tree pulled back on the saddle horn. The horse let out a high-pitched squeal as she jumped straight up in the air again. When the horse landed it was obvious that something was behind her, determined to see what it was the mare stepped to either side trying to get a good look at the swaying object.

Buck hadn't expected the gun shots either and Lizzie was struggling to climb up into the saddle. "Quit!" she said in a controlled manner as she tried to keep him from dragging her through the snowbanks as he headed for the trees. By now she'd lost one of the reins and she knew her only recourse was to grab the saddle horn and hang on for dear life.

"Whoa!" she yelled as she saw her sister out of the corner of her eye. "Don't let her see it, Liza," Lizzie yelled. "She's gonna...!" Before Lizzie could finish her sentence the inevitable happened. "Blow!" Liza hit the ground with a thud.

Liza saw the buckskin take off on a dead run for the safety of the timber just as the tree started to fly by. She knew she had to grab it and hold on. Faster and faster the horse ran as tree limb after tree limb cracked, broke, and laid like deserted arms behind them. Liza did everything she could think of to get the crazed animal to stop. Clinging to the snow filled tree she could see the embankment in the distance.

"No, please, I beg you, no." she mumbled to herself. She had two choices, let go or hang on it took a second to decide. But in clinging to the tree's base, the rope had somehow gotten tangled around her left thigh and around the bottom of her snow filled boot, the one she hid her knife in. She knew what was going to happen she was going over the edge and down the ravine.

But, just when she thought she was doomed out of the timber shot Lizzie like the devil himself was on her tail. Liza could see her pounding the fleshy sides of the buckskin, the steam from his coat and nose looked like fog in the distance as it escaped from his heated body, where was her saddle?

Lizzie knew she was Liza's only hope as she reached down and grabbed the reins of the fleeing horse. "Whoa!" she hollered, pulling back on the strands of leather as hard as she could, using Buck as a shield. But, when she looked back all she could see was disaster.

Liza and the tree shot across the wide-open space like a freshly honed sled her terrified eyes looked like snowballs, her clothes were covered with pine needles and sagebrush. "I'm never gonna live through this one." Lizzie mumbled as her sibling and the broken tree both disappeared from sight. The last thing Lizzie heard was her sibling's high-pitched scream's climb an octave higher and higher and higher as her voice echoed across the open ravine finally fading into complete silence.

Instantly Lizzie jumped from her heaving horse as she peered over the side of the steep embankment. She tried hard not to laugh at the hysterical sight of her identical twin lying headfirst in a snowbank, she hoped there wasn't a rock tucked away inside the huge drift. As fast as she could Lizzie slid down the hillside on her butt. Like a raging bull she pulled her sister feet first from her snowy prison, as far as she could tell there was nothing broken.

"Don't ever scare me like that again, Liza!" Lizzie scolded. "What did you think you were doing flying off the cliff like that? Why, I thought you were dead!"

Liza was a disheveled mess as she desperately grabbed for the front of her sister's coat. Her eyes were aimed in opposite directions as she whispered in a dazed tone, "Am I on the ground?"

"Of course you're on the ground where else would you be?" Lizzie's answer was so curt.

"A bird," Liza rattled on.

"Bird? I didn't see any birds Liza; all I saw was you and that tree go fly…"

"Me you idiot I was the bird." Liza gave her identical sibling a horrified look. "I, I tried to put my feet down to help stop us but there weren't nothin' but air beneath me, air, Lizzie. And, and I was spinning and spinning and spin…" Liza grabbed her stomach and threw up.

"Too much spinning?" Lizzie said in a sympathetic tone.

"Now I know what it feels like to be a bird." She gave her sister a horrified look. "It's awful everything goes by so fast! And then—bam!"

Lizzie grabbed her sibling and gave her a good shake. "Holy catfish's whiskers Liza, snap out of it don't look like nothing's broken. Wait, how many fingers am I holding up?"

"Holding up, are you daft, I nearly died and you're talking about fingers!" Liza fumed. "What took you so long?"

"I was riding as fast as I could didn't you see me; I nearly broke my neck chasing after you." Lizzie confessed.

Liza gave her sister a heated look. "Next time ride faster."

"Hump, this is the thanks I get for saving your life? I should have left you in the snow drift!" Within seconds Lizzie started walking back up the embankment.

"Really?" Liza said in a cunning tone.

Lizzie saw the fire start to build in Liza's darkening eyes. "Now, Liza," she said in a concerned tone, "whatever it is that you're thinking just remember, I'm in a delicate condition."

"So you say!" she hissed.

In an instant Lizzie laid face first in the fluffy snow when she came up for air she was sputtering like a flailing fish. Then both women looked at each other and started laughing. "You look like a snowman, Liza."

"Me, look at you!" Liza giggled.

"I don't care what we look like," Lizzie said in a worried tone, "we've got to get out of here before we freeze to death."

Together the two of them started up the hillside holding on to each other as they slid downward as many times as they crawled upward. Huffing and puffing Liza stated, "I sure hope that lame-brained mare didn't take off."

"Me, too cuz, it's gonna be a long walk home for you." Lizzie gave her sister a menacing look.

Liza was in no mood after all she'd just seen her life pass right before her eyes for the sake of a tree. Stubbornly, she gave Lizzie a good shove as they both rolled backward down the hill. After several tries they finally made it back to the top. Fatigued, they caught their breath sputtering words that weren't befitting a lady. But, when they looked up both women were shocked to see the curious looks on two snowy faces neither horse had moved.

"What just happened here?" Liza asked, dumbfounded at their odd situation.

"Now we both know we missed the fox!" Lizzie was furious. "The shots came from over there on that far ridge dirty dogs. Who do they think they are trying to ambush two defenseless women, with one of us in the family way. Cowards hiding like a weasel in a dirty hole."

"So help me if I find out who that was," Liza interrupted, "they're gonna be wishin' they'd finished the job."

"We need to ride over there and see if we can pick up their trail." Lizzie suggested.

"My mind says we should, but my gut says, no, I think that's what they want, I expect they're just lyin' over there dug in the snow laughing and waiting thinking that's just what we're gonna do as they gut shoot us before we ever make the ridge. It's getting dark sister father will be worried we need to git on home." Once again Liza stepped up on the lanky mare as she spoke to her in words the animal hadn't heard before. The young horse seemed to quiet down. Then she looked into her sister's red face. "Think we should grab a different tree?"

"Nope we got ours," Lizzie answered proudly.

"You know the *'Thankful'* tree won't seem right this year without Emmy and Charlie," Liza half whispered.

"Nope." Lizzie sighed. "But then there's lots of stuff that don't seem right."

With the incident behind them they headed back into the timber to collect Lizzie's saddle as they two of them headed toward the ranch with the new tree. The young horse kept a close eye on the object following behind. Just encase it made any funny moves. After a bit, she forgot all about the tree and never made another bobble.

"Lizzie, what ya think?" Liza asked proudly.

"She looks good on you," her sister said honestly.

"It's the way I sit a saddle," Liza stated in her typically snotty tone.

"Yeah! When you're in it!" Lizzie stated matter-of-factly.

# CHAPTER 33

In the rocky chamber Emmy relit the small torch as she took a good look around the sunless room. Standing there in the corner was a sizeable crate she had to try something, anything, to regain her freedom, she had to get out of here. Frantically, she pulled the heavy box to the side of the wall by the hidden opening, then she stepped up on it. "Ahh!" Within seconds she was lying on the rocky floor.

Jeffrey woke with a start he swore he heard a woman scream but when he looked at the dancing shadows in the room he was the only one there. Purposely, he threw another piece of wood on the fire then like a lost child he passed out again.

Crying, Emmy pulled the large flour barrel over to where she believed the opening was. This time she was a lot more careful as she stood up on the top franticly she felt around for the opening that had cradled the disappearing rope. But, no matter how hard she tried she couldn't find it.

"It has to be here," she wept, "it has to be."

Several hours had come and gone as she frantically held the burning torch up above her head scanning the wall of the small tavern she had to find that opening. But, much to her dismay when she finally found it the hole was too small. "No." she wept as she tried to push her hand in the jagged crevasse.

She could feel the bite of the sharp stones cutting into her skin, it didn't stop her. She had to get out of here she had to find a way out to save the babies. "Jeffrey!" she screamed. "Jeffrey!"

Once again Jeffrey woke with a start, gun in hand, there had to be someone else in this cavern. Suspiciously, he stared at the darkened walls the only sound he heard nothing the constant chomping sound of his hungry horse. Like a fog had settled its chilly fingers into his drunken brain, he shook his head and threw several more splintered pieces of wood on the dying fire. This place gave him the creeps he never did understand what Butch liked about it.

As he settled his bulky frame down against the soggy saddle he pulled the cork from the bottle he'd captured in the hidden storage room. Purposely, he took a long intended pull off of the liquid concoction that he couldn't seem to stay away from, it was the only thing in his life that gave him any kind of comfort. But within seconds the dark liquid spewed from his mouth at a faster rate than he had inhaled it directly at the fire.

"What the devil?" he grumbled that wasn't whiskey. "Butch, you worthless, carpetbagger." he hollered as he stood up. Like a drunken sailor he made his way back to the rope-hinged door.

Emmy's heart was pounding like a hundred drums, she was exhausted, and to make matters worse the stone room kept getting smaller and smaller, harder, and harder to breathe. She could feel the wiry rope at the tip of her fingers she was almost there one more...

All of a sudden the hidden door started to open. Like a moth to the flame she jumped to the ground distinguishing the torch as she clung to the side of the opening. She knew this would be the only chance she would get to escape this rocky tomb. She didn't care if he saw her the risk was worth the chance, she had to get out of here, Emmy wasted no time.

When Jeffrey entered the darkened room he stumbled over the very crate that Emmy had tried to stand on. Taken completely off guard he dropped the burning torch which he held like a saber. "What the...!" The terrified outlaw screeched like a hunting owl as the caged shadow blasted past the inebriated man like a bullet.

In a state of shock Jeffrey captured the torch and flung it in every direction. He was sure that something or someone had touched his shoulder and purposely shoved him to the ground. But once again there was no one there only the reflection of his distorted shadow.

"I hate this place!" he screamed out loud as he scrambled to his unsteady feet. "Stinking spooks!"

The drunken man kicked the busted box out of the way as he rummaged around for several more minutes before he found the right bottle and exited the room shutting the closure behind him. Like a selfish child he took one long pull on the brown liquid as he protectively placed the leather-bound parcel close to his body and passed out in front of the flame.

Emmy shuddered as she sat heaving from the exertion of her flight. She could have died in the darkened room and no would have been any the wiser she could have suffocated. It would have been years before anyone would have found her barren bug infested bones if they found them at all.

"The babies!" she worried. For heaven's sake what kind of idiot thing had she just tried to do? With the sleekness of a hunted cat she slid within the protective shadows and disappeared within the arms of the kind loving walls in the back of the black cave.

After she had tended to the babies Emmy made her way back to the hidden entrance of the large cave opening, she'd sat for several hours as she watched Jeffrey's steady breathing. She couldn't help but feel a certain sadness for the drunken man after all, he must have been awful lonely to want to bring this much pain and sadness to his own family. It was plain to see that he was nothing like Matthew and sometimes it was hard to imagine that they were brothers at all let alone twins. No, something must have happened to Jeffrey somewhere, somehow because he certainly had no loyalty for his family.

Emmy settled herself down for a long night as she leaned her watchful head against the rocky wall. The babies were fed and lay sound asleep, besides if anything was amiss Persistence would alert her. So, the longer that she sat and watched the dozing man, the more curious she became about the leather parcel. It appeared to be awfully important. After all, what grown man would wrap something like that beneath his arm like a hidden jewel, and it not be important? So, she sat for several more minutes contemplating whether she should do the unthinkable. After all, she'd already had one close encounter with the drunken maniac should she risk one more?

But, before the tempting words had even left her lips, Emmy knew the answer to her own question. So with the motionless sound of a cat she wound herself around the cave wall making sure she stayed safely hidden within the shadows.

Jeffrey appeared to be asleep, or rather, passed out as she crept closer and closer to where he lay like a dead log in front of the dimly lit fire. She studied his position for several minutes, trying to figure out the best way to reach under his arm and take out the detached possession. Her heart was pounding out of control as she began to reach for the leather parcel when Jeffrey made a slight roll.

Immediately, Emmy withdrew her hand and stretched like a shadow against the rocky wall praying that he wouldn't roll over in her direction. She stood there barely breathing for several more minutes, Jeffrey never moved. So with trembling fingers she hunched down and quietly reached for the parcel again. This time something strange happened, Jeffrey lovingly touched her hand, Emmy wanted to scream but nothing came out of her terrified throat.

"Hello, there," he said in the kindest voice she had ever heard. "It's been awhile."

Emmy didn't know what to do as she stared into his sea green eyes, but there was something different about them those weren't the eyes that had attacked her they were kind and forgiving. For a brief moment he had the expression of complete surrender if he'd of shown this kind of temperament he could have had any woman he wanted. Afraid to move Emmy sat still as a stone.

"I've missed you," he said sincerely as he affectionately ran his fingers across the top of her hand.

"Oh?" Emmy's voice was barely audible.

"Yeah, I'm sorry for what I said earlier," he said sincerely.

"You are?" she was terrified.

"Yeah, I should'a believed you, I didn't mean it," he whispered as he gently stroked her hand.

"Me neither," she said as she gazed into his love-filled eyes. Emmy couldn't help but wonder who he thought she was.

"I'm tired of hiding," Jeffrey said lovingly.

"Me, too." Intentionally Emmy tried to slide her hand away from his.

"I told you we should have just packed up one night and left," he continued to whisper.

"I wanted to," she continued. Who was he talking to?

"You did?" he sounded so surprised.

"Yes," she swooned.

"Nah, they'd of just found us," Jeffrey said in a forlorn tone.

"Maybe, maybe not," Emmy said softly.

He gave her a queer look. "If mom or Aunt Lizzie ever found out what I'm doing, what we're doing, they'd kill both of us." He laid the parcel on the ground inches away from her and in a worn-out tone he added, "Now, they have to find out the hard way." As he gazed into Emmy's face his smile started to fade he gave her an odd look as a glaze started to cover his eyes.

"I never asked much of you, Mother, in fact, I've always tried to treat you with the utmost respect." This wasn't the Jeffrey Emmy knew.

"Yes you have son," Emmy's voice quivered this was not a good idea.

"Still, you don't trust me, why?" he asked in a calm coherent voice. "I wouldn't have to go behind your back to show you who I am if you'd just listen. I could tell you what I'm doing with a clear conscience I wouldn't have to hide or, or, lie to you. But not you you're always thinking I've got something up my sleeve I think back and I can't remember doing anything but loving you. I know that you've cut me out of my share of the ranch I pretend not to know, but I do." His grip became tighter and tighter.

"And I know that I can thank my so-called loving aunt for that." His tone was getting darker. "You took her side when you should have taken mine, why?" he said with a heart full of hurt. Then he let out a loud laugh like a breying mule. "But, ole Aunt Lizzie, she's gonna find out the hard way I got her pledge of death right here in this leather bag." He paused a moment. Then shook his foggy head. "I'm most sorry about, you. You're my mother, and I love you. In fact, I think you're the only person in this ole world I've ever really loved well, besides, her." He gave Emmy a look that said he was struggling with the choice. "But, you've turned against me my own mother." Again his grip got harsher as his features changed, "Now, you'll pay the price right along with the rest of them."

Emmy trembled as she gently placed her hand on his sweating cheek. Then with fingers of velvet she reached inside the opening and lifted the papers out of the small leather parcel. Not once did she take her eyes off of the man sitting in front of her then like a cat she placed them in her shirt as she whispered. "I wish there was another way."

Jeffrey's empty expression stared at his captive and within a single breath his persona changed again. His warm inviting smile became foreboding the soft green eyes that had been so kind earlier were dark, and hollow, he wasn't talking to his mother anymore.

"No! You! Don't!" Like the snapping jaws of a steel trap Jeffrey released her hand and grabbed her arm. "It's because of you that I'm in this mess." He said in a blaming tone. "Nothing more than a lying bed warmer, I should have gotten rid of you when I had the chance. Baby? I wouldn't dirty my name claiming anything that came out of you."

Emmy knew beyond the shadow of a doubt he wanted to kill the person he was talking to, now she believed everything Nelly had told her. It both shocked and hurt her when he dug his long fingers into her unsuspecting flesh. Emmy let out a loud scream, just as the wolf pup made her presence known teeth barred and growling.

The unexpected yowl startled Jeffrey back to reality as he fell over backward against the rocky floor, scrambling for his gun. Emmy flew back within the protection of the caves shadows.

"Persistence, come!" she commanded. But, the protective dog ignored her command as she squared off at the male intruder.

Terrified Jeffrey would make it to his gun before Emmy could save her trusted friend, she picked up several small stones and threw them at the back of his crawling torso.

It was plain to see that the inebriated man had no concept of direction. Like a mole heading for cover he put both hands over the back of his head screaming in a high-pitched yowls when the spinning rocks hit their intended target. Within seconds the dog disappeared.

"What the...!" he screamed frantically. "What was that?" Finally his trembling fingers found the security of the wooden handle felling the trigger he instantly started firing. "Where'd you go ya nasty witch you've already stole my heart what else do you want from me?" Once again he spun around aiming the gun barrel wildly. "Show your face again!" He yelled. "I dare ya I'll blow you to kingdom come, where are you?" he yelled over and over.

Emmy was holding Persistence back for all she was worth. The animal wanted to inflict bodily harm no doubt, but, there was no way that she could stand up to a bullet. Finally, Emmy took her by the back of the neck and told her *'no'* in a voice that said the dog had better listen. Quietly the protective ball sat by her commander as they both waited for their unwelcome company to leave.

It had been an endless night with no sleep Emmy's heart lifted when she witnessed the first rays of sunlight start to flicker against the tavern wall. Soon the sun would be shining its brilliant beams right over the top of Jeffrey's head. Worried that the babies would be waking soon, Emmy whispered in a determined state. "Time for you to go home, Mr. Jones."

Quietly, Emmy gathered up several small stones and tossed them toward the sleeping man hoping to wake him from his exhausted slumber. No luck he was really passed out this time. So she took a larger stone and popped him a good one alongside the head. Bullseye.

Jeffrey came to life like a snapping turtle. "What!" he demanded angrily as the drunken marauder's bloodshot eyes focused on the empty room.

Emmy saw the hidden pain in those mesmerizing green circles, and for a split-second her heart felt a pang of sorrow as he ran his fingers through his blonde hair. Why did he have such a grudge against his own family?

Jeffrey knew there couldn't be anyone else in this cavern, how could they be no one knew about it but Nelly and Butch, they were both dead, confused he stared at his waiting horse.

Then, as though nothing had happened he recklessly grabbed the startled hairball, saddled up, and left the safety of the warm cavern. He never looked back.

# CHAPTER 34

Abe was just getting ready to ride out as the two rag-tag looking women rode into the barn. There was no missing their disheveled appearance as he gave them both a questioning look. "Trouble?"

"Nope," they said in unison.

"Sure?" Abe stood and gazed into the matching duo's wind burned faces.

"Yep," they answered together.

He'd known that lying look since they'd been babies. "Quite a knot."

Liza touched the side of her head. "Low branch."

"That blood on your boot, Liza?" he questioned.

Both women looked down at her foot at the same time. "Huh. I reckon so."

"Dare I ask?" he questioned with an arched brow.

"Nope," they said together.

"That the tree?" It was all he could do to maintain his demeanor.

"What's wrong with it?" They acted like two cornered raccoons.

Abe put up his horse and walked toward the barn door. "I'll see you inside?"

"Right, shortly," they answered. Baffled the twins looked at each other. Then Liza reached down and took a look at the young mare's front foot sure enough her right leg had been grazed by a bullet.

"Was she limping, Lizzie?"

"Not that I noticed," she said in a confused tone.

"We best tend to that, then we'll take the tree in the house." Liza stated matter-of-factly.

"Yep." her sibling answered.

No one said a word when the two hooligans drug the large tree into the house, well what was left of it. They all pretended not to notice the unruly ceremony going on in the grand room as they listened to the two of them argue about which side looked the best, and where they were going to put it. Liza had several suggestions for her identical sibling which went over like a boulder falling on a person's foot. Then, they'd break out into hysterical laughter by the end of the following evening it was hard to tell exactly what kind of tree it was but it was upright and decorated. The two of them stepped back as they admired their handy work.

"Right, nice," they said in unison as they stood arm in arm. Then, like two children they ran upstairs into their rooms and hurried back. "Father," they hollered. "Everyone, get your memory and come on its time."

When Abe entered the room the twins stepped to either side of him as they placed their hands in the crook of their father's arm. Lovingly, they laid their heads on his sturdy shoulder. "I love you, too," he whispered. For as many branches as there were missing the tree didn't look all that bad. "You did good," he said as he placed a kiss on each of their heads.

Then he took a lone eagle feather braided within a strand of red hair out of his pocket. He looked like a giant when he stepped in front of the tree. As though it was made of glass he placed the token on a waiting limb. "I cherish every memory that you gave me and the token of the love you and Flying Eagle left us here to share." he stepped back.

Clinton stepped forward he placed a handful of dried wildflowers tied with a yellow ribbon on the tree. "I didn't know the lovely young girl named; *'Sarah'* but I've heard so many amazing stories about her. I am forever in her debt for giving me my beautiful wife, Naomi." Clinton stepped back.

Hattie stepped forward and placed a worn-out blue bonnet on the tree. "This was my Emmy's favorite, it still smells like her hair," she sighed as she stepped back.

Luke stepped forward. "Don't reckon' I've ever much belonged to no one cept' I had quite a hankering' for Miss Maria. She always knew what to say when I were needin' words of knowing." Quietly, he placed one of her favorite cotton towels on a waiting limb Luke stepped back.

Matthew stepped forward trembling from head to toe, he looked just like his grandfather. It was all he could do to place the beautiful golden band made of straw that he'd taken from Emmy's jewelry box on the tree. "I gave this to you when we first met. I knew then that I never wanted to be with anyone else but you. My, Emmy." Matthew stepped back.

Naomi stepped forward her large odd colored eyes were full of unshed tears. "I have a token for every one of my memories. A band of leather for my mother and father, Maria's favorite spoon, which I felt on my a... butt more than once, Dancing Bears beaded bracelet, a necklace of wildflowers that Emmy made just for me." She held the strand to her chest before she placed it on the tree. "And Charlie's black neck scarf." Naomi stepped back.

For a few moments time stood still no one made as much as a whisper. Liza and Lizzie looked like identical silhouettes as they stepped forward. Everyone in the room knew that Lizzie wasn't herself.

Liza never let go of her sister's arm as they placed two large eagle feathers with a strand of red hair and a streamer of yellow ribbon braided within the fine tines on one of the lone branches.

"Sarah, the youngest part of our being," Liza said in a loving tone.

"The largest part of our heart." Lizzie whispered in the same tone.

"We miss you every day." They said in unison.

Then, they placed two dried biscuit's on an open limb. "We remember this for you Maria and the scat of your apron." Liza said. Then, they placed Dancing Bears leather poke on the tree.

"The Mighty One knows what was sacrificed on your day of dying, the brutal attack that took your life will not be forgotten. The spirits say justices' bullet killed the filthy pack of wolves that stole your breath, that the greedy hounds of hell drug their evil souls to the underbelly of the fire world, they will dwell in darkness with the evil one forever never to see light again." Liza said in a harsh tone.

Liza started to step back when Lizzie's grip told her not to leave her. Together they stood like two old oaks, one shadowed within the soul of the other. Everyone stood in awe as they held their breath.

It was Lizzie's turn they all held their breath. "I," she could barely speak, "was ta...told," Lizzie's lips trembled as her identical sibling's tears matched hers. "That love couldn't live in an empty heart, a dark heart." Her words sounded so desolate. "My heart."

Liza held her sister even closer. "Lizzie," she started to say. But, Lizzie shook her head no. Liza's voice became silent as tears drifted down her cheeks.

"But the wind tricked me," Lizzie's words sounded like magic, "and blew a gentle-handed tumbleweed right through my fingers," she stared at her hands in bewitching wonder, "And into my soul." Gently, she placed her hand over her heart and let out a deep sigh. Liza did the same thing at the same moment. "Charlie." Within seconds Lizzie felt the support of her father's strong arm around her trembling shoulders as a sob escaped her dry lips.

Instantly, Abe pulled his heartbroken daughters as close to him as he could. Like two broken branches they laid their heads back against his broad chest. Both seeking the shelter of one strong heart.

Within minutes Matthew slid his muscled arm around Liza's waist, Hattie placed her hand in the small of Matthews back Luke placed his hand on Matthews shoulder, Naomi slid her small frame next to her mother as she slid her arm around her waist, Clinton did the same to Naomi. Together they stood, arms entwined, sacrificing their strength, to a torn petal, whose dream was shattered from a jaded lie.

"I miss you," she whimpered. "I do, I, I miss you so much that it makes my heart hurt deep inside like an endless crack in a frozen lake." Lizzie took in a deep breath, so did Liza. "And, you loved me, the whole me you told me so all the time with your soft breath, with the warmth in your eyes." Like a child she unbuttoned her shirt, reached inside, and pulled out a piece of red flannel. "I couldn't bear to part with more than this." Liza saw the red flannel shirt beneath her sister's blouse and smiled. "It still smells like you." Tears rolled down her chaffed cheeks as her trembling fingers placed the delicate cloth on the tree. "We fooled them, Charlie Redbone, you and me, we did it," she sobbed as Abe held her tight.

Then she turned and stared into her father's rugged looking face, she never let go of Liza's hand. "I'm not going to be able to hide behind my secret much longer father. It's time to tell you and everyone else in this room what is going on with me, to explain my behavior, I'm going to have a baby." The shocked 'ohh's' rang through the room. "Charlie's baby."

"I know, Lizzie," Abe whispered as he gently held her.

"How do you know? I've never said a word to anyone," she whispered as both women laid against his chest, she was so relieved.

"Because, you—are—my—daughter, Lizzie," he stated lovingly. "I feel every breath you two take."

The words had no more than left Abe's lips when the front door blew open like the tail end of a tornado. Everyone jumped as they turned around in complete shock as the snow blew through the front door like rice at a wedding then slammed shut with a loud thud.

"Jeffrey!" Liza stated in shock. "What are you...? How did you? In this weather? Why, you can hardly see outside."

"I didn't want to miss the so-called **'Thankful'** celebration." he slurred. "After all, I think I'm still a part of this family."

"Barely," Lizzie stated in an icy tone as she wiped the tears from her face. She also wondered how he'd gotten here unscathed in this nasty storm.

Like a cat that ate the canary, Jeffrey blatantly stared into their surprised faces. "What'd I miss? And, who's knocked-up?" In an arrogant manner he continued. "Not you again, Aunt Lizzie, man you'd think you'd of learned the first time."

It only took a second for the storm to start brewing in her black eyes as Lizzie looked into her father's naysaying face. "Don't do it," he said in a calm hesitant tone, "he's not worth it."

"You—filthy—two—legged—pile—of—horse—dung, you wouldn't know what you missed with that pea brain of yours if it was stuck up the back end of your britches!" she stated in a venomous tone.

"Yeah, well if you were a lady instead of an old hag you'd know how to keep your legs shut!" he snapped back just as hateful.

At first it sounded like a low rumble, then it went to the next octave as a high-pitched, ear-piercing scream echoed like an erupting warrior. Her intimate confession, the moment of truth was ruined as the attack cry echoed across the room like a thunderstorm.

They all heard it; they all knew what was coming. Everyone except, Jeffrey.

"Duck!" Liza yelled as she scrambled to the floor.

"You disrespecting hornet head you're day has come; I'm putting this family out of its misery, let me at him!" she yelled. "I'm gonna tear your tongue out and tie it to your head, after I tear you limb from limb you low lying coward!"

"You're the only misery this family has you knocked-up old prairie grubber." he retorted back in an indignant tone.

After that remark Lizzie turned and pointed her gun at his chest. "Your day of reckoning has come you two headed snake it's time to send your lying soul back where you came from."

"No!" Abe hollered as he grabbed for the pistol, everyone took cover.

Bang!

"You stinking weasel!" Lizzie screamed furiously; she was beyond any rational thinking.

Bang!

Jeffrey jumped like a trapped jackrabbit from one side of the room to the other. "You're crazy." he screamed like a girl.

"Where were you yesterday, huh mister big mouth?" Lizzie demanded skirting his every move.

Bang!

"Mother." Jeffrey yowled, "she's gonna kill me."

Once again Abe tried to take the gun out of the furious woman's hand, but Lizzie was quick and eluded each grab. "This isn't going to solve anything."

"Were you out hiding in a ravine in the snow you stinking coward!" Lizzie demanded.

"Ravine? What ravine?" he squealed. "I don't know nothin' bout no ravine."

"Liar!"

Bang!

"Yes you do you lying skunk, trying to maim two defenseless women!" she hissed.

"Defenseless women?" he whined in a high-pitched yowl. "You two haven't been defenseless since the day you were born." he accused. Jeffrey was so shocked at his aunt's agility she was inescapable.

"Ah, hah so you admit it!" Lizzie countered in a no-it-all tone as she swung the gun in every direction he tried to run.

"Admit what, that you're crazy? Yes, I'll admit that cuckoo, cuckoo." he taunted.

"It was all Abe could do to get the gun away from Lizzie as the bullet's echoed throughout the wooden planked walls, taking the gun away did little good.

Abe couldn't keep her from slugging the nasty mouthed troublemaker in the gut, knocking the wind out of him as he sunk to the floor scrambling to get away from her. The two of them slid like they were skating on ice. Within seconds they were both on the floor, Lizzie right on top of the screaming liar pounding him hard in the chest. "What do you think now you low life lying skunk, still think I'm crazy? You haven't seen crazy yet!"

"I surrender!" he screamed in a high-pitched voice. "Mother! Papa! Help me!"

"I'll show you surrender!" Lizzie screamed like a lioness as she grabbed Jeffrey by the back of the shirt and pants. "Ain't no one gonna save you." Within seconds the obnoxious man landed on the snowy porch in a startled heap. "Let that be a lesson you, you conniving spawn of the devil, next time I won't be as hospitable." The echo of the slamming door sounded throughout the rafters of the large house as she turned and looked into everyone's shocked faces as though nothing had happened.

"Well," she stated in a calm tone, "now that the trash has been thrown out let's have some cream and crumb cake I'm starving." She gave her father a wink. "After all I am eating for two." As though she didn't have a care in the world Lizzie disappeared around the corner into the kitchen.

No one said a word, no none moved all they could do was stare and hope she didn't come back. "Is anyone hurt?" Abe questioned in a relieved tone as they crawled out of their hiding places.

Liza ran to the front door praying that her son didn't have any bullet holes in him. What was her sister thinking she could have killed him. When she stepped out on the porch there laid Jeffrey.

Relieved that he was alive Liza knelt down next to him. "Are you hurt?" she worried.

Furiously Jeffrey pushed his mother aside. "What do you care?"

"What?" Liza stated shocked at his hostility towards her.

"You didn't do nothing." he accused. "To help me, you didn't do nothing, nothing."

"You were told because of your selfish heart never to step foot on this ranch again, why would you have made such a foolish choice put yourself in harm's way like that?" she questioned.

"She could have killed me, and you did nothing!" he accused again.

"Lizzie? She would never kill you. You are my son, my sister would not do that. My ears heard your hurtful words, she's not the one that started the war," she stated matter-of-factly. "That was my son."

All Jeffrey could do was stare at his mother in disbelief. "I hate you."

"What foolishness is this I hear coming from your mouth?" Her tone held a warning. "If she would have wanted you dead my son, you would be."

"She despises me she's always has." his tone was so angry.

"And what of you Mr. Jeffrey? Was what you said tonight kind? No. It was cruel and you meant it to be cruel." She gave her son a knowing look. "We have lost so much this family and now you blame someone else for your misgivings? That's not my son, I have raised my son to be a better man than that."

"Why do you always take her side? She's not perfect." He was so frustrated his mother was like talking to a rock wall.

"When will you learn there are no sides, just truth Jeffrey. And," as though he was a little child Liza continued, "Truth has never been your strong suit." Liza let out a deep sigh. "C'mon, let's get you settled in the barn where it's warm."

Jeffrey was drunk, and it took a lot of babbling drunkenness to get him settled down for the night. "Now, no funny business tonight we'll have coffee and talk about this more in the morning."

"Mother?" Jeffrey said in a cold tone.

"Yes," her tone was so forlorn.

"I won't be here in the morning when you wake up. I don't want to have coffee with you or anyone else on this pathetic ranch." His angry features said he meant it. "You made your choice tonight mother, and it wasn't me it's never been me now you'll all pay the price." He slurred in a fading voice.

Like a broken doll, Liza covered her drunken son and blew out the lamp. "Where did I lose you?"

# CHAPTER 35

"Liza!" Lizzie hollered as she waddled down the length of the wooden staircase taking each step one at a time as she clung to the banister. "Liza, where are you?" she yelled again in a slightly panicked tone. "She'd better not of left!" Lizzie mumbled to herself.

Within seconds Lizzie's identical twin stuck her dark head around the corner of the kitchen wall staring at her sibling with a humorous twinkle in her eye. "What?" she demanded. "A person can hear you plumb out in the barn."

"I woke up and you weren't there," she said simply through dark abandoned eyes.

Liza had noticed a definite change in Lizzie's disposition since her pregnancy an urgency to keep her within eye shot most of the time. Not that Liza didn't appreciate her sister's company, it was just getting old, not having any time to herself, not to mention the snag it had made in her affections with Albert. "Honestly Lizzie I have chores to do, besides what are you doing up?"

"I never said that you couldn't do your chores." There it was the typical ornery disposition possessed by her identical twin that seemed to show up out of nowhere. "And, I'll get up if I want to." Lizzie stated in a highhanded fashion. "I'm not an invalid you know." When she finally made it to the bottom of the stairs she was breathless as she encountered a dignified slightly gray-haired man with a cup of coffee in his hand and a knowing twinkle in his eyes. "Mornin' father," she said sweetly.

Her father gave her a suspicious look. "So you say."

"What's that supposed to mean?" she snapped.

"I don't know," he said truthfully. He didn't want to have a heated encounter with his daughter in her delicate condition. "Maybe because the suns shining and it's a beautiful day?"

"Oh yeah, hold that against me." Lizzie walked to the window in the cozy kitchen and gazed out the clean glass.

It was a beautiful day well at least for everyone else. Not being able to pull her weight around the ranch for the last several months had taken quite a toll on Lizzie's typically cranky disposition making her grumpier than usual. No one said having a baby would be this hard.

She remembered the last time Doctor Slater had made one of his unexpected visits with his mousey wife to the ranch and in no uncertain terms demanded that Lizzie stay in bed the last two months of her pregnancy, that is if she planned on carrying a healthy full-term baby. She smiled cunningly to herself as she remembered what she told him he could do with his leather bag and unauthorized advice.

"Old goat!" she mumbled under her breath.

Lovingly she placed her hand on the top of her once flat stomach. The miracle no one thought would ever happen—did. A token of the veiled love that she and Charlie had made together. Affectionately, she slid her warm hand across the huge lump in front of her she could feel the baby's restlessness to be born as much as she was to have it. It broke her heart knowing that she alone would raise this little blessing that strangers wouldn't understand her decision and brand him with harsh words just like Naomi.

Lizzie let out a deep sigh of longing, it wasn't supposed to be this way, they had so much to tell everyone so much of life to live. Now, it didn't make any difference what would be, would be.

For Lizzie there weren't enough words to express how much she missed the cowboy that use to lay his large, calloused hand securely against her muscled back. Today the tumbleweed that had rode across her heart in less than a whisper was rounding up wild horses just out of her reach.

"Blast you, Charlie, we were supposed to ride the wind together." With a slight mist in her eyes she made a determined decision. "I think I'll go out to the barn this morning," she announced triumphantly. It had been a long winter and she needed to get out of this house for a while. "I feel good, I'm gonna give it a try."

"I knew you were going to say that." Liza knew what her sister had been thinking all night there was no hiding their thoughts from each other.

"What?" Abe echoed in the exact surprised tone within the same breath. "You're not even supposed to be out of bed, no, don't even think about it."

Lizzie gave the two of them a look that showed her determination. "I think I'm old enough to know what I can and can't do." she said in a dark quiet tone just as Clinton came around the corner.

"What'd I miss?" he questioned as his startling blue eyes studied Abe's distraught face.

Lizzie'd been a total pain in the butt whining like a lost pup the past several months and Liza was well past her last nerve. "Well it seems Miss Hardhead is gonna take a stroll to the barn." Liza snapped completely disgusted with her sister.

"Really?" Clinton grinned. "Alone?" All eyes were on him as he confronted the determined woman.

"What do you mean, alone?" Lizzie snapped. "I'm perfectly capable of going out to the barn by myself I've done it my whole life I'm not an invalid you know. What's wrong with you people bossing me around all the time?" she mumbled under her breath.

"Oh I know that for sure," Clinton agreed matter-of-factly. "I've seen people what don't help themselves afore and you're sure not one of them. No you're not. I just came in for a cup of coffee, but what the heck I can grab that later. I'd be honored to walk out there with you," he paused for a brief moment. "If you'd let me."

Clinton rubbed his hand across his bristly chin several times. "But...you might have to wait a bit before we can come back to the house I have a few things that I need to take care of, it might take a bit." He gave her reassuring smile. "Mercy what am I saying you can wait that long; I'll be done before you know it."

"See," Lizzie injected in a dramatic tone, "at least one person in this house has a sense of decency." She gave Clinton a huge smile. "You know you're the only one who understands me."

"I know," he grinned as the deep dimples on his cheeks lined his handsome face. Like the gentleman he was Clinton held out his strong arm as Lizzie waddled like an over-stuffed duck to where he stood.

Like a princess with her king, she gave her father and sister a flippant look. "Now, what was it you needed to get done?"

Abe gave Liza a quick grin, the young mapmaker had definitely learned how to manipulate the dark-eyed rebel without her even knowing it. "This ought to be good," he said under his breath with a chuckle in his voice.

"Matthew and I brought Big Bob down from the Red Clay Ridge, time to shoe the raunchy devil. Albert showed us a quicker way to get it done so I'm quite sure that Matthew is tying up a foot right now. We can always use some good advice with him, but I don't have to tell you what a rascal he is."

Lizzie's footsteps became slower and slower. "Really?" her voice was barely a whisper.

"Oh yeah, then Matthew and I have that wagon of feed to unload, but that won't take us long either, besides," he stated sincerely, "it will be nice to have some female conversation, I get tired of listening to his babbling all the time. Yak, yak, yak, that's all he does without sayin' nothin'."

Like a gallant knight Clinton reached for the knob on the old oak door just as Matthew stepped within the well-lit corridor. "Hey, we were just coming to meet up with you." He gave the man a huge grin.

"What is this?" the tall dark-haired man questioned with concern on his scruffy face. He knew as well as anyone that his Aunt wasn't supposed to be out of bed. Where did she think she was going, what kind of nonsense was this?

"Lizzie is coming out to the barn with us while we shoe Big Bob." The features on Clinton's face told the younger Baxter to play along. "She's dang dog tired of being stuck in this ole house lugging that freeloader round the house, she needs some real airing out."

Matthew had been around Clinton long enough to read the hidden expressions on his smiling face. And it wasn't often that anyone got the chance to undermine Lizzie, he took the lead and ran with it.

"Really, Auntie, that's great I was wonder'n when you were going to get out of that ole bed." he said in a caring tone as he slid his large arm beneath her other elbow. "There's not much that can keep us Baxter's down no siree we learned from the best that stink'n ole skin slayer he don't know what he's talking about, sides I just got ole Bob settled down, you remember ole Bob?" He paused for a brief moment, "Of course you do what was I thinking you and mom were the ones what traded that ornery ole bull for him, by the way it was one of the best trades we've made on this ranch, I mean you and mom have made." With a twinkle in his eye Matthew continued. "Have you heard that story, Clinton?"

Clinton gave him a wide smile. "By golly I don't think I have but I'd sure would like to." He gave Lizzie a loving expression. "You can tell me all about it once we get to the barn."

"Besides Auntie," Matthew added, "any advice that you can give us would be greatly appreciated on that huge ole boy." Just then Matthew let out a quick giggle as the baby gave him a quick thump. "Man, he kicks like a mule."

"Tell me," Lizzie said in an annoyed tone. "I've been feeling it for the last six months." But as the pregnant woman stood there contemplating her next move an overwhelming feeling of exhaustion over took her. "You know," she said honestly, "as much as I'd like to see ole Bob and believe me it's not because I can't get out there."

"Of course," the two men said in unison as they continued to lead her toward the door.

"I'm feeling a little... tired," she said in a dramatic tone as she placed her hand on her forehead.

"Tired? You?" Matthew gave her an odd look. "You're never tired."

"We can pull the wagon around," Clinton said. "It's no trouble."

"We just pulled down some loose hay bales I think they'd be plenty soft enough for you to sit on," Matthew stated matter-of-factly in a concerned tone. "I mean until we're done."

"A hay bale." Clinton interrupted. "She can't sit on a hard old hay bale can't you see what a delicate condition she's in? One of those grain bags would be much softer."

"A grain bag those things are hard as rocks." Matthew argued. "She'll smash that baby's head sit'n on that."

"Oh, I hadn't thought of that," he said honestly.

"No we need something much softer." Matthew injected as he rubbed his bristly chin.

"Really," Lizzie said in an annoyed whisper as she backed away from the door's threshold. "I don't think you two would know the difference between a grain sack and a mules butt."

Ignoring her completely the two of them continued, "I've got it." Clinton stated. "Why don't we pull one of the goose-down bags for her to sit on they're are super soft," Clinton stated.

"Why didn't I think of that?" Matthew countered.

"Because you're both idiots." Lizzie mumbled under her breath.

"What was that, Auntie?" the two of them asked at the same time as they gazed into her annoyed face.

She was sure that the two of them had forgotten that she was even standing there listening to this ridiculous gibberish. Hay bale, grain sack, down feathers who cared they were acting so childish. "Honestly, I think I need to sit for a bit."

It was all Liza and Abe could do to keep from laughing aloud as they peeked around the corner like two naughty mice. It was plain to see that Lizzie was finished with the two misfit highwaymen she had a scowl on her forehead that stretched all the way across the room.

"On second thought, I think I'll just go into the parlor for a minute then go back upstairs."

"What?" Clinton said in a disappointed tone. "I was looking forward to spending some time with you especially since you've been a prisoner in that ole bedroom of yours."

"I said I was feeling a little tired," she injected in a louder tone as she gave both of them a scolding look.

"Are you sure?" Matthew asked surprised at her submission. "You don't look tired do you think she looks tired, Clinton?"

"Beautiful as ever," he said honestly.

"Well auntie I'm thinkin'," Matthew added, "it would do you good to get outside and blow some of the stink off'n' ya."

Lizzie gave them both a look that said the sooner they were out of her sight the better. "I'm not sure that I stink," she said in a dark tone.

"I don't think she stinks." Clinton said in a miffed tone as he squeezed her elbow.

"I didn't mean you stink, stink, Auntie." Matthew gave Clinton a dirty look. "I mean the outdoors would do you good fresh air, sunshine."

"Well if I did stink, which I don't, I sure as a skunks tail wouldn't tell you two!" She couldn't wait to be free from their irritating grasp they were so exasperating.

"Now look what you did," Matthew accused. "She's upset."

"Don't look at me, I ain't the one what brought up the hay bales and told her she stunk." Clinton defended himself.

"I'm sure my decision is in my best interest." she snipped trying to get their attention. Lizzie gave them both a dark intimidating look as she regained her freedom and paddled into the parlor holding her back. "Idiot's!" she mumbled under her breath in an irritated tone. "I must have been out of my mind wanting to be with those two jaw flappers. Pure idiots...!"

"Coffee?" Clinton asked with a twinkle in his devilish blue eyes.

"That's what I came in for." Matthew grinned as the two of them walked into the kitchen.

As Clinton and Matthew sat down at the long oak table they couldn't help but grin. "She's a handful that Lizzie."

"Whew." Matthew whispered.

"That was a close call." Clinton whispered. The kind mapmaker looked directly into Matthew's humored face. "Thanks man I don't know what I'd a done if you hadn't walked in that door."

"Are you kidding?" he said in a soft tone. "I wouldn't have missed that for the world."

"I can hear you two!" Lizzie hollered in an irritated tone from the parlor. "I'm pregnant, not deaf."

"What's that Auntie?" Matthew asked. "You want us to bring our coffee in there?"

"I won't be in here that long!" she snapped. They were so annoying.

Then on a more serious note, Clinton asked, "What time did Naomi and Hattie head for town?"

"It's been a couple of hours," Abe said honestly. "Why?"

"Nothing, I just wish I could have gone with them. I guess they were going to stop and check out the small place." Clinton paused for a brief moment as he looked into Matthew's estranged face. He knew the man hadn't made a trip to the small acreage since Emmy's death. It was time to make sure everything was still alright so Naomi and Hattie went instead. "It's just me," Clinton stated in a concerned tone, "I'm always a little nervous till I see her coming."

"If it makes you feel any better," Matthew said calmly. "I sent two of the new men with them. They're in good hands."

"How so?" Clinton questioned.

"I threatened them with their lives!"

When Abe and Clintons eyes crossed the distance there was no missing the worried relief in the younger man's face. "Thanks, Matthew."

# CHAPTER 36

The air was crisp as it gently whisked across Naomi and Hattie's reddened cheeks. It was a beautiful ride to the Small Place, a soothing journey that never disappointed Naomi. Nonchalantly, she clucked the horse's into a soft walk as the two women gazed at the vastness of the open prairie. Everything about this ride was beautiful.

The two of them sat and listened to the constant sound of the horse's hooves as they echoed with the timely wind. The clip-clop—clipping sound made a rhythmic pattern against the well-traveled road. Naomi gave Hattie a wide grin as she made sure that the heavy wool blanket was tucked securely around the older woman's bouncing frame.

The huge cottonwoods would be budding soon, bringing forth their beautiful incipient leaves, the brown grass would turn different shades of green and the wildflowers would be poking their mismatched blooms upward toward the warming sun. It never ceased to amaze her how one hillside could be filled with purple blossoms and the opposite ridge bore nothing but white and yellow blooms, then another nothing but prairie grass.

How many times as a young girl had she lain within the protection of this amazing meadow listening to the buzzing of the bees as the white fluffy clouds drifted across the wide blue sky above her. And how many times had the small clear creek quenched her thirst as the chilly snow melted filling the fingered streams like a cup of cold water.

Naomi's soft voice broke the silence. "Papa told me a story about this majestic meadow," she said to the quiet woman sitting next to her.

"Really? How so?" Hattie questioned.

"It's kind of sad at least that's what I saw in Papa's face," Naomi said.

Hattie and Abe's affection's for each other had turned into a strong friendship since the truth about Becky had been exposed. She'd lost count how many times the handsome cattle baron had told her what a fool he'd been loving a woman that had never loved him back, how betrayed he felt. All those years of mourning and blame.

Hattie'd told him over and over, "The only fool was Becky for not knowing the love of a good family man."

Naomi broke the silence. "This particular meadow is one of Papa's favorites he calls it, Sourdough. He told me once about a beautiful young woman who had sat right there," Naomi pointed at one of the wider veins of spring water, kneading bread dough by one of the smaller fingers of the clear streams. He'd watched as Becky's thin fingers stretched the moist flour up and down till its texture was just right. He told me how he watched her roll the dough into large flat balls then cover them with a cotton towel as the warm wind whipped the bottom of her red braid.

In the distance he saw two dark-haired dark-eyed rebels running down the middle of that stream like wild horses. I bet you can't guess who that was." Naomi let out a slight giggle.

"Those two are still like that." Hattie laughed.

"Yeah they are. I guess Papa tried to stop the stampede, but he was too late. The collision between two wildcats, one pan of rising dough, and a water-soaked woman was not a good combination. According to Papa she was furious, and mother threatened them both with their lives as they ran toward the timber screaming."

"I'm sensing a but here," Hattie smiled.

Naomi turned and looked into the lovely woman's kind face. "She didn't know he was behind her, Papa I mean, when she picked up a rock and threw it at them, I guess it hit Liza square in the back as she fell in the grass crying.

Within seconds Lizzie picked up the same stone and flung it back like an arrow, it hit Becky right in the forehead. Papa said she'd a throw'd another one if'n he hadn't quietly shook his head no."

"Oh my." Hattie stated in surprise.

"I know. Papa said when my mother stood up soaking wet with a good-sized knot on her head and climbed out of the creek her face was full of sourdough and hatred. So he named this place

Sourdough. Leave it to papa to find the beauty in something ugly." She let out a long sigh. "Of course he never allowed her to touch them; ever, after that day he did the rough-shodden, said he never trusted her after that." Naomi giggled. "Becky, wanted both of them whipped, Papa said he had a better idea, something they wouldn't forget. He made them wash the pots and pans for a week."

"Do tell," Hattie smiled she knew how much they disliked the kitchen.

"Right!" she giggled. "He said that was far worse than any whippin' he could have gived them, I love that man."

"Me too." Hattie whispered to herself.

"So you see, Liza and Lizzie were their own worst enemies from the time they were little." She chuckled.

"Papa says the only'st thing he can figure is, The Mighty One with a stroke of his hand made two beautiful wildflowers, perfectly matched right down to the last petal." Naomi let out a soft sigh. "Papa's always gets emotional when he tells this part."

"Oh my," Hattie said intrigued by the story.

Naomi smiled at the older woman sitting next to her. "With a swish of his hand and a warm breath he blew those two flowers plum across't the open prairie." In a dramatic gesture she threw her hands up in the air, "Search'n for fertile ground to place his moral code of right and wrong, his righteous command of justice, 'a knowing beyond my knowing' Papa always says."

"I can see him saying that." Hattie agreed.

Naomi was quiet for a few moments, she needed to gather her thoughts, to make sure she told the story right.

"There has to be more."

"There is."

Hattie let the young woman collect her thoughts.

"Sitting on a hillside together crying on that very prairie two young girls searched for a place of being, a place only they knew existed, a place where they were safe."

"Liza and Lizzie." Hattie breathed.

"Liza and Lizzie." Naomi said softly.

"Papa says the spirit breath from The Mighty One on that particular day done soaked right deep inside both of them till the day they die." Naomi took in a deep breath, "Safe within each other. One breath…one life… one soul."

"That gives me an even better understanding of the two of them, 'spirit blessed', that makes sense. What a wonderful story."

"I never tire of hearing." She sighed.

"Thank you for sharing that with me."

"Absolutely." She smiled.

# CHAPTER 37

Naomi couldn't help but grin to herself when she thought about Lizzie's little bud that would soon be gracing the family of the old log house. Would the newborn baby bring a healing light upon the souls of those who lived there? Would it shine a light upon the ranch giving it a new breath? She prayed to the Mighty One that it would.

As the twosome plodded along she couldn't help but wonder if the baby would be a wild spirit like her aunt Lizzie, or sweet like Charlie. Would it have red curly hair the color of strawberries or black as the night? Either way she was sure that the baby's presence was going to bring a sense of healing, a new beginning for all of them, she could hardly wait.

But then on the other hand she couldn't help but wonder why her body hadn't accepted the seed of her precious cowboy. They both desperately wanted children but each month her womb was empty of any sprouting seed. Naomi prayed to the Mighty One every night that he would bless them with the magic of their deep seeded love, she had to believe he would.

"You know Hattie we don't have to go to the Small Place today if you don't want to," Naomi said sincerely. "We can pick up the supplies we need and head back to the ranch." Most of her family was buried on that particular piece of ground. "We can just check the house and cellar and be done with it."

"No," she said stubbornly. "I need to check the graves and who knows; maybe some of those pumpkins in the dirt shed will still be worth keeping. A pie sure sounds good."

Naomi knew how hard it was for the older woman every time that they went to check on the small homestead.

Hattie sat silently for several minutes before she spoke. "It's all right you know. I've come to terms with Emmy's death, not that I don't miss her, goodness no. But sometimes in life we don't get to hold all the pieces. You know because of Emmy's death I found you and your family, what would I have done without your kindness to an old woman?"

Naomi loved Hattie she had taken up the void in her life that Dancing Bear and Maria had left behind. She was so warm and caring that Naomi wondered how such a sweet spirit could have survived in such a savage untamed land.

"I think it is us who have come out on the better end of that deal!" Naomi giggled. "I bet papa is thinking his throat has been slit about now, heaven knows who's cooking."

"That man does love a good sit down." Hattie confessed through knowing lips.

"And, let's not forget the rest of the scoundrels." Naomi laughed. "Believe you me, if it's Mother or Aunt Liza cooking they'll be cinching up their belts come nightfall."

"Or perhaps in the privy." Hattie laughed. "I swear between the two of them they can't boil a pan of water."

"Amen." Naomi laughed back.

In the distance they could see the hustle and bustle of the small collection of buildings as the wagon made its way down the dirt road. They wouldn't be here long just a few supplies and they'd be on their way. Naomi nonchalantly nodded her head to one of the older ladies on the street when she noticed someone that looked like Jeffrey in the land office. Immediately, she slowed the team.

"What?" Hattie asked in a hesitant tone she knew that look as her old fingers felt the security of the double-barreled shotgun. She'd die before anyone touched Naomi the way they had Emmy.

Naomi nodded her head toward the land office just as the team slowly plodded by. "Pretend you're getting something out of the back of the wagon Hattie and see if that's cousin Jeffrey walking out of that building." She had an urgency in her voice.

Immediately Hattie did as she was told just as Jeffrey with his arrogant stride, in his fancy pinstriped suit stepped out of the building puffed up and acting important like a mating sage grouse.

He hadn't seen the two women yet as Naomi pulled the team to a casual stop in front of the general store. Hattie gave Naomi a quick nod letting her know that was exactly who had exited the small building.

"I thought so," Naomi said in a suspicious tone. "I wonder what he's up to now."

"Nothing good," Hattie reiterated. The older woman had a definite dislike for the arrogant man.

"Yep," Naomi answered as she stepped down from the wagon waiting to help Hattie when a hand reached over her slender shoulder and took the older woman's arm.

"Here, let me help you," a voice said in a cocky manner. "I wouldn't want you to fall off head first."

"Thank you," Hattie said in a hesitant manner what did he mean, *fall head first*? The touch of his hand made her skin crawl.

"When did you get into town, cousin?" Jeffrey asked in a lighthearted tone. For once he sounded like he meant it.

"Just now," Naomi said in a far friendlier fashion that she felt. "How bout you?"

"Where else would I be?" he stated with an impervious air.

"Do you want to go down that road Jeffrey, here?" she asked in an edgy tone.

"I've been busy doing business you know odds and ends," he lied.

"Really? Business? That sounds interesting." But what she really wanted to say was, "I hope Aunt Liza can pull your sorry butt out of another botched up deal."

"Yep, spending some of that inheritance money of mine," he said trying to get a rise out of his lovely redheaded cousin.

"Good luck with that," Naomi stated in her typically dry tone. She knew that Jeffrey had already spent his inheritance and any extra money that his mother had to get him out of one jam or the other. She was sure that there couldn't be much money left for him. "What'd you do find a gold mine someplace?" she questioned.

"Go ahead, Hattie, I'll catch up," she instructed.

"Maybe," he said in a coy manner. "Why? What have you heard?"

"You're the one doing the talking. Have you told Aunt Liza about this great investment yet?" she questioned as her wildflower eyes penetrated his soul.

"Nope and I don't plan to for a bit needs a little tending to first." He acted so cocky.

"More like jail time is what I'd say," she stated dryly.

The look on Jeffrey's face said he wanted to take her disrespecting head off for her snide remark, but before he could counter her cutting remark a tall thin man walked up behind him and slapped him on the back.

"Jeff...ro my boy, I've been looking all over for you how bout I buy you a drink?" he smiled openly. Then as though he finally noticed that he had interrupted their conversation, the man turned and faced the beautiful redhead. "And, who might this pretty young filly be?"

"My cousin," Jeffrey said in a bored tone.

"Man, she sure don't look like you." he chided. "She's much better looking."

"So you say." Jeffrey said completely disinterested. "So you and big ass's mother going back home soon?" he asked with a smart mouthed attitude, trying desperately to impress his newfound friend.

Naomi's face showed her disappointment and brewing anger with her cousin especially after everything that had gone on within the walls of the Baxter ranch the past year. He just never understood the meaning of family loyalty; she doubted that he never would. "You're a mules butt!" she said in a dark challenging tone.

"Why, cousin." he stated in a flippant manner trying to act offended. "I'm just telling the truth."

"You wouldn't know the truth if it bit you in the back of your britches, Jeffrey." she scolded. "But, to set your mind at ease we'll be leaving soon enough, besides, Clinton and Matthew aren't far behind us," she lied through darkening eyes.

"I should have known," Jeffrey said in a blown-up voice. "Tell me, are you ever allowed out of his sight?"

"I'm his wife Jeffrey, it's nice to be seen," she countered in a frosty tone. "Would you like me to send them over?" Purposely, she nodded toward the noisy saloon. "I'm sure they'd both like to know about your so-called venture."

"Don't bother!" he snapped back at her snide remark.

Jeffrey didn't trust Naomi's changing moods she was just like Lizzie, totally unpredictable. He could never be sure what she would do or where she would do it so instead he tipped his new white hat and headed across the street to the noisy brothel.

"Skunk!" she hissed to herself as she entered the busy general store dismissing him entirely as she looked for Hattie.

"Hello Naomi, what a pleasant surprise," Mr. Dott said in a friendly manner as Naomi entered the small store. "Hattie's right over there." Like a well-schooled butler he pointed in her direction.

As Naomi came around the corner she couldn't help but notice the lovely fabric that the older woman held in her work worn hands. "Pretty isn't it?"

"Blue?" Naomi said as she arched one brow.

"For the baby," Hattie grinned.

"What makes you so certain?" she asked.

"Oh, that Charlie he was a man's man," Hattie said confidently, "it will be a boy."

"How's that?" Naomi asked curiously.

As Hattie looked into Naomi's wondering eyes she couldn't help but notice Mr. Stokes fussing with something on the shelf just inches away, hanging on her every word. "We'll discuss this on our way home," she smiled as she nodded in his direction.

Naomi let out a soft giggle as she gave Hattie a wink.

After several hours of shopping and closing out their business, Hattie and Naomi headed for the livery. The two hired men that had made the journey with them had been waiting for the two women with Albert as they pulled the team to a stop in front of the large building.

"Hey Albert, I've come to steal my men," Naomi giggled light-heartedly as the livery man gave her a big hug.

"Good," he countered, "I'm tired of their nonsense. Hey by the way, how is that Aunt of yours doing I haven't seen her in a month of Sunday's?"

Naomi let out a slight laugh, "Taking care of my whining mother. The baby is due any day now I just hope she doesn't kill her first."

"Which one, Liza or Lizzie?" he teased.

"Believe me it will be a toss-up." she laughed out loud.

"You tell her I said hello," he insisted through loving eyes.

"Oh, I expect she'll be in as soon as this is over." She gave him a knowing look. The livery man and her aunt Liza made quite a smart looking couple and at some point Naomi was sure that they would be married. "When you gonna stop horsing around and make an honest woman out of her?"

"Soon as she'll let me." His smile reminded Naomi of a bashful little boy. "Each time I ask her all she says is, 'we'll see'."

"Ready?" she questioned the two mounted men as the small troop headed for the small place.

Naomi took the long way out of Crocker down the backside of the buildings on purpose. There was no good reasons for Jeffrey to know when or which direction they were traveling in. She didn't trust her cousin; he always seemed to have something crooked stuffed up his sleeve. But more than that the crooked liar didn't need to know that Clinton and Matthew weren't coming to meet them.

# CHAPTER 38

The two outriders watched on a constant basis to make sure that they weren't being followed even though they did their best not to be conspicuous. Naomi had seen Matthew talking to the two new men, she was sure that they had been given explicit instructions on what would and wouldn't be acceptable. She was glad they were here.

They'd gone several miles when the party finally started to relax. "A boy," Naomi coaxed with a smile on her freckled face, picking up the conversation from the general store, Hattie wasn't getting out of this one.

Hattie gave Naomi a loving smile as she took a deep breath. "Now, don't think what I'm saying is written in stone it's not, it's just an old woman's tale."

"Point taken."

"I believe Charlie's life was pretty much coming to an end when he met your mother. You know like the last chapter of a book filled with both adventure, mystery, and endings. He knew some where's deep down within his wily soul that your mother would be the last wild filly that he would tame, and, quite honestly from his modest ways I doubt he'd really tamed that many.

Charlie wasn't the kind of man that hunted around like a heated dog from woman to woman, no Charlie was a disappearing breed, a gentleman, but," she gave Naomi a knowing look, "a cowboy, a kind soul with a hard past." Hattie let out a soft sigh. "This is what I believe just the words of an old woman. Yes?"

"Yes." Naomi could barely breathe.

Hattie gently patted Naomi's leg. "I believe The Mighty One gathered Charlie's soul from the prairie dirt, molded the clay with spring water from several mountain streams, sprinkled it with the smell of pine trees and aspens giving it light, and wisdom from the wide blue sky."

She smiled at her intrigued listener. "Then he blew life into the molded clay, a brand-new soul right out of the Mighty Ones hand." She placed her hand over her heart. "And when the time was right for Charlie to claim his wildflower, scoop up her heart up to join his it was too late for Lizzie to resist.

"She sure wasn't looking for love she'd given up on that part of her life years ago." Naomi's voice had a sad echo to it.

Hattie gave the young woman a caring smile. "Lizzie placed her life's work in this ranch and you Naomi, she wasn't ready for Charlie he snuck up on her when she wasn't looking. He planted a warmth within her barren soul that she'd forgotten even existed I guess you could say he blindsided her. A lot of folks missed his noble spirit silently hidden under the cuff of his shirt sleeve." Hattie paused for a moment. "They couldn't get past his unkept ways." Hattie paused for a moment. "But not your mother, not Lizzie she never scoffed at a person down on their luck, or cared bout the way they was dressed, no siree Lizzie never did that."

"No. Papa wouldn't have allowed that, not Liza neither." Naomi agreed.

"When she finally figured it out, what had happened it was too late. With a soothing voice and a gentle hand..., well the rest is history, you get the picture." She gently patted Naomi's slender leg.

"I have to be honest though, I don't understand why Charlie's life had to be taken he was such a kind soul. Just like my, Emmy." Hattie paused for several minutes,.

"I was mad at the *'Mighty One'*, that's what Dancing Bear called him. I was angry for some time, for years I tried my best to protect her, taught her how to shoot, ride a horse, pull what we needed from the garden, put it up on the shelves for leaner times, everything... but leave me behind. That I couldn't let my heart do." Hattie let out a deep sigh as silent tears ran down her cheeks. "Seems she did it anyway."

She said in a distant voice. "Taking their lives seems so senseless to me I can't see past the feeling. So the only way I can deal with all of this heartache is knowing that there will be another strong gentle soul just like Charlie standing ready at the gates to replace what your mother lost. What we all lost. After all," she insisted through misty eyes, "what would the world be like without one more Charlie or one more, Emmy? That's why I believe Lizzie's baby will be a boy."

Naomi was mesmerized by the woman's analogy as she countered, "And what of me? Do you have anything for me in that wonderful bag of magic words?"

"What I see for you? From what I was told from Dancing Bear your father Chief Flying Eagle was a mighty War Chief in charge of his own kingdom. He was a courageous warrior, a kindred spirit, he saw the loss of many warriors and children whether by his hand or another's, he knew his way of life was disappearing like a soft summer wind. There was no reason to bring forth another to take his place your father and his tribe's existence was vanishing right before his eyes."

Hattie looked lovingly into Naomi's eyes. "You were given your father's wisdom, a gentle caring for life, it's bred in your soul, it comes natural for you and yet... to survive in this ruthless land you needed the teachings of a harder fearless form of life which you wear like a protective cloak." Hattie wiped the tears from her reddened cheeks.

"Mother, Lizzie." She breathed.

"Lizzie. So I believe when your time comes," she stared into the wondering face of her young companion, "and it will, that your child male or female will ramrod this outfit with an iron fist and root out anyone or anything that disturbs their domain."

"You are a most amazing woman," Naomi breathed. "No wonder Emmy was so wise. I chose to believe your story; it plays out much better than the one in my mind." She paused for a brief moment. "Your marriage must have been so wonderful to have such insight."

"Don't let my babbling fool you, child my husband was a hard man. My body warmed his bed on frosty winter nights and my food warmed his belly at the supper table and his hands were harsh when times became hard. He was never interested in the teachings or the babbling's of a young wife; he was only interested in the fleshed production of his brood. That's why I was so pleased when Matthew took a shine to Emmy. I saw what I'd always desired and never experienced myself in the warmth of his eyes every time he looked at her. I wanted her to know that there was a softer place to fall than the terrible ordeal that fate had dealt her. He's an incredible young man that, Matthew I couldn't love him more if he was my own son."

"I'm sorry about Emmy," Naomi whispered. "She was my best friend."

"Mine, too," Hattie stated matter-of-factly as she gently patted Naomi's hand. "That's what I mean about not being able to read the cards that you will be dealt in this life. But, we mustn't dwell on the past, Naomi today is a beautiful day and tomorrow will be its own spring."

"Amen," Naomi whispered as she clucked the horses onward.

When the two women finally made their destination Naomi got an odd sensation in the pit of her stomach a lesson that she had learned to listen to years ago. Purposely, she brought the horses to a slow stop as she sat on the top of the ridge and scanned the grounds below, it was such a beautiful little place. From where she was sitting everything looked normal. Except...

Within seconds of her stopping one of the men rode alongside the wagon. "Ma'am?" he questioned as he watched the expression on her cautious face go from normal, to fearless, to cunning.

"I don't know," Naomi stated as she stared like an eagle at the small ranch house. Something wasn't right she could feel it the smell of the grizzly was strong.

"Want us to go down first, check it out?" he questioned again as he pulled his rifle from the scabbard.

"No," she said in a quiet demanding tone. "I want you to get down off of your horse and stand behind the wagon, both of you right now. Hattie, get in back!" The words had no more than left her lips when they heard the winging sound of a bullet. Naomi scrambled from the seat of the wagon and slid to the side of the waiting team pulling Hattie with her just as part of the wagon seat shattered behind her back, the bullet barely missed the older woman.

"What the dickens," Marty exclaimed. "They would have blown us to kingdom come."

Then another shot slammed into the dirt just in front of the team of standing horses it was all Naomi could do to hang on to them.

"Whoa!" she hollered at the nervous set of sweating flesh as they tried to bolt.

"I can't see where he is." Marty hollered as he lay in the dirt like a wiggling snake. Trying to get a better position.

"Get back Miss Naomi!" Chinsey yelled.

Naomi never took her eyes off of the small house below it was too quiet and too far away for a bullet. The gunman wasn't in the house he was someplace close, he could see them, but they couldn't see him. Like a hunting hawk her wildflower eyes scanned the heavy grasses, but she still couldn't see anything, the flowing meadow looked like an ocean of greens, grays, and yellows.

"Where are you ya skunk skinner," she whispered. "Show yourself."

Then, from out of nowhere the wind changed as the cooling breeze swept across her face lightly walking across the tops of the wavy grasses awakening the very senses that she'd been taught as a child. Patiently she let the memory engulf her, calm her, as she drew in a deep breath.

For a brief moment it was confusing, then, she knew. He was close, no, they were close. There were two of them, she could smell their dirty sweat just like the smell of the grizzly when she was young, only this time she wouldn't ignore the two separate scents. One was in front of them, one behind, clever but not clever enough.

"Marty, can you wiggle your way back toward that patch of willows behind you?" Naomi whispered.

"Yeah," he answered, "but I'm not leaving you here to fight alone."

"I'm not alone, I have Hattie and Chinsey." She admired his bravery.

"Chinsey can't hit the broad side of a leaning barn." he whispered in a worried tone. "He's likely to shoot you."

"That's why I need you behind me," she said in a confident manner as her eyes told him everything would be alright. "Don't miss."

"I won't," he got ready to make his move.

"When I fire out into that there meadow, you skedaddle. he'll come fast, when he does don't hesitate for one second, you put a hole in him."

"You mean kill him?" he stuttered like a scared little boy.

"If you don't he'll put a bullet in you the size of this here ranch. You want to die today Marty?"

"No, Ma'am."

"Then, do like I said ya hear? I'll deal with the other one," Naomi stated with confidence.

"What other one you mean there's two of them ambushing skunks?"

"Marty!" Honestly, where had her mother picked up these two.

"Hattie when I shoot at that red bush in the middle of that there meadow you take this rifle and fire right at the edge of that dirt hump over there." The older woman was afraid too, but she wasn't about to let Naomi down, this girl knew exactly what she was doing. "Chinsey, you do the same thing."

"What? Way over there? I'm not sure I can hit that Miss Naomi," he fussed.

"You can more than hit it, that's where the other one is hiding. He's gonna poke his nasty bush whacking head up like a gofer and you're going to send him packing."

"How do you know he's there?" Chinsey questioned completely taken aback at her cool headedness.

"He's there, be sure of it," she said in a knowing tone. "Get ready, Marty. Run!!"

Bang! Bang! Bang!

Naomi's rapid fire sounded like dropping a boulder in a canyon as she watched the tops of the red bushes go flying. Within seconds of her recoil, Hattie's gun sounded off beside her.

Bang!

She'd hit a little in front of the pile, but she'd gotten close. The ejected bullet sent tiny rocks flying in every direction.

Then Chinsey's loud ole gun went off.

Bang!

He hit the dirt pile and again small rocks flew through the air like splintered glass, his aim was more to the right.

Within seconds a man's head popped up firing wildly just as Naomi put a bullet right between his surprised eyes. The man toppled backward in a heap down the rocky cactus filled hillside.

"Get down!" Marty yelled just as his gun went off.

Like a charging bear Chinsey tackled Naomi as they disappeared face first into the dirt. The bullet missed her, but she knew her protector hadn't been that lucky.

Within seconds they heard the recoil of another shot as Marty's gun went off not more than fifty feet away, then nothing but silence. As Naomi tried to scramble to her feet, Marty was standing over her huffing like a wind broke horse his face was white as a ghost.

I thought he done got you." Instantly, he put his hand over his heart. "Do you know what your grandfather would...," his face turned even whiter, "what your moth...Lizzie...would have done to me?" Instantly his hands covered his manhood. "I might well give up me time right now she's gonna skin me like a cat!"

"You did good." Naomi said as she brushed herself off. "I'm all right no broken bones." Then she turned and gave the downed cowhand a pull up when she released her grip she had blood in her hand. "Are you hit?" she questioned.

"No." Marty stated.

"No? Chinsey, are you?" Sure enough the bullet had missed Naomi and hit the man in the fleshy part of his upper arm. If he hadn't knocked her down the steely billet would have gone through her heart. Instantly, Naomi yanked her scarf from her neck and tied it around the bleeding man's arm. "It's a flesh wound I'll take care of it when we get to the house."

"I'm hit?" he said weakly as he fell to his knees, the color slowly drained from his face, the reality of what he had just done hit him full force. "Marty, I'm hit."

She couldn't help but sympathize with the weak-legged man. "You'll be fine."

"Did you get him?" Chinsey questioned like a kid as he held the gaping wound.

"Do you see him lying here?" Marty said in a disgusted tone to his wounded companion. His eyes told Naomi how sorry he was as he rubbed the blackening circle on his face.

"That looks like it hurts," she stated matter-of-factly. "Seems I'll be tending to both of you."

"Nah, I'll be all right," he grinned. "Takes more than a blow to the head to knock ole Marty out, I'm tough."

"Like the time when your horse dumped you in a pile of cactus?" Chinsey stated. "When'd you couldn't sit for a week?"

"Chinsey!" Marty hollered, completely humiliated.

Naomi couldn't help but grin, this was her protection what a pair. "Where is he?"

"He jumped off'n that there ravine right into the water, jumped like some hopping toad." It was plain to see that Marty couldn't believe it himself.

"He jumped into what water?" Hattie gasp. "Where?"

"Right there," Marty pointed as the three of them walked to the edge of the steep ravine. "I don't care how far he jumped; you can bet he's ridin' with a backend full of buckshot."

"You shot him with the shotgun?" Naomi questioned as the picture started to unfold.

"Yes ma'am, I ain't much account with a rifle I need a little more firing room." His wide smile was unmistakable.

Naomi got a sick feeling in her stomach. A shotgun? What if Marty would have missed? And why was the water so high, it hadn't ever been up this far before?

The cowhand saw the disenchanted look on Naomi's face as he spoke, "I snuck up right in front of him, there weren't no way to miss, ma'am. If'n that's what you're thinkin' nope he's wear'n a butt full of buckshot. I'd of hit him square in the chest if'n something didn't make him turn around and start a run'n. There weren't no way he was getting to you. I'd a died first. I got this," he pointed to his swelling eye, "when I knocked the rifle out of his hand."

"What?" Naomi said, shocked at the man's confession. "Did you recognize him?"

"No, ma'am, he put a boot in my face afore I could get a good look at him, but he had a pile of light curly hair."

Even now Naomi could see how sorry the cowhand was he did the best he could. He didn't miss. He had defended her by placing his body between her and the intended killer, he'd protected her the only way that he knew how.

"You did good, Marty," she said in a tone that told him she meant it. "You too, Chinsey you two saved my life today and Hattie's. Those fellas were laying for us, somehow they knew that we were coming, and we nearly walked right into their trap."

"What do you pose they wanted, Miss Naomi?" Chinsey asked completely baffled.

"I don't have any idea there's nothing to take here…except." Naomi took in a deep breath as an eerie thought crossed her mind. "I guess we'd best go and see who's over the hill."

The small party walked to the top of the dirt knoll and stared at the still body on the bottom of the small ravine, she hadn't missed the fact bushwhacker was dead. All they had to do now was figure out who he was and what he was doing here. Liza and Lizzie weren't going to like this one bit and to make matters worse they would have to stop at the Sheriff's office with the dead body, the gossip would spread like wildfire. "Damn." She whispered to herself.

"Hattie," Naomi said as she helped the older woman back onto the wagon seat, "Are you all right?" The worry showed heavily on her dusty face.

"Yes, child, I'm fine." She gave Marty a grateful smile.

There was no missing the relief that washed across her worried face, "You and Chinsey go on down to the house see if there's something to bind that wound up with, I'll be there shortly." Then those crazy looking eyes gazed at the cowhand, "You did good today, Chinsey, really good my mother will be grateful."

"Tha, thank you, ma'am," he stuttered through reddened cheeks.

"Marty, you best come with me." As they rode to the bottom of the ravine Naomi couldn't help but wonder what plausible reason the thugs would have for being here. When Naomi stepped down and rolled the man over, she didn't know him. Not that she thought she would.

"Ma'am," Marty said, "if you don't mind me ask'n how did you know them there fellers were a hidin' like that?"

As Naomi took the rope from Chinsey's saddle horn and looped it around the man's downed body she said, "The birds told me."

"Birds, ma'am?"

"Didn't you see the birds down in the meadow circle the small ridge then dive in behind us? They told me they was there." The man must have had a baffled look on his face. "Mother taught me."

That's all that needed to be said Marty had been told many a story about Liza and Lizzie Baxter, the fearless set of twin sisters and their mysterious ways, he just never thought that he'd live long enough to actually see it. "Oh," he said quietly.

"We'll drag him to the road and put him in the wagon on the way out, a backstabbing cur like this don't deserve no better," she stated in a disgusted tone.

"Yes, ma'am." Marty agreed.

Naomi gazed around at the small acreage, four graves and two dead intruders, why did such a beautiful piece of ground hold so much heartache? This wasn't what Liza and Lizzie had intended when they purchased this small ranch for Matthew and Emmy, they wanted a family to grow here, live here, love here.

As she gazed around the majestic property she couldn't shake the nagging feeling in the pit of her gut. Thinking this devious ruse had something to do with her cousin's big family business venture. Perhaps they'd be better off getting rid of it, maybe death had taken over the soil. Naomi shook off the feeling, no matter when they got back to the ranch she would talk with her mother and aunt. She knew Matthew hadn't stepped foot on this quaint little place since Emmy's death, she wondered if it was time to get rid of it.

# CHAPTER 39

"Lizzie!" Liza yelled up the long stairwell. "I'm going to go and check on some of the heifers you send Hattie for me if needs be." There was no reply. "Lizzie!" she yelled again. Still nothing. A sickening feeling engulfed Liza's entire body and just as she was ready to bolt up the stairs Lizzie stepped around the corner.

"You were looking for me?" she asked with a smirk on her face.

"What the dickens are you doing?" Liza demanded as she placed her hand over her heart. "You like to scared me out of ten years of my life."

"Huh," she countered unimpressed, "well, we can't have that. Besides, Hattie and Naomi went to town hours ago I was gonna fix some lunch."

"Lunch?" Liza was at whit's end with her cantankerous sister. "You can't fix lunch you're not even supposed to be down here your sorry butt's suppose be in bed. Do you want this baby or not Lizzie?"

Lizzie gave her sibling a cold look. "Of course I want this baby."

"Then you'd better start listening you stubborn ole mule! Honestly, Lizzie, you've been told a hundred times what can happen." she said in a heated tone.

"Liza, Liza, Liza," Lizzie said in a dramatic voice. "I've been in labor most of the night. My water hasn't broken yet, but it will it's just a matter of time now, I've been walking and walking for hours."

The horrified look that ran across Liza's face would have stopped a ten-day clock. "Why didn't you come and get me?" Baffled at her sister's offhanded remark.

"Liza, you have bent over backwards for me these last few months doing my chores, checking in on me, running the ranch, you needed your sleep, too." Her crystal circles said she meant what she was saying. "I know that you will be there when I need you I've never doubted that. So, if you need to go and check the heifers, then go I'll be right here."

"I'm not going any where's now you could explode at any minute I might not get back in time." she fussed. "You need to get that over-expanded butt of yours back upstairs and we need to get ready. My word, Lizzie, what are you thinking?"

Lizzie didn't like her sister's snide remark, but she loved her flustered state. You'd of thought she was the one having the baby. "I'm fine," she countered. "I'll call you when I need you." Then Lizzie saw the panicked look wash across her sister's face. "Liza... Liza!" she demanded in a loud tone. "What?"

"I can't," Liza confessed in a barely audible whisper as she stared into her identical sibling's shaken face. For nine months she'd worried about the delivery of this baby. The risk that it would be for her identical sister. "I can't let what happened to me happen to you I won't risk it."

"Liza," Lizzie said softly, "nothing is going to happen to me."

"I remember calling your name over and over, praying that you would hear me," her eyes were full or regret, "I was so scared." Her breath caught in her throat. "No one knew what to do. I could feel every ounce of blood running out of my body like a melting stream it was so cold and haunting, and then—you opened the curtain and my soul filled with light and, and." She paused for a moment. "I knew I was going to be alright, you were there, the other half of my heart, my blood my being with a heated vengeance, I could breath." She gave Lizzie a heartfelt look. "I would have died if it hadn't been for you."

"Oh, cow turds Liza you're standin' right here so stop that blabbering nonsense. Is there another grave out in the burying patch, no, are you standin' here, yes, ain't no one's going nowheres," Liza's confession was unnerving, but Lizzie didn't want her sibling to know that.

"No, but I remember being afraid," she whispered as her cloudy blue eyes searched her sister's uncaring face.

"Afraid? You'd been nuts not to be afraid especially with Mr. Horseflesh hiding like the jackal he was, hoping you would die the dirty dog."

"Not because of that," she stated sincerely.

"Then what?"

"I was afraid you wouldn't be there with me. You know—to say goodbye." Liza had held these feelings in long enough. "And, when you walked through that door…"

"Walk my ass, just encase you don't member father still blames me because that blasted door don't shut right!"

Liza gave her identical sibling a quick smile. "When I saw the angered relief rush across your face, when I knew was still breathing, from that moment I knew that we had cheated the darkness once again, I could never risk that for you."

"I see," Lizzie said in a tone that tried not to show any emotion, a tone that told her sister that she was being silly. But, deep down beneath the surface of her being she knew they had fought the inevitable darkness together and won. As Lizzie gazed into her sister's confessing face, she was sorry those haunting memories had lingered all of these years.

"Well then, I suppose we should go upstairs and get ready for this baby before you have some kind of episode." Purposely, Lizzie reached for Liza's sturdy waist as the two of them made their way to the top of the landing.

"I'm not having an episode you mules butt I'm confessing my feelings." Liza snapped.

"Well, could you do that later this really hurts." Lizzie whined as she bent over from one of the pains.

"Oh," Liza half giggled, "Just you wait, it gives you a whole new respect for the cows and horses."

"Cows and horses? I'm not a cow, Liza." Lizzie complained in a high-pitched tone. "I have two feet not four."

"I never said that you were a cow." Liza answered off-handedly.

"You just said it, I know I'm not deaf." she accused.

"No, you're not deaf, you're being a stubborn old mule."

"Well, that's easy for you to say, you're not having a baa…by." Another pain racked Lizzie's body before the word had completely escaped her lips.

Liza gave her identical sibling an offhanded look. "I hope Naomi gets back soon; I don't want her to miss this."

"What, her mother in pain and agony because of one weak moment?" Lizzie gave her sister a dirty look. "You're enjoying this aren't you? Of course you are, if I could ...why I'd...ohhh here comes another one."

Liza led her sister to her room as she busied herself with the gathering of the necessities that she would need, everything was in its place as she happily anticipated the inevitable delivery.

"Ohh." Lizzie moaned as Liza dabbed at the small sweat beads on her forehead.

"That was a good one," Liza said matter-of-factly. "Keep that up it won't take long if you keep doing that."

Lizzie gave her identical sibling a warning look as she spoke, "You're enjoying seeing me in pain, admit it."

"No, no. no sister." she said dramatically. "I was just thinking, do you remember Big Betty?"

"Betty?" she moaned.

"Yeah, Big Betty, the old sorrel mare that used to make so much noise when she was giving birth? You just reminded me of her." She gave her sister a huge smile. "Man, I haven't thought of that horse in years."

"I swear Liza when I get out of this bed...ahh! It's coming! I can feel it!"

But, there was no sign of the small infant when Liza checked her. She knew that the baby should have been here, made its gallant entrance into the real world and to make matters worse it was very evident that Lizzie was beginning to tire.

"If I die tell Naomi...," Lizzie said in a traumatized voice just as Naomi and Hattie walked into the room.

"Tell me what?" Naomi asked.

"Good, your back," Liza said in a masterful tone. "Hattie," Liza said, "we're going to need some hot water oh and Hattie could you round up, Luke." She gave her sister a knowing smile. "Just encase."

"Just encase," Lizzie echoed, "encase of what?"

"Your mother is having an episode," Liza said to Naomi in an irritated tone as she got ready to help the baby along.

"Lizzie," Liza said, "now don't go falling asleep on me you're gonna have to push."

"I can't," she whispered. "I'm all out of breath."

Liza gave Naomi a worried look as the young woman sat on the bed with her mother. "Lizzie, I'm going to have to see what the matter is here. I'm going to have to reach up and see." Liza was sweating profusely. "Luke." At the sound of his name he automatically rubbed the special salve up both of her arms. By now Lizzie had no dignity left.

"Am I dying?" Lizzie whispered pitifully as another pain racked her body.

"No," Liza said in a distracted tone. "But don't push Lizzie just let it pass."

"You can tell me the truth I can take it. Am I?" she whimpered. Liza gave Naomi a humored look everyone knew how dramatic Lizzie could be. "It's gonna get your attention for sure by the time I'm done, that is if I can get him turned around," she mumbled to herself.

"What did you say?" Lizzie snapped back to life sitting partway up.

"I said… I might have to turn him around." Liza tried to blow it off so her sister wouldn't panic.

"For crying in a washbasin, he's backwards?" Lizzie fretted in a whining voice.

"Appears to be," Liza answered through unconcerned pinched lips.

"How did he get backwards?" she stated, "I didn't put him in there backwards."

"You need to relax Lizzie." Liza stated in a calm soothing tone.

"Relax, my baby is stuck, sides your'n hand ain't gonna fit up there!" she insisted.

"Why not, yours did!" Oh how Liza was loving this.

"Because, I'm delicate down there." Lizzie whined.

"And, you're saying I'm not?" Liza snapped, irritated at her sister's insinuation.

"I never said that, stop twisting my words, can't you see I'm in a situation here?" she fussed.

"This is all Charlie's fault!" Lizzie whined. "Why did he have to be so persuasive and handsome and gentle and…?" With her last statement Lizzie began to cry something that surprised everyone. "Don't tell me if it's dead Liza, just walk out the door my heart won't take it I swear it won't."

"Oh, stop that bothersome blubbering!" Liza demanded. "You remind me of an old soggy washcloth ain't nothin' wrong that a little twist can't fix, stop being a blubber'n' baby."

"I'm not being a baby!" she hissed. "I'm in pain."

"I'm going to show you pain...," and then just like that the small pink infant made its way into the warm room. Immediately, Luke reached to unfold the cord from around his tiny neck as Liza cleaned out his mouth. Both of them had worried looks on their faces the baby was quiet as a mouse.

Lizzie didn't miss the look of dread that passed between them. "What?" she said worriedly. "He's dead isn't he?" Anxiously, she grabbed Naomi's hand and held it tight as she laid her head back against the pillow and closed her crystal blue eyes. "Don't let him be dead he's all I've got left of h..."

No one said a word, it felt like time stood still, like the moon and the sun collided against the heavens just waiting for darkness to surround them. Liza had tears running down her tanned cheeks as she motioned for Luke there was something stuck in the baby's throat, she couldn't swipe it clean. Instantly, she flipped him upside down, end for end, and gave him a mighty whack. The small infant let out a blast loud enough to raise the rafters as the slippery muck that was stuck in his throat escaped his little mouth and splattered like a raw egg on the floor.

"It's a boy, Lizzie!" Luke exclaimed. "A little boy! By damn girl you did it! Who'd of ever thought!"

"A boy?" she whispered through dry lips.

"A little boy," Liza said compassionately.

"Is he...normal looking?" she wept.

"He's more than normal little sister, he's hung like an old bull far as I can see." Liza stated matter-of-factly as she handed the bundled baby to his mother. "Dang, Charlie."

Then she sat down on the edge of the bed. "See," she said in a caring tone as she wiped her sister's sweating brow, "you didn't die you pain in the a...neck. Although you might wish you would have here in a couple of weeks, but nope, you made it."

There was no missing the unspoken respect that the identical sister's had for each other as Lizzie touched her sister's arm. "We—made it." There was no missing the pride that shone equally through both of their cool blue eyes. There was no missing the fact that they knew this baby would be raised by both of them, just like the other children. But, most of all there was no missing the desolate look that said Charlie was supposed to be here, he was supposed to see what their love had made.

"I know," Liza whispered, "I know."

"Look father," Lizzie whispered through trembling lips. "Look what Charlie gave me." Her blue eyes held his like a warm blanket as a slight sob escaped her dry lips. "It's a little boy. My, little boy. How could Charlie have really died when I'm holding the best part of him? I wish he could see," she wept openly," what we did, I wish he could see."

"The Mighty One see's all," Abe whispered as he continued to hold his broken daughter as she wept. "I'm sure Charlie is standing right in this room, right now." He was so proud of her. Lizzie had finally come full circle. "Charlie knows." Her journey seemed to be so much harder than most, but she'd made it just the same. He was so grateful that for once in his life he was speechless.

"Do you really believe that father," Lizzie said as though she had read his mind as she handed him the small bundle. "My heart aches with both joy and sadness father, are you sure?"

"Yes." His tone was firm and unwavering. "What will you name him, Lizzie?" Abe asked through emotion-filled lips. The baby looked like a pebble in her father's mountainous arms.

"Charles Redbone Baxter," she said proudly.

"Are you sure?" he questioned.

"No one would believe me anyway," she sighed. "They'd think I made it up to save my family the humility, my reputation is already soiled father, let the gossips be damned. I know you know and that's all that matters."

She gazed at the bloodied little boy. "Someday when he's old enough I'll tell him the truth."

"I know you will." Nothing else needed to be said. "Charlie Redbone Baxter, that's a fine name Lizzie, a fine name indeed," Abe whispered proudly.

Then like a gust of wind Matthew and Clinton came barreling through the bedroom door. "Have I no dignity left!" Lizzie whined. "I'm nearly naked here!"

"None," the two men said in unison, not allowing Lizzie time for a rebuttal. "Look," Matthew laughed, "he has red hair, red hair, tons of it!"

"Lizzie," Clinton teased, "He's gonna stand out like a blister."

All Lizzie could do was smile as they fussed over the small infant. They were all here. Everyone that mattered. Hattie, Naomi, Luke, Clinton, Matthew, her father and of course, Liza.

"Thank you, Charlie," she whispered to herself as a silent tear's drifted down her reddened cheeks. Now she understood Emmy's brokenhearted dream.

www.ingramcontent.com/pod-product-compliance
Lightning Source LLC
LaVergne TN
LVHW021805060526
838201LV00058B/3238